TIPTON'S SUGAR COVE - MATTHEW

REBA RHYNE

Reba Rhyne
enjoy!

Tipton's Sugar Cove – Matthew

Cover by Ken Raney

Editing by Sara Foust

Publisher's Cataloging-in-Publication data
Name: Reba Rhyne
Title: Title: subtitle: Tipton's Sugar Cove – Matthew/ by Reba Rhyne
Identifiers: LCCN: 2019920477
ISBN 978-1-945976-69-8
Subjects: 1. FIC042110 FICTON / Christian/ Romance / Historical

Published by EA Books Publishing a division of Living Parables of Central Florida, Inc. a 501c3
EABooksPublishing.com

Dedication

Fiction writers, especially historical fiction writers, must be able to dream — of characters and scenarios. We haven't lived in the time period written about, although we may know people who did.

Information on actions and actors which make up our story — some real, some not — can portray actual events, so copious research and visiting the actual setting is needed. At least, that is my philosophy, delving into the least detail which I can use to validate my story.

I am a product of Tipton ancestors who lived in Cades Cove, Happy Valley, Six Mile, and Chilhowee. All of these are embedded in and around the Great Smoky Mountains of Tennessee, and of a genealogist who wrote the Rhyne and Whitehead family history of the East Tennessee area.

As such, I've heard about this family of Tipton's for years, and in this mountain setting, I've used them to describe how life was in this beautiful scooped-out valley and area.

Matthew Tipton is a *fictional* character, belonging to a real Tipton who lived in the area. He has become the son of Nathaniel Tipton who was the step-brother of my great-grandfather, Noah Tipton of *Chilhowee Legacy*, my last book which is part of The Tipton Chronicles.

Tipton's Sugar Cove — Matthew is dedicated to the Tipton families who lived in Cades Cove and their descendants all over the world. God bless each and every one of you.

Acknowledgements

My mother, Margaret Naomi Whitehead Rhyne must have been responsible for my writing ability, although she was a down-to-earth, practical person with four children to raise and a secret she shared only in her later life, *My Cherokee Rose.*

Missy Tipton Green for her picture of the chimney still standing in Tipton's Sugar Cove and the epilogue of the actual people who lived there.

Robin Rhyne Greenlee, my second cousin, a well-known photographer of the cove area, for the background picture on the cover, of the Methodist Church from Rich Mountain.

Ricky Rutherford for his expertise in hunting and all things hunting, including the Plott's hounds brought from Germany to the Smoky Mountains to track wild game.

Ken Raney for gathering all the information and putting the cover together so beautifully.

Sara Foust for editing the book.

Dawn Staymates, Kristen Veldhuis, and **Cheri Cowell** of EA Books Publishing for another good job, well-done.

Contents

Introduction

The Great Smoky Mountains are many things. Tall, hazy, and the protector of thousands of species of plants and animals. They straddle the border of western North Carolina and eastern Tennessee. Within its massive land area are many scooped out areas called coves. These scars in the mountains were thought to be made throughout the last ice age. During early times, the fertile depressions were inaccessible except for trails made by animals, seeking food and water, and used by the earliest humans on foot or horse.

Near the beginning of the 1800's, a man by the name of William Tipton explored one of these coves, consolidated several earlier land grants, and became the first legal land owner of several hundred acres of mountain, hillside, and prime bottomland within the most famous, Cades Cove. William was a land speculator, as were most of the large land owners in the East Tennessee area, and the western frontier. He never lived within the cove, but did within an area outside the cove called Tipton's Station, which became a stop on the railroad from Knoxville, Tennessee to Maryville, Tennessee.

He sold or gave land within the cove to his family and friends who lived in northeast Tennessee. Coming on horseback, the first settler was named Jobe, and the second one was named Oliver. They built cabins out of logs and during the first winters barely survived the hardships they encountered.

As time went on, the trails were widened into roads, fields were cleared, and the many cove residents prospered. The Jobe's moved from the cove, but the Oliver's stayed, becoming the first permanent settlers in Cades Cove.

Tipton's Sugar Cove is an actual place within Cades Cove, as are Tater Branch and Tater Ridge. There was a red-light district, Chestnut Flats, but it isn't near the fictional setting of Red Oak Flats. Thunderhead Mountain, the highest peak, served as observer, protector, and glowering censor of those nestled in the verdant valley below. The busybody line spread the news, good and bad, through the community with the aid of an internal party-line telephone system.

Matthew Tipton, the protagonist in this story, is a fictional descendant of William "Fightin' Billy" Tipton, my ancestor.

TIPTON'S SUGAR COVE - MATTHEW

REBA RHYNE

❦ Chapter One ❦

Early May, 1917, Cades Cove, Tennessee — A.B.

A.B. sat in a cane chair on the front porch of the cabin at Red Oak Flats, watching as her father rode his favorite horse down the curvy Rich Mountain Trail toward Townsend. His ride would take him two miles to Rich Mountain Road, where he would turn right, cross a creek, and ride eight more miles to the village. The morning sun flooded her covered perch and burned the morning mists off the new growth in the green forest around her home. She looked down at the ground. Three weeks ago, her footprints left trails in a late April snow, covering the ground. The remnants were long gone, melted away by the warm sun. Because of the morning chill, she pulled her jacket closer around her, and shoved her hands into its deep pockets.

Red Oak Flats, positioned at the head of Leading Ridge and almost three miles from the floor of Cades Cove, had been Abigail White's abode for sixteen years. Secluded, she knew it harbored many shady characters, some seeking refuge or protection from the law. As a young girl, she had heard whispers about its occupants, and as she grew older, the actual circumstances became apparent.

1

Her father protected her from the inhabitants who came and went and shielded her from the goings-on, including his *cough syrup* operation. Many stayed only a few days and moved on, preferring more activity than the quiet the mountaintop offered.

Others only stayed the night after getting solace from two painted ladies in one of the cabins above.

"Mornin', A.B," said Jake coming around the side of the house. "Chuck's gone."

A.B. jumped up, and clutched at the porch railing, pretending to be frightened. "Jake, you scared me out of a year's growth," she exclaimed. "Yes. He's gone." She looked at her elderly friend with his scraggly hair and grinned at him. His blue, denim jacket was buttoned firmly over his slightly, rotund stomach, hiding real muscles he'd gained from hard work. He was right on schedule.

"Chuck's headin' to Townsend," he announced again.

Jake laughed and shuffled his feet. His sparse, gray hair was dripping wet and waved tightly on top where he'd combed it to the side.

Abigail noticed his shoes were new. "New shoes, huh?"

"Yep. I been saving 'em." He walked up the steps to the porch and lifted one up so A.B. could get a closer look. The brown leather boots had high tops and leather laces.

"Wow, I like those. They look sturdy. Should last many, many days." A.B. leaned over and gave him a firm hug as the old man looked at her adoringly.

Each Tuesday, he came quietly around the side of the cabin on purpose to scare A.B. Like a child, he was delighted that his charade had worked. A.B.'s friend was a permanent resident at Red Oak Flats. He was Chuck White's right hand and the only man at the Flats allowed near her—besides her father. Jake never fully developed mentally, although he was capable of many repetitive and simple tasks. His love for Chuck and his daughter was fervent and included defending them when necessary. A.B. knew some of the residents taunted him by calling him stupid and ignorant, but her father sent anyone abusing his helper packing down the mountain. They didn't return.

"Jest thought I'd come down and carry some water from the spring for yer washin'. I gotta go to work soon." Jake stood, shifting his weight from one foot to another, mumbling under his breath. Arthritis caused pain, and he moved slowly, limping at times. Both of Jake's parents were dead, and years before, Chuck had offered him a home.

"I see you brought your own buckets." Jake always brought his buckets.

"Yep, I sure did. Are you ready to go?" said Jake, fidgeting and looking at the path to the spring. He never stood still.

Washing clothes was the last thing A.B. wanted to do. There wasn't any reason to rush. As long as the clothes were dry before bedtime, she and her Pa would be pleased.

"Sit down and rest, Jake. I'm in no hurry." She knew he would refuse.

Jake shook his head, and continued to shift his weight from one foot to the other. "Have you had breakfast?" he asked. He pulled a biscuit out of his pocket and held it out to her. Kitty, another resident, always cooked extra for him. "I think I'll go on to the spring. You catch up." Holding onto the porch rail, he was soon on the ground and headed toward the trail, talking as he went.

"Jake, you're my sweetheart. Thanks." A.B. called after him as he disappeared down the path. She walked inside, placed the biscuit on the kitchen table and, hefting the bucket of water already in the cabin, she poured it into a kettle on the iron stove to warm. She picked up the biscuit and looked at it. Known as a cat's-head in the Appalachian Mountains, because it was oversized, the offering was probably a leftover from yesterday, because Kitty didn't always get up early in the morning to bake bread.

Every Tuesday, A.B. acted out the same ritual. In Jake's mental condition, structure was necessary. Doing the same thing every week was familiar and comfortable to the older man, who never veered from his normal routine.

Jake was even responsible for her being called A.B. Due to a speech impediment; he couldn't say Abigail, so her name had been shortened to A.B.

Walking back outside, she stretched her arms over her head and yawned. Music came from a cabin up the hollow. A.B. walked to the edge of the porch to get a better view. The porch boards creaked as she stepped on them. She smiled. Her father kept saying he'd nail them down. But so far, he'd postponed this household chore, much like she put off going to the spring for wash water. He had other more important business in a hollow some distance from the Flats.

The melodic sounds came from Kitty's cabin. This was the closest house to the White's home. It sat at the mouth of the hollow.

Kitty must be playing her guitar. She's up early today. Since A.B.'s mother died, Kitty had acted as her surrogate and often gave A.B. advice and encouragement, including her emphatic, "Don't ever come up here at night. Never! Promise me!" Kitty insisted her home was out of bounds after dark. A.B. didn't question her insistence, or reason, and promised immediately. So far, she was faithful to keep her vow.

Beyond Kitty's cabin, a flatter area opened up where five other cabins sat in a semi-circle.

"Nothin' beautiful about them rough homes," she often heard Kitty say.

The cabins were built by her father of rough-hewn oak logs, the cracks filled with chinking mud. Each had a couple of windows, rough porches covered by tin roofs, which gave off a loud roar in a Smoky Mountain downpour. Inside were cots to sleep on, a rough table with chairs, a counter for miscellaneous pots and pans, a cook stove, and a fireplace to keep warm in the winter.

One of the cabins was given to Jake as his home. This May morning, gray smoke came from his chimney. A.B. noticed its curl was as unhurried as she was.

Wonder if anyone's awake up there? Guess they stayed up late last night drinking. Cough medicine, no doubt. Probably have hangovers this morning.

The men played cards and gambled. Often loud arguments and fights broke out. Her father refereed these brawls by tossing both combatants out of the small community. At least twice, A.B. was awakened during the night by gun shots coming from the direction of the rude shelters. When she asked Kitty what happened, Kitty wouldn't look her in the eye.

"Just men horsing around, A.B. Don't worry your pretty head about it." Abigail didn't push for an answer. She knew it would be useless—none would come. The people on her mountainside were tight-lipped.

She walked back over the creaking boards to the porch steps and turned her gaze down toward the mountain trail where her Pa soon appeared leading the two horses. The large sacks roped to the animal's backs would be delivered to a bootlegger in the Townsend vicinity. She watched as he disappeared around a curve and appeared again down the trail. He would be back in the afternoon—the horses carrying provisions for their home and his business.

~

Charles "Chuck" White, her father, went about his chores like clockwork. He always went on Tuesday to purchase supplies and to sell the last week's production of cough medicine.

A.B. laughed. How many years did I believe that tale?

She remembered overhearing her Pa talking about Prohibition. He'd said, "Bring it on! I'll become a very, rich man."

Someone had asked, "Won't that put you out of business?"

"Heck, no." And then, he'd noticed A.B on the porch. "No," he said, putting his thumbs in his overall straps and nodding. "Cough medicine will double in price."

A.B. remembered thinking the family might move off the mountain and into a nice house in Maryville, maybe next to Aunt Mary Anderson's on Court Street. A.B. laughed again, the sound of her laughter floating through the forest.

How innocent I was.

Would she ever get off of this mountaintop? She loved her mountain home, but —

She always told herself, A.B., there is another world out there.

She'd seen some of it when her father sent her to school in Townsend where Little River Lumber Mill operated. The mill attracted stores filled with the latest fashions, grocery stores, a theater, churches, a barber and a doctor. The train depot especially fascinated A.B. She imagined herself walking up to the ticket office and buying a ticket to Knoxville, Washington City, or New York.

She often thought, wouldn't it be wonderful to go to New York City and see the Statue of Liberty on Liberty Island? Ride the Ferry. See a play on Broadway.

She'd tasted that different life in Maryville, riding down the dusty streets in her Aunt's new Ford automobile. Walking from the Anderson's home to Maryville College, listening to recitals or concerts, and watching budding actors in plays. These activities captivated her.

How I love music, sitting at the piano and touching the keys. At least, I know where Middle C is on the keyboard. I'd love to play the piano.

Aunt Mary owned a piano, and she had taught Abigail the keyboard, plus two or three simple songs. All of her aunt's daughters knew how to play the piano, but none of them were very accomplished at the keys. Abigail's interest in the keyboard included becoming proficient at playing. She knew she could do it.

"Abigail, if you lived with me, I'd send you to Maryville College for private lessons." Aunt Mary refused to call her A.B., saying it sounded boyish. "Would you like that?"

"Yes, Aunt Mary. That would be a dream come true." Abigail hadn't approached her father with the idea.

What was in her future? Marriage and children?

Yes. Marriage and children, she did see them in her life.

But she wondered how she would meet anyone stuck up here on this mountain? No one who came there was acceptable to her Pa or to her. A.B. shook her head.

She was undecided. She loved these hills. She enjoyed the mostly quiet days and years of her life here on the fringes of Cades Cove, especially when her mother had been there. But life in the big city of Maryville seemed exciting and also appealed to her. She didn't think her Pa would keep her at Red Oak Flats, if she wanted to go.

What about Pa?

He will be lonely without me to keep him company.

Maybe he wouldn't. A.B thought about the creaking boards, late at night. Those boards that her Pa hadn't fixed gave him away. Had her father found comfort in Kitty's arms? She really didn't know for sure, and she didn't want to think about it.

She picked up her buckets, stepped off the porch heading toward the spring, and passed Jake coming toward her.

❦ Chapter Two ❦

Red Oak Flats, Noon the Same Day — A.B.

A.B. walked out the screen door. It slammed behind her. She headed for Kitty's cabin, only a short walk away. All morning, she'd washed dirty dishes and clothes, heating gallons of water on the wood stove and pouring it into containers to perform each task. She glanced down at her fingers. They were shriveled and blanched white after many hours in the wash water. Now, as she walked down the back-porch steps, she breathed a sigh of relief — glad for the morning's chores to be over.

Oh, I forgot to empty the wash water.

Turning around, she retraced her steps to the porch and tipped the wooden tub holding the dirty water, pouring it on the ground. She replaced the wash board on a nail driven into the cabin wall and turned the tub upside down on its bench. Her wet clothes hung on lines behind the cabin in the full sunshine. As she passed by the shirts and dresses, A.B. ran her hand over the drying clothes. Some were still sopping wet. She stopped to ring the water out of the legs of her Pa's denim overalls, not an easy task.

Continuing her walk toward Kitty's home, a chirping redbird caught her attention. It flew among the branches of the laurel thicket below the cabin. The male's bright red body stood out among the shiny green leaves. April showers had brought May flowers, and she saw a patch of mayapple nestled in the forest below her. Its umbrella-like leaves hid the white flower underneath.

About the middle of April, the rain had stopped with the last snow, causing an unusual dry spell in the Great Smoky Mountains. In Cades Cove, plowing and planting was done in record time, but rain was needed for the crops to sprout and continue to grow. This early dry period did not promise rain for the summer months. The Cove residents started to pray for "showers of blessing" when they attended church.

A.B worried that their spring would go dry.

Up the hill to the right was a small garden patch her father planted each year. They canned vegetables during summer for the winter.

A chicken coop held a dozen or so candidates for laying eggs or for the frying pan. Their young replacements ran hither and yon on the bare ground. The young chicks could go through the fence wire, leaving the mothers to loudly chastise them for straying. A flying hawk could always swoop down for a quick meal. When this happened the clucking of the hens was frantic.

Looking up and to the left, A.B. noticed a movement on the porch of a distant cabin. The man sitting there, watching her, noticed her gaze and threw up his hand to wave. A.B. turned her head and walked on, ignoring him.

It was Dirk. She wondered how long he'd been sittin' there? Was he watchin' as she washed the clothes? She couldn't explain her aversion to him. The man was handsome in a dark, swarthy way, but she avoided him like the plague she'd read about in the history books at school.

When A.B. looked up toward those cabins, she often saw the residents as they chatted outside on their porches or walked between the dwellings. She didn't advertise her presence due to her father's stern warnings, but the others knew she lived in Chuck's cabin. She stayed outdoors more than indoors.

A.B. followed the path which detoured around two large, drooping hemlock trees and a walnut tree as she approached her older friend's cabin. Besides Kitty and A.B., two other women lived in the small neighborhood. Ginger and Jocelyn shared another of the rough huts in the semi-circle. During the day and night, men came and went from their quarters.

A.B. had overheard talk in Townsend about some women who weren't very reputable in that town and an insinuation that others could be found up in the hills. She recognized the directions being given. No one else lived in her part of the mountains.

Sometimes hunters came through but not often. The terrain, isolated except for the area of the path toward Rich Mountain Road, was rough, steep and rocky—a good place to fall, get hurt, and never be heard of again.

Her father mostly refused to get involved in the affairs of those who lived in his compound. They were expected not to disturb his peace. He did charge a daily or monthly fee for its use and toss the rowdy out when they caused trouble. He didn't need the aggravation or money that bad.

Chuck White worked seven days a week. Sunday was just another day to him. He eschewed church going, although A.B. didn't know why. He didn't have anything good or bad to say about it, at least in her company. A.B. went a few times while she was at school in Townsend. Not regularly, though.

As A.B. approached the steps to Kitty's cabin, she thought about her hard-working father. The only day Chuck didn't work in the woods beyond the Flats was Tuesday, when he made his regular run to Townsend. The other days, he left after breakfast, picking up Jake on his way into the forest. He chose a new path each day, preferring not to make a permanent path for anyone to follow. No one knew where his manufacturing operation was located, or so he thought. He returned in the early afternoon, hungry as a bear.

Chores for A.B. started as soon as she got out of bed. After her father built a fire in the cook stove, she cooked breakfast, washed the dishes, and made the rumpled beds. Her father liked order in the house, and she liked the neat appearance of things in their proper places.

"Hi, Kitty," said A.B. as she entered her friend's house. A.B. usually went over for dinner since her father didn't come home to eat. She never knocked when she entered the door.

"Come in A.B. Dinner is about ready. Are you hungry?"

"Starved." A.B. felt an answering rumble in her stomach. "Want me to set the table?"

"Sure. Use the good china." Kitty laughed at the hodge-podge A.B. set on the table. Her table wouldn't know what to think if two pieces matched.

A.B. watched her friend put the finishing touches on lunch. Kitty moved with a graceful amble, waving her plump hands through the air in flourishes as she talked. Kitty wasn't fat, A.B. decided, just well-rounded.

"What did you say?"

Kitty turned to look at her. "I said do you want cream in your coffee?"

"You know I don't drink coffee."

"You do now. I asked your father if you weren't big enough to start, and he said it was alright." Kitty was pouring the dark brew as she spoke. "You ready to try?"

"I reckon so." A.B. took a sip of coffee out of the cup Kitty handed her. "Ouch, that's hot."

"I should've warned you, I'm sorry."

A. B. tested her tongue against the roof of her mouth and then stuck it out to look at it. Her eyes crossed and Kitty laughed.

"It's definitely singed, but I'm sure it'll heal," said A.B. "Let's eat." The two sat down and ate leftover fried chicken, green beans seasoned with fatback, and buttered biscuits with honey.

"Well what do you think?" asked Kitty.

"About what?"

"About the coffee, silly!" exclaimed Kitty. "What else?"

"Oh," laughed A.B. "It's alright. I'll have to get used to it."

"It's a taste you acquire." Kitty got up from the table and started to clear the dishes. A.B. joined her.

"You got somethin' on your mind, A.B? You seem a little addled today."

"I did want to talk to you. I wonder if Pa would let me go live with Aunt Mary in Maryville? She said I could come and stay with her." There, she had said it out loud.

"Why do you want to go live in town? Aren't you happy here at Red Oak Flats?" Kitty was looking at her — questions in her eyes.

"I love the mountains, but if I want to get married, how will I find a husband? I'm not interested in someone from here, who'd sit down, expect me to wait on him, and have babies. I don't want my husband to learn the art of cough syrup making," A.B. said, the last a little sarcastically. She rushed on before Kitty could interrupt her. "I don't want him to join this crowd. I want someone who makes a respectable living, a young man who doesn't break the law to support himself. There's no one here Pa would approve of, and, besides, I don't want to stay here on this mountain for the rest of my life."

"What brought this on?"

"I've been thinkin' about it for awhile." A.B.'s thoughts started tumbling out, one after the other. "I'd like to travel, go to recitals, plays, and learn to play the piano. I can't do that here on this mountain." At that instant, A.B. knew exactly what she wanted.

"Whew. That's a mouthful. Did your aunt put this in your head?" Kitty seemed miffed at the 'respectable' part.

"No." A.B. bristled a little at the comment. "She didn't. It's been on my mind a bunch. I just haven't said anything about it. Actually, I hadn't made up my mind for sure. I'm sure now."

A.B. noticed that Kitty was quiet as she continued to clean off the table.

"I didn't mean to make you angry."

"No. I'm not mad. I'm thinkin' about what you said and what I should say." A.B. realized she was Kitty's only confidant here on the mountain. If she left, Kitty would be lonely, but it was necessary to convince her of the truth of the situation.

"Sit down, A.B." They both sat at the kitchen table.

Kitty's next words made further talk unnecessary. "I do see the truth in what you say. I jest didn't think about you bein' of marriageable age. My, you've grown so fast. It's my fault you aren't off this mountain. Guess I wanted to keep you all to myself. The one we have to worry about is your Pa."

What *would* Chuck say about the subject?

A.B. started toying with the tin pepper shaker as she waited on Kitty to continue. She knew Kitty's influence with her father always helped when his daughter needed something. That's why she decided to approach Kitty first.

～

Kitty was busy thinking. Of course, A.B. was right, and she could go live with her *rich* aunt in Maryville. Or, Chuck could rent a place for his daughter there, but it wouldn't be respectable for her to live alone. Money wasn't a problem. Chuck had plenty. A.B.'s youth was the issue. Staying with her aunt seemed to be the only solution.

"I'll help with your Pa, if that's what you want. You're of the age when a girl of the mountains starts to think about gettin' married, and I know it can be lonely here in these hills. I can't see how he would stand in your way, if you've got your mind made up to go."

A.B. jumped up, ran around the table, and gave her friend a hug. "You know I'll miss you. You're the only mom I've known for over two years, and I've learned to love you as such."

Kitty's eyes welled with tears as she hugged her young friend. No, she didn't want A.B. to end up like her, and if she didn't leave this mountain, she might. When she could talk, she said, "I've been considerin' you as my daughter for some time. We'll talk to your Pa when he comes back from Townsend." Kitty smiled and got up from the table. "Run along, I got work to do."

A.B. gave her a quick kiss and went out the door.

Kitty followed and called from the porch. "A.B., I love you, too."

Chuck's daughter stopped and turned around. She waved and blew Kitty another kiss as she walked on home.

Kitty returned to the kitchen and started getting flour, lard, and baking powder from the cupboard. Love was not a word she used often. In her line of business, love wasn't involved.

For almost two years, she'd not been with another man. She liked A.B.'s father and as a kept woman, she was content to be with one man. Well, almost. There was still that nagging longing to make it official and legal. She couldn't shake that feeling, although she had tried.

She put more wood in the stove and placed her oven on top. Jake was out of biscuits, and she needed to bake some for the rest of the week.

✤ Chapter Three ✤

Earlier That Same Morning as A.B Sat On the Front Porch — Dirk

Dirk Johnson rode his horse slowly up the path, heading for Red Oak Flats. He felt sluggish after several days of carousing. His trip to Townsend on Friday had lasted five days and included wine, women, and song.

Well, forget the song, and the wine had actually been hard liquor poured liberally into his glass.

He didn't run after women that much, but when he did, it was with gusto. For several days, maybe weeks, his thoughts about women were concentrated on the young filly at the Flats — Chuck's daughter.

During the last few days, he'd gambled day and night but hadn't won a penny. Now, he was broke and ready for some peace and quiet on the mountaintop at the Flats. Rounding one of the sharp switchbacks on Rich Mountain Road, he saw Chuck White coming toward him leading his loaded horses. They met in the center of the straight stretch.

Chuck was on his normal Tuesday run to Townsend, but he was later than usual. Dirk wasn't about to mention that fact, because White would know he was keepin' tabs on him. He threw up his hand.

"Good morning, Dirk. Are you headin' for the Flats?" Chuck didn't like this young man. There was something hidden and mysterious about him. Of course, he might think that about most of his residents—but with Dirk, yes, he was different.

"Yeah, I was in Townsend for a few days. Needed some excitement after a month of Flats peace and quiet." Dirk nodded his head and smiled knowingly at Chuck.

"I see." Chuck decided not to use his imagination concerning this man's last few days. "I'm headed down to get supplies, and I'm late. I'll see you later today." Small talk was not something he felt like exchanging with Dirk as he led his horses past the surprised man.

"Yep, see you later." Dirk realized he and Chuck didn't have a lot to talk about. *He could be a little more social.* He turned around in the saddle and watched until White was out of sight. Dirk rode on but continued to think about this brief encounter.

Chuck acted like I'm not civilized. Well, I don't plan on staying at the Flats much longer. The place is boring, and I want to move on. I just need some money, and I think I know where to get that.

Dirk turned off onto the trail to Red Oak Flats and rode for several minutes. Rounding a curve, the first cabin came into view. Chuck's daughter sat on the front porch of the White's cabin. He stopped his horse to drink in the sight.

She looked delicious, even from this position, with her slight frame and dark hair. Her full skirt, pulled slightly above her knees, moved in the breeze. The women of Dirk's acquaintance were plump, painted, and well-used. A.B. was beautiful without makeup. The longer he stayed on the mountain, the greater his desire for her. He continued up the trail before she saw him.

During his stay at Red Oak Flats, he'd become familiar with the territory, its occupants and their habits. He laughed out loud into the empty forest.

The old man doesn't think anyone knows where his moonshine still is located. But I know.

Dirk often sat watching as the two men, Chuck and Jake, worked at making their brew in a flat space at the head of a valley below Cerulean Knob. He heard their voices clearly from his perch above, and often thought how easy it would be to put a bullet in both the men and take the fruits of their labor to sell. He knew exactly when a new batch was started and when one was ready to load. Those were the days, when Chuck and Jake led the horses out of the compound on their twice-a-week trek to the still.

He also knew where White stashed his money; at least, some of it. Not far from the moonshine still, a stump stuck out of the ground. During one of his visits, he saw Chuck and Jake lift the stump out of its hole. Underneath was a gallon jar. After stuffing a wad of bills into its open mouth, the lid was replaced and the jar and stump placed back into the ground. Dirk guessed there were other hiding places in the forest, but this was the only one he cared about. From what he could see, this stash was hefty.

Because he prowled around at night, he knew that Chuck often visited Kitty's home after everything quieted down on the mountain.

He knew that Jake helped draw water for A.B. to wash on Tuesday. He'd followed, maybe stalked was a better word, them many times to the spring and watched as they laughed and worked together. He observed the couple as the young girl threw back her head and laughed, filling the forest with the beautiful sound of her voice. He looked until he knew every curve on her body.

~

Dirk had never known love. He was a late, unwanted arrival. His mother and father argued about everything, including his father's numerous liaisons with women. When they weren't arguing with each other, they turned their anger on him.

"Dirk, get up. You lazy child. Go carry wood for the fire." His mother would grab him by his hair and push him out the door. A rebellious and unenergetic child, some of the anger was deserved.

"Dirk, haven't I told you five times to draw water from the cistern and water the cow and chickens? You're worthless." He had hurried to water the cow and kicked her unmercifully, imagining it was his mother or father, whoever had called him names.

The last straw was a tirade from his father over a plate of beans. His father had accused him of not doing his work and not deserving to eat. Dirk had picked up the dish and thrown it squarely in his father's face. Beans splattered everywhere and a loud crack was heard as the bowl hit the floor, breaking into a hundred pieces. His father jumped up from the table and headed in his direction.

"You're an ungrateful wretch of a son, get out of this house and don't come back!"

Dirk escaped from the room, knowing that his father meant exactly what he said. In his bedroom, he packed what few clothes he had and left out the back window. He never went back.

When his father kicked him out of the house, he was sixteen, had a terrible temper and was broke. He set out on his own. With no job skills, he found that stealing was the easiest way to make a living. The months passed by. At first, he stole to eat. He remembered the satisfaction he got out of taking the food he wanted without being detected.

He got tired of walking and decided to steal a horse and saddle, he'd found in an unattended barn. He rode all night, putting distance between him and the scene of his misdeed. Having transportation, he had determined to see the rest of the country. He was on the move. What else did he have to do? Dirk had no dreams.

As he made his way slowly through Ohio and into Kentucky, he learned the art of gambling and won money. He won a gun, a small derringer he kept in his boot. Because he was dark-skinned and good-looking, women fell into his arms. And when they didn't fall, he forced them—young ones especially. Now, he considered himself a real man.

After traveling through Kentucky and western Virginia, he entered Tennessee. He learned how to fight. In Kingsport, he left a man dead after a barroom brawl. Hiding out, because of his numerous escapades, he had ended up here in the foothills of the Smoky Mountains. At twenty-two, his heart was hard— unreachable.

With Dirk everything was physical, and satisfying those desires was his whole life. If he couldn't buy it, he took it with force. Remorse was a word he wasn't familiar with.

~

Dirk rode into the Flats. Jake came out the front door of his cabin, munching on a biscuit. Down below, A.B. hummed as she washed clothes on the White's back porch.

"Mornin', Dirk. You been to Townsend?" Jake had a lop-sided smile.

Dirk had an urge to ride on past the smiling, senile old fool. "Yeah, I went down for some excitement, you know, gambling and women," he said roughly. "It's too quiet up here on the mountain."

Though slow mentally, Jake recognized a bad mood. He walked down the steps and prepared to head back to work. "I see."

"I'm thinking," Dirk continued. "This is my last day in Red Oak Flats. I've decided to move on. Probably in the morning." Or before, thought Dirk. It depended on how events turned out this afternoon.

"I'll tell Chuck when he comes home." Jake said, wondering if Dirk owed money on his stay, and if he planned on settling up before he left. He decided not to say anything to Chuck. "I gotta go to work."

"Sure, Jake. Maybe I'll see you later."

Dirk dismounted his horse at his cabin and sat down on the porch steps.

I'm glad this is my last day here. Tomorrow, I'll move on with another notch in my belt and plenty of money in my pocket.

Dirk never made long-range plans. Plans tied a man down, regulated you, and confined a person to a specific way. No, he always played it by ear.

He looked down at the White's cabin. A.B. was washing clothes on the back porch and hanging them on the clothes line behind the cabin. He sat and watched her for several minutes before going in to eat.

When he came back to the porch, he saw her walking to Kitty's house. He knew she was going to dinner. When she looked up the hill toward the cabins, he waved. He was sure she saw him.

Hum-m, Miss Prissy Pants. Ignore me. Soon, you'll get to know me better. Dirk leaned back against the house in the cane chair, his hat pulled over his eyes. His nap lasted several minutes. He dreamed of A.B. When he woke up, he felt better.

Wonder where she is now?

Dirk didn't have to wonder long. A.B. walked out on the back porch and down the steps. She checked the clothes to see if they were dry. He watched as she pulled everything but Chuck's overalls off the line. She went back into the cabin. An hour passed before he saw her again.

A.B. walked from the side of the cabin, headed for the woods. In the direction she was headed, Dirk sensed she would end up in a depression where flowers grew in profusion. She went every week to see what was new. He waited until she was out of sight, then he walked into the woods and started toward the hollow. If he walked fast, he could beat her there and watch her arrive.

~

After pulling the dry clothes off the line and folding them, Abigail looked in the direction of a favorite hollow, where trillium, lady slippers, and phacelia grew in excess. It was late in the afternoon, and the yellow sun caused gentle shadows in the forest.

Maybe the Robin's-plantain and Jack-in-the-pulpits are in bloom. Last week, they were very close to opening up.

Her father wouldn't be home for another two hours. If she hurried, she could be there and back with enough time to start supper. A.B. decided she needed to check them out. She placed the folded clothes on the kitchen table. Walking out the front door, she headed to her left and down the mountain. The hollow was a thirty-minute walk from her home.

❧ Chapter Four ❧

Same day, afternoon at Red Oak Flats — A.B.

A.B. walked often in the woods. She did this without feeling fear or being threatened. Bears roamed the forest, but hunting had reduced their numbers, and the chances of seeing one was little. Mountain people talked about hearing the wild cry of a panther, but these large animals didn't exist in the Smokies, killed off long ago by bounty hunters. Sightings were only stories—tall tales told by the inhabitants seeking attention.

She followed the path until the edge of Pawpaw Hollow appeared. This was A.B.'s name for the place, because she often saw the black-and-white, swallowtail butterflies flitting about, and because a pawpaw tree grew here.

She looked down the deepening depression, where the terrain grew more rugged, and where a spring emerged from underneath a large rock embedded in the hillside. A.B. never went that far, because about one-half mile below the bubbling stream's appearance, it cascaded off the face of a rock bank and ran under Rich Mountain Road. Boulders, strewn helter-skelter as if deposited by a giant hand, blocked the path.

Copperhead snakes lived in holes under the smaller stones.

A.B. walked into the hollow, heading for a large patch of yellow trillium she knew well. She bent down to get a closer look and smelled its lemon scent.

"Hi, yellow trillium. Hum, you look like you're turning brown. Time to store food for next year. Remember the ants and bees," she cautioned as she touched one of its three petals. She always talked to her flowers. Some of the old-timers said they grew better if you talked to them.

The yellow lady slippers hadn't changed from last week. A.B. imagined each as a fair maiden with a prominent chin, their hair hanging in wisps down their cheeks. "Ladies, are you ready for the spring ball next week?"

Yes, they nodded in the thin breeze which blew down the hollow. "I'll be by to pick you up on Friday. Don't forget the date." A.B. waved goodbye.

Leaving them, she saw that the Robin's-plantain was blooming. Their yellow centers surrounded by a white halo of tiny, thin spikes. She picked a handful and threw them into the air, wondering if they might turn into stars in the night sky. The Cherokee used the leaves or roots in a poultice for headaches. She never had headaches and didn't know if it worked or not.

Abigail continued her slow walk down the hollow, stooping at times to check for new arrivals and doing a pirouette because she felt as light as a feather. She felt a wonderful happiness and freedom here in the woods in the midst of her wild flowers. If she left her mountain home, walks to this hollow would cease. She felt a quick stab of sorrow because she wouldn't see her old friends.

"I promise to return each spring to say hello," she called up the hollow.

The Solomon's seal arched its back in long fronds from the side of the bank.

"Now don't get miffed and be upset with me. I do promise to be back. Really, I do." Abigail raised the stem to see the white, bell-shaped flowers beneath the opposite leaves and shook the frond to ring them.

She said hello to the green-suited Jacks who stood in their striped, hooded green pulpits. "Dear Sir, what's the title of your sermon today?" Abigail listened, cocking her ear, but the gentleman answered nary a word.

Abigail checked the position of the sun and decided there was time to sit down under an old hemlock tree, a favorite place where she could look back up the hollow. The ground was covered with a thin bed of short needles which had fallen from the aged patriarch. She eased down to the ground, using them as a mat and trying not to get her clean skirt dirty.

My friends are here.

For the first time, Abigail realized that she was lonely. There were times when she was glad to be alone. But there were also times when she needed a soul-mate. She studied this new feeling as she sat under the shelter of her hemlock tree. The problem, she thought, was that the beautiful flowers couldn't talk back. Her conversation was one-sided.

Of course, she had Kitty. But this feeling was different. She needed someone with which to share more, share herself, share — something. She couldn't put her finger on it. She laughed aloud and stretched out under the boughs of the hemlock, placing her hands under her head.

I'm a creature of habit. I always sit here, and I always lie back and watch the puffy, white clouds through the drooping limbs of this elderly hemlock.

Abigail looked up the huge tree trunk. It had so many boughs that a hard rain couldn't penetrate to the ground. She decided it was as old as the hills surrounding her.

A.B.'s thoughts turned to her father. What response would he make when she and Kitty talked to him? Would he go to Maryville and make arrangements for A.B. to live at her Aunt Mary's or refuse to listen to her plan? She closed her eyes for a minute. When she opened them, a man stood before her.

Dirk.

Fear stabbed at her startled heart. What reason did he have for being here? Dumbfounded, she couldn't speak.

"Hello, A.B."

"How—how did you find me?" Abigail stood quickly to her feet. He was within three steps of her and blocked her way home.

"Oh, I followed you." Dirk leered at her.

"Well, I'm getting ready to go back to the cabin." She didn't like the look he gave her, running his eyes over her face and body. She felt cold chills on her arms.

"Let's don't go just yet," he suggested, saying each word deliberately and nodding at each one.

Abigail tried to bolt past him, but he caught her arm and drew her to him, trying to kiss her on the mouth.

A.B. tried to break free. "Let me go. My father will kill you, if you touch me!"

"Oh, I'm going to touch you."

A.B. struggled.

Dirk pinned one of her arms against his body. The other was free. "I'll enjoy this."

Abigail smelled his breath. It reeked of alcohol.

He started to tear at her blouse, ripping some of the buttons loose and exposing part of her chest.

Abigail struggled against him, pushing hard, and struck at him with her free arm. She landed one hard blow to his head.

He let go.

She didn't see the fist as it flew through the air. She landed on her back, struggling to stay conscious, with the taste of warm blood in her mouth. Still woozy, she felt him tug at her clothes, and then the weight of his body was on hers. She struggled but to no advantage. A.B. closed her eyes as his greedy, searching mouth, smelling of alcohol, covered hers. She couldn't scream, and even if she did no one would hear her.

She continued to struggle, but when the assault was over, he was gone. She turned over on her stomach and sobbed. She had expected she would die during the attack, but she was still alive.

A terrible thought ran through her mind. Thinking in horror that he might be back, she jumped up. Still crying, she ran blindly through the forest. Small limbs caught at her skirt and tore her skin. Anywhere was better than under her hemlock tree.

She headed for a part of the mountain not familiar to her. She kept running.

Running.

On top of the mountain, she came to an opening in the thicket and pushed through to a small, rocky overlook. Down below, a church sat nestled within Cades Cove.

It looked so peaceful.

Her world was shattered, but below there was a peaceful valley. She didn't understand it at all. She couldn't think—couldn't put it together. She sat down on the warm sunlit rocks. Her sixteen-year-old world was crushed.

Abigail started to cry again, sobbing deeply from her hurt. She rocked back and forth, her head down. Each time she thought about what happened she started to sob again. She felt dirty, soiled. Never had she felt unclean or impure in her life. When she quieted down, she started to think a bit clearer.

How can I go back to Red Oak Flats? How will I tell my father? What will he say? Or maybe I'll go to Kitty. Yes, that's what I'll do. I'll go to Kitty.

She was ready to get up when suddenly there were sounds behind her in the forest. She leaped up, pulling her blouse together with her hand and adjusting her dirty skirt. Oh, no! He was back again. She glanced around. She couldn't go. She was trapped.

When Matthew appeared before her, for a second she was relieved. Fear replaced the relief immediately. It wasn't Dirk. She was glad of that.

"Hello, I'm Matthew Tipton." If Abigail hadn't been so terrified, his deep voice would have soothed her, but she was in no condition for small talk. She kept silent, watching his movements. She had no idea what he was saying. The attack was all she could think about. She couldn't concentrate on his words.

When he passed her and sat down on the rocky outcrop, she bolted past him down the path. All she wanted to do was get away.

At the top of the mountain, she paused a minute, got her bearings, and headed toward home. She was eerily calm. Focused on reaching Kitty's, she cleared her mind of everything else and followed the ridge of the mountain. The path was unfamiliar but this was good. It reduced the possibility of Dirk finding her in the forest again.

Coming into familiar territory, Abigail walked faster, almost running toward home. Climbing the steps, she rushed in the door of Kitty's house, relieved to be there, and broke into sobs.

I'm home. I'm safe.

Kitty took one look at Abigail and ran to the crying girl. "Abigail, what on earth has happened?"

Abigail sobbed. She couldn't speak.

"It's okay. It's okay." Kitty held on tight to the shaking, overwrought girl. "Settle down."

For several minutes, the two stood, arms around each other. Abigail felt Kitty stroke her hair and rub her back. *Like a child,* she thought. Abigail calmed down.

"He hurt me." Abigail said. "He hurt me. He hurt me."

"Let's sit down."

Abigail followed Kitty to a couch.

Telling Kitty was the hardest thing Abigail had done in her life. She was exhausted when she finished. She leaned against Kitty, the weight of her body resting against the curve of Kitty's arm. They sat there, the sound of the ticking clock filling the room. Each tick meant her father was closer to home. What would he say?

Abigail shook her head. What happened to a day that started so beautifully? If only she had left this mountain; days, months or years ago, this horrible experience wouldn't have happened. She started to cry again.

"Kitty, I want to go home and lie down." Abigail wanted the warmth and safety of her own bed. Kitty walked her home, helped her change her soiled clothes and wash up. Then, she put A.B. to bed.

"Kitty, don't leave me." Abigail clutched her hand, a desperate look in her eyes.

"I wouldn't think of leaving you. I'm going to stay right here, until your Pa gets home." After Kitty spoke, a relieved look appeared in Abigail's eyes, but she refused to let go of her friend's hand. When she slept, it was a fitful, restless sleep.

∼

Kitty got up and paced the room. When Chuck got home, someone would pay for this act. Walking out the back door, she started to cry. Through her tears she pulled Chuck's overalls off the clothes line. They were dry.

∼

Chuck arrived just before dark. In fact, Kitty had lit the lantern in the White's cabin because she couldn't see to get supper ready for the table. Abigail didn't awaken as Chuck came up the back steps and opened the door.

"Kitty, what are you doing here?" He was puzzled. Kitty's form blocked his sight into the room.

"Sh-h-h." Kitty put her finger to her lips. "Abigail's sleeping. Let's go out onto the porch to talk." She turned him around and gave him a push out of the door before he could say anything else.

"What's wrong?" Chuck sensed the problem was serious. "Is A.B. sick? Does she need a doctor?"

Kitty went straight to the problem. "Dirk followed Abigail into the woods today."

"What! Did he hurt her?" Chuck yelled loudly. He looked intensely at Kitty.

"Sh-h-h, talk lower. I'm afraid he did." Kitty nodded her head.

"I knew there was something I didn't like about him." Chuck turned around and kicked viciously several times at a clump of grass in the ground, sending it flying into the air. He clenched and unclenched his fists. "What exactly happened?"

"He trailed her into the hollow where her wildflowers grow, grabbed her, hit her with his fist when she struggled, and attacked her there. She has a big blue bruise on the side of her head where he hit her with his fist and a cut on the inside of her mouth. She's exhausted, and I put her to bed. I'm going to stay with her tonight. You can stay in my cabin."

"I won't rest until I find that low-life." Chuck went into the house and got his revolver out of a drawer. He paused to look at his daughter, who slept with the quilt pulled up to her nose. His little girl was now a woman, by the worst possible manner. He intended to take care of the man who did this. "Don't worry, daughter, I'll see that he doesn't do this to anyone else," he said under his breath. "But, what good will that do Abigail? The worst has happened."

Kitty heard him mumble and met him at the door. "Be careful. That man has no conscience. He won't think twice about killing you, and you probably wouldn't be the first one to die by his hand."

～

In his anger, Chuck pushed past her and stomped up the path to Dirk's cabin. He slung the door open — hard. Wham! It broke off its cheap hinges. The sound of it falling echoed in the stillness of the forest. The room was empty.

Of course, he isn't here. He's long gone. I wonder if he's in Townsend, bragging to his buddies. I'll saddle up and go see.

"Chuck, what's wrong?" Jake was standing outside the cabin door in the twilight, alerted by the loud noise of the door falling on the porch. "Is it Abigail?"

He waited for Chuck's answer, but he thought he knew the problem. Abigail was sick. Abigail was asleep in the daytime. He had an uneasy feeling that something was badly amiss.

"He hurt Abigail," Chuck nodded toward the cabin where Dirk stayed. "If I find him, I'm goin' to make sure he never hurts anyone else, the braggart." Chuck looked down the trail toward Townsend.

Jake, eyes wide-open, stared at the gun in Chuck's hand. "Are you gonna kill him?" He didn't often see his boss this angry.

Chuck didn't answer Jake's question. "I'm headin' for Townsend. With any luck, I may find him there."

"I'm goin' with you."

"No Jake, you stay here and take care of Abigail and Kitty. He might come back, and they'll need you." Chuck didn't need Jake tagging along. He intended to ride fast. If Dirk was there, he might catch him. Jake didn't need to know what might happen next.

~

Later that night, Chuck returned to the Flats. He was glad to be home. His search for Dirk was unsuccessful. He'd poked his head into every watering hole, including the women's houses, and come up blank. His stomach was empty, and he was drained of energy.

I need to check on Abigail and Kitty before going to Kitty's cabin to sleep.

He walked up to the back-porch steps and stopped in his tracks. He saw Jake stretched out across the door's threshold with a quilt wrapped around him. Sound asleep, Jake was snoring as he lay on the hard, wooden floor. Chuck shook his head. Even though the situation was grave, he smiled in the darkness. Trust Jake to do the best he could to follow orders.

Chuck walked around to the front porch. The boards creaked as he crossed them and opened the front door.

Never did fix those confounded, creaking boards. I'll nail them down tomorrow.

"Who is it? I have a gun." Kitty's voice was clear and steady.

"It's me. I wanted to check on you both before going to bed."

"Oh, Chuck. I'm sorry. This whole situation is like being in a bad dream, especially for Abigail."

"How is she?" Chuck walked over to his sleeping daughter. "Has she been up? Did she eat anything?" he whispered.

"She sat up for a short period, but she wasn't hungry. She's still so tired. She has no strength. I put her back to bed. I still can't believe this happened to her. What a dreadful nightmare, especially for her."

"It's all my fault. I shouldn't have insisted she stay up here on this mountain with all this riffraff living here. I should have known this would happen."

Kitty ignored the "riffraff" part. *Is that what he thinks of me?* "Abigail talked to me at lunch about going to live with her Aunt Mary in Maryville. I told her we would both talk to you. Her thinking was that if she was going to get married, no one here was acceptable. Guess we didn't know how unacceptable they were." Kitty sighed and went on, "Did you find Dirk?"

"No. Not even a hint of his presence in Townsend. He's probably in the next county or North Carolina. Do you have any food left from supper? I'm hungry. I suppose Jake ate with you."

"Yes. He did. He's been guarding us ever since you left. He insisted on sleeping on the porch. He'll be sore in the morning." Kitty fixed Chuck a plate of food.

"He wanted to go, but I convinced him, he was needed here, the old geezer." Chuck looked affectionately in the direction of his aged friend. "I'm exhausted. I'll take the food to your cabin to eat, but I'll be down early in the morning. I think I'll send Jake to tend the still and stay here at home tomorrow. Good night, Kitty." He turned toward her and gave her an awkward hug.

"I, uh – you know how I feel about you." He said this to soothe the "riffraff" comment. Then he was gone.

❦ Chapter Five ❦

Afternoon on Tater Hill Same Day — Matthew

Matthew stopped and cocked his head. *What's that?* Coming from the direction of his destination, a small rocky outcrop ahead, was the faint but distinct sound of sobbing.

He'd spent the afternoon working on his rusty hunting skills, walking along the crest of Rich Mountain, listening for sounds of animals in the forest.

The noise of sobbing was the last one he expected.

Coming home, after the mad rush of finishing his last year in preparatory school in Maryville, he had headed for his secret haven. Walking there was an enjoyable, annual ritual after months of concentrated study. In this sheltered place, he rested and thought about life, while renewing his acquaintance with his beloved home, Cades Cove. Down below his intended perch was a small, white-framed church — the one at which his father preached and where he hoped to speak in the future. Cautiously, he went toward the uncommon sounds.

He'd never encountered a soul during many trips to his hidden, craggy bluff on Rich Mountain; part of the low hills which framed one side of Cades Cove. The scooped-out cove nestled between ridges on the western side of the mile-high Smoky Mountains. This undulating, blue range straddled Tennessee and North Carolina.

Sobbing.

Deep and uncontrollable, it assaulted his ears and cut to his soul as Matthew crept forward through the dense forest.

The heart-wrenching sounds grew louder. Despair, tragedy, he heard both in the loud weeping.

Coming near he stopped and parted the shielding leaves. Matthew stood within ten feet of the shaking, crying girl. He waited. *Maybe she'll calm down.*

She was sitting on the ground, her forehead on her folded knees and her arms crossed over her head. He watched her slender figure as she rocked back and forth in her dirty, cotton-print frock, the deep sobs racking her body.

Embarrassment rushed through him. He felt like an intruder watching a forbidden scene through a laurel-leaf-framed window.

In his seventeen years, he'd never had an experience like this. *Think Matthew. What would Dad do?* His father ministered to his congregation, wrapping his long arms around those who were sick and dying, whispering words of comfort.

Remember Aunt Annie's grief when she lost grandpa. I was so young, and death was a notion I was just startin' to understand. I ran to her, grabbing her around the waist, holdin' on for dear life as she cried her heart out . . .

Matthew watched, feeling compassion and foreboding.

The sounds had lessoned, although the rocking kept on. He turned to go.

"No, Matthew." He shook his head after taking one step. "You can't leave her here. Not without tryin' to help her. Maybe you'll mess up, but she needs to know someone cares, and you're the only one to lend a hand," he said softly to himself.

He decided not to walk into the small clearing unannounced, so he kicked at some twigs lying along the trail — making noise while eyeing her reaction.

The young girl looked startled, jumped up, and clutched at her torn clothing. Her eyes darted around the opening, but escape was blocked by his presence in the path and the surrounding thick laurel underbrush.

Seeing the terror on her pale face and in her eyes, Matthew realized she expected the worst from her intruder. He guessed her age to be around fifteen or sixteen, only a little younger than he.

Stepping into the small, open space, he spoke to the startled girl.

"Hello," he said. "I'm Matthew Tipton. My home's on Tater Branch and my father preaches at the church you see down yonder." He pointed in the general direction of the steepled church, hoping this would put her at ease.

She stood, staring uneasily at him.

Matthew waited for the trembling girl to say something. Instead, she looked at him from reddened eyes underneath long, sweeping lashes which glistened with tears. With the back of her hand, she wiped tearstains from her cheeks. Even in her disheveled, dirty condition, she was a beautiful girl. Pushing wavy chestnut hair from her suntanned face, she looked at him with deep, brown eyes, wide with dread.

"I don't intend to hurt you," Matthew said clumsily. "This here's my resting place. I come here every chance I get."

Should I ask about her trouble?

Prying for answers wasn't like him; at least not in this situation. *Heck, I've never been in this situation.*

He sensed she was not a person who easily trusted a stranger. He would not ask, not yet. Maybe she would volunteer the information.

"I come here to enjoy the view," he said trying to gain her trust.

Still no response.

Now what? This talkin' is one sided.

Matthew stepped a little closer and said awkwardly, "Sure is hot today. Everyone says the summer will be a scorcher, and Abrams Creek will go dry. There's less water already."

Silence.

Matthew continued to stand in the path to the ledge, and the girl watched his every action.

He held up both hands and, with one, gestured toward the rock at the edge of the drop. He made the first move. The frightened girl took one step sideways, standing hemmed in by the laurel bushes at the side of the clearing. She clutched her clothing tighter around her.

Smiling at her, Matthew walked over and eased himself down in the place the girl had left only minutes before.

Maybe this will show her I can be trusted; that I'm not here to hurt her.

The young woman eyed him, shuffled her feet and turned as she followed his movements. Satisfied that the man was firmly on the ground, she bolted past him and disappeared out of sight.

Matthew twisted, catching glimpses of the fleeing girl through the forest foliage.

Air gushed into his lungs and rushed out as he sighed. He'd been holding his breath in expectation of—he didn't know what. An explanation? A conversation?

The peace of his rocky outcrop was broken by the woman's presence.

Matthew turned around, his long legs dangling over the short, eight-foot drop. Leaning forward, he rested his hands on the rock ledge and looked off into the distance. He hardly noticed the church as it sat against a large clearing in the cove before him. His eyes didn't follow the curving dirt road to the west or look to see the rock chimney top of his mountain home on Tater Branch. He didn't look at the tall, magnificent mountains beyond, where hunter's feet had walked for centuries, making paths for future generations to explore. He didn't think about the former gatherers of the forests' fruits of nuts, berries and wood, as they worked in leather-fringed clothing or loin cloth. His mind was stuck on the present.

Matthew's uneasiness continued as he remembered the young woman's terror-filled eyes. What prompted her outburst? Where did she live? What was her name? Why haven't I seen her before?

Questions.

Questions crowded his mind. Jumbled together, unanswerable questions.

Matthew sat thinking. *I don't recollect seeing her in the cove, at school or my father's church. There are cabins in many isolated areas on this side of the Smoky Mountains. Most of the residents I know. I'm sure I would recall this striking, dark-haired girl. I wonder if she comes from Red Oak Flats. I've never visited the area, but if I remember rightly it's not too far away and off Rich Mountain Road.*

Could she live there?

He didn't know anyone from the Flats area, and no one he knew ever went there. It was the red-light district of Cades Cove. The busy-body line said loose women lived there.

"That's what I've heard, but it may not be true." Matthew said these words out loud, willing to give the settlement the benefit of a doubt.

Then he remembered. "Dad said no respectable, church-going man or woman ever sets foot in the place."

He shook his head. "I hope she isn't from there."

Frustrated, Matthew ran his fingers through his short, light-brown hair and decided it was none of his business. And yet, he realized the haunting look and tear-stained cheeks of her terrified features would disturb him for many days. He pulled his knees up and wrapped his long arms around them, assuming the vanished girl's stance.

"Pshaw." This low statement was accompanied by a two-chuckle laugh. "I'll never see her again . . . still." He dropped his head onto his knees and uttered, "Dear Father, please protect and surround this young woman with your love. If it is Your will, may I be a help to her in the future." He paused for reflection then continued. "Bless this summer as I start preparation for Your service. In the name of Your Son I pray, Amen."

Matthew shivered.

The sun had disappeared behind the mountains. The rapid change in temperature always amazed him. It was his signal to return home.

If I hurry, I'll get there before dark.

He arose, and after one last look at the interrupted, pastoral scene below, took a different trail down the mountain. After traipsing over the hills and valleys of Cades Cove for several years, he wasn't afraid of getting lost.

❦ Chapter Six ❦

Same afternoon, the walk home — Matthew

The encounter with the girl filled Matthew's thoughts as he left his rocky retreat. He stumbled as he descended the steep slope. Grabbing at saplings to steady his progress, he stepped carefully to keep from tripping and tumbling headlong down the sharp incline.

Reaching the gentler elevations of Tater Ridge, his pace picked up and, keeping to the woods, he left the mountaintop behind. The darkness deepened in the woods as he skirted the plowed, planted fields of the verdant valley and arrived at Tater Branch.

Picking his way along the brush and fern-covered banks of the trickling creek, he disturbed a whitetail deer grazing at the edge of a grassy meadow. He watched the deer rush away, the sounds of its hooves thudding against the forest floor until they faded into the hushed woodland. He stopped to catch his breath and look for the rest of the herd in the woods. They should be close by and, as twilight deepened, the animals always appeared and grazed in the open fields.

Matthew saw no movement under the trees.

Quiet.

Quiet, he thought. How could there be silence after the events of today?

His mood became lighter as he crossed the meandering, clear waters of Tater Branch and intersected a well-worn path following the creek.

"Thank goodness, I'm only a few minutes from home, and I'm hungry. Food's on the way." He told his grumbling stomach. His appetite hadn't been fazed by the afternoon's happenings at all.

Turning left, he headed toward the valley of the cove. Several hundred feet later, he came to a cleared area, walked down to the water's edge and knelt beside the stream. Cupping his hands for a cool drink, he noticed his broken reflection in the moving waters.

"Matthew, you've got crooked ears." He smiled at his reflection in the water, revealing deep dimples in his cheeks. Earlier that morning, he'd placed his city britches in the bottom drawer of his dresser and put on his clean, patched overalls. He noticed the soft, blue material, faded from many washings, matched the color of his eyes.

Stuffed in the pockets of his clothes, when he'd left the cabin, were his pocket knife, a small box of matches, and his red bandana handkerchief. These items were stored in the top drawer of his dresser while he was at school. Two newspaper-covered ham biscuits, handed to him by his mother as he walked out the door, finished off the items needed for his walk in the woods. At lunchtime, he'd stretched out under a pine tree and eaten them with great pleasure.

Matthew cupped his hands and drank deeply. The water was cool and satisfying.

A movement on the other side of the creek bank caught his attention. Leaning back on his haunches, he stared at a small animal which moved in the underbrush. It was a full-grown squirrel. He sat quietly watching it forage for food beneath the low-hanging branches. The squirrel's appearance brought back memories of another stop at this very spot.

"Here's where I found Nibbler." Nibbler was a half-starved, baby squirrel. "Mom was ready to run out of the house when I brought her inside. No wonder after the snakes, frogs, and bats I've carried home." He laughed at his words. He'd nursed the little squirrel with a medicine dropper until it was grown and released it to the woods. The squirrel stayed close to the Tipton house for several months. "I wonder if this one is her offspring."

Most spots hereabouts were attached to some favorite happening. All it took was visiting them to nudge his memory.

Matthew stood up. The squirrel scampered away.

The frame Tipton house was visible through the trees. *I wonder if Dad's back from visiting Mrs. Burchfield?* The elderly lady, one of his flock, was bedridden with rheumatism.

A few steps later, Matthew emerged from the woods. He crossed a barbed wire fence and traversed the grassy field until he came to the pasture gate which swung on stout hinges as he opened and closed it. His long legs soon covered the distance home.

❧ Chapter Seven ❧

Same Day — Matthew

From the curve of the path, Matthew saw his father and waved.

Nathan Tipton sat under the wood-shingled roof of the front porch. Although many of the mountain homes sported the new tin roofs, his father preferred wood shingles on his frame home. As Matthew approached, his father stood up to greet him.

"Whew, I need to catch my breath."

Nat walked over to the wooden porch steps, where his son dropped down to rest.

"You've been gone some time, son."

"Walked up to Rich Mountain Road to sit a spell." Matthew wondered if he should relate the girl's presence and condition. He decided against it. Most likely, he'd never see her again.

His father glanced toward the mountain. Only the top was visible from the porch. In the twilight, this side of the mountain turned green-black against the darkening sky.

"Do you remember your first trip up there?"

Matthew nodded his head. How could he forget? He was seven years old. After the long climb up the trail, he was tuckered out and his father carried him on his broad shoulders most of the way back home. He remembered ducking his head when they encountered low-lying branches and his father letting him cool his bare feet in Tater Branch before they arrived home. He had kicked the water, splashing it from one side of the brook to the other. He'd caught crawdads and minnows with his hands and played skip-rock on the surface of the water.

"When we arrived home, Mom complained because I was soakin' wet." Matthew smiled in the gathering twilight.

"Has it changed any? I haven't been up there in years," said his father, leaning against one of the porch's supporting posts, his face settled and serene as it often looked when he'd been reading his Bible and talking to God.

Matthew glanced over at the chair his father had vacated. The Bible rested on a small table exactly where he expected to find it. On top were his father's spectacles.

"No. Just about the same. Maybe the overgrowth is denser. The view is still beautiful . . . " Matthew hesitated to add peaceful after today's encounter.

"It's beginning to get dark."

Both men turned to look across the pastureland to the low-land hills below the towering sentinel, Thunderhead Mountain. Thunderhead was the highest peak on the other side of Cades Cove. In the new dusk, lanterns flickered from the resident's homes. Some were high upon the hillsides. Others appeared along the unseen road at the edge of the planted fields. They reminded Matthew of the lightning bugs he'd caught as a young boy.

"Dad, when do the lightnin' bugs come out?" Some people called them fire-flies.

His dad laughed. "I was just thinkin' the same thing. They'll be out next month, in June, along with the June bugs. Those times are long gone, aren't they son?"

Those times were when his mother loaned him one of her precious Mason canning jars. He and his dad caught lighting bugs and put them in the tinted-green, glass container. Later in the night he watched from the haven of his bed as the bugs lit up his coverlet with a green glow. The next day he released them into the air.

~

At least, there was peace here on Tater Branch, he thought, sniffing the air.

Nat noticed Matthew's nose wriggling. "Mother's getting' our meal ready."

In the dim light, Matthew grinned at his father. For as long as he could remember Nat had called his wife, "Mother." After seven children, this was an aptly applied name; one she deserved. Matthew thought how good it was to hear the familiar term again.

Martha Tipton was the most industrious woman Matthew knew and the perfect minister's wife. Her home was immaculate, her cooking delicious, and her faith in God steady as a rock.

"I'm hungry," he responded. It was good to be home.

The two men continued to sit on the front porch, waiting for the call to supper, and resting in each other's company.

"I hope you enjoy your summer. It's the last one you'll have, especially if you go to summer school."

Matthew nodded, agreeing with his Dad. "Yes, when college starts this fall, I won't have any time off for three years and then my pastorate will begin here in the Cove."

Nathan smiled at Matthew. "This summer will be like a rite of passage from young man to adulthood. A putting off the old and putting on the new is the way the Bible says it."

❦ Chapter Eight ❦

Same day, nighttime at the Tipton's home — Matthew

When the dusk turned to dark, Matthew smelled a strong cooked cabbage aroma coming through the screen door of his summer home. He peered into the cabin's dark interior, but his mother could not be seen. A light shining from the doorway of the kitchen was momentarily interrupted, as she moved about the room.

Before leaving for his afternoon walk to Rich Mountain, he'd gone to their winter vegetable storage, which was nothing but a deep hole dug in a cool, shady spot. The hole and the vegetable layers were lined and layered with straw. Matthew had knelt down and removed the boards atop the hole. They served as weights on the thick top layer of straw. Last year's extra cabbage, turnips, and carrots were placed inside. He fished a head of green cabbage and some carrots out of their resting place and took them to his mother.

"Dad, my stomach's rumbling from the odor of cooking cabbage. I didn't know I was so hungry." His mouth watered as he thought about his mom's cabbage dumplings.

"Your Mom makes the best ones I've ever eaten. And I'm more than ready to eat them and the fried squirrel I shot this morning.

At daybreak, his father had killed and dressed two squirrels before his son was out of bed. Matthew smiled, remembering what his uncle, Lazarus Tipton, often said, "One squirrel will not feed two hungry men."

His thoughts were interrupted by his father's question.

"Are you ready for the hunt tomorrow? The others will be over early in the afternoon. When they get here, we'll head for Thunderhead Mountain. The walk will be brisk, but we plan on arriving on top before dark."

"Yes, Dad, I'm ready."

"I'm glad we could wait until you got home. I haven't been bear huntin' in years. Can't wait to see what my new Winchester 30-30 rifle will do. The Maryville gunsmith claimed it was a newer model and good for huntin' large animals. I spent yesterday afternoon settin' its sights. It's loaded and ready to go. We're provisioned to stay several days. Have you packed your heavy coat? It'll be cold on top of Thunderhead."

"I'm ready." Matthew nodded from his seat on the porch steps. "My blanket, rifle, and other supplies are sittin' beside my bed, all set to be loaded in the wagon. I'm excited at the chance to see Spencefield and Thunderhead again."

But that was all he was excited about. He'd managed to avoid bear hunting expeditions. Matthew looked over at his father and wondered why he hadn't refused to go on this trip.

But then, he never refused his dad. As the dutiful son, he followed in his father's footsteps. He was the example the young man looked up to and admired.

"Dad, do you remember me preaching to the congregation after your morning service was over."

Nathan laughed and reminisced, "Yes, you were determined as a young four-year-old child to preach, much to the embarrassment of your older brothers. After my sermon, you sent the church people into gales of laughter as you stood in the pulpit and mimicked my actions. Raising your arms, speaking forcefully in a loud, childish voice, you proclaimed the Word of God as best you remembered it."

His father stood up and pulled a box of Diamond Matches from under the shingled roof. Taking the glass globe off the kerosene lantern hanging on a nail beside the door, he struck the match on the side of the box. After lighting the wick, he replaced the matchbox where he'd found it and trimmed the woven wick to give off enough light but not darken the globe with soot. A golden glow lit the men's faces and the porch area.

In the darkness, they heard scurrying feet in the yard. The smell of a skunk wafted on the gentle breeze, and two eyes peered at them from the hedge beside the road.

"We have a visitor." His father laughed, disturbing the skunk. Its eyes no longer seen, he said, "Only one thing worst than seeing a skunk's eyes, and that's not seeing 'em. Then you have no idea where the varmint is or which end is pointed toward you."

"Supper's ready," his mother called from the cool interior of the house. Father and son went in to eat by lamplight.

Matthew went to bed early that night.

❦ Chapter Nine ❦

Preparations for the Hunting Trip — Matthew

Matthew opened his eyes. His father was shaking him by the shoulder.

"Get up, Son. We must start chores early so we'll be ready to go this afternoon. You'll need to drop by the church and make sure everything's been prepared for Sunday's service. We may not be back until Saturday night."

"O.K., Dad. What else do you want me to do?" said Matthew as he got out of bed. He stretched his arms toward the ceiling and yawned.

"Milk the cow and feed the chickens, hogs, and horses. Be sure and set extra feed where your mother can get to it. I'll tend to the garden and make sure she has provisions while we're away."

"Mother," Matthew's father called as he left the room. "Do you have your list ready for the store? I want to go after dinner."

Matthew looked into his bedroom mirror. He grinned at the tall, lanky young man with light brown hair and twinkling blue eyes.

"You look a little sleepy-eyed, Matthew," he said out loud and laughed. This caused tiny crow's-feet to appear at his temples and deep dimples to emerge on his cheeks. He made a funny face in the mirror and checked the stubble on his face.

Splashing water from a basin on his dresser, he lathered up to shave, which didn't take long. Following his nose, he headed for the kitchen.

The aroma of bacon cooking on the wood stove and fresh bread baking in the oven made his mouth water. His mother was making extra biscuits filled with sausage, bacon, and country ham for their trip. These were placed in a tin pail with a lid. Eggs, boiled in his mother's iron pots, would be added to the supplies. Onions, sardines and cheese would be brought from Burchfield's store and added to the growing stack of provisions placed on the back porch for the hunt. His dad always purchased a few pieces of stick candy for a snack.

∼

Matthew tiptoed up behind his gray-haired mother who stood at the stove turning over the bacon she was frying in her iron skillet. She alternately cooked and fanned her face with her calico-colored, bib apron.

"Having one of your *spells*, Mom?" He grinned. Martha used this expression to explain about being in the *warm-stage* of life as she called it.

"Good morning, Son." Martha chose not to answer his question.

Matthew was totally ignorant when it came to female problems, spells, and warm stages. Intimate details of bodily functions weren't considered a proper subject to talk about between men and women unless you were husband and wife. Martha was the only woman Matthew was around, and she wouldn't breathe a word to her son. Most of his acquaintances were men. He didn't know much about women at all.

He'd never liked any girl, unless Sally Adams would qualify. But like many short-lived cove families, hers had left before anything serious happened between them other than hand-holding in the moonlight.

"It's wonderful to have you home for the summer." Martha Tipton wiped her hand on her apron and patted her son's cheek when he came up behind to hug, nuzzle, and kiss her. She loved it. "I miss you while you're at school."

"It's good to be home in my own comfortable bed. I slept like a log last night. Don't think I moved a muscle from the time my head hit the pillow." Matthew picked up a piece of crisp bacon from the warming plate resting on the stovetop and munched on it.

Martha turned around to get a good look at her son. "I can't get over how tall you are. I think you've grown three inches since Christmas. Isn't there something I can do to keep you from growing up and out of the house?"

Matthew reached for another piece of bacon. "That's good stuff."

His mother slapped his hand with the fork she was using.

Matthew dropped the warm slice back into the plate.

Standing sentinel over her plate of freshly cooked bacon was a necessity when Matthew was around.

"I'll whack your head if you reach for bacon again."

"Aw, Mom, I'm your favorite son. Could you let me have one more piece?"

"No. Haven't changed a bit, have you? Wait until breakfast. Make yourself useful and go tell your father to come on and eat. The eggs and biscuits will be ready by the time you get back." Matthew was laughing as he opened the screen door and started outside. He and his mother played the same game . . .

"Son," Martha called after him. "Do you really want to go on this hunt? You've only gotten home, and you're out the door again. I hoped we could talk about school today." She was a former school teacher at Townsend and interested in his school events.

"Dad wants me to go. He's been planning this trip for months. I can't disappoint him. We'll have all summer to talk about school." Matthew closed the screen door and bounded down the back-porch steps calling for his dad.

$\sim$

Martha watched her tall, good-looking son open the screen door and disappear from view. She loved her son, who was an accident—born ten years after the last child. Martha Tipton's nest was empty except for Matthew, who lived in Maryville while school was in session and attended Bill Joe Henry's Academy. The rest of her children lived in Townsend or Maryville with their families. Each moved from the Cove as jobs opened up for them. Some worked for Little River Lumber Company in Townsend and others for the Aluminum Company of America in Maryville.

Turning back to the frying bacon, she used her doubled up apron to remove the iron skillet to a cooler part of the cook stove. Lifting each piece out with a fork, she poured most of the grease into a container sitting nearby.

Cracking eggs on the edge of a mixing bowl, she added milk and beat them with her bacon fork. Pouring them into her warm pan, she stood stirring as she thought about today's trip to go bear hunting.

"It's enough for Matthew wantin' to please his dad. Goin' hiking will please Matthew, but bear huntin', I just don't see that," she said to the cook stove. She often talked to it.

She piled the eggs high on a platter and turned to look out the sole window in the kitchen. Matthew wasn't anywhere to be seen. Going to the table, she placed the plates, knives, forks, and spoons at three places. "Matthew's never been one to kill living things unless we have a need for them. Hogs, cows, or chickens are another matter. We raise our own, 'specially to eat. We don't need bear meat. Anyway, I don't like its taste."

She set the platter of meat on the table with the rest of breakfast. A huge sigh escaped her lips as she turned back to the stove and pointed her finger at her stove-top oven. "Mark my words, Matthew doesn't want to go, and I wish he wasn't." She heard the voices of the returning men on the back porch. She pulled the browned biscuits from the warmer.

🌿 Chapter Ten 🌿

That Same Morning at Red Oak Flats — Jake

Jake headed in the direction of the moonshine still. He was alone. Chuck intended to stay around home and comfort his daughter.

"I might come out later in the afternoon, after I've finished some chores around here," he added.

Bewildered by the previous day's happenings and his secure world turned upside down, Jake struggled to make sense of yesterday's events. His rote life was interrupted. He talked to himself and the forest as he went.

"Abigail's hurt. I saw the bruise on her head. Chuck's angry, really angry. Don't like Dirk. He brought heartache to the Flats." Jake raised his fists into the air and punched at an imaginary target.

Jake walked on. He was sore and limping from his overnight rest on the back porch. "My girls were safe last night," he said, nodding and looking at the trees in the forest. "I protected 'em." He nodded his head at a dogwood tree. "Protected 'em."

Arriving at the still, he busied himself with housekeeping chores.

Several times each day, Chuck sent Jake to check on the money deposited under the stump — not far out of sight in the woods. Since Jake mumbled constantly, these trips were mostly to get him out of his employer's hair. The constant, one-sided conversations annoyed Chuck, who couldn't understand a word being said. Chuck wasn't enamored with money or even checking the stump, but he did love peace and quiet, and he wouldn't hurt the old man's feelings by telling him to be quiet.

Jake headed in the stump's direction, deep in thought and talking out loud. A sound to his left caused him to look up the mountain. He stopped to listen.

Jake shrugged his shoulders. "Probably a squirrel or turkey rummaging around in the leaves," he mumbled.

~

Jake couldn't know that Dirk had changed his mind about leaving the Flats area, although he'd ridden almost to Townsend. Dirk needed money, and he knew where he could get a fistful. He turned his horse and rode slowly back across the treacherous, boulder-strewn mountains, staying away from the main road and stopping when darkness arrived. Travel off the main trail was dangerous at night.

He sat down under a white, pine tree and spent the night cold and cramped in the dark. After taking the saddle and pack off his horse, he wrapped a blanket around his shoulders. Building a campfire was dangerous if Chuck was out looking for him, and he most surely was looking for him, and the smell of wood smoke carried a long way through the forest.

He thought of Abigail. Forcing himself upon her was the most pleasurable moment of his life. A wild sound came from his throat and echoed through the forest. It was the sound of triumph, turning into crazed laughter.

Dirk waited until daylight and led his horse in the direction of the moonshine still. The going was rough, and the trip took longer than he thought it would. He was working feverishly on the stump when he heard Jake coming.

~

Jake entered the steep area where the stump sat. He sucked in his breath! To his horror, the huge piece of wood was out of its hole.

"I need to tell Chuck," he mumbled.

But he couldn't tell Chuck, because he was at the cabin with Abigail. Instead, he limped over and looked into the cavity. The jar was still in place. It hadn't been removed.

"Who did this?"

Jake looked around the cleared space. He saw no one.

"I've got to put the stump back over the jar."

He pushed at the stump, trying to replace it in the cavity. Grunting and sweating, Jake managed to move the chunk only an inch or two. Dirk came up behind him quietly.

"You'll need this to pry it into the hole." Dirk held up a long pole he'd found in the forest. The stump was heavy, and one person couldn't move it. Using the pole as leverage, he'd managed to move the chunk of wood far enough away to get at the jar. That's when he'd heard Jake mumbling as he came to check on the hidden money. For some brainless reason, he carried the pole with him to hide.

"Stupid old man, I'm going to kill you!" He swung the pole at Jake, who ducked. The pole was too cumbersome to strike again. Dirk threw it aside.

Jake heard the word "kill" and knew he was in for trouble.

When Dirk jumped onto Jake, he made one fatal error. He equated senility and old age as an advantage. He was wrong! After years of hard work, the old man was strong, and today he was fuming mad. Dirk was lazy, but he had youth and cunning on his side.

Anger, an emotion Jake did not feel often, welled up as Dirk moved toward him, grabbing him by the neck in an attempt to strangle the elderly man. Dirk intended to make this fight short but sweet.

The violence of Dirk's lunge caused the two struggling men to fall into the hole vacated by the stump. Jake fought back. He managed to loosen Dirk's grip and push him away. Jake jumped up. Dirk came at him again, starting to realize the strength of his opponent. The two men, locked in a life and death battle, fell to the ground and rolled down the steep hill.

Slamming hard into a tree, Dirk lost his grip on Jake's throat.

If I'm going to kill the old goat, I've got to do it with my gun. He's strong as an ox. I didn't count on that.

He reached for the little derringer he kept in his boot. Jake saw the gun as Dirk pulled it out and started to aim it in his direction. Forgetting his arthritis, he kicked at the gun, which dropped out of Dirk's hand into the leaves on the forest floor.

Dirk went for the gun, and so did Jake.

Got to keep him from finding the gun.

Jake was tiring as the two men kept struggling. He knew it wasn't long until he couldn't match Dirk's strength.

Not finding his gun, Dirk's hands were on Jake's throat again. Jake felt funny. He'd fainted before, and he was about to lose consciousness.

Underneath the leaves, he felt a hard object — the gun. He had one shot. Putting the gun to Dirk's chest, he fired the weapon. A strange look passed over Dirk's face as he looked into his opponent's eyes. Jake scrambled away as Dirk collapsed against the side of the tree. Blood oozed onto his shirt.

Jake didn't move for several moments. He stood up and looked at the gun in his hand. Instead of throwing it into the woods, he carried it back to the moonshine still. Dazed and worn-out, he laid it on the bench where he often sat to relax. Jake sat down beside it. Looking down at the ground, he realized his new boots were muddy. He got angry all over again.

Worthless skunk. Dead is good.

Jake leaned back against the red oak tree and closed his eyes.

～

When Chuck arrived later that afternoon, Jake stood up to greet him. He hadn't moved since he sat down.

"I kilt him," said Jake simply.

"Killed who?" Chuck asked, looking at the subdued man.

"Dirk." Jake pointed to the small gun on the bench beside him.

"What are you talking about, and where did you get that gun?"

Instead of telling Chuck, Jake headed down the trail toward the stump and motioned for Chuck to follow.

Wondering what had happened, Chuck put the gun in his pocket and followed.

∼

Totally subdued, Jake wasn't mumbling.

What on earth has happened? Thought Chuck, following Jake into the forest.

The two friends didn't speak as they walked toward the stash area. Chuck saw that the stump was out of the ground and ran to the hole. The jar appeared to be intact.

Jake pointed down the mountain.

Chuck turned. A hundred feet below the stump, Dirk's body rested against the trunk of a tree.

Dear God, has the senile old man actually killed him as he said?

Chuck hurried down the mountain and looked in astonishment at the motionless body. He squatted and touched Dirk's arm. It was cold and the eyes stared back at him unknowingly. Dried blood covered the shirt and pooled on the ground in front of the body.

Chuck looked at the dead man, satisfied he would never hurt anyone again.

The body couldn't remain where it rested. Chuck thought quickly as he and Jake replaced the stump over the jar.

He wasn't going to turn Jake in. He couldn't imagine his helper in jail, but the body couldn't remain next to the tree. He and Jake needed to dispose of the corpse. But where? "Jake, we need to take the body to Crooked Arm."

Crooked Arm was about a mile away where the mountain dropped off steeply and undergrowth was sparse until half-way down the gully. Huge trees were plentiful. He and Jake carried older parts of the moonshine still to the place and rolled them off the mountain. It was their dumping ground.

Good place for that piece of trash, thought Chuck as he prepared to raise Dirk's legs so he could grasp them and carry the man.

"Jake, come and help me. We'll carry the body toward Crooked Arm and toss it down the steepest part of the mountain."

Jake never questioned his boss. He always did as told.

They hauled the body up the hillside and over to the still. Wrapping it carefully in a piece of canvas being used as a canopy over their bench area, they tied each end with a rope and looped it around their shoulders. Taking a deep breath, they raised the body off the ground and trudged in the direction of Crooked Arm. Several minutes later, they arrived at the top of the steep hill. There wasn't any need to tarry.

"Take the canvas off the body, and we'll grab it by the arms and legs." Chuck pulled at his end.

"Shouldn't we say some words over the body?" said Jake as they unwrapped it.

"I don't think so," said Chuck. "What would you say?"

"Don't know. What a shame to be so cruel."

"I think you just said 'em."

Swinging the body back and forth, they loosed it into the empty air and listened until the crashing sound faded away into the distance. The gun followed.

Was this justice or vengeance? Probably a little of both, Chuck thought; *mountain justice and a father's vengeance.* He doubted if anyone even cared about Dirk Johnson. In their limited conversations, the man never mentioned his father or mother. Chuck didn't even know where he was born.

The men returned to the still area. Both of them sat down on the bench. Chuck's chest heaved as he sighed.

Whew!

Will this nightmare ever end? First Abigail and now Jake. That roguish vagabond brought gloom and death to Red Oak Flats. It'll take many days for this to end.

Chuck sighed again and rose from the bench.

Might as well get on with life. Hopefully, we'll never see another two days like these. I'm exhausted.

"Jake, we'll never speak of this again. Do you understand?"

Jake nodded his head.

"I don't want Abigail or Kitty to know what happened."

"Okay, Chuck."

"Are you ready to head for home and supper?"

"Yes."

∼

Walking along behind Chuck gave Jake time to think. Jake was better, because he was muttering again.

Dirk said yesterday was his last day at the Flats. He was wrong. Today is his first day of forever.

Jake smiled. He was rather proud of himself for thinking up such a profound statement. He analyzed it, turning it over and over in his mind. He thought about telling Chuck. He'd certainly be surprised.

No. Chuck said we would never mention today's happenings again. Better to let it go.

It was three o'clock as the two men plodded on toward Red Oak Flats and home.

❧ Chapter Eleven ❧

Back to the Hunt — Matthew

At three o'clock, the hunters assembled at Nat Tipton's home. Lazarus Tipton arrived early so he could help his brother gather and load their hunting supplies.

He slapped his favorite nephew on the back and shook his hand. "Hi, Matthew. Are you glad to be home?"

"I sure am. I always miss my Mom's home-cooking while I'm at school."

"You don't look like you've lost any weight," Lazarus joked. "Are you lookin' forward to college in the fall?" Lazarus was proud of his nephew's accomplishments and the fact that he was the first in the family to go to college. He intended to finance his nephew's continuing education.

At that moment, Nat arrived from the garden and ended the conversation about college. He stopped in front of the tool shed to unharness the plowing apparatus from the horse.

"Nat, where's the tent? Matthew and I'll carry it over and put it into the wagon bed." Lazarus could have furnished the tent, since he made part of his spending money setting up campsites and guiding people in the Smokies. His tourist business flourished in this beautiful valley.

"And good afternoon to you, brother," said Nat, smiling at his brother's directness. "And how are you today?"

"Guess I did get right to the important part, didn't I?" Lazarus teased his sibling. "The last time I checked I had all my faculties and parts. I'd say I was doing great. Now where's the tent?"

Did Matthew detect a little bit of brotherly rivalry? His dad was older than Lazarus by a few years.

"It's in the tool shed on a shelf over the workbench." Nat laughed. He was busy unhitching Shorty, his favorite plowing horse from the plow. He'd worked a garden section to plant corn and tomatoes when the hunt was over. This new ground was hard to turn over. Tired and thirsty, he led the horse to pasture, returned, and disappeared into the barn to hang up the harness. "The rest of the equipment is on the back porch," Nat called over his shoulder as he walked to the spring. "Load it, and while you're at it, hitch the black mare to the wagon."

Matthew watched as his father reached for the large tin cup that hung on a nail outside the spring house and disappeared inside. *How many times have I seen my hardworking, sweating father do that?*

Nat reappeared with the tin cup, spilling water as he drank long draughts to cool his parched tongue. Dark blue streaks ran down the front of his blue bib overalls where the cool water dropped, and he used his blue, bandana handkerchief to wipe his brow.

"Matthew, are you with me?" Lazarus stuck his head out the tool shed door.

"Coming, Uncle Lazarus."

~

Most of the hunting supplies and equipment were loaded when the other work wagon appeared. It kicked up dust as it traveled toward Nat's. Putting his hand over his eyes, Matthew squinted to see who was riding in the back. Donald Razor came with his father, John. Ike Shields brought his twin sons, Paul and Peter. The three young boys were childhood friends of Matthew.

"Whoa," yelled John Razor as they pulled up in the Tipton's yard.

Matthew walked over, greeted his friends, and looked into the back of the wagon. The bed of the farm wagon was bulging at the seams. It was a tangled mess of dogs, leashes, and young men stuffed together with hunting supplies.

"I'd shake hands, but I don't have a free one." Donald was grinning at his playmate from years back.

"I can see why."

Matthew started laughing at the antics of the Plotts-mixed hunting dogs. The bunch of them were barking, sniffing the air, and leaping around. The young men attempted to restrain them with ropes tied to their collars, but they were determined to jump out of the wagon and search this new territory, looking for new smells and trails.

"They probably smell the perfume of the skunk that was runnin' around here last night," said Matthew.

"Perfume, huh. That's the first time I've heard the odor of a skunk called perfume," laughed Donald, making a grimace.

Matthew counted six dogs in the wagon bed.

"Paul your dogs are raring to go." Matthew had heard that this kind of dog was a hunting fanatic.

"Yeah. They need a good run." Paul pulled on his leads, trying to settle his charges down. "They're crazy when it comes to huntin'. Don't have a lick of sense."

"If they're like most of us, the excitement will wear off, and they'll tire out soon enough," said Matthew.

"No, they won't. These hounds are known for their grit and stamina when chasin' wild game, whether it's a bear or 'coon or anything else their noses can latch onto," Paul replied, holding tightly to his two charges.

"My father always says they're as important as a rifle in a bear hunt," Donald volunteered. He had given up and sat in the middle of the tangled mess, while swatting at a slobbering hound.

"Dan, settle down." Peter Shields, the quietest and shyest one of the group, yanked on the dog's leash and promptly lost his balance when he tripped over another dog. Falling hard, he made a thud in the back of the wagon. "Crazy dog," he exclaimed.

Paul, Donald, and Matthew laughed at him as he sat, disgusted, on the wagon floor.

"I'm ready to git out of this wagon and git this hunt underway." Peter was unhappy and embarrassed. The loud sound of his fall caused the older men to look his way and grin. All eyes were on him.

Another of the hounds named Daisy came over to get acquainted with Matthew. She stood sniffing at his hands and clothes. Matthew felt the softness of her nose as he patted her on the head and scratched around her drooping ears. She was the friendliest of the six.

"Whew. She's definitely odiferous," exclaimed Matthew, using a word he'd learned in preparatory school and waving a hand back and forth.

"Hound dogs have a distinct smell," Daniel said, holding his nose.

The other boys laughed.

Matthew put his hand under the dog's chin and looked into her eyes. "Don't you ever take a bath, Daisy? A little lye soap would do you good." He patted her on the back, making dust fly in every direction.

"She rolled in the dirt when we let her out of the pen. She has her own favorite dusty spot that's for sure." Donald tightened her rope lead.

"No baths at all, big girl?" Matthew continued to scratch her head. Daisy was in dog heaven, eyes closed and head leaning to the side.

"Only if she accidentally falls in the creek or wades in up to her belly when she's thirsty," said Donald, keeping her rope taunt. "I usually jump in and wrestle with her." He changed the subject.

"Are you glad to be home from school?"

"Yes. It's great to be home. Speaking of jumpin' in, I miss hiking with you guys, especially to Abram's Falls and swimmin' in the deep pool below. Have you been there lately?" The falls was two or more miles down the creek from Razor's gristmill. The swiftly moving water fell off the face of the high cliff, creating a deep swimming hole below. The young men usually took lunch and skinny-dipped in the cold water.

They continued to talk as they waited on the four older men to finish loading the equipment. When they were ready to leave, Matthew climbed into his father's wagon for the short trip to Nat's birthplace. Lazarus rode his horse. The other wagon trailed behind.

~

In the middle of the cove, the group crossed rain-starved Abrams Creek and continued on toward Annie's.

The unusual dry spell had caused the ground to become bone-dry and crack. Matthew brushed dust off his clothes. It was powdered dirt as fine as flour kicked up by the wagon wheels.

He sneezed.

Turning his head to the right and left of the roadway, he saw the early corn. Not far above the ground, its new fronds curled together. Mounded dirt hills, recently planted with corn seeds, showed little evidence of germination. Here and there a sprout appeared above the ground.

He turned to his father. "If it doesn't rain soon, the crops may be lost."

"Yes, we need to harvest good crops this year since last year's harvest was scanty. There was barely enough to feed our animals through the winter." He flicked the reins on the mare's back. It trotted a little faster, throwing the dust farther up in the air. "Won't be long until we'll be at Annie's."

Aunt Annie was his father's sister, who lived on the ancestral home place where Nat was born. John "Jack" Tipton, Matthew's grandfather, Nat and Annie's father, had passed away only a few years ago.

As Matthew bounced over the ruts toward his Aunt Annie's, he remembered the way his father had explained Tipton roots in Cades Cove. Jack's father, Jacob, was the first Tipton to live in the house. The land was given to Jacob by his father, William Tipton. Although he never lived there, William was the first man to hold a deed to property in Cades Cove. William lived half-way to Knoxville at Tipton Station, a railroad stop on the route to Maryville and points south, or north.

Cove heritage and love for this land ran deep within the Tipton family, as deep as the Smokies were tall. His dad had tried to explain this feeling.

"Don't forget what I've told you. Being landed is important on this earth. Think of it as a picture of the Promised Land in the Bible, a future inheritance."

"Yes, Dad," he'd answered. Matthew looked over at Uncle Lazarus who had promised his land to his nephew when he died.

"It's like you can expect or look forward to something in the future. Something you didn't work for but will get. It's promised." His father's voice trailed off as he tried to explain his thoughts. Lazarus had given his land to Matthew, so Nat could give larger inheritances to his older sons, who all lived outside the valley.

~

Upon arriving at Annie Tipton's, the dogs were tied to individual fence posts. Lazarus tied his horse to Nat's wagon, and he and Nat went inside to say hello to their sister. Matthew drove his father's wagon to the cantilevered barn, positioning it under the eaves. This type of barn was common in Cades Cove.

The first-time Matthew saw Annie's barn it fascinated him. He'd walked around it and asked his father about the odd shape. A cantilever was created when several beams making up the loft floor extended far out from the sides of the main barn. The long, sturdy timbers weren't supported, making the area underneath a perfect place to store machinery or other supplies out of the rain.

Matthew had no problem putting his farm wagon in the dry. "Mr. Razor, put yours behind mine." Matthew pointed to the spot.

Matthew helped the men unhitch the horses and transfer the supplies to the horse's backs. The huge tent was lashed onto Lazarus's horse, along with the ropes they needed. Each hunter still carried a large, heavy pack.

As the men returned to the road in front of the house, Matthew looked up at Thunderhead's dark, brooding face.

"Have you been up on Spencefield this year? I'm anxious to see it." Matthew walked with Donald toward the house.

"No and if'n we don't hurry now, we won't see it until daybreak. We'll be putting up our tent in the dark. I'd like to git there and rest a bit before turnin' in for the night." Patience was not one of Donald's virtues. He untied Daisy from the fence and paced up and down the road.

Granny Whitehead, Annie's elderly charge and friend, sat in the front porch swing, crocheted afghan tucked around her legs. The swing squeaked as she moved back and forth. She watched as the men adjusted the load on the horses.

"Matthew," called Granny W., recognizing her favorite from church and motioning him to the seat in front of her. Everyone called her Granny W. She was gifted in mountain ways and a loveable old lady. The swing continued to move gently.

"Yes, Ma'am," said Matthew, leaving the group of men and heading for the front porch.

"Matthew, are you goin' on this bear huntin' trip?" Granny W. pulled her shawl tighter around her shoulders and frowned at him.

"Yes, Ma'am." Matthew dropped into the cane chair in front of her. He could have said he was reluctant to go but didn't.

Granny stopped swinging and leaned forward. She lowered her voice and spoke almost in a whisper.

"Be careful. My knees are hurtin' and that means there's rain acomin' and Thunderhead didn't git hits name for no reason. That hill is a good place for lightnin' to strike. Heed my warning." The silver-haired old lady pointed her long, arthritic finger in the direction of the mountain.

"Yes, Ma'am. I'll be careful," said Matthew, leaning over to give Granny W. a hug. If what she said was true and rain was on the way, the men needed to keep a watch on the skies. Thunderhead Mountain was a dangerous place in a storm.

Granny W. continued, "I never did like for the men to hunt for animals that could turn on 'em. Too much danger of gittin' hurt." She paused, rubbing her neck as she sometimes did when thinking or planning some mischievous suggestion. "Now, if'n a bear steps out in front of you and your gun is loaded, cocked, and aimed, then shoot it." She paused, grinning at him as if she'd made a big joke. She was serious again as she said, "Guess I've always been skeered after that episode when Harry got kilt. Things can turn bad fast."

Matthew opened his mouth to ask her who Harry was and what happened to him, but at that moment the men appeared from within the house. They carried more food in a tow sack. As they passed Matthew, the smell of fried apple pies and cinnamon lingered in the air. Aunt Annie followed behind laughing as usual.

"Hi, Matthew," she said, putting her arm around him as he stood up to greet her. After everyone went out the gate to the road, she whispered in his ear, "There's two extra fried apple pies in the bag for you," and winked at him. Turning back to the group she said, "Have a good trip, everyone. I'll see you when you come back down on Saturday. I'll have dinner ready."

Matthew bounded down the porch steps and hurried to the road. He lifted the heavy pack and placed his arms through the straps, hurrying to catch up to the moving group. He knew they must walk fast to reach Thunderhead Mountain before dark. Donald was right. They needed to set up camp before the light was gone.

"Bring me a piece of bear meat," called Annie as they crossed the road headed for Rowan's Creek, the start of their long walk.

Matthew threw up his hand and waved.

Reaching around, he adjusted his pack and remembered that the old timers used to say 'the fat's in the fire.' He couldn't turn back now.

Rowan's Creek ran in front of Isaac LeQuire's home. He sat on his front porch with his felt hat pulled down over his eyes. Matthew thought he might have been napping, but with the noise of the barking dogs, tromping, talking men, and snorting horses, he didn't stay that way long. He pushed his hat up on his forehead and stood up as they approached.

"Can't talk now, Isaac." Matthew heard his father say. "We've got to reach Spencefield before dark." Nat kept walking while holding his horse's reins and waved. The others followed his lead.

"You goin' bear huntin'?" called Isaac. "Isn't it late in the season?"

"Yep, but we waited until Matthew came home from school." Nat kept walking, with Matthew close on his heels. Matthew realized if they stopped to talk to Isaac, the group would never get to Spencefield.

"Bring me a piece of bear meat." Isaac sat back down and watched the group as it passed. Finished with work for the day, he rested on the porch of his log home in the midst of a grove of hemlock trees.

∽

Matthew looked back at the group. There were eight talking men, three clomping horses and six barking dogs as they walked up the creek past Isaac's gristmill. Once the men, horses, and dogs got on the trail, they could spread out and the confusion would decrease. Matthew smiled at the noise the procession created.

If there's any kind of animal or a bear within a mile of us, it'll be on the other side of Thunderhead Mountain in a jiffy.

Not far beyond the mill, the path crossed Rowan's Creek and, farther along, over Cooper Branch. Matthew noticed the streams had slowed to a trickle. Crossing these two streams wasn't hard since there was a lack of rain.

After walking another mile, the trail veered sharply right to parallel Anthony Creek. Matthew started to get excited. After following this creek for two miles, the climb to Bote Mountain began. He was half-way there.

The final stretch, another two miles to Spencefield, was the hardest. He trudged along with the others.

Chapter Twelve

Dog and Bear Talk — Matthew and Donald

As the hunting group approached Spencefield, Matthew peered into the thick underbrush. Ten steps off the path, the dense heath and laurel thicket made walking impossible. Matthew turned to Donald, who walked beside him. "What do you do if your dogs corner a bear in the midst of that mess?"

Donald chuckled. "You git down on all fours and crawl to cover the ground to the fight, and you hurry as fast as you can."

"Doesn't sound like much fun to me."

"It isn't. Once a dog corner's a bear in the laurel, its main objective is to keep nipping at that bear until it starts runnin' again. But if the animal has other ideas and your dogs are in there fightin' it, you gotta go in."

"Why?" asked Matthew.

"Well, here's the main reason. Since your dogs will fight to the death, you don't want to lose them. Good bear dogs are expensive, so you want to save 'em."

Matthew didn't want to appear stupid, but he asked the question. "How do you save them if they're fighting a bear?"

"The only way you can. You sure can't choke a bear to death. No, try to git a clear shot and shoot."

"What if you don't kill it?"

"Then you got problems, big problems." Donald indicated this by spreading his hands apart. "Some hunter's crawl into the midst of the fight to kill the bear and don't come out. Thank goodness this doesn't happen often. Trapping a bear in the heath, well, it's dangerous to man and dog."

Matthew shuddered at the thought of chasing after an animal in the shadowy thicket.

He responded a bit sarcastically, "I don't like bear meat that much."

Matthew wanted to tell his friend he'd have to be starving to go into the midst of the tangled mess. He'd take a chance on getting another bear, another day.

Donald continued, "The best way to kill a bear is to let the dogs do their job. Let them run it up a tree. Once the animal climbs a tree, one good shot will bring it down."

"How often do people go in the thicket after the hounds?"

"Not often, because the hounds usually run the bear out. But if it sounds like a dog or dogs are gittin' kilt, a hunter won't hesitate. He'll take care of his dogs. I've heard of some hunters dying to defend their dogs."

The two friends walked on in silence.

"Spencefield hasn't changed," He told Donald as he looked around at the large grassy area where cattle were taken in the summer to feed. Fattened up until fall, they were driven to the Knoxville market to sell. The fatter the cow, the more money the owner got, and Spencefield grass was the best.

As he walked out on the lush pasture, Matthew heard the tinkling of cow bells. Some were nearby. He looked to his left where the dark and rockier tops of Thunderhead could be seen in the distance. The plan was to hunt between Spencefield and Thunderhead on both sides of the mountain's crest. Straight ahead was North Carolina. If he turned around, he looked across to Rich Mountain.

To the right, or west, was Russellfield, another potential hunting area much like Spencefield but smaller.

Huh, there's dark clouds on the western horizon.

He remembered Granny W.'s warning and smiled.

It looks like Granny W's knees might be right.

❦ Chapter Thirteen ❦

Back to Red Oak Flats — Abigail

Late in the afternoon, Abigail walked upward to the ridge above Red Oak Flats. Here she could see across Cades Cove to the dark mountains beyond. Her steps were no longer light and happy. With great effort, she lifted one foot and then the other, plodding along, burdened with heavy emotions, and the weight of her new world on her shoulders.

"I'll go with you," Kitty had said.

But Abigail wanted to be alone with her thoughts. Alone, just as she had been most of her sixteen years. She knew she would survive this terrible shock, because she was a survivor. But there wouldn't be a quick bounce-back from yesterday's happenings.

Anger welled up within her. She clenched her fists as she walked along. Right at this moment she hated the man who'd attacked her. If she could get her hands on him, she would kill him herself.

Never in my life have I felt such violent emotions. It scared her.

Why! Why did this happen to me? Abigail wanted revenge — yes, and restoration. She wanted her life to return to yesterday morning when everything was innocent and normal.

The anger left her as quickly as it had come.

She sat down on a grassy area and sobbed, but it was the quiet crying of resignation, of accepting yesterday afternoon's happenings.

Healing will take time. But part of me will never get over this dreadful attack, without a miracle taking place.

Pulling her knees up to her chin, she wrapped her arms around them and looked across the deep valley that was the cove. Thunderhead's shadowy contours stood out against the darkening sky. Looking west, over her shoulder, she saw a bank of clouds. "Rain's a-comin'."

After such a prolonged absence of rain, the storm'll be fierce. I'm glad to be here and not there.

Only last summer, two hunters killed by lightning on Thunderhead's peaks were carried down from Spencefield. She was coming home from Townsend and remembered passing a wagon containing their covered bodies. The smell of burnt flesh was strong as the makeshift hearse drove by. She remembered thinking people should be more careful if they had reason to visit the mountain's crest. *I hope no one is on the mountain tonight.*

Abigail stood up and breathed a deep sigh. Below in the lengthening shadows of the forest, the distinctive chirp of a robin could be heard. Stepping a little to the right, she saw the dark-colored bird with its orange breast, pecking at the forest floor. *Guess it's after a worm or grub.* The robin's hunt for food reminded her that she was hungry too.

Time to go home. Kitty will have supper waiting.

～

Two things Abigail didn't know as she sat looking out over the cove. Her attacker was in his makeshift grave off Crooked Arm and the young man who'd tried to comfort her the day before stood looking back at her from Spencefield, below Thunderhead and across Cades Cove.

❧ Chapter Fourteen ❧

Spencefield and Camp—Matthew

The ramshackle herder's cabin at Spencefield was slightly off the mountain on the North Carolina side. This was where the hunters would pitch their tent and set up a rough camp.

"Hello there, Frank Gamble," yelled Ike Shields as they approached the cabin. Matthew saw a short, thin man emerge from its dark interior, wearing long johns. He had a full beard and walked toward the group barefooted.

Frank Gamble was rubbing his eyes and yawning. Although it wasn't quite dark, he'd already turned in for the night. "Who's there?" he said, still sleepy-eyed.

"It's Ike Shields and a group going bear hunting."

"Oh, Ike," he said, squinting at the men. "Glad to have you." Frank approached the tired men. Even the dogs were more subdued, their tongues hanging out as they panted.

"Pitch your tent over there in that flat place." He pointed to an area where hunters always stayed and straw covered the ground. "That's where the group of men stayed last week."

"Thanks, we'll do that." Ike walked his horse toward the area and started unloading it. Nat did the same. Matthew and the other young men dropped their packs and prepared to put up the tent.

"You may have trouble finding a bear. The last group didn't get a smell. Isn't it late in the season to be huntin' bear?"

"True. True, Frank." Nat was getting tired of answering that particular question. "But we wanted to include Matthew in the hunt, and he came home from school in Maryville on Monday. We couldn't get here any earlier."

"It's *all* my fault," mumbled Matthew so no one could hear. He was tired and a little on the grumpy side.

"I see," said Frank, looking over at Matthew and then transferring his gaze back to Matthew's father. "Pastor Tipton, how are you?"

"Doing well. Where do you want me to tie the horses?"

"Come along and I'll show you." Nat collected the horse's reins and followed Frank, who headed around the back of his rough home. The two men soon returned.

"John. Glad to see you. Guess you aren't busy now." Frank, his hands thrust deep in the pockets of his sleepwear, paused to speak to John and Lazarus. Razor's gristmill always ground his grain after it was harvested.

"This is my slow season at the mill. But I've been plantin' a garden and my own fields. I have a family to feed like everyone else." John was tying his three hound dogs up to a convenient tree.

"Hush up," he shouted as his dogs started to bark at the cow bells ringing in the forest around them.

Daisy, Spot, and Hank plopped down on the ground to watch the activity around the camp. "And besides, I need something for my boys to do, besides eat, swim, and hunt."

Donald looked at his father and rolled his eyes. *There was always a-plenty to do around the farm and mill,* he thought, looking down at his calloused hands. *They proved it.*

Ike walked over and hefted the tent, carrying it to the spot Frank pointed too. John and the young men laid the well-worn item over the previous site. Ike placed the side poles in position and tied them down to stakes driven into the ground.

While Donald held the center peak up, Matthew walked the center poles into the tent and placed them square with the ground. Their new home was ready.

Frank walked over in his red long johns, peered inside and laughed. "Eight men and their belongings in that small space will take a miracle, Pastor."

"You're right, Frank. It's a good thing were friends," said Nat, grinning. "Help me tie this rope around the neck of this sack. It contains provisions the group won't need tonight." Nat was preparing to stash their food in a tree.

"Here, Pastor. Let me help you pull it up over the limb. The higher the better, if you don't want a bear or other varmint to reach it." The two men worked together to secure the supplies.

"Who was here last week?" asked John.

"W.B. Townsend and a group from Little River Lumber Mill stayed four or five nights. I don't think they did much huntin'. But they did tromp all over these hills. I got to wondering if they were cruisin' for more timber."

"I guess anything's possible. They're lumbering in Elkmont right now. One of my sons is helping 'em cut timber." John watched as the two adjusted the final height of the group's food cache.

"Son's," called Isaac, "check for wood to start a fire."

Paul and Peter left in the dwindling twilight to forage for wood under the trees nearby.

"Yer welcome to use some of my store for your big pieces," Frank called after them. He turned around, watching as the two boys toting their hatchet and axe disappeared down the trail.

Nat called to his son, "Matthew, find the kerosene lanterns and light 'em."

Matthew rummaged around in his belongings until he found the Diamond matches in their cardboard box. He lit the lanterns, placing one in the tent and the other between the tent and the intended campfire.

Matthew placed the latter lantern on the stub of a convenient tree branch and turned the wick down. It would stay lit so the men could take care of business during the night. Heading into the dark woods without a light wasn't safe or relished by any of the men. Matthew headed back to where his father and Frank stood beneath the suspended food bag. He caught the end of Frank's sentence.

". . . a shame it happened to that church, Pastor."

"Yes. Every pastor lives with the possibility of this kind of problem." Nat had shoved his hands deep in the pockets of his jacket. His head was down.

"Must have been goin' on quite awhile."

"I really don't know any of the details. I decided long ago if a hint of scandal touched my ministry, I would resign. Tearing up my church isn't an option. A pastor should get out at the very onset of a problem. Let the church deacons and membership see if the problem can be worked out. Pastor Clucke should have left months before he did."

"That he should." Frank headed for his shack. "Good night."

"What was that all about, Dad?" questioned Matthew, wondering what kind of scandal was going on.

"One of our sister churches over in Sunshine ran into a problem with their pastor. I don't know all the details, but my advice to you in your future ministry is to resign or step down until problems within your congregation are solved, especially if they involve the pastor. No pastor should continue to preach if he's a hindrance to God's work."

~

Darkness descended on the camp, accompanied by a sharp drop in temperature. The moon cast long shadows under the trees, and from a distance, Matthew heard the lonely hoot of an owl and, closer, the silvery tinkle of a cow bell. These were accompanied by the distinctive chirp of crickets at the campfire. There was no camaraderie around the warm campfire that night.

Tin pails of already cooked food appeared from within the camping supplies. Exhausted after the day's activities, the men sat on the hard ground, ate their supper of biscuits stuffed with meat, and turned in to bed. What was left of supper would be breakfast in the morning and the noon meal. As Matthew pulled the covers up to his ears, he heard a rumble in the distance. Was it a warning of things to come?

We need the rain to end the drought. I hope it's not a bad storm.

He closed his eyes and dreamed of a sobbing girl on a rocky outcrop.

⁓

Boom! Matthew thought dynamite had blasted him out of bed. Another flash of bright light, followed immediately by the deafening crack of thunder, scared the living daylights out of him. In the distance, the distinct sound of something crashing onto the ground was heard.

Jarred out of sound sleep, everyone was sitting up on their blankets, looking at each other. John braved the coming storm and went out to retrieve the lantern from the tree next to the campfire, where sparks flew into the air from the mound of glowing coals.

Flash! Boom!

Matthew wanted to run for the forest around him, but knew there wasn't any safety on top of the mountain. Up here, cattle in the woods and on the field were often killed by lightning. He gritted his teeth and sat still, as did the other inhabitants in the enclosure. He noticed in a flash of lightning, that his father had his head down—praying.

The wind whipped the canvas tent, trying to tear it loose from its moorings, and finally the rain came down in torrents. A trench dug around the tent diverted the rain water, but a fine mist filtered through the cloth, dampening those inside.

Lightning flashed and thunder roared.

The whole mountain shook with the storm's fury. As the worst passed, Matthew peeked out the tent flap and saw a streak of white hit Thunderhead. Over a mile away, the flash lit the mountaintop as if it were daylight, exposing each rugged curve in a perfect silhouette. The storm spent its fury and moved on. Shivering beneath his blanket, Matthew was cold, damp, miserable, and sleepless the rest of the night.

❧ Chapter Fifteen ❧

Hunting on the Mountaintop — Matthew

At daybreak, everyone piled out of their cold, damp beds. A fire started with dry wood from Frank's lean-to felt mighty good to Matthew. He warmed both sides of his body and dried his clothes by turning around slowly next to the fire, becoming toasty on one side and icy on the other. The men hung their damp blankets on bushes or limbs, expecting them to dry in the rays of the sun.

Hurrying to eat their quick breakfast, they warmed their biscuits in a large iron skillet laid on the fire. They needed to hit the trail. Bear hunting was on their minds.

While they were gobbling down their victuals, the men discussed the setting of standards. Standards or lookouts were assigned to the gaps in the mountains, in case a bear started to run from the dogs. Bears usually headed for these lower areas or gaps, to cross over and get to safer territory and try to get away from or lose the howling, snapping animals.

The standard heard the dogs barking long before he saw them and knew which way the hunt was headed. If he saw the bear coming, his job was to kill the bear before it ran through the gap or turn the animal back to the dogs so they could tree it. A treed bear was much easier to kill than a bear on the move or fighting the dogs on the ground.

The older men decided to send the four young men to stand in the gaps. Matthew, along with his friends, picked up their hunting rifles and set out in the early morning mist. Clouds hung low in the valleys as they walked along the rocky ridge, heading toward Thunderhead. The mountaintops surrounding them looked like giant ships on a sea of white fog.

Matthew imagined them sailing along, toward the sun now peeking over their tops. Its first rays not yet warm on his face.

Matthew reached his assignment at Bee Stand Gap while the others continued on. Within an hour, everyone was in position and Matthew could hear the dogs barking somewhere down the mountain. Matthew's position was here until the hunt was over.

⁓

After the standards disappeared out of sight, John, Ike, Lazarus and Nat set off with the dogs. They worked their way to the headwaters of the west prong of Little River. The dogs were divided between the four men, who restrained them until they picked up a bear scent. After that, the hunt was on.

The four men covered as much territory as possible within the assigned hunting area. They walked through hardwood, evergreen, and laurel forests. Trekked up creeks and over hills until they were sure not a single bear was in their vicinity. Coming out on the steep, rugged trail to Thunderhead, a single shot alerted the rest to join the men with the dogs. The men sat down to eat and rest.

"We didn't get a single prospect; not a sniff," said Ike, looking around at the rest. He continued, "I think we should hunt on the North Carolina side along the headwaters of Eagle Creek before we return to camp. In fact, we'll come out below the camp and the walk back won't take long."

"I'm all right with that," responded Nat. "How about you, John?"

"I came to hunt. So, I say let's do it. The boys can maintain the same standard positions, except for Paul. He needs to move past Spencefield toward Russellfield, in case the bear goes that way when we hunt toward our camp."

"I'll go that way," offered Lazarus, surprising the rest. Although he hated to admit it, being dragged up hill and down by one young hound was taking its toll.

"That's a good idea. Paul can find another, smaller gap down the trail," said Ike getting up and stretching. "Let's get started."

Nat looked at his younger brother with a question in his eyes but said nothing.

∼

Later that afternoon, the dogs picked up a faint scent along De Armond Ridge. The animal appeared to be headed in the direction of Russellfield or thereabouts. Following the scent for several miles, up ridges and down streams, the dogs finally lost it in a creek bed. Last night's gulley-washer had obliterated it. The time being late, the men decided to return to camp. The hunt would start here tomorrow morning.

Disappointed, they set out toward camp, but they were pretty sure there was a bear in the area. Tomorrow, they would continue hunting on the North

Carolina side of the mountain in the direction of Russellfield. For now, a hot supper would taste good.

~

Matthew checked his bedding. During the day, the sun had dried out his blanket, and it felt warm against his skin in the fading sunlight.

Wrapping it around himself, he stood up and walked out into the grassy field. For several minutes, he looked toward the North Carolina side. Somewhere down there was a bear they might find tomorrow. He noticed an area to his left filled with hemlock trees, growing on top of a nearby ridge. Last night's rain had washed the sky of dirt and grime, and each tree was clearly outlined against it.

Not a cloud in the sky. Tomorrow will be great. "No smoke or fog on the mountains tonight." A bit of wind ruffled his blanket as he breathed deeply of the clean mountain air, filling his lungs to capacity. The air rushed out. He inhaled again. *How I love these mountains.* Turning he walked quickly back to camp. He would be expected to do his part of the chores.

~

After eating biscuits filled with meat for several meals, the men were ready to fry some bacon, eggs, and potatoes with onions in the large iron skillets they'd brought with them. The homemade bread they'd packed in was toasted in a bit of the bacon drippings. Matthew could smell the meat all the way to the spring where he went with two, three-gallon buckets to get drinking and wash water.

I hope they have enough eggs and potatoes. I'm as hungry as a bear.

He laughed.

After eating their fill, the men lounged around the campfire. Daisy, who was tied on a lead, came over to Matthew to be petted. She was a beautiful brindle-colored dog with friendly brown eyes. Her ears flopped down from her flat head and her body was covered with short, silky hair. When he sat on the ground, Daisy was eyeball to eyeball with him and immediately showed her interest by licking him in the face.

"Hey, I don't need a girlfriend." He was startled by her sudden movement and pushed her away.

Daisy tried again.

Matthew laughed and, putting up his hand to protect his face, said, "Get back you hound, you're slobbering." But she insisted on sitting in his lap.

She stretched out.

Her long legs dangled off into the air. Soon, she was sound asleep and snoring.

"Ike," he said. "Where does the Plott hound get its unusual name?" Matthew rubbed Daisy's velvet ears. She didn't move a muscle.

"Well, if I remember correctly, a man by the name of Jonathan Plott brought them over from Germany in the mid seventeen-hundreds. He'd bred 'em to hunt wild boar in Europe, but when he came to America there weren't any wild hogs. Plott settled in the mountains of North Carolina and started breeding his hounds to hunt bear."

"They're a well-known, rare, and expensive breed. That's the reason most of the dogs we hunt are mixed-breed Plotts. They're still fierce hunters and once on a trail, it's almost impossible to get them off. You can't find a dog anywhere with as much strength or determination on a hunt. I've seen them lure a bear away from many a man who was being mauled because they kept snapping and snarling at it, and they're willing to die in the process."

John added, "If you don't keep them penned up, they go off and hunt for days. Run miles in the process."

Ike continued, "Yep, hunting is what they're bred for and hunt they will. Give 'em a scent and they'll track until they've cornered their prey."

"That's true. Once out of their pen, they must be kept on a lead," added John, motioning to the leads on his dogs.

The men sat for several minutes talking about their experiences when bear hunting with dogs.

"There's one thing you youngsters need to know. Ike, do you remember the greenhorn that we guided here in the mountains about three years ago? He was from Chicago, I think. He was determined to refer to the bear's scent all the time?" asked John.

"He's the one we kept correcting? We told him the proper term was bear track or bear trail, but he never caught on."

"That's the one. He stuffed his pant's legs into his high-topped boots. You lads must remember the proper term, because no experienced bear hunter uses any other.

∼

The sun went down beyond the mountain, and more wood was added to the fire. It crackled and popped as the hickory wood burned. The faces of the men shone in the firelight as the stillness of the forest closed in around them. It was cold again. Matthew and some of the others went to retrieve their blankets from the tent.

"Uncle Lazarus, what happen to Granny W.'s son, Harry?" said Matthew during one lull in the conversation.

Lazarus sat cleaning his gun while listening to the talk around the campfire. "I reckon your dad can tell that story about as well as anybody, even me."

"It's a sad story, son," said Nat, who got up and stretched a bit. Returning to his seat, he sat back down. "Have you other youngsters heard about what happened to Harry?"

Donald, Peter, and Paul shook their heads. As Nat began to relate the story, all was quiet—except for a distant cowbell and a screech owl, trilling down one of the hollows radiating from Spencefield. "Harry went out hunting one night with his single-shot 22 rifle. He took his dogs, hatchet and his carbide light, because he was looking to tree a raccoon. After walking about a mile from his home, the dogs picked up a scent and began to run a trail. The dogs stayed with the scent, but the trail went further than most 'coons would go. Harry began to suspect he was on a bear track. When Harry's dogs finally treed the animal in a huge hemlock tree, all he could see were two eyes shining amongst the branches. The carbide light wasn't strong enough to light up the tree, and the bear's color blended into the dark hemlock limbs and the even darker night. Harry needed to make a decision, and he made the wrong one."

Nat knew how to keep his audience spellbound. None of his worshippers went to sleep in his church services, so he paused to take a drink of water from a tin cup. Nine sets of eyes were pointed in his direction, because Frank sat with the group. Nat was enjoying the attention as he narrated the story.

At that moment, there was a particularly big pop from the fire, and everyone jumped, except Peter. He leaped so far; he fell off the log he was sitting on.

All the men laughed.

"He's a might touchy," said Frank.

"Looks like I'm goin' to have to take him back to sittin' and standin' school," said his father, remembering Peter's earlier thud in the wagon. He slapped his son on the back. Peter looked down at the ground, so the others couldn't see his red face.

Nat continued.

"Harry shot at the bear, but the shot glanced off a branch in the tree and barely grazed the animal. The angry bruin came rapidly down the tree, and the two dogs, which stood leaping at the trunk, jumped on it. A fierce fight broke out while Harry reloaded his gun in the dim light of the carbide lamp. The bear was killing his dogs. He shot again, but his gun didn't have enough power to kill the bear, which quickly turned in the direction of the shot.

"The bear's first blow knocked the carbide light out of his hands, and without it Harry couldn't see anything clearly. The animal grabbed him, tearing at his arms, legs, and body. Harry felt his flesh give way. He knew he was being torn apart by the animal.

"Although he fought back, there wasn't much he could do. Earth, air, and forest became one in the black blur that followed. The dogs kept snapping and snarling at the bear. Thinking Harry was dead, the bear turned to fight with them, and in the midst of the ruckus, Harry managed to crawl away. From a painful fog, Harry heard the fight continuing as he stood up." Nat was talking so fast, he paused to swallow some coffee from his cup and get his breath.

"Then what happened?" asked Donald, John's son. Everyone listened intently.

"Harry started to walk. Bleeding profusely, he staggered toward the closest house. It was around midnight when he got to Rube Whitehead's.

"'Uncle Rube,'" he called. Rube was Granny W.'s brother. "'Uncle Ruben.'" When Harry yelled and approached the house, Ruben's dogs began barking excitedly. Ruben didn't hear his nephew yell, but the animated barking of his dogs woke him up. That sound indicated an intruder, so Ruben went to the door.

'"Who's there?"' he called, cracking it a bit and holding his rifle in his right hand.

With his last bit of strength, Harry called to his uncle, identifying himself.

'"Harry, where are you?"'

When Harry answered back, Rube recognized his nephew's pained voice as he added, '"I'm hurt."' Harry collapsed beside the tree he'd been leaning against."

Nat stopped as John rose to tend the fire.

John poked at the fire with a long stick and added more wood making sparks fly into the air.

"And sparks flew up to heaven," said Lazarus watching the brilliant spots of light race upward and extinguish themselves in the air. He got up to place his gun in the tent, and returned to take his place by the fire.

"I was gettin' a chill, and I thought I might as well put backlogs on the fire. Won't be long till we turn in to bed." John apologized as he worked the fire, adding two huge logs and working the coals into the middle of the fire pit. He placed more sticks over the coals and sat back down, rubbing his hands together. The flames licked slowly between the open spaces of the stacked wood. "This cold makes my rheumatism hurt." He nodded at his friend to continue.

"Rube hurried to get his sons out of bed. They found Harry lying beside the tree where he had collapsed. Gently, the men carried the young boy into the kitchen and placed him on the table, which was covered with an oilcloth. In the light of the lantern, the terrible extent of his wounds could be seen. Rube realized that Harry probably wouldn't live. He'd lost a lot of blood. Ruben and his son, George, cleaned Harry up as best they could and bound up his wounds.

"Right before daybreak, Harry regained consciousness and told his kinfolks this story. At first light, someone went to fetch his mother. While she was on her way to her son's side, he went into another coma and died a short time thereafter. She arrived too late to say goodbye."

It was quiet after Nat quit speaking.

"Guess I'll hit the sack," said John. The four young friends followed him, whispering in the dark.

John turned around to look at them. *Were they up to foolishness?* he wondered.

"Me too," said Frank, getting up and heading for his cold, cheerless hut. He was enjoying the rapport around the warm fire. "Hope you have better luck tomorrow."

"Can't be any worse than today," Ike called after his disappearing figure.

The last three men moved closer to the blaze and its intimacy.

"Ike, I hear you and Barbary are planning a trip." Lazarus, the oldest of the group, lounged on the straw-covered ground. His frame stretched into the darkness beyond the fire.

"What?" exclaimed Ike. "That's news to me. Where did you get your information, the busybody line?" He meant the telephone exchange in the cove.

"Maybe. Edna Akkins . . . "

Ike shook his head, held up his hand and stopped Lazarus in mid-sentence. "Enough said. You can't believe anything that woman says. She twists and bends a truth or lie easier than Gate's bent barbwire. The woman wouldn't recognize the truth if it stood in front of her and introduced itself!"

"Mean you're not planning to go to Atlanta for the opening of the silent film *Straight Shooting*?" Lazarus was teasing his friend.

Ike guffawed at Lazarus's suggestion. "No! Where does that scheming, eavesdropping female get her information? Sorry Nat, I know she's one of your flock, but—"

Nat threw up his hands and looked toward heaven, as if pleading for mercy. He knew it was true, but he refused to comment on Edna and her cohort, Precious Tipton.

"Sounds more like something you'd do, Lazarus." Ike chuckled, looking at his longtime friend.

"Yep, it does. Do you suppose Edna got her wires crossed?" The two men laughed at Lazarus's joke. Nat remained silent.

Lazarus reflected on Ike's comment about something he'd do. He was a devoted bookworm, as was his deceased wife who passed away not quite two years back. When thinking of his wife, he felt a strange, sweet sadness. While Sarah was alive, they often went by railroad to see plays at Maryville College or theatrical performances by famous stage actors at Knoxville's Staub Theatre. Boarding the train, they rode to Chattanooga to see her parents and siblings, getting off at the majestically domed Terminal Building of the Southern Railway. It was the same building where the Chattanooga Choo Choo regularly pulled into and unloaded passengers.

Goin' to Atlanta is something Sarah and I would do if she were still here.

Sarah loved going hunting, tramping the woods, wading creeks, and climbing mountains as much as he did. Leaving early in the morning, they stayed all day, looking for game or soaking up the mountain atmosphere. He knew their activities and union were a curious combination, but he didn't care. They were lovers who were deeply in love.

Lazarus had land. His wife had money. Since they were childless, he and his wife decided to sponsor Matthew's college education. Recognizing his aspirations and bright mind, they approached him with the idea. Matthew met their suggestion enthusiastically, and Nat agreed to the proposal. Whether his pastorate was in Cades Cove or New York was irrelevant to them. Knowledge was precious.

"Laz, are you still with us?" John asked, since he'd asked a question without getting a response.

"Sorry, what did you ask?"

The conversation went on as the men sat in comfortable friendship around the warm fire.

∼

"Men, I'm tuckered out. I'll see you in the morning." Nat got up and headed for the tent. Once inside, he carefully threaded his way through the crowd of snoring, prostrate bodies.

He whispered into the darkness, "Father, please give us a perfect day tomorrow. And, is it possible to close Edna's mouth or through a miracle straighten out her meddlesome ways?"

He turned over on his side and went to sleep.

❧ Chapter Sixteen ❧

A Second Day of Hunting — Matthew

The next morning, after breakfast, standards were set toward Russellfield, which was almost three miles from Spencefield. Matthew was assigned Maple Sugar Gap, over halfway to the other grassy field. The young men headed for their posts as the older men walked the dogs in the direction where they'd lost the trail the day before. Lazarus decided to join the young men and take up a stance on top of the mountain. He didn't tell anyone, but during the most strenuous part of yesterday's hunt, he'd had chest pains.

John, Ike, and Nat walked the dogs to the spot where the hunt had ended the day before. Leaving there and heading down the creek for more than five miles, the dog handlers came to its intersection with Tub Mill Creek. The dogs hadn't picked up a bear's track. Because of the rugged terrain, the men stopped to discuss the situation.

"Do you think the scalawag might have gone over Nuna Ridge?" asked Nat, heading for the creek bank.

"Anything's possible at this point, but one thing's for sure, we don't need to travel down the creek any farther. I don't want to get caught out in the woods overnight, and if we go any farther, we'll be sleeping under a dogwood tree," said John, pulling out his handkerchief and mopping his sweating brow. Climbing over rocks, wading creeks, and hiking up and down mountains was hard work.

"Let's go on over to Lawson's Gant Lot and walk back toward Russellfield," suggested Ike. "Sometimes the dogs have struck a bear trail there."

"We could do that, but if we do, our standards won't be in position to help us," responded John. "What do you think, Nat?" He looked in Nat's direction.

Nat squatted beside the creek, drinking water, which he scooped up with his cupped hand, as he swatted gnats with the other. He splashed water on his face, sending droplets in all directions. They flashed in the sunlight. Wiping his hands on his shirt, he replied, "I'm with you fellows. Anywhere away from these flying insects." He swiped at the air again. "You're the experts."

John looked at Ike.

"What do you suggest, John?" asked Ike.

"This area of the mountains is really rugged. It'll be hard goin' no matter which way we go." John paused and thought a moment. "I believe we should continue up Tub Mill Creek. At least, until we run into Burnt Ridge Branch. Then we can decide on whether to head in the direction of the gant lot, and we'll be close enough to reposition our standards. We'll also cover most of the possible area where a foraging bear would travel."

"That's a great idea," said Ike. "Why didn't I think of that? Let's go."

Nat stood up. He looked up the creek where they were headed. All he could see were laurel thickets, gray boulders, and rushing water. The men walked in the creek until a space appeared alongside in the underbrush. There the group climbed out upon the bank, leaving wet footprints upon the river rocks and pine needles. They headed upstream through a pine and hardwood forest. The laurel thinned out for a short distance and within a mile, the dogs picked up fresh bear track.

The men looked at each other. The eager dogs were jumping up and down while straining at their leashes. This was what they were trained to do, track 'coons and bears. With a deep breath, they turned the dogs loose.

"The hunt's on," said an excited Nat, looking at the other men and staring after the disappearing dogs.

Within minutes they were out of sight, but their short, high-pitched barks could clearly be heard.

"Hurry, men," said Ike who was ahead, bounding up the mountain like a goat. "Let's don't let them get out of our hearing."

"Ike," John called after his friend, "we need to climb the ridge so we can listen to the hunt. That bear will wander hither and yon on its way to the top of the mountain. We can hear the dogs running it from the hilltop and decide where to intercept them." John was all for taking the shorter route, saving his arthritic joints.

Ike threw up his hand and waved, continuing after the dogs.

"Ike's ready to go," laughed Nat, watching Ike's back as he disappeared up the mountain into the underbrush. "Nothin' like gettin' your second wind."

"Yep. It's this way every time we hunt. He gets excited and wants to run after the dogs. Those dogs will travel double what we'll walk on the ridge. They'll follow every move the bear makes. Ike will tire out soon. That second wind will blow through fast enough." John thought a moment then added, "But, he's one of the best bear hunters in these parts, no doubt about it, even if he's old.

"Which way do you think the bear will go?"

"There's no tellin' this time of year. Fresh food is scarce. Sounds like the dogs are heading in the general direction of the mountaintop, but that might change. Chances are it'll keep headin' up the hollow."

The men walked on in silence. It took all their effort to breathe since it was almost a mile high where they walked. Soon Ike joined them. He looked a little sheepish.

"Guess his second wind's worn off," whispered John to Nat.

Off in the distance and still on the bear's trail, they could hear the dogs high-pitched barking. John, Ike, and Nat's part in the hunt was to keep the dogs within hearing and follow as best they could.

Three hours later, the three friends still trudged up the west side of Nuna Ridge.

"That bear seems to be going up the creek toward Maple Sugar Gap," said Ike.

"I think you're right," responded John, mopping his brow with his dripping handkerchief. "The barking is coming from that direction."

"Isn't that where Matthew's standing?" Nat felt a cold chill run up his spine. He didn't like the idea of his inexperienced, bear-hunting son confronting a running, angry bear alone. "What's our best plan for gettin' there fast?"

"We're not far from the main trail between Russell and Spence fields. Let's head toward it and walk along the ridge. It'll be faster travelin' since the area below Maple Sugar Gap is steep, rocky, and full of dense laurel thickets. We don't want to get tangled up in that mess," said Ike.

"Denser than these," said Nat, motioning to an area close to where they were standing.

"Yes. That hillside is the worst place hereabouts to traverse. It's got laurel, heath, and huckleberry bushes, plus other low-lying shrubs. If that bear remembers this fact, it'll head straight for it, and bears aren't stupid."

"Ike, I hadn't thought of that." John started in the direction of the trail. "We need to hurry. My dogs will follow a bear into a dense laurel thicket, and I'm sure yours will too. Someone won't come out of the fight that'll start within. Let's hurry."

"All right, lead on. I'd like to get to Matthew before that bear does," said Nat. He wanted to strike out ahead, to plunge down the ridge to the trail, but he wasn't as familiar with this part of the mountains. He must trust these men to get him quickly to his son.

Dropping off Nuna Ridge, the three men heard the trailing dogs about one-half mile away. The pitch of their barking meant they were on the bear's heels. Soon, the bear would turn to fight.

Fifteen minutes later, the group reached the main trail and headed toward Russellfield. They picked up Paul on the way.

"That bear is heading up the hollow to Maple Sugar Gap," he said.

"Yeah," said his father. "We know. Come on, we've got to hurry."

"Is Matthew guarding the gap?"

"Yes, we need to hurry. Listen, the dogs are barking wildly. The bear has turned to fight."

At his first step down the trail toward Maple Sugar Gap, Nat started praying for his son's safety.

After breakfast that morning, the standards walked away from their camp at Spencefield, and the sounds of the impatient dogs faded away. Five sets of feet made little noise on the dirt path. Each of the men, even the young ones, knew how to walk in the forest. At each gap the group grew smaller, until only Matthew and his Uncle Lazarus continued their walk toward their watch areas nearer to Russellfield.

"Matthew, are you coming over to spend some time with me this summer?" said his uncle in a quiet voice. Those were cherished days for Lazarus. Matthew was the child he never had.

Since Matthew was six years old the two tromped the mountains, enjoying the summer days spent together. During these walks, Lazarus taught his nephew the names of wildflowers and trees. They worked the fields in Tipton's Sugar Cove and picked the bounty of the land. At night, after a delicious supper cooked by his Aunt Sarah, the trio sat in the lamplight discussing the merits of new books each was reading. Sarah kept her bookshelves stocked with reading material—all types, sent from her family in Chattanooga, Tennessee.

"I've been plannin' on it," said Matthew. "Do you have any particular time in mind?"

"Oh, what about around the 4th of July? We'll ride our horses into Townsend and take the train to Knoxville for the Declaration of Independence celebration. They'll have fireworks off the Gay Street Bridge, and we'll bum around town and stay the night at our favorite hotel on Gay Street."

"Wow, that sounds great. I don't know of any reason why I can't." Matthew stumbled down the path, tripping on a root he didn't see in the worn trail. "So much for silence," he said with a sheepish grin on his face.

"Then it's set. I'll talk to your Pa." Lazarus was grateful to Nat for sharing his youngest boy.

The two walked on, deep in their own thoughts.

"I miss Aunt Sarah." Matthew wasn't sure he should bring up the subject.

"I do too." Lazarus breathed deeply. "Sometimes I go in the back door of our house, and I could swear I heard her hummin' and the pots being stirred on the stove. Then I realize if I want a hot supper, I gotta fix it myself." Lazarus was misty-eyed as he looked off the mountain in the direction of his home. His hurt hadn't healed very fast.

"Do you ever think about marrying again?"

"A woman like her is hard to find. I'd always be measuring another up to Sarah. That wouldn't be fair to anyone. Sarah was like the woman in Proverbs. She was smart and kind, and I trusted her. I never got in her way, and she never got in mine. We grew together in every way."

"I hope I find someone as wonderful as she."

"An enduring love and a woman you respect and who respects you is a rare jewel, Matthew. Most men and women tire of each other in a few years. They just live together because of convenience or family, not necessarily because of love."

"I understand Uncle Laz, or at least I think I do."

"If you find her, that perfect wife, treasure her, for there aren't many like Sarah. We were alike in so many ways. Remember what the Holy Bible says, *'Who can find a virtuous woman? For her price is far above rubies. A woman that feareth the LORD, she shall be praised.'* I've raised my hands many times in thanks for my beautiful wife."

Matthew heard the pathos in his uncle's voice. What could he say?

"Here's your gap. I'll see you later." Lazarus continued on toward Russellfield. He was quickly out of sight.

🦋 Chapter Seventeen 🦋

The Bear's Attack — Matthew

Matthew sat under a huge white oak at Maple Sugar Gap. He hadn't heard a sound except for some chattering squirrels and chirping birds since he'd arrived. In fact, it was so warm, quiet, and peaceful, he struggled to keep from napping.

For several minutes, he had watched a yellow, swallowtail butterfly as it flittered in and out of the bright sunlight. Finally, it disappeared into the quiet forest. Closing his eyes, he relaxed and let his mind wander, and as it had done the last two days, he thought of the young girl's presence on Rich Mountain. He saw her frightened eyes and her torn clothing. The same questions ran through his mind.

～

Matthew awoke with a start and rubbing his eyes wondered groggily why he was sitting under a tree on top of the mountain. Then he grinned wryly and jumped up, thoroughly awake.

Some bear hunter I am.

He could hear the dogs barking in the distance. The sounds came from far down the mountain.

Wonder if they're comin' my way?

He listened for over an hour as they gradually approached. The dogs and bear were heading in his direction. He was sure of this.

The sounds of the chase are much closer. Wonder where they'll come out?

Matthew peered into the thicket below him, making sure his gun was ready to shoot. He couldn't see a blamed thing.

No way can I get in there without crawling on hands and knees.

The dogs were closer. Their excited barks said they were on the bear. They were coming toward him, faster and faster. He could hear crashing in the laurel below. Suddenly, he heard the sound of a terrible fight in progress.

The bear must have turned on the dogs in the midst of the thicket.

Matthew remembered Donald's advice. The dogs must be protected. He took a deep breath and plunged off the mountain. Heading for the sound of the fight, he elbowed his way toward the midst of the thicket. He heard clearly the sounds of the fighting – snarling dogs and growling bear. The fight was close.

He heard the popping and gnashing of the bear's teeth as they caught thin air. Standing up he poked his head above the thicket. Within the laurel patch the tops of the bushes were moving violently.

I must head for that spot.

A dog was yelping pitifully. Mortally wounded, it grew silent.

Hurry, hurry, Matthew.

In the dense laurel thicket, Matthew dropped to his knees and crawled toward the crashing, barking sounds. Focusing his eyes straight ahead, he struggled as he inched forward to maintain his balance on the steep hillside. Seeing a black blur ahead, he felt the hair stand up on the back of his neck. He held his gun tighter and pulled himself forward – always forward.

Something soft under my hand.

Matthew drew back his hand. Looking down in the dim light, it was Daisy. She was the dog he'd heard yelling. There were puncture wounds on her neck. Daisy had made a mistake, and she was dead. He couldn't make a mistake.

There was no time to feel sorrow or anger. He crawled over her and emerged into the fight area, exposing his legs. He'd lost his concentration. The bear, smelling his scent, was upon him.

Matthew didn't have time to think or shoot. The huge bear grabbed him by the calf of the leg, sinking its canines in deep and throwing him around in the narrow opening like a dishrag. In the tight area, he bounced off bushes, rocks, and dirt. Dust clogged the air.

In the shadowy light, he caught glimpses of the dogs snapping and snarling at his adversary. He tasted blood on his lip. The bear loosened its grip on his leg but continued to claw at his body with lashes so quick Matthew couldn't see them coming.

The dogs increased their furiousness attack, and the bear momentarily turned its attention toward them. Snapping, whirling and foaming at the mouth, it knocked another of the dogs into the bushes. The dog returned to the fight. Matthew thought he saw blood on its side.

During the bear's brief attack, Matthew hadn't thought to scream. Lying on his side, he saw his gun and crawled toward it. Searing pain came from his wounded leg.

Matthew groaned loudly as he moved toward his gun.

That was a mistake. The bear saw the movement and heard the moan. It twisted around toward its wounded prey.

The enraged animal went for the kill, heading for the throat.

Matthew threw his arms up over his head, and this time he screamed. He felt hot air as the animal panted in his face. He smelled its stinky breath. As the bear clamped its dripping teeth onto his left arm, slime ran down to his elbow. He felt the bone snap, like breaking a twig. With one arm, he could no longer defend himself.

This is it! The end of my life. Oh, God! Help me.

The loud report rang in Matthew's ear and the three-hundred-pound bear collapsed on his torn body. Mercifully, Matthew passed out.

Breathing hard from running and crawling, Nat hunkered over the bear in a daze. He could feel warmth coming from its still body. His son's scream still echoed in his ears. Blood and bear covered Matthew.

Tossing the smoking Winchester to the ground, he grabbed the dead bear by its hind legs. Adrenaline flowed through him as he rolled the huge bear off Matthew's body. The dogs danced and snapped at the bear's lifeless carcass, which leaned against a laurel trunk. Nat bent over his son.

Guided by the sound of the barking dogs, Ike, John, and Paul arrived at that moment. They were detained by a fall which left Ike limping.

With hunting knives, a spot was cleared to enter the heath. Pushing Nat gently aside, Ike and John knelt in the confines of the tiny spot. Man touched man and bear.

They examined Matthew's body. This wasn't a job for his father. It was best left to them.

Matthew's clothes were almost torn off. His body was covered with dirt and blood. Still, it was easy for their expert hands to inspect his wounds. Matthew was alive. He had a broken arm, deep puncture wounds on his arms and legs, and ragged, bloody claw marks on his torso. But, the worst damage, they agreed, was done to the calf area of his leg where the bear had grabbed Matthew first. Miraculously, no major blood vessels had ruptured or torn, but serious damage was done to the leg's tendons. He would live; the men assured his father, but he needed to be moved swiftly down the mountain.

~

Getting Matthew home quickly was the biggest problem the hunters faced now. Each time they touched him, Matthew groaned in his unconscious state. They decided to make a stretcher of part of the tent at Spencefield and sent Donald to fetch the canvas, Nat and John's horses, and Frank. It was just past noon. If they hurried, they could be down the mountain before sunset.

Six of the men would carry the injured young man off the mountain, taking turns carrying the homemade litter. Donald and Paul would stay behind. They would skin and dress the bear, sinking the meat in a deep, chilly pool at Anthony Creek. The horses, dogs, and meat they would return to pickup tomorrow.

"Hurry, Donny," called John as his son left for Spencefield. "We need to leave here as quickly as possible."

"How do we get Matthew out of the laurel thicket?" called Nat, hovering anxiously over his son, his hand over the worst gash on his leg.

The standards, hearing the shot, started to arrive. After hearing what happened, Lazarus rushed into the thicket to see his wounded nephew.

"How bad is it?" he asked Nat, squeezing into the thicket beside his brother.

"He's torn up pretty bad. Nothin' that won't heal. The calf of his leg, the muscles look like the worst wound. You can see the claw marks on his chest. And he has a broken arm."

Lazarus examined the claw marks on Matthew's body.

"We're gettin' ready to move him," called John from the trail.

"Nat, if you want to help with the preparations for removing Matthew, I'll sit with him." Laz was glad Nat took him up on his offer. At the sight of his beloved nephew's body, tears coursed down his cheeks. He knew many days would pass before the damaged muscle, claw marks, and puncture wounds healed. He fervently wished it was him instead of this young man. *Thank God, the bear didn't get to his face.*

Outside the thicket, he heard John giving orders.

"Get your hatchet, Ike, and we'll cut some hemlock boughs. Then we'll use the rope to tie them together and make a pad to pull him out, unless someone else has a better idea. I'm open to one. I don't think we should wait until Donny gets back with the canvas."

No one else came up with a plan.

"John, I think I'll cut away the trunks of the laurel bushes so we can get in to Matthew before we look for something to make a litter." Ike hefted his hatchet and cleared the brush from the shortest way to the young man. The others pulled brush and piled it outside the thicket.

Ike headed for the nearest hemlock tree, and the men followed. They came back with several long boughs and soon a makeshift litter was pulled into the thicket. Lazarus got out of the way as they attended to moving his nephew.

It wasn't long until Matthew was beside the trail. He was a bloody mess. Paul and Peter gasped at the appalling sight. The imprint of the bears teeth was clearly seen on his leg. The leg bones, exposed by the torn skin, had saved him from more serious damage.

"Paul, take the empty lunch bucket and see if you can find a creek. Bring some water back. We'll wash out Matthew's wounds while we wait for Donald to return."

Using their salty, sweat-drenched handkerchiefs, John started cleaning Matthew's wounds the best he could. The touch of the cold water made Matthew shiver as he lay on the grass at the edge of the trail. With the cold water on his face, he regained consciousness.

"How do you feel, Son?" asked his father. "Don't move your arm. It's broken." Nat gently pinned Matthew's arm so he couldn't move it.

"What happened? Am I alive? My ears are ringing." Matthew put his right hand up to his ear and rubbed it.

"You had a fight with a bear and almost lost." Lazarus was standing over his nephew and smiling down at him. He continued, "Your Pa got there just in time and shot him. He's lying dead down on the trail where you got hurt."

"Son, were getting ready to carry you out so the doctor can treat you. I'm afraid the trip will be painful. I'm sorry."

Matthew nodded his head.

As the men continued swabbing him down, he was aware of excruciating pain. It was over most of his body. He couldn't tell which part hurt the most, and he didn't see how the trip down could be worse.

The sun was warm on his body, but Matthew started to shake. When he was cleaned up, the men took off their shirts to cover him and took hold of the makeshift stretcher, moving it to another sunny place along the trail and closer to Spencefield. They met Donald, leading the two horses by their reins, with Frank walking behind.

The men constructed the stretcher, cutting holes in the canvas to thread the rope and using two, sturdy poles Ike cut with his axe. Finally, they were ready to start down the mountain. They would take Nat's horse with them to pull the wagon when they arrived at Annie's.

"Donny, I'll be back tomorrow," said his father, and they hefted Matthew and started the arduous trip off Spencefield. "Take care of the bear. Use the horse to carry it into camp."

Because the first part of the Spencefield trail was rough and steep, carrying Matthew out wasn't easy on any of the participants. The men tried their best to be gentle, but Matthew wiped off beads of sweat from his brow caused from the stabbing pain. He gritted his teeth and bore it. At last, the trail hit more moderate grades. The going was easier and less painful, if that was possible.

When the group reached Annie's, she almost passed out.

It's a good thing she can't see the extent of Matthew's wounds, Lazarus thought as he went inside her home to get an old quilt to cover his nephew.

Of course, Granny W. was in one of her I-told-you-so moods, but she managed to keep her mouth shut, mostly because the group headed straight to the barn.

Nat's horse was hitched to his wagon, and Matthew was loaded into the back on a hurriedly made bed of sweet-smelling hay. Nat paced up and down under the cantilever of the barn. He was anxious to start toward the doctor's house.

But, before Nat mounted into the wagon seat to head for the doctors he walked over to Peter, shook his hand, and said, "Thanks Peter for helping. You did a fine job." Not once had Peter lost his footing, and he had performed with true grit and determination, on par with the rest of the men.

Peter smiled at Nat. He felt vindicated from his recent clumsiness.

"Thanks, Pastor," he said.

Matthew recalled little of the next three days. By the fourth, he sat up in bed, although he was a bundle of pain.

❧ Chapter Eighteen ❧

Five Weeks Into Recovery — Matthew

On the fifth week, his father had helped him to a chair in the kitchen, because he'd complained about staying in his bedroom until he could climb its walls. The going was rough and painful because every place Nat touched on his son's body was sore. Afterward, Nat had complained to Martha, "The only words Matthew knows are ouch or that hurts."

∼

Standing next to his dresser were two new crutches. Matthew tried them out, feeling the wood pressing against his arm pits. He couldn't use them, because of his broken arm, and although his leg was healing nicely, it still hurt and took his breath away to walk.

∼

Two months went by and most of his body was healed and the danger of serious infection had passed. He felt the thin strip of bandage wrapped around his torso and the smaller one twisted around his leg. These were stubborn areas with open wounds, refusing to heal. His broken arm had mended, but he was afraid to place a heavy burden on the newly knitted bones.

No need in tempting fate. Go slowly and let them strengthen –muscles and bones.

Taking a few cautious steps, he walked to his dresser where his shirt lay. Before putting it on, he looked in the mirror. His reflection revealed the angry red scars and healed puncture wounds, ghastly reminders of the bear's furious attack on that terrible day below Thunderhead Mountain. He ran his hand down the lumps and bumps of his formerly smooth chest. The sight of his body, once young and attractive, repelled him when he looked and felt it with his hands. Matthew's face tightened in resignation. Months, even years, would pass before the scars aged to white streaks, the lumps would flatten somewhat and the garish redness disappear.

For several days, his mother, using a healing salve the doctor provided, massaged the areas on his stomach and side. She gently pressed the tender flesh back and forth, up and down, to loosen the tautness of healed claw marks on his skin.

When Matthew could stand the pain, she massaged his leg, working the damaged muscle with pungent horse liniment the doctor left in a brown bottle.

"If that horse liniment doesn't help your leg, it'll clear up your head," Matthew's father commented, laughing the first time Martha rubbed it on. "I could smell it on the front porch it's so strong. Whew!"

Something in his tone of voice caused Martha to look up at him and roll her eyes.

"Get down here and put it on. Then you'll really smell it, Nathan Tipton." She sat in the floor, her gray head nodding back and forth as she worked steadily on the leg muscle, the bottle of liniment tucked securely in the pocket of her apron. Matthew was stretched out in a cloth-covered chair, gritting his teeth and holding on for dear life. His face was ashen with pain.

"Now, Martha. Don't get your hackles up." Nat knew how much he could push his wife and backed off. "I didn't intend a criticism by the remark."

"Actually, I like the smell." Martha pulled the bottle out, stuck it under her nose in a defiant gesture, and waved it back and forth for effect, while eying her husband. He changed the subject.

"Son, when you exercised this morning, could you put your full weight on your leg? I saw you walk out on the back porch."

"No, I can't. It hurts too much." Matthew had bit his lip to keep from groaning loudly from the pain. He didn't want to worry his mother. He did manage a half-hop, half-walk across the floor with his crutches. Once on the back porch, he looked at the steps to the ground and grimaced. No way was he in condition to negotiate those.

The doctor's advice was to continue with the massages and exercise the leg by walking. "He's to walk short distances at first and put more weight on his left side. The doctor said to increase the length of the walk as the muscle loosens and strengthens."

"What did the doctor say about recovering the use of the muscle? Should you expect a quick response to exercise or walking?"

"He was extremely happy with Matthew's progress, wasn't he Son?" said Martha, still on the offensive, her hands continuing their feverous activity on his leg.

Matthew's mouth formed the word stop, but he didn't utter it.

"Yes, he was, but I don't want to be using crutches when I go to college. I'll need to get around campus quickly, or who will carry my books?" This was a conundrum; one that needed to be worked out. Matthew was looking at the top of his mother's head as he voiced his concern.

"Son, don't heap trouble on your head," Martha replied, looking up at him. "You still have two months until school starts. By then, your leg may be healed and well enough for you to walk without a crutch. Let's wait and see what happens."

"She gives good advice, Matthew. Mother, I'm going to the garden. I may need to hoe the corn." His son watched as he left the room.

"Dad, I wish I could help." Matthew had called after his father.

Martha continued, "Matthew, you didn't ask for this to happen to your leg. I know you didn't want to go on the bear hunt. You did it to please your father. I'm glad you're alive, and I'm sure he's glad also. He's still strong and vigorous. He'll manage."

His mother didn't know her soothing words were better medicine than any jar of cream or liquid out of a bottle. Because of them, Matthew didn't slide into bitterness and despair, and he might have done both after the attack.

∾

Several days had passed since the first liniment was rubbed on his sore leg. It was Sunday, and Matthew felt well enough to attend church. He never missed church and over two months had passed since he'd gone.

Leaning his crutches against his dresser, Matthew pulled his shirt over his head and secured the buttons.

He turned from the mirror and wobbled toward the bed, easing down slowly, he sat on the edge. After fumbling around several minutes, he pulled his bib overalls over his knees, stood up and balanced on his good leg. Drawing the straps over his shoulders, he locked the front clasps in place. The overalls and shirt were loose fitting clothes which wouldn't restrict his movement or chafe his body. He wouldn't feel out of place today, because most of the men wore overalls to church.

"Good morning, Son. Are you ready for church?" Martha stood at the doorway to her son's room. "My, you look handsome today."

"I'm ready except for my socks and tying my shoes." Matthew shrugged his shoulders, shook his head in resignation, and smiled at his mother. He felt embarrassed at not being able to perform a task he'd been doing since he was five years old. Bending over *that* far was still very painful.

"Aren't you glad your mother knows how to carry out that chore?" Martha knelt in the floor, put on his socks, and tied his shoes. "Your father has the buggy at the back porch. We think you'll be able to step off and into the floorboard without a problem. Are you ready to try?" She reached out to help him, but he ignored her extended hand.

"Mom, I'm determined to start moving on my own," he said. "Hand me my crutches from the dresser." He was a bundle of emotions as he thought about returning to the church. "But you can carry my Bible," he added, smiling again.

They headed for the porch. Perspiration gathered on Matthew's lip. He wasn't sure whether it was from his exertion or the heat. After all, it was late June. Matthew entered the buggy with minimum difficulty. His father slapped Old Jack with the reins and drove down the shaded lane toward the church.

How will I ever get out of this buggy once I get to the church grounds?

That was the problem, since not many places on his body could be touched without pain and his skin hadn't totally regained its elasticity. Jumping or sitting down to slide out of the buggy was impossible.

He shouldn't have worried. Men from the church had been busy constructing a set of steps for him to negotiate, and they sat in new, white wood splendor next to the road and close to the open church door. The horse and buggy pulled up to the steps. Donald and Peter came running from the church. Matthew, steadied by his friends and crutches, stepped gingerly down to the dirt road. Together the buddies walked the short path to the church's two steps. Secreted in the church, several men immediately came outside and applauded Matthew as he walked slowly up the steps. The group followed him as he entered the sunlit sanctuary.

More than one attendee said, "Glad to see you back, Brother. We've been praying for you," as he entered the door and started down the center aisle.

Matthew walked along two rows of wooden pews separated by the center aisle. As was the custom for many years, men sat on one side. The women and children sat on the other. Three glass windows on each of the church's side walls let light into the interior. On cloudy or rainy days, the worshippers sat in semi-darkness with lanterns lighting the pulpit and congregation. When it was cold, a pot-bellied stove, sitting in close proximity to the minister, warmed the area, and at times it seemed him.

Matthew walked through the sunlit patches on the uneven, worn church floor as he made his way to the front pew. This was his favorite place to sit. In fact, most of the men in church had favorite places where they sat. As he went forward, Matthew looked around to determine who was present and who wasn't.

Halfway to the front, he passed by the pew where the notoriously snooping pair, Edna Akkins and Precious Tipton, were sitting. They were whispering to each other as he approached. The ladies nodded in recognition and welcome.

Stirrin' up some mischief, I imagine. Hope it's not about me.

How his distant cousin, Precious, got her name was a mystery to Matthew. If her parents had waited until certain traits of character surfaced, he was sure they'd have named her Nosy.

She and Edna are cut from the same cloth. That's for sure.

In anticipation of Matthew's coming, his Uncle Lazarus was waiting at the front pew. Matthew eased down on the wooden bench and Donald placed his crutches at the end of the seating area. Lazarus sat down and put a protective arm around his nephew.

Finished with greeting his congregation, Nathan came by and stopped, "Brother, you're planning on coming to the house for dinner after church, aren't you? Martha's expecting it. She's fixing your favorite, country ham and redeye gravy."

"If he doesn't go, I'll come, Nat," said John Razor. He was sitting about two seats behind Matthew and heard the conversation.

Everyone close by laughed, but Lazarus replied, "Yes, I'm coming. I couldn't miss that feast. Besides Sarah, Martha's the best cook I know."

"Now I see where I stand," said Joanna Graves, feigning disgust. She was a widow who had designs on the widowed, Lazarus.

"Shot out of the saddle again," replied John, slapping his knee. And then, "How are you feeling, Matthew? It's been awhile since that fateful afternoon under the dark face of Thunderhead."

Nat left the group and continued to the front. He sat in a cane chair with his head bowed as was his custom before the service started.

Matthew turned gingerly to face John, "I'm much better, but I still have a ways to go. There's still healing to take place and my movement is hampered because of pain here and there."

"You definitely look much better than that day we carried you off the mountain. That was a hard trip. The trail's so rough in places, especially where the dirt washed off and exposed the slate crossing the path. It's slippery and after the deluge we survived the night before . . . well."

"Thankfully, I don't remember much about that trip. With a broken arm and so many wounds, the pain put me in a fog."

Nathan stood up to start the service.

"Ready to go bear huntin' again?" asked John, whispering to Matthew. He was teasing of course.

"No," said Lazarus. "I don't think he'll ever go again. Right, Matthew." Lazarus turned to look at his nephew.

Matthew shook his head as his mother hurried forward with his Bible, forgotten in the meeting and greeting session before church.

"Thank you, Mom." Matthew placed it on the pew beside him.

Nat asked for announcements and when it became known the widow Howell was sick in bed with pneumonia, several women volunteered to take food and help with the children. The men made plans to hoe her garden and take care of her livestock. Until she was better, the cove people would care for her. No one went without, if the church people knew about it.

"Let's stand and pray."

Rustling and scraping of wooden benches was heard in the church. The elderly remained seated while the rest of the congregation stood with heads bowed.

"Brother Taylor, will you lead us?" The prayer was not long.

"Please stand and turn to page sixty in your hymnal and let's sing, *Showers of Blessing*," said Nat, looking directly at Matthew and smiling. "We're glad to welcome our brother, Matthew, back to our congregation this morning."

When his father finished his sermon and gave the altar call, Matthew whispered to Lazarus, "Help me to the altar. I want to pray." Although his pain was severe, Matthew intended to thank God for extending his grace through the last two months' trial.

Lazarus and Donald placed an arm under each of Matthew's and half carried him to the altar, where he carefully knelt to pray. The elders gathered around him, laying hands on his shoulders. As they prayed out loud, Matthew prayed silently.

Father, I thank You and praise You for Your protection over me during the last two months. I don't know why this happened, and I wonder how You will use this scarred body to Your glory. But I realize You have a purpose; one that will bring honor to Your name. Give me patience to accept the continued pain and recuperation period.

And thank You for my mother's serenity and concern; for her determination to help me recuperate, the gentleness of her care, and her kind words.

I honor You for a father who prays for his children and supports them in all things, and most of all for his dedication to being a Christ-follower and for the tremendous example of His life.

May I continue down Your Son's path and one day stand in His pulpit as a shepherd of His people, as Jesus stood and as my father is now standing. I love You, Lord. You are my all in all.

"Amen and amen." Matthew spoke inaudibly except for the last amen's. Slowly, he arose from the floor and, with the aid of his crutches, hobbled out the door and down the steps of the church. Back in the wagon, his father drove home and, after exiting the wagon, Matthew went straight to his room. When his father went to call him to dinner, he was fast asleep.

Nat gently shook his son. "Matthew, dinner is ready."

Matthew opened his eyes and looked groggily at his father, "I'm sorry, Dad. I'll eat later. I'm worn out. Tell Mom it smells delicious."

∾

Matthew awoke with a start.

Uncle Lazarus stood over him. "Matthew," he said. "I want to plan on a trip to Maryville College around Labor Day. That's over two months away. You need to meet my friend Dr. Elmore. Do you think you'll be up to this?"

"I'll have to feel better than I felt today. I've got to get out of this house and walk. I didn't realize how weak and puny I'd become."

"I'll come over and walk with you a couple of times a week. Do you think this would help?"

Matthew nodded his head. "Dad doesn't have much time except later in the day, and then, most times, he's studying. Tending the garden and caring for the livestock is a full-time job, especially in this heat. But I know he'll help when he isn't worn out. Mom's not a walker."

"O.K., it's settled. We'll work hard and you can spend your yearly two weeks with me at Labor Day. I-I look forward to your coming." Lazarus hid his emotions as he reached down and gave his nephew a careful but loving hug and left the room.

Matthew listened to him telling his mother and father goodbye and then heard the sound of horse's hooves on the gravel road.

∾

On Wednesday, Joanna Graves came to see Martha. Matthew heard her arrive from the back porch where he sat shucking corn which his father had pulled from the stalks earlier in the morning. This wasn't the first time Joanna had visited his mother in the week. Something was going on, and he couldn't put his finger on it.

Their tête-à-tête came from the kitchen, where his mother readied the brushes to be used in silking the corn and collected knives for cutting the kernels and milking the juice from the cob. This task was taking much longer than necessary.

Matthew heard snatches of the conversation — enough to get deeply irritated.

Joanna was reporting what she'd heard through the busybody line. First item was that Matthew knew he would never walk without crutches again. He couldn't even carry his Bible, so assuming the church pulpit was impossible. He, in fact, had said as much to his friend Donald Razor. And second, the group that carried him off Thunderhead Mountain made the trek in a thick fog and stumbling had broken his arm in a fall on the slick trail.

Martha came back to the porch with more pans and sat down across from her son. One glance at his face told her volumes.

"You heard?"

"What do you think about that, Mother?" questioned Matthew in disbelief.

"I tried to straighten her out on the front porch, before she left for home."

"I never said anything of the kind to Donald, and there wasn't any fog or fall."

"I'm sorry you heard her words," his mother tried to soothe his annoyance.

"Well I did," said an indignant Matthew.

"Must be sort of slow in the gossipin' business this week," mused Martha, picking up an ear of corn to silk with her brush. "You'd think Edna and Precious would be busy fixin' corn out of the garden, wouldn't you?" She waved the ear of corn in the air.

"I don't understand what they get out of telling lies, flat-out untruths." Matthew tore the shucks off an ear with a vengeance. "Maybe they should put their talent to use and write books."

"Wait until I see her later this week. I'm goin' to take those two ladies aside and talk to them. I'll do it with love, but they'll know how I feel when I get done. The very idea!" Martha brushed the tender corn a little too vigorously. Corn milk flew in every direction.

"May well be better not to say anything," Matthew observed. "They'll just think up more untruths to go with the first, and you'll turn into the brunt of the conversation."

"You might be right, but someday they'll go too far and somebody'll put those two in their place. You wait and see."

The mother and son shucked, silked, cut off, and milked ten dozen ears of corn. This was only the first of many to come. After dinner, Martha used the waterbath and canned the corn in glass jars. When the containers cooled, Nat carried them to storage in the root cellar under the house, where it was cool and dark.

Nat commented after his return, "Son, you're moving much better this week."

Matthew laughed, "Yes, I am. May be able to carry my Bible to church on Sunday."

After supper, Nat went outside to sit on the front porch, and Matthew lingered at the kitchen table while his mother cleared the dishes and prepared to wash them. Neither one had said a word to Nat about the gossip they'd shared earlier. Martha opened the kitchen cupboard, where the jellies and jams were stored.

Matthew was startled. "Hum-m, where did the blackberry jam come from?" Suddenly, the pieces of the puzzle fit together. "What have you and Joanna been doing?"

"Son, I wasn't trying to keep it from you, but we've been swapping jellies and jams."

"I wondered why you were making so many jars of peach preserves." Matthew shook his head. "I miss picking the berries. I guess Joseph is picking them." Joseph was Joanna's son. "I could tell him about my favorite places, where he can pick berries as big as his thumb."

"I'll let Joanna know later in the week when she comes again." There was silence in the kitchen for several minutes. Then the rattle of dishes grew louder as Martha continued washing them.

"Mom, I'll help you dry the dishes. That is, if there's any left."

Martha started laughing. "I *am* clanging them together, aren't I? I can't help but think about Edna and Precious. I declare those two women make me so angry." Martha stopped and looked down at the soapy dishwater, "Lord, forgive me for unkind thoughts, and help me not to make rash judgments or take actions for which you would not be proud."

Martha handed the drying towel to her son. "You know I love you, Matthew." She never missed a chance to tell him this.

"I know, Mother."

❧ Chapter Nineteen ❧

A Trip to Tipton's Sugar Cove — Matthew

Although a hint of orange glowed beyond the tops of Thunderhead Mountain, it remained dark outside. Matthew limped quietly around in the shadows of the room, pulling on his pants and shirt and drawing a light jacket over his broad shoulders. On this September morning, he wished to enjoy the sunrise alone. His Uncle Lazarus would be up and moving around soon enough.

In stocking feet, he treaded softly across the room, carefully opened the front door and sat down in a chair on the front porch of his uncle's home. Even after his mother's massaging and the long walks with his uncle, his leg continued to be stiff when he got out of bed in the morning. Bending over, he rubbed the calf of his leg to loosen the muscle. With the morning's activities, it would soon free-up and he would walk limp-free. After five long months, he'd made tremendous progress.

Matthew's desire was to watch the sun come up and feel the peace of the waking valley. Several minutes passed. He sat watching as Tipton's Sugar Cove appeared out of the morning mists hanging low in the valley before him. In early September, the humid air still clung to East Tennessee, and the first frost hadn't pocked the grass with ice crystals. Within days, this would quickly change. Even now, there was a chill in the morning air.

Matthew shivered.

I'm cold.

He hunkered over, his arms wrapped tightly across his chest, watching the scene developing before him.

My position is much like the hills enfolding the low-land cove in the cool, pre-autumn haze.

"Your attempts to hold yesterday's warmth close to the ground will be a losing battle," he advised the hills softly.

Matthew looked down into the valley. His eyes followed the path to the barn and machinery shed. They appeared as large, shadowy ghosts against the flat, harvested fields behind them. Dark corn shocks stood as sentinels over the cows and horses, grazing in the meadow below. The only sound he heard was the muffled gurgling of the nearby trickling stream and the lowly but insistent mooing of a cow for her calf.

"Such a beautiful, peaceful place," he murmured.

He loved this place, Cades Cove and the Smoky Mountains. The Tipton heritage ran deep and was a vital part of Cades Cove; plowed deep into the soil. Sitting here on his uncle's front porch was a good time to think back to his Aunt Annie's comments.

She often related the family history that John "Jack" Tipton had told her. "Remember this, Matthew," she would say, "your family has lived here for almost one hundred years. Your great, great grandfather, William Tipton, was the first legal landowner in Cades Cove after the Calhoun Treaty opened it up for settlement. William was a land speculator and never lived here, but he sold or gave his holdings to his brothers, relatives, and friends. Your dad lives on land handed down from generation to generation. So do I."

She kept pondering these facts, as she sat and rocked on the front porch a few minutes and then continued to speak. "Your roots grow as deep as the ones of the oak and hickory trees in the Smoky Mountains. It's important to establish those same roots for yourself and your future family. They'll give your family strength. Now I'll hush up."

Those same roots have grown into a deep affection engrained in my very soul. Nobody can live here and not feel a profound attachment tugging at your heartstrings and drawing you back when you leave.

He often wondered if any of the other Tipton ancestors related stories of their heritage. He knew some of them lived in Jamaica, Barbados, and England. What were their stories, how did they live in these different worlds he'd only heard about? Would he ever know?

~

Positioned at the western end of the greater area known as Cades Cove which nestled in the Smoky Mountains, Tipton's Sugar Cove was a small side cove.

In Tipton's Sugar Cove, maple trees were abundant and the early inhabitants tapped the trees in early spring, much like the ones growing in the northeast of the United States. This natural sweetening, discovered by the Eastern Woodland Indians, and bee's honey were the two main sources of flavoring for the sometimes-monotonous foods of early mountain folk. Matthew knew of many sugar coves scattered over the

Smoky Mountains where maple sap was gathered and converted into sugar.

The maple sugaring process had diminished with the introduction of cane sugar purchased at cove stores. Buying sugar meant that Matthew's mother could devote her time to other areas of her cabin life.

Giving up the old methods of producing necessary staples for maintaining life in these hills lessened the camaraderie of making those products like maple sugar, lye soap, or apple sauce. As each household bought mechanical equipment to make their jobs easier, they became more independent, and social networking grew less and less.

But that didn't mean anyone went hungry or without in Cades Cove. Families gathered around and helped each other when difficulties arose.

Down to the left of the front porch of Lazarus's cabin and past the sumacs, whose green leaves were turning maroon, the misty road led out of Tipton's Sugar Cove. It would connect with Parson's Branch Road.

From there, depending on where you were headed, a left turn crossed Hannah Mountain. At its end the traveler must make a decision on going north into North Carolina or south to Chilhowee. This was where the Aluminum Company of America's dams were being built along the Little Tennessee River, and where his Uncle Noah Tipton had a mercantile store.

If you didn't take the Parson's Branch Road, a right turn took you back to Razor's Grist Mill in Cades Cove, where John and Donald Razor's home was located. Their home was smack at the middle of the lower, western end of the mountain depression. This area was once swampland, but due to the efforts of former owners, much of the land could be planted and now contained some of the richest soil in the valley and the best-looking crops.

Tater Ridge, where his father lived, was toward the middle of Cades Cove on the northern side of Abrams Creek, about five miles in distance.

Later this morning, Matthew and his Uncle Lazarus would head to Townsend. They would pass Razor's mill, Burchfield's store, Nat's house, and cross Tater Branch. At the Missionary Baptist Church, they would turn left and ride up the face of Rich Mountain, traveling the curvy Rich Mountain Road, where the locals laughingly said you met yourself coming and going on the road's switch-backs. After crossing the mountain, a rider came out into Dry Valley and finally into Townsend, which nestled in Tuckaleechee Cove.

To access the outside world, the Cades Cove residents must cross a mountain in any direction.

~

A slight noise behind him disturbed his thoughts.

"Good morning, Matthew." Lazarus Tipton joined his nephew on the front porch of his cabin. "Are you 'soaking in the mountains' as Granny Shields always said?"

"Yes Sir, I am. I'm soakin' in the noise of silence this morning." Matthew loved his uncle, but he would've been happy to sit a few more minutes in solitude, enjoying the pastoral scene before him. It wouldn't be long until he went to college. There the opportunity to sit and enjoy the cove wasn't available.

"I heard you get up. Gave you a little alone time and then thought I'd join you."

"It's chilly out here this morning. Guess fall is on the way." Matthew rubbed his hands together."

"Before Sarah passed away, we sat here each morning before cookin' breakfast and enjoyed the changing seasons. Life passes before you here on the hillside." Lazarus looked wistfully across the fields. He had a large garden which he tended, but the bigger fields, what few there were, he rented out to friends. The cows and horses were his.

Matthew looked at his uncle and smiled. Turning his gaze back to the dimly lit fields, he said, "Guess it must be lonely without her."

"Yes. I remember after we returned from Chattanooga, where we were married, she insisted I carry her across the threshold. I thought it was a silly custom, but she was adamant, and so I picked her up and carried her in that door." Lazarus pointed to the front door. "I've lifted hay bales heavier than her. She was light as a feather." He paused in reflection. "I've been doin' a great deal of reminiscin' lately."

Matthew laughed at the thought of his aunt as a hay bale. "Aunt Sarah probably wouldn't be happy at being compared to a hay bale."

"Maybe not. But she was happy living here at Tipton's Sugar Cove. I was afraid after livin' in the hustle and bustle of the big city she might feel lonely, misplaced here. She always said 'there are still sounds, just different sounds.' The creek replaced the noise of travel on the street. The crows cawin' and cows lowin' spoke volumes in a language she didn't understand but loved to hear. The wind, sighin' in the pine trees or rustlin' leaves, was the overall hum of the big city."

Lazarus paused and then continued, "She fit right into life here. She sure did."

"Aunt Sarah always said she loved her cabin home, the farm, and the people. They were the dough, but, you, she called the spice. I remember her laughing and blushing at the same time. She was quite a lady." Matthew looked at his uncle uncertainly.

"You'll know what that means, someday. It's about time for you to add some spice to your life."

Matthew didn't open his mouth, but two red spots appeared on his face, disclosing he did think about women.

"Have you considered what kind of wife you want and need for your future in the ministry? You'll meet many types of women when you go to college."

"I'd imagine so. A minister's wife is not the easiest life, especially here in the cove. But I think my mother is a good example to follow and my revered aunt, of course. I miss Aunt Sarah." Matthew tried to change the subject. Lately, he'd begun to wonder if there was a woman out there for him — one who'd look over the rough, red scars on his body.

"Women are a-changin' these days. Sarah was a good example of that change. May I emphasize good? When the Bible talks about a help-meet, I believe she was a first-class example of that lady." Lazarus nodded his head. "We met each other in all things. Had a lot in common. There was healthy give and take in our marriage. That's what made it special — spicy." Lazarus grinned from ear-to-ear.

Both men were silent for several minutes, each thinking their own thoughts.

"But enough of reminiscin'. I'm hungry. It's time for breakfast, and we have a busy day ahead; a day at your new school. We need to get started." His uncle immediately arose from his chair but paused before going in the door. "Are bacon and eggs O.K.?"

Great," said Matthew, getting up and following his uncle into the house. It was his job to stir up the biscuits. Calling his uncle's flour creation by that name was comical.

～

Matthew and Lazarus boarded the Little River Lumber Train at Townsend. The train trip from there to Maryville necessitated several stops at small stations along the way, and a change to the Southern Railway System at Walland.

Kinzel Springs was the first stop. "I'm always fascinated by this place," said Matthew as he looked at the impressive Kinzel Springs Hotel. The huge, three-story spa offered many amenities for the rich and famous. It was advertised nationwide in magazines, along with other large hotels in the area. They were speedily becoming a watering place for thousands of vacationers each year.

Attracted by cooler weather, mineral water, horseback riding with mountain views, hiking and social gatherings, people stayed for days, weeks, or whole summers in the foothills of the Smokies. The only way to access the inn was by train or the road on the other side of Little River. Driving from Maryville meant walking over the river on a swinging bridge, once you parked on the other side.

"I've ridden on the train with people from New York, Philadelphia, and Washington D.C. Many are doctors, lawyers, and transportation barons," said Lazarus.

Matthew pushed his head through the open train window. He watched as several people who stood under a wooden canopy waited until their time to embark. This didn't take long.

"All aboard," yelled the conductor, hanging off the back step and waving his hand at the train engineer who stood at the controls in the cab of the steam engine.

The warning whistle blew, steam hissed, and the train lurched forward, moving slowly down the narrow gorge where it wound back and forth with the Little River's meandering bank. Moving to the opposite side of the railroad car, Matthew heard the muffled laughter and squeals of children and adults swimming in the clear, cold river below. Above, a swinging bridge offered a sure footpath for residents to access Tuckaleechee Pike. The gravel road snaked along the river on the opposite side from the railroad and inn. Women carried parasols, sheltering their heads from the sun beating down on them as they stepped onto the planked surface, held on to a heavy cable, and cautiously moved across. Several rental cabins dotted the riverside next to the road.

"How did the road get its name?" asked Matthew, looking at the other side of the river where he caught glimpses of a lonely automobile traveling bumpily along the road. It was headed in the direction toward Maryville.

"Because the road originally went to an area known as Tuckaleechee Cove before the city of Townsend was built, and thus the road was named for it. A dirt road was the only route from Maryville to the cove, until the railroad was constructed. Townsend was established after the lumber mill went into operation and was named after W.B. Townsend, the mill's primary owner. He's the one who oversaw the building of the railroad and train system we're riding on now," replied his uncle. "He and his Pennsylvanian group built the Little River Lumber Co. It's the supplier of most of the jobs in the immediate area, unless you work at the Schlosser Leather Company in Walland."

Walland was the next stop. On approaching, the train's whistle was blown to alert passengers of its imminent arrival. Here a railroad spur ran across Little River to the tannery. Car loads of animal hides came in by rail. These were processed, and leather was shipped out by train all over the United States.

"Are you ready to get off here, Matthew?"

A turntable used to head the engine of the train back to Townsend stood off the track to the left.

"I'd like to tour the tannery. I think it would be interesting to see how they mass produce raw hides into leather." While the passengers loaded and unloaded, Lazarus looked across at the smoke coming from numerous chimneys protruding from the huge buildings making up the complex. "I know they use large amounts of water in the process."

"Guess that's why they built next to the river. Doesn't the tannery flood? It is built on the flood plain," observed Matthew.

"I know of at least one time when the water came up into the buildings."

The employees, several hundred of them, lived in the company village and up East and West Miller's

Cove. Chilhowee Inn, a large, white-framed building with lots of windows, sat on the other side of the river. Its occupants were tourists or businessmen calling on the tannery.

"Walland School looks down on all from its perch above the growing community." Lazarus pointed to several buildings, barely seen through the tall oak trees on the hill.

While waiting to board the Southern Railway cars, Matthew noticed an automobile pulling into the gasoline pump at the Esso Station across the river. It was the same one he'd seen earlier at Kinzel Springs. He saw two men come running out to the car. One started pumping gas into the customer's tank, and the other wiped the windshield of the car with great vigor. Money changed hands, and they stood watching as the car drove out of sight.

"Matthew, did you realize that this train connects with a network that hauls goods all over the states? Specialty Smoky Mountain woods, such as walnut and cherry, are found all over Europe."

The train whistle blew. They boarded, and after fifteen minutes, a jolt signaled the start of the rest of the journey.

The terrain flattened out immediately after leaving Walland, but the train hardly had time to pick up steam until it came to the next stop, which was Hubbard. Before the railroad was built, this community was the last one before traveling on to Townsend. It was also the last railroad stop into town. Matthew heard the whistle blowing, but although the train slowed, it didn't stop. Today, there was no one to board and no one to get off.

"Ha, we don't have to stop. There's no one to board the train." Matthew said to his uncle.

Looking out the window, he saw the car that seemed to be keeping up with the train's progress pass over the tracks just before the train arrived at the crossing. He wondered if that was the driver's aim and if he did this often.

"Look, Uncle Lazarus. I wonder who's driving that car. Will he beat us to Maryville, do you think?"

"If he doesn't find a ditch or field first," said Lazarus shaking his head. He only caught a glimpse of the speeding vehicle.

Matthew was delighted as the train sped onward toward Maryville, whizzing through the pastureland until it slowed at the depot in town.

"Time to get off, Matthew." Lazarus grabbed his hat off the rack above his head and waited for his nephew to push his way into the aisle.

"I always love the fast ride in from Hubbard. I can't imagine what it would be like to ride to Knoxville or even Chattanooga. Does the train go faster between those cities?"

"Yes, it does. We'll have to travel to Chattanooga. Maybe as a graduation present from college. We'll go see Sarah's sister or brother and stay a few days. We might take a steamboat ride on the Tennessee River in celebration. Would you like that?"

"Would I. I'll hold you to it," said Matthew as they walked toward the road taking them to the college. They started across the street when a car came careening around a sharp curve on the dirt road. Matthew jumped back, almost knocking his uncle down. Dust flew all over the startled men.

"Looked like your cousin D.H. in John Anderson's car." Lazarus was staring after the rapidly moving vehicle. Men in vehicles were rather scarce in Maryville. The car was easy to identify, but, "I didn't get a good look at the man driving. I don't think it was Mr. Anderson though. That reminds me I need to go to the bank before we go home."

"Was he the one who followed us from Townsend? He sure wasn't doin' the speed limit. What is the speed limit any way?"

"In town, it's 5 miles per hour. He was doin' at least 15 if not 20," said Lazarus. "I'll say something to him the next time I see him. By golly, he needs to slow that contraption down before he kills somebody."

"That might not be too long. Isn't that him comin' back?"

D.H. Tipton pulled up at the side of the road next to his kinfolk.

"Sorry about that, Uncle Lazarus. I almost ran over you. I'm coming from Townsend, and I'm late. How about a ride to wherever you're goin' to make up for the dust?" D.H. was the handsome cousin from Chilhowee, who worked downtown at Blount State Bank. Mr. Anderson was the president of the bank and his boss.

Matthew looked at his uncle with a knowing look in his eyes. He *was* the driver following the train.

D.H.'s father, Noah, was custodian over Lazarus's last will and testament, mainly because he had a safe in his mercantile store. Maybe ten years earlier, Noah Tipton moved out of Cades Cove over Chilhowee Mountain and into Happy Valley. His final move, a few miles down the road toward the Little Tennessee River, was to Chilhowee, where he bought a mercantile store from a man named Lowe.

Lazarus always saw Noah in May on Decoration Day at the Primitive Baptist Church in Cades Cove and other important times. The church was where his father and Noah's mother were buried. Lazarus's mother had died in Joplin when John Jack moved to Missouri for several years. Lazarus, Noah, and Nat were step-brothers.

"We're only goin' to the Maryville College campus. That's just a short walk. We'll be O.K. I heard you were leavin' for the war in Europe."

"Soon, I think. I haven't gotten my papers yet. Sure you don't want a ride? I've got to get back to the bank. The college is only a shortcut away."

"No. I'm taking Matthew over to tour the campus. He's starting school there in a few days, and we're meeting Dr. Elmore for lunch. Why don't you go with us? I haven't seen you in some time. I'd like to catch up on the news and hear all about what's happening in Chilhowee."

"Uncle, I'm so sorry, but I really don't have time. If you want news, you ought to go and visit Melva. I'm sure she'd love to see you and talk to you." Melva was his sister. "You could take Parson's Branch Road and come out close to Alcoa where she lives with her husband, Burl Whitehead. Burl's driving a team of mules and snaking wood off the areas being developed for the Alcoa dams, and Melva's tending store for her father at the new town."

"Where exactly is this?" asked Lazarus, who hadn't been to Chilhowee in several years.

"The town sits on the old Howard farm at Tallassee, where the ferry crosses the Little Tennessee River."

"Oh, yes, I remember where that farm is located, and I think I remember Nat saying something about Alcoa being built there." Turning to Matthew he continued, "Time's getting away from us. Guess we'd better be goin' or we'll be late. That is, if we can make it across the road without being run over by a car."

D.H. laughed. "It won't be me. I'm already by you. I'm sure John's wondering what's happened to me. It's good to see you. Give my regards to Uncle Nat," said D.H.

"We'll be by the bank later in the afternoon. By the way, you'd better slow that contraption down," suggested Lazarus as D.H. put it in gear to make a u-turn in the road. "You look a lot better with your head on your shoulders."

D.H laughed and threw up his hand as he disappeared down the road. The car's tires kicked up dirt as he went.

"He'll never learn." Lazarus shook his head as he turned toward the college and this time looked right and left before starting across the road.

❧ Chapter Twenty ❧

Experiencing Maryville College — Matthew and Lazarus

From the train depot in Maryville, it was a short walk to the Maryville College campus and its tree-lined avenues. The plan was to meet Dr. Edgar Elmore for dinner in the dining area of Baldwin Hall and tour the campus after eating.

Lazarus gave Matthew a description of his good friend as they continued toward their meeting place. Dr. Elmore, a graduate of Maryville College, was appointed a teacher at the school in 1884. At present, he served as pastor of Second Presbyterian Church in Chattanooga and was Sarah's father's personal friend. As chairman of the Board of Directors, his ties to the college were still strong, and he visited as often as he could, using the boardroom as an office.

"I met Dr. Elmore when he officiated at my wedding in Chattanooga where Sarah lived," said Lazarus, who was in his early thirties at the time he and Sarah met. "When we attended functions at Maryville College, which we did regularly, we often sat with Dr. Elmore and his wife."

"If Sarah lived in Chattanooga and you lived in the cove, how did you meet?" asked his nephew.

"Oh, the Moore family came up to camp and hike in the mountains. They needed a guide and someone to tend camp for them. I put up the tent, hauled water, and kept the fire going. At the same time, Sarah and I found out that we had a lot in common. She was twenty-four years old, ten years younger than I. During the two weeks the family spent in the mountains, we often walked in the woods and talked about books, just ordinary talk. When she went back to Chattanooga, I realized I missed her. So, we started writing, and after several months, I finally confessed my love for her and asked if I might come to see her."

"Let me tell you the next few days until her letter came were harrowing ones for me. But she wrote giving me a date to come and meet her family. It wasn't until I proposed that she told me she returned my affection, although the little things she did and said made me think so, and you know the rest."

"It's one of those love conquers distance stories, isn't it?"

"Love does conquer many things, maybe more than you'll ever know." Lazarus had been observing his nephew out of the corner of his eye. "Matthew, you're walking much better."

"I know, but I still have a limp that's noticeable. I hope my hop will go away by year's end." Matthew laughed at his favorite phrase describing his affliction, but he was pleased that his uncle had noticed.

"Keep exercising your leg. That's the secret." Lazarus paused in the middle of the lane, checking his directions.

"I think we turn here, and that's Baldwin Hall sitting at the end of the road. I hope I'm right. This campus changes each year. So many new buildings have been built. I understand there are several hundred students going here now. You're going to meet many new people, make lots of friends, and some will remain lifelong buddies."

"Look Uncle, there's a sign about the college." The two men stopped to read it. The bronze marquee placed atop a pole read:

MARYVILLE COLLEGE

Established in 1819 by the Presbyterian Synod of Tennessee as a preparatory school, four-year college and three-year theological seminary. It was first known as "The Southern and Western Theological Seminary." In 1842, a charter was issued by the State of Tennessee, officially calling the school Maryville College.

"I didn't realize the school was *that* old. It won't be long until it celebrates a one-hundred-year anniversary."

"Yes, they're planning a big centennial celebration in two years. Maybe you'll be a part of that."

They had arrived at Baldwin Hall. After asking directions of a student, the pair walked into the dining room and sat down, waiting for the arrival of their host. It wasn't long until he entered the room.

Meeting Dr. Elmore became the highlight of Matthew's visit to Maryville College.

"Lazarus," Dr. Elmore said as he strode in the dining hall door. He was exactly on time, which Matthew would grow to expect during his years at this school. He shook hands with Lazarus and said, "This must be Matthew." Dr. Elmore turned his full gaze on the younger man and extended his hand. He quickly sized up Matthew, whose broad smile was infectious. Dr. Elmore was sure he'd learn to like the young man immensely.

The feeling was mutual. "I'm really pleased to meet you," said Matthew. He gazed at a fine-looking older gentleman with deep-set, blue eyes, Greek nose, and thin mouth. His even teeth could be seen as he smiled in return. The shock of thick, white hair gracing his head was parted to the side. He carried himself elegantly and looked scholarly. Matthew soon found out that he was.

"I'm so sorry about Sarah, Lazarus. There are no words to explain the loss of a spouse. How are you doing?" Dr. Elmore put his arm around his friend as they headed for the cafeteria line.

"It's hard. Hard to give up someone who's been a part of your life so many years. She was too young to die. But the sickness, we think it was flu, took her so fast." The conversation continued as the group selected their food items.

"When you feel like it, I hope you can join us at some of the activities here on campus. We should get together like we used to. Maybe Matthew would like to come also." Dr. Elmore was smiling as he talked.

After going through the cafeteria line, the threesome sat down at a table. Before they could continue talking, a tall, thin distinguished gentleman with brown eyes and balding head came over to the table. His hair was white, and he wore black, wire-rimmed glasses. A snow-white mustache was clipped firmly above his lip, shortening his long, slender face.

Everyone stood up. Dr. Elmore extended his hand and shook hands with the visitor who stood before him.

"President Wilson, I intend to come by your office before heading back to Chattanooga," said Dr. Elmore.

"That's the reason I stopped by, to make sure you did."

"Let me introduce you to the Tiptons. This is Lazarus and his nephew, Matthew. Matthew will be a student here this fall. Lazarus and Matthew, this is Dr. Samuel Wilson, president of Maryville College."

Dr. Wilson shook hands with the two men and said to Matthew, "Welcome to 'The Hill' as everyone affectionately calls our campus. I'm pleased you've selected us as your school."

"I'm anxious to get started, Sir." Matthew stood, smiling at Dr. Wilson. He was awed by the man's presence and at a loss for words.

Regal. Yes, that's the word for President Wilson.

"I've got to get back to my office for my afternoon appointments. Don't forget to come by, Edgar. I have some important matters to discuss with you. It's been a pleasure meeting you gentlemen." Dr. Wilson bowed slightly and headed for the dining room door, only to be engaged in conversation by someone else.

"Dr. Wilson and I were given professorship's here at the college the same year. He taught English Language, Literature and Spanish. Let's see," Dr. Elmore did some quick figuring in his head. "He's been president for sixteen years."

The threesome sat back down and ate a leisurely lunch while Dr. Elmore talked about the school. It turned out that he was a walking encyclopedia when it came to Maryville College.

"Matthew, Maryville College started with the noble aim of preparing ministers for the frontier, which at that time included the territory east of the Mississippi. The staff of the college soon learned that its students were woefully lacking in the skills and knowledge needed to participate in a theological seminary. Because of that problem, a Preparatory School, we would call it a high school today, was added along with a basic college education. Only then could men be trained for the ministry for which it was established.

"The college has been in continuous operation except for during the Civil War when it closed for five years. The hostilities ravaged the old buildings in downtown Maryville when both North and South used them as bivouacking areas. After the war was over, the college might have closed permanently except for the efforts of Dr. Thomas Jefferson Lamar. He was a professor before the fighting and became Chairman of the Directors and taught Languages after the conflict was over.

"The first $1,000 contribution to the college, by William Thaw of Pittsburgh, allowed the school to buy these acres where the school sits today. Others joined Mr. Thaw with generous endowments and by 1871 several buildings were erected, constituting the new core of Maryville College. In 1875, I graduated from the college and I can attest to the fact that nowhere in the South was a school so modern, and it was debt free.

"Two years later, the first February meetings were held. These winter days were the major evangelistic thrust on campus, with emphasis on the spiritual lives of our students. I'm humbled to say, I've had the opportunity to lead many of them since they were started." Dr. Elmore paused to finish his meal.

"Matthew, you're getting a serious history of your new school," said his uncle. "I didn't know much of what Dr. Elmore has said."

"We'll know more than that because Dr. Wilson is writing a history of the college for the centennial. That may be what he wants to talk to me about." Dr. Elmore stood up. "Are you ready for your walking tour, Matthew?"

"Ready and waiting, Sir."

The tour of the campus included a visit to Carnegie Hall, newly built in 1916. Upon entering the lobby, a desk was positioned to the side where a young man sat reading or studying. He looked up when the group walked forward.

"Timothy, I'd like for you to meet Matthew Tipton and his Uncle Lazarus. Matthew will be a student this fall."

Timothy Brackett walked around the desk and shook hands with both men. "Are you staying in the dormitory?" he asked Matthew.

"No. Off campus," replied Matthew. "But I'd like to see the building, if you don't mind."

"My pleasure," said Timothy. "Let's go up to the third floor. I need to take my books to my room and then go eat at Baldwin Hall. I have just enough time to give you a quick tour."

"We'll be waiting for you here," called Dr. Elmore. Turning to Lazarus he said, "We'll have time to catch up on Cove news." He put his arm around Lazarus, and the two walked to a bench on the opposite wall while the students disappeared around a corner at the end of the hall.

Matthew followed Timothy to the top floor of Carnegie Hall. As he topped the stairs, he noticed a telephone on the wall at the end of the corridor. They had a few internal telephones in the Cove, and a sometimes access to the outside world. Maintaining the lines over the mountains was almost impossible.

The room he entered was sparse but practical. A window on one side let in light. A table lamp and overhead fixture lit the room when it was dark. Maryville had electricity and running water. Both were utilized when the new building was constructed. Each suite of four beds had a bathroom between, another innovation of this dorm.

"This is a nice room. Are you a freshman?" asked Matthew.

"Technically, I am. But I started spring semester, this year. The fall semester is my second one. You'll like going here. I do." Tim deposited his books on his bed and picked up a laundry sack sitting beside the door.

"I don't do laundry," he said, "or iron. My dad always said that it's women's work."

Matthew laughed. "I do. My mother taught me just in case I needed to know. Who does yours?"

"One of the ladies in the Maid Shop. She takes it home with her. She or her mother does it."

"What's the Maid Shop?"

"It's part of the system established here at Maryville to help women student's pay for their education. They do some type of sewing. When I work on the reception desk downstairs, my hours help with my tuition."

Matthew walked over to the window. "Hum, I see the courthouse clock."

"Yes. How are you paying for your tuition?"

"My Uncle Lazarus is taking care of that part." Matthew walked back to the center of the room.

"I see," said Tim. "I wish I had a rich uncle."

Matthew took no offense and replied, "Oh, he's not rich. He has no children, and I guess I'm like a son to him."

"Let's head back downstairs. How do you know Dr. Elmore?"

"He's my uncle's friend. Dr. Elmore performed his marriage to Sarah Moore of Chattanooga. It's sort of a complicated story."

"I see. Have you had dinner?" asked Tim. Tim was taking the stairs two-at-a-time until he noticed that Matthew couldn't keep up. He slowed his pace.

"Yes, we ate at Baldwin Hall."

"I was going to say we could have dinner together. Maybe some other time?"

"Sure, I'd love to. Where are you from?" asked Matthew as the two walked downstairs to the lobby.

"I'm from Asheville, North Carolina. My father is a doctor there."

"Are you going to become a doctor like your father?"

"No, blood always makes me want to faint. I don't think my patients would go for that. I plan to teach school. I'm seriously thinking about majoring in English."

"Ugh, I don't envy you. English is not my best subject. My father is a pastor, and I will take over his pulpit when I graduate."

"How did you get the limp?" Tim was curious about Matthew's slight hobble.

"That's a long story also, and I'll be glad to share it with you someday. Anyway, the bear got the worse end of the fight."

Tim raised his eyebrows and looked at Matthew with new interest. He wanted to ask several more questions, but they had arrived at the lobby and were approaching the two waiting men.

"Do you stay in the lobby much?" Matthew asked of Tim.

"Yes, I call myself the director of questions," said Tim, who gave a short laugh. He added, "I'm really thankful for the opportunity, since mountain doctors aren't the richest in the world."

"Ah, you're back," said Dr. Elmore as the two young men joined them in the hall. "What did you think of our new building, Matthew?"

"Tim's got a great room — with a view."

Everyone laughed.

"Of course, the old Carnegie burnt. Our board decided that when we rebuilt our building would be the most modern building possible. Our insurance and an intense campaign to raise funds let us do that."

"Matthew, Dr. Elmore and I have been talking about one other serious matter. The college has a chapter of the Students' Army Training Corps."

"What's that?"

Dr. Elmore answered. "At present, the Selective Service System is registering men over twenty-one for drafting into World War I. Most of our students have graduated by then, but we do maintain a Company A made up of students, who train under an assigned army officer. They're mustered into the Army, with pay. Men under military age can register in Company B and drill. Barring a serious turn in the war, the government doesn't plan on calling our students."

"Dr. Elmore says that being in Company B doesn't interfere with your studies. You might want to think about joining."

"Are you in Company B, Tim?" asked Matthew.

"No. I have enough activities without adding another," replied Tim. "I barely have enough time to study now."

"Okay, I'll think about it."

"Matthew, we'd better go. I'm sure Dr. Elmore has lots of important work to do while he's here." Lazarus and Dr. Elmore started for the door.

"Tim, I'll come and see you soon. I'm going to need a friend." With that Matthew shook hands with his new buddy-to-be and followed his uncle and Dr. Elmore out of the building. Outside, the trio stood on the steps saying goodbye.

"Please come to me if you encounter any problem with your courses or if you need other resources. I may be able to help you." Dr. Elmore was shaking hands with Matthew. "You know where my room is located, although I'm not there all the time."

"Edgar, I've enjoyed our visit, and I promise to keep in touch. Let me know when you're coming to college functions, and I'll try to meet you here. Since

Matthew's staying nearby, I could stay with him overnight." Lazarus looked at his nephew, who was nodding in return.

"Goodbye, my friend." Edgar shook Lazarus' hand warmly.

Matthew's visit was over.

❦ Chapter Twenty-One ❦

The Final Hunt — Lazarus

Lazarus Tipton rose early on Tuesday, February 12, 1918. Although he'd slept several hours, he was still tired. It was his fifty-fifth birthday. He and Nat had made plans to go hunting, but at the last moment, Nat was called to the bedside of an ill parishioner. He couldn't go.

Hunting alone never stopped Lazarus. He put on his warm socks, heavy wool coat, and old felt hat. He picked his gun off its rack over the fireplace and, placing his two hounds on short leases, headed for Gregory's Bald. This was about a two-mile distance as the crow flies and where the two men originally planned to go hunting. Maybe not quite to the bald, but wherever the track of a 'coon led them. He planned on being back in early afternoon.

A light blanket of snow had fallen overnight and each step was accompanied by a soft crunching sound, hard to hear over the din of the prancing, barking dogs. Soon Lazarus left the headwaters of Tiptons Sugar Cove Branch that started high above where he lived and ran by his hillside cabin. He left clear tracks in the white mantle covering the ground. Heading up a valley between High Point and Gregory's Little Bald, he came out at a saddle between the two elevations. He stopped here at this level place.

This was as good a place as any to turn the dogs loose.

"All right, you lazy hounds, go find a 'coon," he said as he loosed the dogs near Bower Creek.

Running up the creek, they immediately picked up a raccoon trail, and, barking loudly, ran out of sight.

Hunting today was an excuse for coming back to this spot, and he knew his dogs would return even if he didn't follow them.

Lazarus paused for several minutes, looking around at the familiar setting, where he had met his future wife, Sarah. He was a landowner, farmer, and hunter who guided Sarah and her family on a camping vacation under Gregory's Bald. When he first learned the family was coming, he'd hiked about a mile to this area and spent several days clearing the brush and ground of obstacles so their camp would be comfortable upon their arrival.

This wasn't the first time Lazarus had been a guide for vacationers. He made good money in the summer doing this and met many fine people in the process. He had suitable tents and camping equipment just for these occasions.

Lazarus thought back to those few short days. They were as clear today as when he lived them. He couldn't help himself, although he knew the hurt would return as each scene passed before him.

Sarah's father, Peter Moore, was a prominent doctor from Chattanooga, high in society and rich far beyond Cove standards. With his handlebar mustache, brown hair, and dark eyes, he was a distinguished looking gentleman. He and Lazarus hit it off immediately. Late in the afternoon and on their second day at camp, Mr. Moore approached him with a request.

"Laz," Peter preferred a shorter version of his guide's name, "I want to walk to the Bald tomorrow and pick some huckleberries."

"Of course, Mr. Moore. We'll leave early in the morning and be back with buckets full by noon."

Mr. Moore continued, "Do you suppose the flame azaleas are in bloom also?"

Lazarus looked down toward the creek where Sarah watched her nieces and nephews as they splashed in the shallow creek. "James! Don't do that!" he heard her say.

Turning back to Mr. Moore, he replied, "We're sure to pick huckleberries and see flame azaleas. The last time I was at Gregory's Bald we shared the picking with a black bear, and there was sign of wild hogs in the vicinity."

"How do you know they were wild hogs?"

"The hogs make furrows in the ground with their long tusks, looking for wild roots and bugs to eat. Sometimes large areas are so torn up they appear to have been plowed. We'll see signs of 'em somewhere along the way. That's for sure. I'll see you tomorrow."

When Lazarus arrived the next morning, the family invited him to help eat their pancake breakfast.

"There's nothing better than pancakes cooked over an open fire on a campout," said Peter. "I hoped you'd get here in time to eat."

Lazarus walked over to the spot where, twenty years earlier, the fire pit was located. The rocks and rusty grates were still there. After they were married, he and Sarah often came here with supplies and relived those particular moments when they first met.

He remembered two large skillets, one with bacon and one with pancake batter, being placed on low racks over coals. Another deep pan with syrup heating up and a pot where coffee was brewing completed the early morning meal. Even now as Lazarus thought back, he could smell the aroma of maple syrup, coffee, and bacon drifting in the air. His mouth watered.

Reticent at first, Lazarus had sat down and enjoyed the family atmosphere. Being a bachelor, he didn't have the opportunity to share a meal except on special occasions. His own cooking left a lot to be desired, so he thoroughly enjoyed the meal. As soon as breakfast was over, an eager group of people left for the bald.

"You'll have blueberries to mix in your batter tomorrow morning," he remembered telling Mrs. Moore.

Except for Peter's wife and the youngest grandchildren, everyone else hiked to Gregory's Bald.

Sarah fell in step beside him. "I love the mountains, Mr. Tipton. Chattanooga is very noisy compared to this atmosphere. I envy you for being able to live here all the time." She continued to walk beside him until the trail narrowed to a single rut up the mountain.

Later during the week, Sarah asked Laz why he wasn't married and he replied, "When you've had your heart broken once, you shy away from having it done twice, and anyway all the good ones are taken." Lazarus remembered thinking, when his standard reply was out of his mouth, that he regretted having spoken. But he couldn't take his words back.

Despite his embarrassing blunders, he and Sarah were immediately attracted to each other and found time during the two-week trip to walk and talk about things in their lives that mattered to them. Lazarus found himself sharing information he'd never shared with anyone else, including the story of his first love. This was a story that didn't come easy.

"You love deeply, Laz," Sarah said simply after he told the story.

He only shook his head and asked, "So why haven't you married? You're a handsome woman. Here in the mountains someone your age would have three or four younguns runnin' underfoot." He'd stated the fact teasingly, but Sarah hadn't said anything or even smiled at his comment. Had he gone too far? "Sarah?"

"I can't have children." She made the statement simple and final.

Taken aback, he'd stuttered and said without thinking, "A-are you sure?"

"Absolutely," and then she'd changed the subject.

Lazarus realized this was a closed subject for her, although he wondered at the circumstances of her barrenness.

"I'm sorry, I didn't mean to pry."

She'd waved her hand as if to shoo the subject away.

Sarah learned that Lazarus was an out-and-out book worm and, upon her return to Chattanooga, forwarded a carton of books with an invitation to write if he had time.

Several days passed after the receipt of the books. A long, suppressed yearning began to stir in his soul, and Lazarus became conscious of a strange need for Sarah's companionship.

I miss her. If I write her, our correspondence might escalate into something beyond letter-writing.

Do I want that?

Finally, he made a decision to trust again.

Immediately he wrote, starting a correspondence of several months. Lazarus asked to come to Chattanooga and return the books she had sent. Sarah's father extended an invitation for him to visit and stay several days. Mr. Moore suspected an ulterior motive behind Lazarus's trip and waited patiently for the results.

In March, Mr. Moore welcomed Lazarus at the train station and included him in the week's activities, including target practice at a local gun club. Lazarus was admired by the club's members when he beat every participant.

"I wonder, Mr. Tipton, if you could give me some pointers this afternoon?" These words were uttered by an elderly gentleman who stopped by their table as Mr. Moore and Laz ate in the elegant club dining room.

"Well, I . . . "

"Jacob, I'm sure Laz will be glad to stay if you can bring him home. I need to go to the office this afternoon." Peter was looking back and forth between the two men.

"Then it's settled. I'll bring him home."

Laz had spent the rest of the afternoon giving instructions to a number of the club's participants and receiving numerous invitations for dinner, supper and other activities.

One of the gentlemen was the skipper of a steamboat on the Tennessee River.

"Laz, I'd be honored to have you come aboard our afternoon cruise this weekend. We have a Dixieland Band and supper about dark. I can't think of any other way to repay you for your instruction this afternoon." Their conversation continued, and the arrangements were made.

∽

Sarah sat down beside him on the parlor settee.

"How was your afternoon?"

"Most enjoyable. I ended up adjusting the sights on most of the guns at the club. After that, the target shooting improved."

"Aren't the grounds beautiful around the club?"

Sarah continued to chitchat about the day's happenings, and Lazarus answered perfunctorily. He recognized his current feelings as a growing love for Sarah. He had come close to telling her so in his last letter but wondered if she returned his feelings.

"Sarah," he interrupted her in mid-sentence, "do you know the captain of the Dixie Belle."

"Why, yes. I do."

"He invited me on the supper cruise Friday night. Would you go with me?"

∽

On the steamboat ride, they'd enjoyed an intimate supper while sitting in the upper level dining area. The captain had positioned them close to the stage where they could look down on the band as it played songs from the South.

Laz looked at Sarah. Her eyes danced with the music.

It was time to share his heart.

Reaching for her hand, he whispered across the table, "Let's go outside and walk along the rail." Underneath the reflection of the moon and the stars on the shimmering water, he declared his love and asked her to be his wife.

It was then she told him again she would never have children.

"Why?" he asked.

Sarah related the story.

Five years ago, a man had forced himself upon her and had touched her in an inappropriate way. She'd become pregnant. Going to her mother, she told the story. The man was influential and scandal touching the family was something her mother couldn't tolerate. Because her father was a doctor, her mother knew many men in the medical field. One in particular, she'd heard, would terminate an unwanted pregnancy.

"I went with mother so the doctor could take the child from me. I've always regretted that decision."

The doctor preformed the operation, but a terrible infection set in and her father barely saved her life.

"You don't hold a grudge against your mother?"

"No, I've forgiven her and our relationship is closer than ever. My father was the one who took the longest time to forgive her. He wanted to prosecute the man. But I never told him who it was."

"Sarah, you're amazing. Forgiveness comes hard for most people."

"*Forgive them for they know not what they do.* Wasn't that Jesus' words? I couldn't do any less."

They were silent for a few moments. Sarah moved closer, looked at him, and touched his arm. "Do you still feel the same way?"

"Do I still want to marry you? The question is the same," he'd said looking down at her lovely face.

"Then my answer is a simple yes."

He picked her up and whirled her around the deck.

"I love you," she'd whispered, her soft breath against his neck.

∼

Closing his eyes, Lazarus could almost feel her in his arms as he stood in the snow at their former campsite. He ached to hold her again.

Ah, Sarah, how I miss you.

The sound of his dogs barking brought Lazarus down to earth with a hard jolt.

He laughed out loud. The sound was strangely close and intimate in the snow-covered forest.

I'd better get to my reason for being on the mountain today.

The dogs were still running slowly along the creek. He hurried to stay within hearing. When they headed for Panther Gap, the area was slick with snow, steep, and much too strenuous for him to rush up the mountain. He pushed on, too strongly, and came out on the Gap. By this time, he was weak and strangely breathless.

"Lazarus, you're losing your grip," he said to himself.

He could hear his dogs in the distance and could tell by their excited barking the raccoon was up a tree.

The pain started with a sharp stab under his ribs.

I need to sit down and rest. It'll pass. It always has.

Lazarus kicked at the ground underneath a huge oak tree, sending snow in all directions. Finally, he had a decent, fairly dry spot. He clutched at his chest, sat down, and closed his eyes, his breath coming in short gasps.

I feel a strange heaviness in my chest. I'll just sit here a spell and get my breath. That 'coon's not going anywhere.

Lazarus leaned back against the huge tree trunk, pulled his knees up almost to his chin, and placed his gun between them. He steadied the gun and leaned it to his shoulder with the barrel against the tree's trunk. Spasms of pain rushed over him. He gripped the barrel of his gun and held on tight.

The dogs are barking. I need to get up. I can't move. I have no strength. I can't move. Need to go home.

His hat fell off as he struggled to get up. He didn't realize it. He settled back down, drew his knees up again, and looked out at the darkening sky.

Is it night already? Everything's going dark.

❧ Chapter Twenty-Two ❧

The Hunt for Lazarus — Lazarus

Finding Lazarus Tipton turned out to be easy. When he didn't turn up to help John Razor at the gristmill the next day, John sent Donald to tell Nat.

"Dad's worried. Lazarus never misses," said Donald.

"Yes, I know. His favorite pastime is watching those millstones turn and greeting the customers. Help me saddle a horse, Donald. We'll go to Tipton's Sugar Cove."

"Dad said he'd go with you to make sure Lazarus is all right."

Nat led his horse to the back porch. He had a bad feeling about this.

"Martha," he called loudly.

When she walked outside the kitchen door, wiping her wet hands on her kitchen apron, he said, "I'm going to Tipton's Sugar Cove. Lazarus may be in trouble. I'll be back as soon as I can." Martha walked to the side of the porch and watched as the two men rode out of sight. She felt a chill, and it wasn't from the cold.

It was after noon before Nat, John, and Donald headed down Parson's Branch Road for Lazarus's home. During the previous night, the skies were clear and the temperature dropped into the twenties. Nat prayed they would find him at home. If not—he didn't want to dwell on that possibility.

One of Lazarus' hound dogs was lying on the front porch. The dog jumped up to greet them as they rode up to the house.

"That isn't a good sign. He never lets those hounds roam free," Nat remarked. The other men were silent.

John went into the house while Donald and Nat looked around outside.

"Mr. Tipton," called Donald. "Come here. There are footprints leading into the woods."

Nat walked over. "What do you make of them?"

"It's pretty clear. One man and some dogs went into the woods."

"Let's make a bigger circle around the house and see if we can find tracks coming back." Donald started a circle around the house.

John came out of the cabin. "He's not inside. The fire's out and the cabin's cold. It doesn't look like he's been here last night."

"I don't like the looks of this," replied Nat, verbalizing his concern. He tried not to worry.

"I can't find any returnin' tracks," said Donald, coming up to the two talking men. "I think we need to follow the trail we saw, Mr. Tipton."

"Do we need any help, Nat.? I'll send Donald after some. You just say the word."

"The signs are clear. I'm sure we'll find him without any extra help."

There was a short discussion about taking the horses. They decided to take them—just in case.

"If we have to carry Lazarus out of the mountains, God forbid, we'll need them," said Nat as he disappeared into the house to get blankets and a cup from which to drink. He busied himself with tying them to the horse and getting another length of rope hanging on a peg on the back porch.

The frozen trail led them under stands of hemlock, their branches drooping with the weight of the snow. They walked through pine thickets and laurel stands. The rhododendron's once glistening leaves were curled and dark in the bright sunlight. The forest was a fairyland of imaginable creatures and snow-draped scenery. Today, its beauty was lost to the three apprehensive men.

Lazarus's dog ran on ahead, following the icy trail. The men and horses followed him at a fast pace. Over an hour later, they came out at Panther Gap.

Lazarus appeared to be resting. He sat naturally against the big oak tree trunk, knees up and hands on his gun. His head leaned back against the tree. His hat lay on the ground beside him. His eyes stared at the blue sky but saw nothing. The second hound dog lay at his feet and didn't move as the men approached.

They examined the body.

"Do you think he froze to death?" asked Donald.

"No broken bones that I can tell," observed John, checking Lazarus's arms and legs. He was reminded of a time not too long ago when he'd done this for another Tipton man. "It's probable he had a heart attack or some kind of heart trouble and died here."

Nat walked off a little way and sucked in a deep breath. It gushed out of his lungs. "He's been having some pain in his chest. Wouldn't go to the doctor, mind you."

"Wasn't yesterday his birthday?" asked John.

"Yes. We were to go huntin', but Ira Whitely was sick, and I was called to his bedside. Maybe if I'd been along—"

"There are lots of maybes in the world, Nat. It's not likely you could have done a thing. It looks like he died quickly, and the Lord knows huntin' was his favorite pastime. Why not die doin' what you love most?"

There was a long pause while Nat walked to Bower Creek to compose himself.

He's with Sarah now.

There were times he envied what Sarah and Lazarus had together, and Matthew loved his uncle . . .

Matthew, I'll have to get news to Matthew. How will he take his uncle's death? They were so close.

"How do you want to move the body?" John was standing nearby and placed a hand on his pastor's arm.

Nat turned around and walked back to his brother. There were things to be done. He was Lazarus's pastor too.

The men spent some minutes covering up their charge and tying him to a horse. The trip back took longer than the trip going into Panther Gap.

"Where do you want to lay him out, Nat?" asked John. "Here in the sugar cove?"

"No, I'll take him home with me. We'll put his casket in our parlor until we can bury him. Would you pick up one for me and bring it over? I'll alert the ladies to come and prepare him for burial as I ride home."

"Nat, we'll do that. What else do you need done?"

"I need someone to notify Noah this afternoon. I'm sure he will want to come. Could your wife stay with Martha while I go to Maryville to tell Matthew? He's going to be shocked, and I want to tell him in person. If I hurry, I can get there before supper, and we can ride the late train back home. I'd like to bury Lazarus tomorrow afternoon."

"Sure, my wife will be glad to help. I'll send her over as soon as I get home. There's some more of our church family who'll want to help. Leave the plans for preparing the body, digging the grave, and sittin' with Martha to us. And Donald can ride to Noah's."

"Thank you, my friend. I'll hurry home and tell Martha. Then I'll ride to Townsend to catch the train."

Nat rode toward home, leaving Lazarus in the capable hands of John Razor. Telling Martha wasn't easy. But Nat dreaded telling his son. Nat boarded the three o'clock train for Maryville.

～

Tim Brackett and Matthew walked out of Carnegie Hall. Classes for the day were over and Matthew was tired. He had studying to do and needed to go to his room to eat and relax.

"Sure you don't want to eat with me in the dining hall?"

Matthew hesitated and then replied, "Thanks for asking, but my landlady will have supper cooked when I get home. We'll do dinner tomorrow."

Matthew walked the short distance to the road and waved at his friend as he prepared to cross Court Street. He didn't have far to go, and he was glad because it was freezing out in the wind. Entering his boarding house, he was shocked to see his father sitting in one of the parlor chairs. He knew immediately something was amiss.

"Is something wrong, Dad?" he said looking at his father's cheerless face.

"Matthew, I have some bad news."

Matthew prepared himself for the worst.

～

The funeral took place on a raw, cloudy February afternoon. The wind whipped through the pine trees behind the church with a dreadful sighing sound. Thunderhead Mountain stood over the scene, a dark participant to the ceremony. Snow mottled its face. As Nat pronounced the last rites in the graveyard, a black crow flew overhead, adding its own comments to the service.

Matthew was glad when the meeting was over and he could go home. He felt oddly detached from all the last day's happenings. His eyes didn't tear when his father told him of his uncle's death. Nor did he feel a thing when he viewed his uncle in his walnut casket. In his short eighteen years, he'd never experienced the death of a close loved one, especially one as loved as his uncle. The shock insulated him from the hurt.

After the service, the family and several friends gathered at Nat's home for a last meal before returning to their residences.

Noah approached Matthew.

"Matthew, I need to read your uncle's will before I go back to Chilhowee. I have it with me. Is that all right?"

Nat came near and sat by his son, placing a protective arm around his shoulders.

Something's wrong. Matthew shows no emotion at all. I hope it's the shock.

"Go ahead, Noah, and read the will." Nat answered for his wordless son.

Before nightfall, Matthew headed for Tipton's Sugar Cove under leaden skies. He wanted to be alone. He'd just inherited a house and one hundred forty-nine acres of bottomland, cove, and hillside. Also included were four horses, a mule, several head of cattle, and a bank account. He had no idea how much money was in the account.

As Matthew rode up to the well-known cabin, there were no barking dogs to greet him. Smoke didn't come from the chimney nor did anyone come from inside the cold, dark home. This was the first time he hadn't been greeted on the back porch. He walked his horse to the small barn that stood close to the house and unsaddled it. Picking up the small basket of food his mother had prepared after the mourners had gone home, he walked back to the cabin and sat it inside the unlocked door.

Matthew busied himself by carrying wood from the porch to light a fire; first kindling, then larger and larger sticks of wood. Soon the warmth from the blazing hearth spread through the room and kitchen as the first drops of rain beat against the metal roof of the porch.

Walking to the door he retrieved the food his mother had packed for him and placed it in the kitchen. The ceramic chicken and rooster salt shakers belonging to his Aunt Sarah sat on the side of the table where Lazarus had used them last. Matthew reached out and touched them and the hand-whittled rolling pin Lazarus had painstakingly made for her.

Familiar objects began to appear in the firelight. Matthew walked back to the fireplace. A tintype sat on the mantle of his aunt and uncle just after they were married. She wore a long white gown, and he was handsome in a suit with a bowtie. His uncle's gun hung on the chimney in a rack over the picture, and his walking shoes rested on the hearth.

Looking around the room, he noticed the floor-to-ceiling, hand-made bookcase by the bedroom door. It was full of books that Lazarus and Sarah had read. Matthew walked to the book case, selected a book, and went to sit in his favorite seat by the fire. Closed in by the warm darkness, he sat looking at the leaping flames.

Opening the book, he turned a few pages but he couldn't concentrate on the words. A great sadness overwhelmed him. Tears ran down his cheeks and an eerie noise filled the room. The sounds were manly sobs from a profound loss. The book fell in the floor with a thud as Matthew leaned forward, his head in his hands.

🎋 **Chapter Twenty-Three** 🎋

February 1920, Life at Maryville College — Matthew

It was the second anniversary of Lazarus Tipton's death at Panther Gap. During February last year, Matthew had gone back to visit his uncle's grave, and he planned to do so this year. He'd sent word to his father to pick him up at the depot on Friday afternoon in Townsend. There was only one missing piece, or rather human, for his trip.

He bounded up the steps to the third floor of Carnegie Hall. Since his uncle's death, Tim Brackett had become chief confidante and advisor to Matthew. Their relationship was one of trust and admiration.

Tim's door was open.

"Hey buddy, why's your door open?" asked Matthew, who was now in the last semester of his junior year.

"Aw, one of the guys down the hall came by and didn't shut the door on the way out. I was just too lazy to get up and close it." Tim was turning the pages in a big book. It rested on his lap as he sat in the middle of his bed. Other single sheets surrounded him. Matthew realized Tim was cramming for a test in one of his classes. Getting his friend to go would be harder than he'd anticipated.

"Tim, pack a bag and spend the weekend at Tipton's Sugar Cove." Matthew suggested to his friend. On long weekends, although there weren't many lengthy ones, the two best friends often packed a bag and took the train to Townsend. There they met Matthew's father. His mother always cooked a big meal and the two ate their fill before riding by wagon to Tipton's Sugar Cove.

"I can't do that. I have a humongous test in one of my classes next week."

"But, wait a minute. You don't realize the benefits of getting away for the weekend. There's home cooked food at Dad's house."

Tim groaned but didn't answer.

"We'll hike in the woods, ride the horses, and do our homework at the cabin." Matthew continued tempting Tim by throwing inviting scenarios before him.

"It's too cold to hike or ride horses." Tim shivered just thinking about it. He liked hot weather, preferring to stay indoors when it was freezing cold outside.

Matthew ignored his comment, "And just think, we can pick up some marshmallows at Townsend Mercantile and roast them in front of a rip-roaring fire," continued Matthew. "And—"

"Okay, okay, don't say anymore." Tim knew it was no use. Matthew would keep on bugging him until he said yes. "I'll pack a bag and go with you, although I really need to stay here and study. My English Literature test will be a tough one on Tuesday."

"Oh, come on. I'll coach you if you bring your notes," volunteered Matthew, something he'd done before. "What's the test over anyhow?" He knew it was hard for Tim to stay ahead on his studies and work the front desk at Carnegie Hall. Tim often crammed for exams. But on this trip home, Matthew needed the comfort of his friendship.

"How about Shakespeare?" said Tim, who got up to pack a few belongings into a small suitcase. He placed the big book and notes into a canvas bag he often carried to the library and classrooms on campus.

Matthew let out an audible, "Ugh." Bending over, he picked up Tim's notes from the floor and handed them to him. "Maybe you'll teach me something."

Tim looked up from packing. "Ugh is sort of the way I feel, but I have to take the course to major in English, and I have to take this test." Tim planned to teach English grammar in high school. "I put this course off until my senior year on purpose and this is my first test in the class. I'd like to make a good grade."

"Quit whining and take your notes. I'll help." Matthew headed for the door.

Tim made a face and threw a piece of crumpled up paper at Matthew as he paused at the door.

"I'll go home and finish packing," he said. Calling over his shoulder he added, "Meet you downstairs on Friday morning after your last class," he closed the door on his way out.

~

Turning off Parson's Branch Road, Matthew drove up the ascending lane to the entrance of Tipton's Sugar Cove. After topping the hill, he dropped gently down into the hollow and drove straight along the gurgling creek toward the upper end. The unique landmark he looked for after entering his property was a tall tulip popular tree situated at a bend in the road where the fields opened up before him. From there he gazed upward to the right and across the cleared fields. There he saw the hillside cabin at the end of the road.

Something was sacred about this picturesque setting. He always felt *it* as he rounded the bend where his home was framed in the branches of one of the largest trees that grew in the Smoky Mountains. Awesome and breathtaking, the scene certainly was both. Blessed and hallowed, it positively was with the love of two people he respected and cherished. The tradition of love found here would be hard to continue or match.

Ah, home. The only thing lacking is smoke coming from the chimney.

The cabin at Tipton's Sugar Cove was spacious. The large corner fireplace in the living room heated the kitchen and three bedrooms.

Before unharnessing the horse, Matthew and Tim immediately built a fire, using wood stacked on the back porch and carried in the back door. The interior of the house was as cold as the outside air.

Heading out to the front porch, Matthew untied the horse from the rail and led it to a small shed next to the house. Pulling the buggy under the shed's overhang, he unhitched the horse from the wagon and walked the animal into the open-ended building. Making sure there was grain in the feeding trough and water in a bucket, he returned to the house.

"It's already warmer in here than it is outside." Matthew rubbed his hands together, crossed the room, and stood in front of the fire. Palms extended, he enjoyed the flickering flames.

Tim sighed and said, "All the food we ate at your Mom's and Dad's has made me sleepy. I could curl up in this chair and not wake up until morning." Tim promptly did as he stated.

Matthew walked over and pushed his feet out of the chair.

"Why'd you do that?"

"Because you've got studying to do or so you told me." Matthew pointed to the huge book resting on the table beside his friend. Tim had already unpacked. "I'm ready to help you. That way we'll have plenty of time to enjoy the outdoors tomorrow."

Tim groaned. "Oh, boy. I can't wait."

Matthew pulled off his coat and hung it on a peg by the door. He lit two kerosene lamps, setting one on the kitchen table and bringing the other to place on the table beside his friend. Picking up the large volume, he opened it, turned a few pages and read,

'I must be cruel only to be kind;
Thus bad begins, and worse remains behind.'

Matthew laughed. "I believe Shakespeare accurately describes our studying time together. Where do we start?"

"The test is over chapter's one and two. Do we really have to do this?"

"Yes," said Matthew. "Shakespeare also said, *'Action is eloquence,'* so get your thinking cap on. You're going to make an A on this test."

Until bedtime, the room was filled with studying and friendly banter. One verse from *Romeo and Juliet* caused the two some questions and conversation.

Matthew read:

> 'My bounty is as boundless as the sea,
> My love as deep. The more I give to thee,
> The more I have, for both are infinite.'

"Tim, do you think we'll ever find the right woman for each of us?"

"I certainly hope so. I've never thought about not being married. Companionship, especially when associated with love for another, is the highest goal I can think of tonight, and since my brain's quit working, I think we should call it a night."

~

On Saturday morning, Matthew and Tim were out of bed not long after sunrise.

After a leisurely breakfast, they had another round of Shakespeare and then Matthew was ready to go outside. His friend knew exactly where they were headed.

Tim didn't mind the walking after he warmed up, but he shivered from the cold until he did.

Matthew, on the other hand, would go without his coat if he could. But he knew better. Once wet with sweat from the exertion of walking, he would cool off and possibly get hypothermia. He always wore his coat.

The two young men made tracks to Panther Gap where Uncle Lazarus had died. They sat down near the tree where he was found to catch their breath. Each shoved their hands deep in the pockets of their coats.

"You were very close to your uncle, weren't you?"

Matthew reflected a few seconds before he answered. "Yes, I was. I have to admit there were times when I wished he were my father. I'm sure he probably wished I were his son."

"Why didn't he and your aunt have children?"

"I've thought about that same question many times. I have no idea. I never did ask either of them. Someday, I'll ask Mom. She might know." Matthew was shaking his head at the mystery.

"Weren't they married several years?"

"Almost twenty." Matthew sat thinking about them. "They got along really well. My Aunt Sarah was only forty-five when she got the flu and passed away.

Tim decided to change the subject. "What do you plan to do with Tipton's Sugar Cove? Do you plan on living here after you graduate from college?"

"Of course. I plan on moving in permanently. This comin' and goin' for a few days at a time will stop. This summer, I'll finish the repairs to the kitchen and barn."

"It'll be really lonely here in this secluded cove. You're goin' to need a companion. Have anyone in mind?" Was Tim leading up to something?

Matthew laughed. He was embarrassed. They'd never talked about women, except for the few words exchanged last night. "Come on, buddy, we need to head back to the cabin." He got up and started down the path. Tim jumped up and tagged along behind.

"You didn't answer my question, *buddy*."

"No, I don't have anyone in mind. You know that." Tim knew as much about his affairs as anyone. They shared their dreams and most of their thoughts.

"Well, I've noticed a gorgeous freshman who seems to have her eye on you. If not you, she must like the way you dress or something. She's certainly not checkin' me out." Tim was walking behind Matthew and grinning like a Cheshire cat. Matthew felt the smile in his words as he walked up the path toward home.

"That's news to me. Who is it?" Now Matthew was curious.

"If you'd open your eyes, you'd see her. You have to practically shove her off the steps of Voorhees Chapel when we come out after devotions. I'm telling you she's interested in you."

"So! Who is it?" demanded Matthew stopping in the path so quickly that Tim ran into him and stumbled on past. Matthew wasn't in the habit of ogling fellow co-eds.

Tim walked backwards down the trail, teasing his friend as he went. "She's drop-dead gorgeous with big blue eyes, luscious red lips, and strawberry blond hair. And what a figure. She puts an hourglass to shame." Tim followed each characteristic with suggestive motions.

"Tim-m-m," said Matthew with a threatening gesture.

"Her name is . . . her name is . . ."

At that point, Matthew took off after his friend, running down the path toward home. Eventually both of them were out of breath, but the house was in sight as they paused at the edge of the clearing.

Tim bent over and put his hands on his knees and between sucking in his labored breaths, he said, "Her – name – is – Alice –Davis."

"Alice? You're kidding. Every guy at Maryville College is after her." Now Matthew was laughing. He knew his friend was touched in the head. This proved it. "Alice Davis wouldn't look at me twice."

"Just wait and see if I'm not telling you the truth." That ended the conversation, because they had arrived at the cabin with company in the house.

Donald Razor was at the house to check on the cattle and horses. It was his job to make sure everything was in good condition while Matthew was at school. The three young men fixed supper, mostly opened cans and heated leftovers. Mrs. Razor had sent some slices of apple stack cake. With full bellies, they sat around the comfortable fire and enjoyed each other's fellowship.

"Donald, go home and get your clothes for church tomorrow. Stay all night," offered Matthew.

Donald was hoping for an invite. He didn't often get to spend time with his school chum, and Tim was always fun.

"Don't mind if I do." Donald left for home, and Shakespeare took center stage until he came back.

When Donald returned, he brought a present.

"What's that?" asked Tim looking at a large mass of black fur.

"Matthew ought to remember where this came from." Donald held the heap of hair out to him.

Letting some of the pelt fall in folds to the floor, Matthew looked wonderingly at the bear skin. The hair was coarse but not stiff.

"Why should I remember this?"

"He's a little slow today, isn't he, Tim?"

"I'm afraid he is," Tim teased, although he didn't have a clue about the fur skin.

Matthew examined the skin again. "Is this — is this skin off the bear that mauled me on Spencefield three years ago? Surely not," exclaimed Matthew, astonished.

"Surely so," said Donald. Tim got up to examine and feel the fur. "Dad said to put it in front of your fireplace. He's been saving it for years." Donald took the skin from Matthew's hand and placed it where his father had suggested.

There was something eerie about having the skin of that particular black bear in front of the fireplace. Suddenly the fear and pain of the encounter below Thunderhead flashed through his mind. He saw the bear's head moving back and forth and the white teeth coming toward him — Matthew winched. He hadn't thought about that meeting in a long, long time.

He had put the attack behind him. At least, he thought the emotional scars associated with the assault were gone. The bodily ones remained, including the slight limp which returned when he was physically tired. For a brief instance, he considered asking Donald to take it back home with him tomorrow.

No, that won't do. John's saved this for me. It's supposed to be a trophy; some kind of badge of courage, but this will take some getting used to.

The young men were seated around the fire again.

"Matthew, how long do you have left in college?" asked Donald as he reclined, toasting on the bear rug. Donald's job was helping his dad at the grist mill and farming his fields. His education consisted of eight years of school and his apprenticeship with his father. He was a clever man and knowledgeable when it came to running his father's affairs but not book-learning smart.

Tim looked over at Matthew and replied, "Is it possible you have only a few months over a year to go?"

"That's true. Hard to believe college is almost behind us. I remember meeting you when I toured the school with Dr. Elmore. Seems like yesterday. Almost three years have passed. Where has the time gone?"

"Tim, I know Matthew will pastor our church when he graduates, but why don't you come and teach in Townsend after you finish school? I'm sure the population of Townsend could support a high school. That way the children wouldn't have to travel to Maryville and board at the Academy or Maryville College. Getting a little more learning wouldn't be so expensive for their parents. You could set it up and run it."

"I'm afraid you've simplified the possibility of starting a school. Anyway, the school children of Asheville need me too, and I promised my father I would come back and teach there."

Matthew knew that his friend was unwavering in his commitment to his father and to his mission in Asheville. He'd already approached him with Donald's suggestion.

∾

Church the next morning was interesting. The busybody line wasn't seated in their regular pew. Matthew briefly wondered how everyone would get the church news the following week. Aunt Annie and Granny W. were at church, seated half-way down the left aisle.

"Hi, girls," said Matthew teasing the two elderly women, who gave him broad smiles. Matthew leaned over to hug each of them.

"Matthew, I'm so proud of you," said Granny W., looking over the top of her spectacles and squinting up at him.

Matthew noted that she looked frailer than the last time he'd seen her. He gave her an extra squeeze.

"Haven't been running any sack races lately, have you?"

"No, Matthew," giggled Granny W. "But I have been swingin' on the front porch. You need to come by and sit with me."

"Wait until the summer, and I'll be by. I don't have much time when I come home during school."

"Summer might be too late," whispered Granny so no one else could hear.

Aunt Annie, waving her hand, caught Matthew's attention and mouthed the words, "She may be right." She nodded her head at the same time.

"Granny W.," said Matthew, "I promise to come on my next trip to the cove. Is that all right?"

"I'm holdin' you to it, young man," said Granny faking sternness as well as she could for her years. "You know you're one of my pets."

Matthew leaned down for a goodbye hug.

"I'm not a spring chicken anymore," Granny called after him as the walked forward, heading for his favorite front pew.

Those who heard her chuckled at the comment.

"Mr. Shields, it's good to see you. Are you hunting this winter?" Matthew leaned over to shake hands with the three Shield's men as Paul and Peter said, "Hello."

"Yes, we went a week ago, up on Hannah Mountain in your neck of the woods. We wasn't lookin' for no bear. Just about froze to death it was so cold." Isaac laughed. "We didn't stay overnight. I was sure glad of that."

Chapter Twenty-Four

Alice Davis and Maryville College — Alice

It turned out that Tim was right about Alice Davis.

People go to college for different reasons. Some go to lock in every scrap of information so they can become more intelligent. Some go to escape their families and live the freedom not available at home. Some go to play sports, hoping to achieve or grab hold of fame and fortune.

But . . . Alice Davis wasn't in any of those groups. Alice was at college for one purpose only. She was there to snag a man, get married, and quit school. Not just any man, but the most handsome, most intelligent man she could find. She needed someone who would appreciate her beauty and overlook her faults, one of which was her manipulative skills.

Alice wasn't intelligent in the book-learning sense. Her grades were passable, but she had no desire to earn a college degree. Where Alice excelled was in sizing up a person and deciding if that person was the type of male she looked for. She was schooled in that knowledge by her mother, whom she disliked but mirrored exactly. After all, if Mrs. Davis could do it and be a wealthy socialite, so could Alice. She'd checked over the possibilities and made her decision.

On Monday, tired of the subtle approach, Alice decided to try something more drastic to get Matthew's attention. His face filled the portrait of her perfect man, and she knew his grades were excellent, because she'd asked around.

"Oh, I'm so sorry," she said after bumping into Matthew on the steps of the chapel and knocking two books from his hands. She rushed around on the steps, collecting one of the books and presented it to him.

"Don't worry about it," he said as he stood from retrieving the other and straightening a crumpled corner. He looked straight into the beautiful blue eyes of the woman in front of him. Meanwhile, Tim had the same Cheshire cat smile—the smug I know everything look on his face. Matthew couldn't really see him standing behind on the top step, but he felt it.

"I'm Alice Davis. I hope I didn't ruin your book. I'll be glad to buy you a new one." Alice could afford to buy several, because her family was arrogantly rich. She was craning her neck, trying to see the extent of the damage to the book.

She smelled good.

"I think it's all right." Matthew covered up the crumpled corner with his hand.

"You're Matthew Tipton, aren't you?"

"Yes, and I'm going to be late to class. Thanks for picking up my book." Matthew turned around to tell Tim goodbye and saw the smile he dreaded.

"Remember what I said, buddy," called Tim, acting as if he were tipping a hat on his bare head. Matthew headed off toward Anderson Hall for his Bible history class.

"You're going to Anderson Hall, aren't you?" said Alice, hurrying to catch up with her prey.

Matthew nodded.

"I'm going that way too. Could we walk together?"

"Sure," said Matthew as Alice fell into step beside him. Being a gentleman, he couldn't turn her down. Matthew felt a little uncomfortable at her suggestion.

Having the most beautiful woman on campus walking alongside will do that to a man, he thought. They walked side by side down the gravel path toward the building.

Alice kept talking.

"I'm from Knoxville. I've lived there all my life. Do you live around here?" asked Alice, attempting to make conversation.

"My home is in Cades Cove. That's on the —"

"Oh, I know where that is. It's across the mountain from Townsend. Sometimes, my family vacations in Kinzel Springs; not at the hotel but across the river in the cabins. Isn't Cades Cove very rural?" That was her kind way of saying primitive or backward. "You don't have electricity, running water, or a telephone system, do you?"

"We have a private telephone system. That's about all. I really don't miss electricity. We work when there's light and sleep in the dark. My water is piped in from a spring above the house. Many of the houses have the same free-flow system. Of course, we must heat our water."

"Doesn't it take a long time to heat water for a bath? I can't imagine doing that."

"Who takes a bath?" Matthew said with a grin. He was teasing of course.

Alice drew back. "Summer's must be bad, the smell I mean."

Matthew started laughing, but this didn't seem to bother Alice, who thought his laugh was delightful. He teased, "We just take our lye soap to the creek, strip our clothes off, and jump in for a bath. The cold water and the suds wash away any grime of the day. Then we wash our dirty clothes and hang them on bushes next to the flowing water to dry. When we get out, we climb into our damp clothes and head for home. That way you don't have to own but one set of clothes."

"I suppose that's done on Saturday." Alice could tease, also.

"Sure, is there any other day for a bath?"

"I couldn't stand to take a cold bath. I don't even like to swim in Little River," said Alice, turning her head and making a face that Matthew couldn't see.

"Here's my class," said Matthew. "I'll see you later."

"I hope so," said Alice. She actually meant meeting again was a sure certainty, but she didn't want to come across too strong.

That afternoon after classes, Matthew met Tim at Lamar Memorial Library. If they weren't in class, the library was a good place to find them. This was a daily custom, except for gym on Tuesdays and Thursdays when Matthew had physical education at Bartlett Hall.

During the winter, intramural sports, part of the physical education program at the college, kept Tim and Matthew in shape. Basketball was Matthew's choice. The athletic director explained it was a new game developed by a clergyman named Naismith who also taught athletics in Canada. This active sport exercised his damaged leg muscles, and Matthew's limp had disappeared. Tim elected to swim in the indoor pool, joining the swimming team. The prospect of exposing his scarred body kept Matthew from the pool.

The heavy and distinct smell of old books greeted him as he entered the building where the college's extensive collection was housed. He headed for a rear section where he and Tim typically hid out. Tim was there in their usual place, an area surrounded by book cases on both sides of their library table. He looked up as Matthew spread out his papers, produced a book to read, and started to take notes.

Matthew's half-hearted attempt to start studying ignored the fact Tim was watching his actions intently. Matthew looked up at his friend.

Might as well get this over with.

"What?" Matthew uttered lowly but forcefully.

The first whispered words out of Tim's mouth were, "Well, didn't I tell you she's been watching you?"

There's that feline grin again, complete with half-closed eyes and nodding head.

"Yes, you did," returned Matthew. "Congratulations, but I don't think one little encounter backs that up, do you?" Matthew was irritated with his friend and upset with himself for letting it bother him. After all, he should be excited at Alice's attention. Like Tim said, she was the most beautiful woman on campus.

"I guess we'll have to wait and see what tomorrow brings, huh, buddy?"

"Sure," said Matthew wishing Tim wouldn't rub it in. Totally ignoring his friend, he reopened his book and started reading until time to go home and eat.

On Tuesday morning, Alice was nowhere to be found. Matthew briefly wondered where she was. He couldn't help but admit he was a bit disappointed and a bit relieved. Unlike most men, her attention confused him.

If she could see underneath my shirt, would she be interested in me?

Matthew realized the scars held him back from becoming involved in a serious relationship with the opposite sex. Sooner or later, any women attracted to him would have to know. He dreaded that future disclosure.

The next morning, Matthew hurried to school and chapel on a dreary, cloudy day. During the service, the rain started to pour down in bucketfuls, and since he hadn't brought his umbrella, Tim volunteered to walk him to class under his. The two boys waited to speak to Pastor Evens to tell him they appreciated his message on discipline. Then they exited the building and started down the chapel steps. Alice was standing outside in the cold rain waiting for Matthew to appear. She held her big, black umbrella.

"Matthew, do you want to walk with me? I have plenty of room," she called from the top step where she stood.

Matthew looked at Tim and started to refuse. He only got his mouth partly open.

"Thanks, Alice," said Tim. "That will save me a trip." Tim walked away, leaving Matthew rooted to the spot, his mouth half-open.

Matthew stood there in the pouring rain watching Tim's back as he disappeared down the sidewalk.

Traitor! I can't believe he did this to me. I have two choices: stand in the rain and get soaking wet or walk under Alice's big, black umbrella. I'll show him.

Already the water was dropping off his eyebrows. He opted for the umbrella and Alice. What else could he do?

That afternoon, after practicing the speech he intended to make to Tim, he went to the library. The table was empty.

It was Friday before he cornered his friend in his room at Carnegie Hall.

"Have you been avoiding me?"

Tim was ready when Matthew walked into the room. "Now, Matthew, if you're here to bless me out, let me say this. You are definitely the envy of every male that I have talked to on campus. They're green-eyed with jealousy. You've made the biggest catch of the year." Tim had thrown up his hand in defense and was waving it erratically as he talked.

"I've made the biggest catch. You sound like Alice is a fish," sputtered Matthew. He couldn't help but grin at the analogy. The anger started to dissipate. "That's not quite correct though, is it?"

"Look at it this way, she's a beautiful young woman that any man would be glad to call a girlfriend, including me. I only wanted to give you the chance to be first."

"Humph," said Matthew as he sat down on the edge of Tim's bed and thought about his friend's words. Could it be that being with Alice increased his stature in the eyes of his classmates? She was beautiful and looked adoringly at him. Was she the spice his uncle had talked about some years ago? Would she be the love of his life?

There's only one way to find out. Pursue the relationship. Maybe Tim's doing me a favor. Still, there's no fatal attraction here. My heart doesn't tug for her. Maybe love sneaks up on you. How do I know? It's a place I'll admit that I've never been to before, a place I've avoided.

Tim watched anxiously as Matthew's thought process progressed. He knew that Matthew would analyze what he'd said. Matthew was practical.

I won't say anything until he finishes mulling his predicament over.

Finally, Matthew was ready to talk. "I must admit it's been nice to have some female companionship, besides having to listen to you all the time," Matthew teased, giving his friend a playful punch with his balled-up fist. The anger was completely gone.

Inwardly, Tim let out a "whew." But to his friend he said, "I'm glad you see it that way, I think."

"Tim, why don't you come home with me?" Matthew said enthusiastically, glad a confrontation was averted. "Mrs. Blount is making a big pot of potato soup for supper. She makes the best in the world, because she fries bacon and crumbles it up with the other ingredients. She said to mention she'll also have fresh milk to drink, hot cornbread, and lots of butter. She'd be glad to have you come. She told me so this morning."

"Now there's a real girlfriend," said Tim, continuing his sentence, "a single woman who can cook. I believe I will." He arose and put on his coat, gloves, and toboggan.

Out in the hall, Matthew asked Tim, "I'm going to walk in the morning, if it isn't bone chilling cold. Why don't you come over and walk with me?" He knew if he pursued a relationship with Alice, they wouldn't be seeing as much of each other. He wondered if his friend realized this.

"You know I would, but tomorrow I'm standing guard in the entrance hall again. I'll have to pass."

When Matthew and Tim arrived at the boarding house, Matthew checked to see if he had mail on the front hall table while Tim walked to the kitchen to greet Mrs. Blount. Picking up his letters, if any, was a daily ritual. Most of the time, the table was empty. To Matthew's surprise, two white envelopes rested there. Matthew looked at the return addresses. One was from Dr. Elmore and the other from his mother. Matthew tore open his mother's letter, fearing bad news. He read,

Dear Matthew,

I hope this letter finds you well and your studies progressing nicely. Your father and I are managing to stay warm on these cold days. We enjoyed Tim's visit last week and hope you will bring him again soon. On Wednesday, it rained really hard. The next morning, there was a dusting of snow on the tops of Chilhowee Mountain and on Thunderhead. Thunderhead reminded me of my rather large grandfather with his white nightcap on.

I have some bad news. During the midst of the downpour, Granny W took sick. We don't know what caused her problem, but death was quick and peaceful. By the time you receive this letter, she will be buried in the cemetery behind the church. I remember Granny W. saying this was a fittin' resting place for a Christ-follower. She will be sorely missed for her wry humor and cantankerousness. (Hope I spelled that right.)

As ever,

Love, Mother

P.S. She'll also be missed because of her weather-predicting knees.

P.P.S. Come home soon.

Matthew stood in the hall, rereading the letter. The front porch swing at Aunt Annie's would never seem the same without Granny sitting in it.

"Matthew, are you O.K.?" asked Tim, noticing Matthew's downcast face.

"Oh, yes." Matthew didn't realize that Tim had entered the room. "Do you remember the aged gray-haired lady I spoke to at church the last time we went to Cades Cove?"

Tim nodded his head. "The one who said she wasn't a spring chicken?"

"That's her. She died Wednesday. Mom says she was to be buried at the church graveyard. I'll miss her when I go home. She sat in that same seat every time the church door was open. When I was a young boy, she would grab me each Sunday and give me a big hug, even though I struggled to pull away. She always said,

'You'll be sorry some day when Granny can't give you a hug.' She's right. I am already."

"It's like losing an anchor," said Tim.

"That's exactly it." Tim had hit a sore spot with Matthew. "The old, the familiar are disappearing. I regret and mourn the passing of the elderly influences, including the old ways of living. When I'm as old as Granny W., what will the world look like? Can you imagine it?" asked Matthew.

"It's hard too. Who would have dreamed of the Bell Telephone, Ransome Olds or Ford automobile? The airplane may be another kind of future passenger travel, traversing long distances, like the railroads we ride so casually. Even now the U.S. Post Office is flying mail from the east to west coast in the old planes from the war. Just this last fall, I read an article on Leo Baekeland's bakelite. It's a hard plastic with many uses. How many other inventions will quickly change our lives?" asked Tim.

Matthew shook his head. "What will tomorrow bring? Will the church change too? This possibility has been preying on my mind this year."

"I hope not," said Tim wondering where this conversation was headed.

"We've been preaching the same message for two thousand years, since Christ died. Christ doesn't change, and neither should His message," observed Matthew.

"Are we having a theological discussion in here?" The cheerful voice of Mrs. Blount broke their somber mood.

"Matthew just lost one of his elderly friends in the Cove."

"I'm sorry, Matthew. How did you know her? Was she a relative? Did she go to your church?"

"Yes, she did go to my church. Her name was Granny Whitehead. And no, she wasn't a relative. She was a sweetheart, an old sweetheart."

"Those old ones are hard to lose," said Mrs. Blount. Matthew nodded his head.

"Supper's ready." she said gently and led the way to the dining room.

The young men looked at each other and grinned.

"Time to eat, buddy," said Matthew, putting his arm around Tim's shoulders. They stood head to head.

"Sure thing," said Tim.

~

Later that night, Matthew opened the letter from Dr. Elmore, who hadn't attended the February Meetings this year. Matthew and Tim missed the last part of the meetings when they went to Cades Cove for the anniversary of Lazarus's death.

The gathering consisted of ten days of evangelistic thrust established by the college many years before. Dr. Elmore and others were asked to speak. The preceding year, Matthew had enjoyed the professor's company for several days when Dr. Elmore was the featured spokesman. The letter stated that Dr. Elmore was coming with his wife for a week's stay, and that they wanted the pleasure of his company at a concert by the music faculty in April.

Hum . . . I'll ask Alice to go. I hope she likes music.

Matthew took off his clothes, turned off the light, and got into bed. He could see Granny W. sitting in the pew on the last Sunday he saw her alive. "Summer might be too late," she'd said, and the elderly woman was right.

Matthew caught his breath in the darkness. "I should have gone over that afternoon to see her," he said out loud before he fell asleep.

Chapter Twenty-Five

Maryville College — Ollie

Saturday morning dawned cold and clear but not as chilly as customary for February. Matthew jumped out of his warm bed. Leaning on the window sill, he stuck his head out the open upstairs window.

This is a perfect day to walk. I wish Tim could have gone.

Pulling on his clothes, he opened his bedroom door and headed down the hallway. The delicious smell of sausage and biscuits greeted him on the top step as he bounced down the stairs.

I'm hungry.

His mouth watered.

On Friday afternoons and Saturdays, Matthew walked around his neighborhood for exercise and to explore the area. After eating breakfast, he asked Mrs. Blount if he could go run her errands.

"If you want biscuits in the morning, I need flour and baking powder," she said as she cleared the table. Mrs. Blount disappeared into her back bedroom and came out with money for the items, and Matthew left the house with money for a nearby market.

Walking into town wouldn't take long, but Matthew intended to go a longer route.

During his travels around the vicinity, one particular house stood out from the rest. It wasn't the outside décor, because it lacked any, being one of a row of ordinary frame homes off Court Street. This company house was painted white and had the customary porch with a railing. Four short columns, part of the railing, supported the porch roof. Three concrete steps led up from the somewhat grassy yard to the centered front door.

What made the house stand out was what came from within. Beautiful music, the most passionate organ music Matthew could imagine. Played with feeling, the sound was captivating and marvelous.

Each time Matthew passed the house, he stopped outside to listen. And today, the beautiful music drifted forward through the half-open windows of the parlor and out to the sidewalk where Matthew stood listening.

Inside, the young man who played the organ was a few years older than Matthew. His name was Oliver Miller. Ollie, as everyone called him, played a pump organ, a very old but serviceable specimen that sat between two front windows of his small home. His feet moved rhythmically up and down on the foot pedals, pushing air into the bellows. His nimble fingers danced over the sixty-one yellowed ivory keys with dexterity and precision. He played by ear. He played any tune he heard, usually without missing a note, and he played for anyone who would stop and listen.

"Mother," called Ollie into the kitchen. "The young man is standing outside my windows again, listening to me play. Would you invite him inside?" Ollie's hearing was acute, almost supernatural. He knew the rhythm and sound of footprints, and these he'd heard before. The last time they approached his home, his mother had described the owner.

"I'll go and see, Ollie," said his mother, throwing on her coat, opening the door, and walking out the path to the road.

"Hello, young man," she said as she approached an embarrassed Matthew. "I'm Nellie Miller. My son Ollie wants you to come inside. He would like to meet you."

"Oh, I don't want to bother you. I love listening to the organ music. Is he the one who plays?"

"It's much warmer inside," said Mrs. Miller, holding Matthew by the elbow and steering him toward the door. Her son didn't often ask for listeners to be brought inside their house. He must sense this person was special.

～

Matthew let himself be led to the house and ushered into the parlor.

There sat a young man at an organ, grinning from ear to ear. "Hello, I'm Ollie."

"I'm Matthew Tipton from Tipton's Sugar Cove. I'm a student at Maryville College, and I enjoy your music. I usually stop and listen when I'm on my way into town." He stepped forward, stuck out his hand to shake hands, and immediately realized that his movement would not be met.

"Ollie, Mr. Tipton wants to shake your hand."

A hand was immediately extended as Ollie stood, and Matthew took it in his.

"It's an honor to meet you, Mr. Tipton. What college year are you completing?" asked Ollie, shaking

Matthew's hand firmly and exploring the hand offered him with his sensitive fingers.

When Matthew got close enough to shake Ollie's hand, he saw the clouded over and sightless eyes of his new acquaintance. Ollie was blind. "I'm a junior. I have one more year," he said as he looked Ollie Miller over.

Ollie was tall, almost as tall as he, with a receding hairline. Even though he didn't look much older than thirty, there were a few gray hairs at his temples. His plain face and thin body didn't add any mystery to his demeanor.

"Please sit down, Mr. Tipton," said Mrs. Miller, "and excuse me. I must tend to dinner in the kitchen." She disappeared through a door at the back of the room.

"Do you like school?" continued Ollie, sitting on his stool and enjoying the sound of Matthew's voice.

"Yes, I do."

"What will you do after you graduate?"

"I'll take over my father's pulpit in Cades Cove."

"Ah, you will be a minister, then?"

"That's my plan."

"Being a minister is a noble and called undertaking."

"Ollie, have you had any schooling?" asked Matthew. He was curious because Ollie appeared to be educated.

"Oh yes, I can read Braille. Helen Keller has nothing on me. Do you know who she is, Matthew?"

"Yes, I know. I believe someone, maybe Miss Keller, has written a book of her life. Have you heard of it, Ollie?" He would have said read, but for Ollie that was impossible.

"No. I haven't. Do you think the college has a copy?"

"I'll find out," said Matthew.

"Miss Keller is my heroine. She said something about the most beautiful things being unseen and untouchable. She said they are felt with the heart. When I play, I feel things with my heart." Ollie put his hand on his chest.

"Those feelings come through in your music," replied Matthew.

"Miss Keller was also deaf. God has blessed me with hearing. I want to play beautiful music, and I'm thankful that I can hear it. I always wanted to go to college and take music lessons, but alas—" He let the subject drop.

"Does your mother read to you?"

"Yes, she does. But we can't afford to buy many books. Could you get us some from the college library? Would that be hard to do?"

"Ollie, you're asking too many questions," said his mother, who returned from stirring her pots. "The young man will be sorry he came in to meet you."

Matthew laughed. "No, I'll never be sorry about that. But I'd love to hear you play the organ."

No one ever had to ask twice when it came to playing music. Ollie twirled around on his revolving seat and played one of his favorite hymns, "In the Sweet By and By." Then he said, "Would you like to hear one of my compositions?"

Matthew listened as Ollie played a lovely piece. It was short but very tuneful.

"I'm not through with it yet. Guess I'm stumped, but it will come to me."

"Matthew, do you like music?" asked Mrs. Miller.

"Yes, I like all kinds of music. It's the outward expression of the emotions of the soul, don't you think?"

"Yes," said Ollie. "When I'm sad, I play poignant hymns, laments, and dirges. When I'm happy, I play marches and lively tunes. My organ fairly dances around the room."

Mrs. Miller laughed. "That's the truth. We periodically push it back in place."

"Matthew," said Ollie his voice very serious, "I can hear your voice and step, but would you let me feel your face so I can know what you look like."

Ollie was facing the direction of Matthew's voice.

The request shocked Matthew.

Ollie stood up and reached out his hand.

Matthew took it awkwardly and placed it on his cheek. Ollie's fingers explored his face with delicate touches to his hair, forehead, ears, eyes, nose, mouth, and chin.

"You have very smooth features, Matthew. No tightness around the eyes and mouth. You're very relaxed even though I'm touching you in a personal way, and I believe we are the same height. I think you may weigh more than me. Your hair has waves and is very thick. Is it brown and do you have blue eyes?"

Matthew looked at Mrs. Miller. "How does he do that?"

"Touch is the only way he can see, and he does see very well with his fingers. They're very sensitive to the slightest imperfection."

"I can't understand his kind of perception."

Mrs. Miller smiled and continued, "He hears extremely well. He recognizes your footsteps each time you pass the house. Last week, he asked me to describe the one standing outside his window. That person was you. It's not often we ask in complete strangers, but something about your step assured Ollie you were a good person."

"That's uncanny," said Matthew as he watched Ollie return to his stool at the organ. He had known this young man only a few minutes, but he realized that Ollie had more insight than many men who could see.

"Ollie, I hope you will let me come by and see you again. I would be honored to call you friend."

"I don't have many friends, Matthew. People don't want to be the friend of a blind man, especially one who needs to touch them. You're my friend already."

"And where do you go to church? I'll be glad to stop and walk you to my church. Would you like to go? They play beautiful music and sing the newest songs. I think you would enjoy going."

"Goin' to church would be great. Mother can't walk long distances now because of her rheumatism, so I haven't been in several years. No one comes to get me." Ollie's smile was almost as wide as his face. It made wrinkles at the sides of his eyes which became narrow slits he was so excited.

"I'll come by in the morning around nine o'clock." Matthew stood up and looked at Mrs. Miller with raised eyebrows.

"He'll be ready, Matthew," she said and walked him to the door. "Plan to stay for dinner. I'll cook something really special."

"Bye, Matthew. It's been very nice meeting you," said Ollie, who turned back to the organ to play again. "I'll see you tomorrow."

Matthew hurried down the street to the strains of another well-known hymn.

~

The next morning Matthew arrived exactly at nine, and Ollie sat on his circular stool, ready to go.

"Glory be, Matthew, he's been ready for an hour," said Ollie's mother laughing. "He's sat on the organ stool so long fidgeting that I was afraid he'd wear out the seat of his pants." She laughed louder.

"Mom," said Ollie indignantly. "What an unkind statement."

Matthew chuckled along with Mrs. Miller. "We'd better go, Ollie. How's the best way for me to help you walk?"

"I'd like to hold your shoulder when we walk." Ollie got up. "Here, unkind Mother, let's show him."

Mrs. Miller came close to Ollie. "I'm ready, annoyed son."

"I believe you mean anointed one," said Ollie who was smiling. Ollie put his hand on his mother's shoulder, and they walked around the parlor.

"That looks easy enough. Now help me with the steps outside," said Matthew.

In a few minutes, Ollie and Matthew were walking down the street, hand to shoulder, as Mrs. Miller watched anxiously from the porch.

"Dear God, protect them both," she said before turning to reenter the house.

Chapter Twenty-Six

Summer Vacation — Alice

After her freshman year at Maryville College, Alice Davis went home to Knoxville, determined to keep her liaison with Matthew ongoing throughout the summer. Their relationship had gotten off to a slow start and hadn't escalated much from there. They attended Tim's swimming meets and some other sporting events; enough to know sports weren't her thing.

In April, she and Matthew went to the faculty recital with Dr. Elmore and his wife. She made a point to be around so they could walk to class, and sometimes he ate with her in the school cafeteria, although Tim was usually present.

Alice was perplexed. What was wrong with Matthew? Why wasn't he pursuing her? That's what most men did. So many, in fact, she was known for pushing men away.

I'm going to write long letters everyday with descriptions of life here in Knoxville. He's not going to forget me.

~

Alice walked to the upstairs landing.

Mrs. Davis stood in the downstairs hall. "Mommy, are you going to town today?" Alice knew her mother didn't appreciate being addressed by "infantile prattle" as she called it.

"Alice, you know I don't prefer to be called Mommy," she said sternly, knowing her daughter used the term to irritate her.

"I'm sorry, Mother. Sometimes I forget. Are you going?"

"Yes, I'm driving down to the corner of Gay Street and Union to Millers Department Store. I need a dress for your father's private gathering before the concert Thursday."

"Will you take the letter I've written to Matthew and post it?" asked Alice.

"I will, but why don't you come with me? You need a dress too. We'll have a mother-daughter talk."

Oh, whoopee. Mother-daughter talks usually turned into mother-daughter arguments.

Mrs. Davis planned to ask about Matthew. She needed to find out about this man, the one her daughter was interested in making her son-in-law. He was all she could talk about after arriving home for summer break.

"How long do you intend to be gone?" asked Alice.

"Oh, we'll spend the morning in town. We can eat at the Farragut Hotel Restaurant or the S & W Cafeteria. After dinner, I want to stop by your father's office. Then we'll come home." Mrs. Davis was an avid shopper who loved being seen on Knoxville's main street and especially going into her husband's banking office.

"O.K., I'll go. What time are you leaving?" *I can always use a new gown for functions at Maryville College. A new gown and hanging onto the arm of the most handsome senior at school sounds good to me.*

"In an hour," said Mrs. Davis, heading up the circular stairs from the house's foyer. "I'll meet you at the car," she replied as she passed Alice in the hall, the sound of her voice and steps echoing down the corridor.

Alice grimaced. Her mother wasn't known as a good driver.

That will be my next attention-grabbing experience.

She followed her mother down the hall while thinking about Matthew. He'd turned out to be everything she wanted in a boyfriend *and* future husband; smart, thoughtful and not exactly poor.

Yes, and he's malleable enough until I can change him.

This was important if Matthew was to fit into Knoxville society. Everyone at school knew she and Matthew were seeing each other. She'd proclaimed it.

"My boyfriend," she said in the safety of her bedroom.

Alice loved referring to him as such.

But Matthew had a fault. He studied too much and made excellent grades. Alice wondered if he might be valedictorian of his class. That certainly would look good on his résumé, especially if he applied to a large church in Knoxville or the surrounding area. When they married, he'd need a large church and salary. She wasn't going to Cades Cove and attend a dinky little church or live in a house without hot water.

Only one more year before he graduates. Time is short. I've got to set my plan in motion as soon as school starts. I think a June wedding after he graduates is perfect.

"My husband," she said as she smiled in the mirror. Hardly a minute went by that she wasn't thinking, scheming, or devising plans to snag her intended victim.

It will take all my female wisdom to trap him, but next year at this time I'll be Mrs. Matthew Tipton.

~

Passing the columned homes of Knoxville's wealthy and famous, the new Buick Roadster careened down Kingston Pike's paved boulevard, headed for downtown. Narrowly missing poles holding electrical and telephone lines, it flew along the tree-lined street, weaved through the University of Tennessee campus, and ended up at the southern end of Gay Street. This was near the Gay Street Bridge that crossed the Holston River, and it was where Mrs. Davis turned left.

Insisting on having a car of her own, Alice's mother took a few brief instructions from her husband and decided she knew how to drive. Lucky for her, automobiles were sparse in East Tennessee, so she usually had the road all to herself, both sides.

Alice hung on to her cloche hat and the door of the forest green vehicle, her knuckles turning white with her effort. She often swore to others that her mother didn't know the car had a brake.

"Mother, can't you slow this thing down a little?" Alice said in desperation.

"Dear, we're just about there. Hang on a little bit longer." Mrs. Davis passed a traffic tower where the light had turned red and pulled toward the parallel parking in front of Miller's. Alice hid her face in her gloved hands and peeked through her fingers as her mother maneuvered around a street railroad car. Somehow, she wiggled her way into the parking space. Parking wasn't one of her mother's strong points either.

"There, we're here." Mrs. Davis turned off the key in the ignition and patted her daughter on the knee. "Didn't think we'd make it, did you, sweetie?" Then she laughed.

Alice shook her head, opened the car door, and stepped onto the sidewalk, breathing a sigh of relief. Not until she felt the concrete under her feet did she feel safe.

"Come, dear. Let's go see if there's anything that catches our eye." Mrs. Davis took her daughter's arm, steered her like a child through the revolving door at Millers, and headed for the fashionable and expensive clothing section.

～

The saleslady saw her coming. She hurried down the jewelry aisle to greet the stylishly coiffed and richly dressed woman *before* she arrived at her sales area. Although Mrs. Davis was a difficult customer, she bought a large amount of her wardrobe from this particular store and this precise lady.

"Mrs. Davis, may I help you?" she asked, hurrying to meet her.

"Yes, Mrs. Clark. My daughter and I need to look at eveningwear." Mrs. Davis, who still had her daughter by the arm, led her toward comfortable chairs by the fitting rooms. The sales lady followed at the rear.

Her mother often told Alice, "A well-bred lady never rummages through the racks but expects the clothes to be brought to her. If she sees something that attracts her interest, she gets up and tries it on."

Alice heard her mother say, "We're having a small party on Thursday before the concert at the university."

"Do you have a color in mind, and have your sizes changed?" The subject of color was a safe topic, but when sizes were mentioned you were on dangerous ground. Mrs. Clark used the same tactic with all her affluent customers. Color first, coupled with size.

This seemed to soften the blow.

"I believe I'll look at black and the size is still the same." Mrs. Davis expected the saleslady to remember her size. She turned to look at Alice.

"What interests you, my dear?" she said.

Alice's thoughts were racing. "Blue I think, any shade."

"Alice, since it's evening, dark or medium blue would be the best. They'll bring out the gold highlights in your hair." Under her mother's gaze, Alice squirmed in her chair.

Why can't she let me make my own decisions? I'm not five anymore. I'm so tired of her bossing me around . . . and leading me around by the arm.

Mrs. Clark hurried off in the direction of the evening clothes racks, while Blanche Davis continued to check out her daughter. "Have you done something to your hair? It looks different."

"Not really, Mother. The girls at school used a heated iron to straighten it out and put waves back in." When wet, Alice's hair curled in mad confusion over her head. The high temperature tamed it somewhat.

"It's not bad," said Mrs. Davis. "I wonder if my stylist can achieve that look. We'll stop by there on the way home."

Oh, wonderful. Now we'll be twins.

For years, Alice managed to bottle her anger, pushing it down inside her. Sometimes, it bubbled to the surface, like effervescent soda water, but dissipated before she unleashed it.

I'm scared at what will happen when the cap comes off and my anger spews out. That won't be a pretty sight.

Two hours later, four dresses lay on the sales counter next to a mound of discards. Unable to decide which one to buy, Mrs. Davis took them all. She could afford to be extravagant. Her husband made good money.

The sales lady grinned. After all her hard work, she was happy to sell her client all four. She proceeded to place the dresses in shopping bags.

"We'll take our purchases to the car and walk to eat. I don't want to find another parking space." The Farragut and the cafeteria were on the opposite side of the street.

Alice didn't open her mouth. She was in agreement with this plan.

Matthew's name hadn't been mentioned during the Davis's shopping spree.

When shopping was on the agenda, nothing sidetracked her mother's concentration.

～

After placing their purchases in the roadster trunk and locking it, the two ladies crossed the street and walked a short distance to the entrance of S & W Cafeteria. Because they were early, the line wasn't long and the spot they chose was away from the other diners.

After ordering their respective meals, the conversation turned to Matthew Tipton. Mrs. Davis said, "Alright, I want to hear all about the young man who's been squiring you around at the college. What's he like?"

"He's from Cades Cove. Do you remember where that's located?" said Alice, starting at the basics.

Sure, that's over Chilhowee Mountain from Kinzel Springs, isn't it?"

"Yes."

"Isn't that area backward or very rural? Do they have electricity, telephones and running water?" The way her mother said it, the area sounded like it was unfit for habitation.

Alice ignored her mother's comment.

"Mother, Matthew is intelligent and very handsome. He owns almost one hundred and fifty acres and a home in Tipton's Sugar Cove." Alice hurried on to explain, "I'm sure these could be sold and a suitable residence purchased here in Knoxville."

"The young man may have some money, but not like Horace Blackwell. And Horace will inherit a bundle."

"Mother, I don't want to go through that discussion again," said Alice forcefully, her clenched hands in her lap underneath the tabletop. Horace's father was a well-known lawyer, practicing in Knoxville and Nashville.

"Have you seen Matthew's land and home?" asked Mrs. Davis.

"No, I haven't, but I don't plan on living in Cades Cove after we get married."

"Married, huh. You seem to have it all planned. You know the kind of home Horace owns. He'll make sure you live in the style you're accustomed to, and he has a fixation on you. I can't see you carrying water from a spring, washing clothes on a scrub board, or using an outhouse."

"Mother, Horace is twenty-five and still has a face-full of pimples. He's chubby and slow. He never smiles. He's not at all the kind of man I want to marry."

"He doesn't smile because he's a serious person." Mrs. Davis plunged on. "Alice, you're used to money. I don't think you'd be satisfied without a good portion of the green stuff flowing around you. It can buy an easier life."

"Matthew can make plenty of money." Alice was on the defense, a place familiar to her when sparring verbally with her mother.

"Really?" said Mrs. Davis in sarcastic disbelief. "What makes you think that?"

"Matthew wants to be a minister. With his qualifications and, after graduating from Maryville College, he should be able to find a very prestigious position."

"He's really that good?" asked Mrs. Davis, her ears perking up a little.

Alice saw an opening and plunged on with her explanation. "Yes. I wouldn't be surprised if he graduated with honors. He might stay here in Knoxville, or move to Nashville, or even Atlanta." Alice had gone from dreaming, to fantasy, to the impossible.

Suddenly Mrs. Davis could picture a conversation with her friends, *My son-in-law is the minister of a church on Donaldson Avenue close to Andrew Jackson's Hermitage in Nashville. Or his church is on Peachtree Street in Atlanta, Georgia. Hum . . . that would be of benefit in Knoxville society.*

Mrs. Davis was skeptical but said, "I'm beginning to see what you're saying. So how do we proceed from here?"

Alice outlined her plan, but only part of it.

"Next year is Matthew's senior year. After graduating, he's going back to Cades Cove and stand in his father's pulpit. If a better offer arises here in Knoxville, I'm sure he would take it. Why wouldn't he? We need to keep our ears peeled for an opening in one of the local churches."

"What if nothing opens up?"

"Something will, I'm sure of it."

"Has he mentioned marriage?"

"No. But he isn't seeing anyone else. I can't imagine why he wouldn't."

Alice wasn't going to let the opportunity of marrying Matthew pass. Not if she could help it. Alice continued, "Our relationship hasn't progressed that far."

"Are you sure you want to be a minister's wife?"

"I'm not opposed to it."

"Somehow that lifestyle never occurs to me when I think about you being married."

"I know. You've always pictured me as a banker or lawyer's wife." Alice intended to choose her own husband, even though her mother was determined to do the same. It was a war of wills.

"I think a pastor's wife needs patience, tolerance, and a love for the less fortunate."

Alice bristled, "Do you think I don't possess those traits?"

"Now Alice, let's not argue. I was only explaining the qualities of a —

Alice cut her mother short, "I think I'll manage. Davis's are always good at faking their feelings."

"What an awful thing to say. I hope you don't believe that statement." Before Alice could answer, the meal ticket arrived, and her mother busied herself with paying for their meal, counting the money out to the last penny. When they got up to leave, Mrs. Davis had forgotten Alice's comment.

Alice was relieved. She didn't often express her feelings about her family. The comment slipped out before she thought about it. But it was true. Her mother's societal airs hid a very insecure woman who needed money, a lot of money, to feel safe. She was willing to love anyone and do anything to be accepted. Alice doubted if her mother had ever been happy in her life. The surface life she lived looked like happiness abounded, but Alice knew the truth. Down deep, there was always an underlying tension, expectation, or goal to be met. Mrs. Davis lived a pretend life.

Being her mother's daughter, Alice was becoming like her. This transformation was gradual, and Alice did not recognize the warning signs.

Becoming like her mother was the last thing Alice wanted to be in life.

～

After leaving the cafeteria, the twosome crossed Gay Street to the opposite side and walked a short distance down the sidewalk to the bank's entrance. Mr. Davis sat at his desk, as his wife and daughter approached.

"What a pleasant surprise," he said as he stood up to greet them, buttoning his suit coat together.

While Mrs. Davis talked to her husband, Alice gazed at him. Graying around the temples, he stood straight as an arrow. This was his custom when he greeted customers, his way of showing respect. Twenty years older than his wife, he was in his late fifties and contemplating retirement, much to his wife's dismay. Mrs. Davis married for money and not love. She wasn't sure she could handle her husband living at home day after day.

Alice truly loved her father, because he was dependable, trustworthy, and strong. She found many of these traits in Matthew.

"Alice, your mother says you have a new evening dress for Thursday night. Do you like it?" said her father. "Alice?"

"I'm sorry, father," said Alice, nudged out of her inward thoughts. "I had my mind on something else. What did you say?"

Mr. Davis repeated his question.

"Oh yes. I do like it. It's teal-blue, and the color of the ocean when we went deep-sea fishing at Myrtle Beach. I believe you'll like it too." The family vacationed on the South Carolina coast each summer. Her father loved the ocean, spending long hours walking on the beach and jumping the waves.

He'd even taken his family deep-sea fishing, although Mrs. Davis begged off. Alice loved the trip. She didn't get seasick and even caught a few stinky fish. Her father had removed them from her hook. Red snapper, grouper, and flounder were the names she remembered. She found this interesting, because she often ordered fish with these names at local restaurants. Now she knew what they looked like.

"I can't wait to see it, sweetheart." After twenty years of marriage, Mr. Davis accepted his wife's lackadaisical attitude toward him. He eased his disappointment by knowing that she was the youngest and most beautiful wife among his friends.

His daughter, Alice, was the spitting image of her. He loved Alice with all his heart. He hoped she had deeper feelings toward other people, deeper than her mother. His biggest regret was not having more time to spend with his daughter and his young son.

Mr. Davis's next appointment arrived.

"I'll be with you shortly, Mr. Walker."

Alice said, "We wanted to stop by and say hello since we were in town."

Taking his daughter by the arm, he walked her outside to the sidewalk as his wife followed them.

"Where are you parked?" He turned around to ask his wife. He intended to walk them to the car and help them inside.

"We're across the road in front of the department store." Mrs. Davis pointed down the street.

"I'll not walk that far since Mr. Walker is waiting for me. I'll see you two ladies at supper." He gave each a kiss on the cheek, followed by a short bow and walked back to the bank.

"Goodbye, Father," called Alice before he entered the door.

Mr. Davis paused, threw up his hand, and waved goodbye.

∾

Isaac Davis was a self-made man. He began as a helper in the mailroom at Knoxville Bank and worked his way through the hierarchy. He couldn't remember not working there.

He was too busy climbing the corporate ladder to devote quality time to his personal life. This meant that

Isaac was ripe for picking when Blanche Boring paid attention to him at church over twenty years ago. Life was rapidly passing him by, and he was actively looking for a wife. Blanche was beautiful and young. When he proposed, she didn't hesitate. They were married within six months in the society wedding of the year. That they weren't head-over-heels in love wasn't important. Each was looking for the right kind of mate, and each found exactly what they were looking for.

Sometimes he regretted his rash action of marrying Blanche, but he wasn't sorry for his two children. When he had time, he doted on both of them. He remembered this as he waved goodbye to Alice, before he went into the bank. Mr. Walker was a good customer. He didn't want to keep him waiting any longer.

Alice's ride home was as horrendous as the one in but interrupted by a stop at Mrs. Davis's hair dresser at Bearden. This stop became an opportunity to make an appointment for Thursday afternoon. Both Mrs. Davis and Alice would have their hair dressed for the evening's activities.

❧ Chapter Twenty-Seven ❧

The Dinner — Alice

On Thursday evening, Alice stood in the Davis's expansive parlor with its floor-to-ceiling windows. She wore the new slinky, teal-blue gown. It was shoe length, low-cut and revealed the creamy texture of her skin.

The guests would be arriving shortly.

At one end of the parlor was the entrance hall and foyer. It was here the curved, pink-marble staircase led upstairs where several bedrooms shared the central hall. Her younger brother, Isaac Davis, Jr., and Alice slept at the end of the hall. Her mother and father's bedroom appeared on the left after topping the stairs. This split sleeping room fronted Kingston Pike and had a clear view of the long, circular driveway in front of the house. His and hers bedrooms were joined by a sitting room.

Alice walked across the parlor and opened a set of French doors, revealing a glassed-in patio floored with pink marble slabs quarried in the Knoxville area. The moneyed people of Kingston Pike and Fountain City floored many parts of their homes with this local stone. Knoxville's nickname was The Marble City.

It was here in the marble patio that Mrs. Davis practiced her one talent. She grew flowers in profusion, even in the winter when the doors were opened to warm the area.

At that end, before leaving the parlor to access the patio, a right turn through an open archway allowed you to enter the dining room.

As Alice returned to the parlor, she heard the tinkle of crystal and the rattle of silverware being placed on the table.

"I'll sneak a peek."

The room was adorned and perfumed with flowers and candles. The cherry buffet held several silver trays with assortments of hors d'oeuvres and canapés. The Davis's heirloom silver coffee urn sat on a nearby server, which could be moved to the kitchen for a refill. The large summer bouquet, picked that afternoon, rested in the middle of the matching cherry dining table, which was festooned with the best silverware, crystal, and white placemats. The glass chandelier's bright lights glistened on the silver service spread throughout the room. Guests could stand, stretch out in the comfortable parlor, stroll around the flagstone patio, or sit at the dining room table. Candles, spread tastefully through the rooms, added warmth to the camaraderie of the occasion.

All the guests had arrived when the Blackwell's made their appearance. 'Fashionably late' was Mrs. Blackwell's motto and she did everything possible to live up to it. Her punctual husband complained that they never went anywhere on time. Although they had many fights over this one attribute, the battles never made any difference. The Blackwell family was *always* the last to arrive.

Horace T. Blackwell, III followed his mother and father into the parlor. Horace's nickname was Three, which Alice thought was ridiculous considering his solemn and restrained demeanor. When Alice saw Horace come through the door, she tried to conceal herself behind one of her mother's tall green plants. Much to her chagrin she did not move fast enough to reach her cover.

"Alice," called Three, after searching the room with his eyes to find her, "It's good to see you. How are you?" he called as he hurried across the room, extended his hand, and pulled her from behind her protection, oblivious to the fact that she might not want to see him. *Wow! his mind screamed. She's ravishingly beautiful tonight,* but his facial expression never wavered, although his blue eyes glowed with feeling.

Alice came out, looking a bit sheepish and shaking the fronds on the green plant. "I'm doing well," she said, noticing that he was still pimply-faced, chubby, slow, and unsmiling.

I wonder what makes him so unhappy.

"Are you finding college to your satisfaction?" He stood stiffly, holding her hand and patting it with the other.

How old mannish.

"Absolutely lovely," said Alice. "Very much so," she added.

I'm satisfied because it keeps me out of your arm's reach. I'm sure you hope I'll say no, because then you could pursue your case for courtship and marriage.

~

When Alice turned eighteen last year, he immediately went to Mr. and Mrs. Davis for permission to court their beautiful daughter. The problem he encountered was with Alice and not with her parents.

Mrs. Davis, true to her dollar-driven personality, was happy that he showed an interest in her daughter. The Blackwells had more money than she dared hope her daughter would marry, and they were well respected with prestige that extended to the greater community around Knoxville. Alice overheard her mother tell her father, "What a catch he'd be for her little girl."

On the other hand, Alice bucked up when it came to her mother's pushiness. She finally told her mother in no uncertain terms, "Horace T. Blackwell, III turns my stomach. He makes me want to vomit." After that, her mother's comments were short, snide remarks, and Alice's mother did sarcasm very well.

Alice didn't know her mother advised Horace to be patient. "Alice doesn't know her mind. She's young and immature. She's sure to wake up to her foolishness and realize you have many charms. Give her a year or two at college."

~

"Come, Alice," said Three. "Let's go see what we can find to eat in the dining room. I'm hungry. Our case load at the office was heavy today, and I didn't take time for dinner." He placed her hand, the one he still held, on his arm and guided her into the spacious, glittering room.

He needs more food like I need another evening dress. He's a pudgy ox.

Three filled his plate to overflowing, pulled out two chairs at the dining room table, and continued to talk between bites. "Will you return to college next year?"

"Of course, I will. I really like college, and I've made a lot of friends."

Including a young man who's handsome and smiles most of the time.

"What's your favorite course?" Three was trying his best to make a good impression and be interested in her activities.

"Dessert, of course," said Alice, being flippant.

"You know what I mean, your college course. What's your favorite?"

"I like history the best," said Alice, thinking that any other human being on earth would have made a face at her sarcastic remark—not Three. "History's easy."

And boys, especially one boy. If you would quit stuffing your face, you'd be more attractive.

Three almost smiled. "History was my favorite course when I was in college. But I ended up in my father's law office. At least, you and I have one thing in common."

Three moved his chair from the table. "I believe I want more coffee. May I get you some?"

Alice managed to contain her laugher.

Now he thinks of coffee when he didn't even ask if I wanted food.

"Do you think I'm old enough?" she said sarcastically.

Horace wasn't only slow at moving, he was slow to pick up voice nuances. Looking at Alice in surprise, he exclaimed, "Of course you're old enough."

What a dunce. And my mother wants me to marry him.

Alice shook her head in disgust. Horace took the action to mean she didn't want coffee and filled his cup to the brim, adding cream and sugar.

"Please excuse me, Horace." Alice got up and hurried out to the kitchen as Horace returned to the table. When the swinging door closed behind her, she burst into gales of laughter.

"What's so funny, Alice?" asked her mother as she came into the room to replace an empty tray of hors d'oeuvres. Alice looked at the empty tray.

Horace probably emptied that one when he filled his plate.

"Nothing, Mother," said Alice, laughing again. "Absolutely nothing." Alice headed out the back way and went to her room. Her mother gazed after her, wondering what ailed her headstrong daughter.

Upstairs in the safety of her room, Alice threw herself on her bed, being careful not to wrinkle her dress.

How on earth could I be interested in Horace when Matthew is perfect?

While upstairs, Alice completed her outfit by pulling on a matching gauzy covering which partially hid her exposed ivory shoulders. When it was time to drive to the concert, she reappeared, carrying her bejeweled evening bag.

Downstairs, she paused to look into the full-length, hall mirror and straighten the folds of her long dress. Checking her makeup, she saw a beautiful face with blue eyes and strawberry-blond hair. She didn't see the hint of hardness at the corner of her eyes and around her mouth.

On Friday, she wrote Matthew a long letter, complete with all the details of her night, *sans* Horace.

Chapter Twenty-Eight

Summer at Tipton's Sugar Cove — Matthew

When Matthew returned to Tipton's Sugar Cove for the summer, he intended to build cabinets in his kitchen and replace the shingled roof of his barn with tin. This project called for two men, and he needed expert help.

"Dad, do you know of anyone looking for work who knows carpentry?" he asked when he visited his father the first time.

"I'll ask around, son, and see if I can find someone," replied Nat.

The next day, father and son went to Burchfield's Store to buy supplies for both homes. The cane chairs on the front porch were all occupied by men. They sat whittling, talking, and chewing tobacco.

"Good morning, men. The weather's fair today."

"Mornin', Pastor. Good morning for plantin'," said Jim Hall, one of the socializing men. "Guess I'd better git along and do jest that. I suspect I'll see you at church Sunday and you gentlemen too." Everyone called goodbye as he walked down the store's steps, took his horse's reins, mounted, and rode off. The sound of his horse's hooves diminished in the distance.

"Matthew's looking for a good carpenter to help build cabinets in his kitchen and replace the roof on his barn. Do any of you know of someone?"

"I usually do my own repairs," said one man who was a new resident of the cove, a tenant farmer of several acres at the upper end of the long valley.

James Coffey spoke up. "I heard that Squeaky Benson's lookin' for work. He'd be a good hand if you can stand the way he talks."

"Is Squeaky his real name?"

"His given name is David."

"What's wrong with the way he talks?" asked Matthew.

"Something about his teeth causes his S's to emit a strange low-pitched squeal when he speaks. Do you know him Frank?" James looked over at his carving mate.

"Naw, I sure don't."

"I've met him." Bill Johnson threw the core of an apple towards the stand of woods growing by the store. "But I've known his parents for years. And I didn't realize he had a problem."

James Coffee continued, "His mom told me the whine became noticeable when David got his permanent teeth. After several years, she gave up trying to figure out how to eliminate the problem."

"Where does he live?" asked Nat.

"Well, Pastor, the last I heard he was livin' for the time being around Rowan's Creek, jest before you pass your sister Annie's. He might be helpin' Isaac Lequire at the grist mill. I've seen him there recently." James punctuated his comment by spitting tobacco juice off the porch.

"Has he worked for you, James?"

"Naw, but my cousin who lives in Townsend said he did a fine job on his cabinets. He'd hire him again, I'm sure."

"That's good enough for me," said Nat. "Thanks for the information, James."

"Glad to be of help, Pastor.

Nat and Matthew headed into the store.

"See you at church Sunday," called James.

The sound of his chair scraping against the worn porch boards said the whittling session was breaking up.

~

After dinner, Nat and Matthew rode out to Annie's to see how she was doing. Traversing Cades Cove on Sparks Lane, the men traveled through hundreds of acres of planted corn and wheat. Part of the road followed the fence rows, making sharp-right or left-hand turns at their corners. Every bit of bottomland had a useful crop.

As they passed through the flowing water of Abrams Creek, droplets flew in all directions, and the reflections of the two riders were mirrored in the surface of the stream.

On the opposite side of the cove, mountain cabins nestled in clearings against the wooded hillsides. Corn cribs, smoke houses, and huge barns confirmed the agricultural nature of the community.

They rode past mountain gardens with vegetable plants in neat, straight rows, lush and green. Long rows of white-washed beehives their frames being filled with honey stood in lines or singularly somewhere around the house or barn. A rock weight held down the top of the hive. Barbed wire or split rail fences kept cattle in their pastures.

"Dad, you've had plenty of water for growing a garden this year, haven't you?"

His father gave a short chuckle. "Yes, we have. I always wonder why we have feast or famine. This year we could use a little less rain and more sun. Tomatoes don't want to ripen, and the okra won't grow well. They both need lots of sun."

"When sin started in the Garden of Eden, it brought a lot of heartache to man and to the world," observed Matthew. "Nothing's ever perfect, except Jesus, of course."

"Have you ever wondered what a perfect world would look like? How would perfect trees, flowers, and grass grow?"

"Maybe they wouldn't grow. They might be caught in a moment of perfect time," said Matthew, deep in thought. "I always think the word grow is coupled with change. Why would anything need to change, if it was perfect?"

"I can't imagine it, but my father, John Jack knows, and Granny Whitehead knows."

"And one day we'll know for sure," said Matthew.

"Do you still intend to be a pastor and stand in my pulpit?" Each year, his father asked him the same question as if Matthew would change his mind.

"Of course, Dad. When I received my calling, I said, 'Yes.' I don't intend to go back on my word to God."

"Next year, Lord willing, I'll step down around summer. You'll have graduated from college. Do you think you will be ready by then?"

"Dad, I hate to see you give up your ministry so soon. You should preach several more years."

"Oh, I don't intend to quit. I'll only focus on different ways to accomplish God's work. I'll visit new folks more often, help feed the needier families in the cove, and sit with your sick members. I think this will benefit you greatly. That is, if you feel comfortable with my participation. My intention is to give you an opportunity to prepare your messages with greater detail. That's something I never had."

"I believe we'll make a good team, if that's what you have in mind."

"It is. With your college education, your sermons should be much better than mine were, with more illustrations and understanding."

"I never felt cheated when you spoke. You have a grasp of the scriptures that can only be God-given." Matthew was speaking with conviction. "I only hope the Holy Spirit will give me that discerning ability."

There was a brief pause before Nat spoke again.

"Get ready to speak some next year. Sorta do practice sermons." Nat turned a little and looked at his son. "I wish Lazarus could be here to see you preach. That was a vision he and Sarah shared. He often spoke to me about your decision to be a minister and their wish for your education. I'm glad they could send you to school."

Matthew didn't know what to say to his father's comments. There were days when he rode into Tipton's Sugar Cove only to be disappointed when his uncle and aunt didn't greet him. At those times, a strange loneliness and a feeling of loss enveloped him.

⁓

The rest of the trip to Annie's was spent in enjoying the passing scenery beneath the steady gaze of Thunderhead Mountain. Matthew craned his neck and looked upward and to the right. He hadn't returned to the top since the fateful day of the hunt. He didn't have any plans to go back to its heights.

If I have a son, someday we might go. Matthew, are you thinking what I think you're thinking?

Well, I do have a girlfriend, don't I? Those thoughts come naturally.

～

Annie sat on the front porch swing. She stood up and greeted her brother and nephew with a big smile.

"I was just wishin' you two would show up," she said. She always made the same comment no matter who appeared.

"Ha! Annie, I'm glad we fulfilled your wish," said Nat. "How are you?"

"I couldn't be better," and Annie laughed. "Come in and sit your weary bones down." Annie was always the same, jolly and accommodating. Matthew enjoyed being around her. If he felt down, a trip to her house shooed away any sad moods.

Matthew noticed that Granny W.'s part of the swing was empty. On a recent trip back home, he had visited her grave and pondered the life of this knowledgeable lady. As a young man, he called her his sweetheart. She loved being teased by him and visa versa. He missed her.

Matthew and his father sat down in two chairs close to the swing.

"Matthew, come and sit next to me. You haven't visited me in months." Annie patted the empty space next to her. "Next year's your senior year at the college, isn't it?"

Matthew moved over to the swing and answered her question. "Yes, it is."

"Will you be sad to leave or glad?" asked Annie, placing her arm on the back of the swing and turning toward him. She started to swing again. The chain creaked as she went back and forth.

"A little of both, I guess. I've some very good friends. They'll be hard to leave. But getting back to the cove fulltime will add permanence to my life, instead of living like a nomad; in one place for a few months and then another. I'm looking forward to it."

"There's no place like home," said Annie. "When I went with my father to Missouri to help farm our grandfather's place," Annie looked at Nat, "I wanted to come back to the cove. Living on the shores of Shoal Creek in Papaw Jacob's big farm house was enjoyable, but I missed the familiar hills overlooking the cove, especially old Thunderhead up there. Joplin can't compare with these hills." She turned her head to see the dark tops towering over her house.

"Can't say I miss Thunderhead, but I do miss the people here in the cove. Sometimes even the busybody line," said Matthew.

Everyone laughed at the preposterousness of missing those two women.

Annie turned to Nat. "How's Martha? You need to bring her over for supper. In fact, why don't all of you come to eat on Saturday? I've got a hen I need to kill and eat. I'll make a pot of chicken and dumplin's outta her. Fresh green beans are comin' in, and I think they'll be enough for a mess of 'em and young, roastin' ears of corn. My mouth's waterin' already."

"Martha will be glad to forsake the kitchen. What does she need to bring, Annie?"

"Some of her mouth-waterin' cornbread and cold tea will be plenty. I'll fix everything else. You can come, can't you, Matthew?"

"I'll be here with bells on and hungry—" Matthew started to say, "as a bear." He decided not to. It seemed the thoughts and comments today dredged up references to that infamous day long ago.

"Are you stayin' in Tipton's Sugar Cove or with your parents?" Sometimes Matthew went to the sugar cove only to check on things. His bedroom was always ready and waiting for him if he wanted to stay with Nat and Martha.

"I'll be at the sugar cove, which brings us to the reason for this visit," said Matthew. "We need to find a man named David Benson. Do you know him?"

Annie thought for a minute. "I know someone named Squeaky Benson. Maybe David is a relative."

"No, he's one and the same man. His name is David Benson. Everyone must call him Squeaky. At least, it seems that way. Do you know where we can find him?" asked Nat, getting up and stretching his arms and legs.

"The last I heard he was in-between jobs and helpin' Isaac LeQuire. That's where I'd start first."

"Guess we'd better go and see. Is there anything I can do for you this week?" Nat headed for the porch steps. Matthew gave Annie a hug and prepared to follow.

Annie thought a minute. "One of the old slat doors in the barn is gettin' mighty loose. I'd appreciate it if you could tighten it up."

"I'll do that on Saturday."

"Matthew, if I see Squeaky, what do you want me to tell him?" asked Annie.

"Tell him I need to build kitchen cabinets in my house and repair the roof on my barn, and I'm ready to start now."

Nat started down the front porch steps with his son close behind. "Tell him to come by my house, and I'll take him to the sugar cove."

"I'll tell him if I see him." called Annie who rose from the swing and followed her relatives down to the gate. Nat gathered the reins of his horse and started walking toward the grist mill.

"Why are you fixin' kitchen cabinets, Matthew? Are you thinkin' about gettin' married?" called Annie.

Nat stopped in mid-step and turned to look at Matthew. He'd wondered about this same subject but hadn't approached his son with a question.

"No, Annie. I'm not in any hurry to get married," said her nephew, quickening his step towards Rowan's Creek, and passing his father to put distance between him and the question sure to come.

"Do you have anyone in mind?"

Matthew was far enough away so that he could throw up his hand and ignore the question.

But Nat noticed his cheeks were a bit redder. He needed to have a conversation with his son in the near future and find out for sure if there was a woman in his life.

"We'll see you later," called Nat, hurrying to catch up. He wouldn't ask the question now. He'd wait for a more opportune time.

"Don't forget supper on Saturday." Annie waved her hand, stood at the gate, and watched as the two men continued walking in the direction of Isaac's grist mill.

~

To Matthew, there was something too familiar about the direction they were going.

He felt a cold chill and shivered as he ran his hand down his chest, feeling the irregular scars, the consequences of his last trip to Rowan's Creek.

❦ Chapter Twenty-Nine ❦

The Hunt for Squeaky Benson — Matthew

Isaac LeQuire was covered with flour dust. He'd already ground several pounds of wheat flour and was on the last run of the day.

"Isaac," called Nat as they entered the dimly lit and noise-filled mill.

"Up here, Pastor," said Isaac, shouting over the din as he emerged, looking like a ghost from behind a set of the large grinding stones that were turning on the second floor of the mill. Flour dust flew off his overalls and remained suspended, floating in the shafts of light coming through the powder-coated upstairs window. "I need to finish loading the wheat grains, and then I'll come downstairs."

"We're not in a hurry, Isaac," said Nat over the racket of the turning, grinding wheels. The frame building shook with their movement.

The old, gray mill wasn't the most beautiful one in the world. The building had never seen a lick of paint. The oak boards from which it was built were sawn from trees cut on the LeQuire farm, and after many years of weathering, had became tough as nails. The building blended into the picturesque landscape of stream, hemlock, and cool, dark places.

Nat and Matthew watched as ground flour fell into a box by the huge lower wheels. Nat reached his hand into the container to feel the whitish mixture.

"It's almost as fine as store bought," he observed. "Isaac is known for his excellent product."

The men waited for several more minutes, until Isaac appeared at the upper end of a rough wooden staircase leading downstairs.

"I'm almost ready. I need to get a flour sack from my bin." He disappeared again into the semi-light and reappeared carrying the cloth bag over his shoulder. Slowly, he descended the steep, narrow wooden steps until he was on the level with them.

Isaac came striding toward them. "It's my rheumatism," he said as he shook the hands of both men. "Gettin' old jest ain't no fun. I got an old rooster out in the chicken lot, and I swear he moves jest like me."

The men laughed together, and Nat said, "I can relate to gettin' old, Isaac."

"I guess you've been over to see Annie." This was more of a question than a statement.

"Yes, we've walked here from there," replied Nat.

"How was she?"

"She's Annie. What more can I say? We found her sittin' in the squeakin' swing on the front porch." Turning to Matthew. he said, "Remind me to bring some grease on Saturday, and we'll stop that noise."

"I wouldn't mind doing the same thing, sitting on the front porch I mean. If'n you've got a few minutes, I'll be through here, and we can go to the house. I'm sure Caroline would like to see you both. She might even scare up some of her famous pound cake and coffee."

"Sounds wonderful, but we came for a specific reason. Do you know a man named Squeaky Benson?" Nat decided to leave off his real name.

"Sure do. He's probably over at his intended's house today. She lives over on the old Cooper place."

"I know where that's located. Matthew wants to get him to do some carpentry work this summer."

"He won't find anyone better. He's a hard worker. I use him as much as I can," said Isaac, looking at Matthew. "Tipton's Sugar Cove shouldn't need much fixin' up. Lazarus took good care of the place."

"It doesn't. I want to expand the kitchen."

Isaac thought about Matthew's statement. "Are you gettin' married, Matthew?"

Oh, here we go again.

"Can't someone fix up their kitchen without everyone thinkin' he's gettin' married?" Matthew was on the defensive, because marriage was a possibility. It was a prospect he hadn't discussed with anyone, not even his dad.

"Well," drawled Isaac, "it is one possibility." Isaac had stated Matthew's thoughts out loud. He grinned. He was sure he hit a sore spot with Matthew. He wondered who the lucky young lady could be; a college woman, no doubt.

"Matthew and I need to be going. We want to find Squeaky and get on home to eat supper. I'll come some other time when I can stay longer," said Nat, tired of the questions on marriage.

～

The Cooper house was a short ride away. When Matthew and Nat arrived, a young man stood on the front porch of the house, and an old man sat on the porch steps. Work for the day was over, and resting was on the minds of the tired men. The strong smell of meat frying in grease came through the open door.

The men introduced themselves. David "Squeaky" Benson was tall and lanky. Matthew guessed he was only a few years older than he. When Matthew shook hands with him, he felt rough calluses on his palms, and Squeaky's smile revealed spaces between his teeth. Matthew wondered if that was the reason for his strange talk.

"My dad and I've been looking for you. We hear that you're one of the best carpenters around."

"He sure us," said the dad of squeaky's intended.

"Well . . . I thank everybody for their faith in me. I like to think I do a good job." said Squeaky, not the least bit proud and not squeaking because he hadn't used an S.

"Matthew's got some work to be done around his house. We're interested in your schedule so we can hire you." Nat stood on the ground looking up at the young man.

"You're in luck if you need someone soon." Squeaky squeaked twice. "The job I had lined up will have to wait until summer's end." He squeaked twice again.

"That sounds great," exclaimed Matthew. "Oh, I'm sorry you lost your job but glad you're available now."

"What did you need done, Matthew?"

"Cabinets. Cabinets built into my kitchen. The ones I use now are free standing."

"O.K., when do we start?" He squeaked once. "Next week?"

"Great, where do I come too?"

"My home is in Tipton's Sugar Cove."

"That's off Parson's Branch Road, isn't it? You go past Henry Whitehead's place. Laz Tipton lived there."

"Exactly. How did you know him?"

"He knew my brother, Benjamin Benson. Ben and Laz cruised some timber for Little River Lumber Company over in North Carolina. I don't think Little River was interested in the property after that."

Nat said, "I remember your brother. Lazarus brought him by the house. I think Martha fed him a meal. Where is he now? I was impressed with him. He's older than you, isn't he?"

"He's my oldest brother, and now he lives in Virginia. He went up there to be with his wife's parents. So, do we start Monday, Matthew?" It was obvious the two young men liked each other already.

"Yes, we'll start Monday."

"Matthew, we'd better go." Nat shook hands with both men. "Mother will have supper ready." Nat walked over to his horse and prepared to mount up. He was ready to head home. Cold food wasn't something he enjoyed.

"See you Monday, Matthew. About daybreak?" said Squeaky with a short wave as Matthew put his foot in a stirrup and swung his leg over his horse.

Matthew was comfortably seated as he said, "Sure thing," and both men threw up their hands and rode toward Tater Branch.

"Your mother will be wondering what's keeping us, Son."

"Our horses might like a good run," said Matthew looking at his father with a question in his eyes.

"Let's go," said Nat.

~

The horses were galloping as they rode into the barn area at Matthew's former home.

"We haven't had a father-son race in ages," said Nat as he dismounted. "Let's take the horses into the barn. After our run, they deserve some dessert."

Tipton horses were usually turned into the fields of Tater Hollow, but today these were to be fed store-bought food as a reward for their run. Nat led his horse to the watering trough, getting ready to unsaddle it. Turning around, he noticed Matthew wasn't doing the same.

"Aren't you going to stay for supper, Son? We'd be glad for you to stay all night with us," said his father.

"Think I'll ride back to Tipton's Sugar Cove," said Matthew, who stood next to his father while his horse drank its fill.

"Aw, come on. Your mother's goin' to be plenty disappointed if you don't stay. What's your hurry?" said his dad, heading toward a barn stall. He unsaddled his horse, hanging the saddle over a stall side board. Taking an old coffee can off a nail driven into the wall, he plunged it into a sack of feed and filled it up. He poured the sweet feed into the wooden feed trough.

The horse gave a snort and plunged its nose into the box. Giving his horse a pat on the rump, the two men started for the house. Matthew was leading his horse.

"I don't have a good excuse for going," said Matthew. Except that Tipton's Sugar Cove had become his home these last three years. He enjoyed being there, being comfortable in its surroundings.

Martha heard them coming.

She stood on the back porch, wiping her hands with her apron. "It's about time you two showed up. Wash up. Supper's ready to eat," she ordered, ignoring the horse her son was leading. Matthew didn't get a chance to refuse, because Martha disappeared into the house.

Nat grinned and slapped his son on the back. "Guess that settles it," he said and started roaring with laughter.

Matthew tied his animal to a porch pole and climbed the steps to eat. After supper, Matthew headed for the sugar cove and home — with plenty of leftovers.

⁓

Since Matthew was eating at his Aunt Annie's on Saturday, he decided to stay that same night at his mother and dad's and go to church with them on Sunday. There was something else he wanted to do.

He rode over before lunch, packed some of his mother's leftovers in a bag, and headed out toward Rich Mountain. He hadn't been to his favorite overlook in almost a year, and he needed a little bit of restful contemplation.

Although the route was grown up with weeds, the trail was still recognizable, and Matthew walked slowly, enjoying the smells, sights, and sounds of the forest. He brushed by mountain laurel and walked under tall rhododendron bushes, climbing steadily through the pine-oak-maple forest.

Stopping briefly, he watched two squirrels as they played in the high branches of an oak tree. Barking in excitement, they ran from limb to limb and down the tree, closely following each other. Jumping to the ground, darting right-and-left, they ran among the leaves on the forest floor, where they soon disappeared out of sight.

During a windstorm last winter, several trees were blown down across the trail. He skirted around these, hoping the small red chiggers were out for dinner somewhere else. Chiggers made large, red whelps on his skin, because he scratched them furiously.

After climbing the steepest part of the hill above Tater Branch, he walked the gentler crest of Rich Mountain until he turned downhill for several feet and pushed through to his well-known perch. The large, flat rock, resting on the edge of the short bluff, was the only resistance to his overlook being overcome by encroaching bushes. At its edge, a six-to-eight-foot drop was followed by large rocks in helter-skelter array down the steep hillside. This confusion of rocks kept large trees from growing below his perch and afforded him the view Matthew loved so well.

He sat down, his eyes drawn toward Thunderhead Mountain.

Memories. Suppressed memories surfaced.

Why has this place been on my mind so much lately?

Involuntarily, his hand went to his shirt. He unbuttoned it.

Looking downward, he saw the white scars running across his chest. Taking a finger, he traced the largest one, an ugly, ragged line twelve inches long. It ran from one side of his chest diagonally across to the other. Others paralleled it. He buttoned up his shirt and turned up the loose leg of his pants, exposing the area where the livid bear had latched onto his leg.

For several seconds, Matthew relived the horror of being tossed through the air like a wet dishrag. He closed his eyes, and the feeling of empty space broadened around him.

He felt dizzy.

Sitting on the edge of the short drop wasn't a good place to feel woozy.

He opened his eyes.

The holes left by the bear's fangs were visible on his calf. One depression was almost one-half inch deep. That puncture wound was the last to heal.

Matthew shook himself mentally.

"Gee, let's change the subject here," he said out loud. The only answer he received was from a woodpecker in the forest below him.

"Rat-a-tat-tat, rat-a-tat-tat," was the sound as the bird pecked into a decaying tree. The hollow sound echoed through the hot, afternoon forest.

Matthew smiled. "I hear you, and you're right," he said, tossing the words in the direction the sound came from. "I came here for a peaceful meal. Thank you for reminding me of that."

"Rat-a-tat-tat, rat-a-tat-tat," said the bird

It's time to eat the sausage biscuits and apple fritters I packed.

He opened his rucksack and pulled out a newspaper-wrapped biscuit. The paper rustled as he opened it. Before he took a bite, he said a short prayer and then withdrew a quart jar full of his mother's sweetened tea from the cloth bag he'd carried up the mountain. He sat it down carefully on the rock.

As he ate, he examined the faded cloth bag. His mother had made it from a flour sack. Tiny red and blue flowers were printed in rows on its surface. The interior was lined with heavy denim. Her irregular stitches were visible at the inside seams and on the straps, he slung over his shoulder or around his neck. On short trips around the mountains, it carried enough food for a day.

The rustle of another paper caused the smell of pie spices, cinnamon and nutmeg, to waft through the air.

When the bag got dirty, he washed it and hung it over the clothesline to dry. The flowers weren't very masculine, but he couldn't insult his mother by not carrying it, especially after her painstaking effort to make it perfect.

Something about the bag caused him to think of the sobbing young girl he'd encountered at this place several years ago.

It's the color. She wore red and blue that day.

The apple fritters were delicious.

I wonder where she is now and what she's doing. It would be nice to see her again and find out if she's well.

Matthew's heart went out to her, as it had on the day he'd found her crying her eyes out and dirty tear stains on her cheeks. He remembered dark, brown hair and brown eyes, but her facial features had dimmed with the years.

Her eyes. Her beautiful eyes were what he remembered most. Even today, the terror pictured there flashed through his consciousness.

Matthew put the remains of his lunch back into his rucksack. It was time to head down the mountain and get ready to go to his Aunt Annie's for supper. He took one last look below at the peaceful scene with the steepled church in the center, then he turned, and walked toward the main mountain trail, heading for home.

❦ Chapter Thirty ❦

Summer of 1920 at Tipton's Sugar Cove — Matthew

During the summer, sawing and hammering were heard coming from the house at the upper end of Tipton's Sugar Cove. At the end of August, the final repairs to the kitchen and barn were done.

Having Squeaky around turned out to be a pleasant experience, and during the summer, Matthew got a taste of how a permanent companion could make his home less lonesome. Along with the noise of making repairs was the clatter of everyday happenings.

After the two young men got to know each other, Matthew offered Squeaky a room, and he accepted. Squeaky's biggest problem was the lack of roots. His father was dead and his mother had remarried. The rest of his family was scattered in many directions, including Virginia.

"Matthew, are you planning on gettin' married?" asked Squeaky as they sat on the front porch at the sugar cove. "I've been wondering why you're fixin' up the kitchen. Shelves are jest fine for a man." Squeaky felt like he knew Matthew well enough after working over two months to ask him this personal question.

"Oh, I don't know, Squeaky. There's this girl at school, Alice, and she's been hangin' around me. It's really obvious that she likes me, and I like her. But I'm not sure there's a future for us."

Squeaky sat chewing on a sassafras twig and Matthew's words.

"I think what bothers me about your statement is the word 'like,'" said Squeaky. "I get the feeling you doubt yourself concerning this girl."

"How so?" asked Matthew, wondering what his new friend was getting at.

"I never use the word like when referring to my future wife. I always use the word love. Can you use the word love in your sentence?" asked Squeaky.

Matthew made the swap. "I love Alice. No, I can't say that it's a comfortable switch. Don't you think love can grow on you?"

"Sure, that's a possibility, but where's the enthusiasm? Where's the excitement of being in the glorious state of love or on the verge of it?" Squeaky threw his hand into the air with a looping flourish. He was half-serious and half-teasing.

Matthew laughed. "She's fun to be around most of the time, but there's a tension, a strain in our relationship. I don't think it's me, but I can't describe the feeling. Let's change the subject."

The two sat in comfortable silence while the sun disappeared behind the Chilhowee Mountains.

"O.K., but be careful, Matthew. I'd hate to see my new friend make a mistake, especially one who plans to be a minister. That blunder would be fatal. Make sure she understands your future plans. Some people marry thinkin' they can change you. That kind of union never works out. Turns into a dog and cat fight. And, that's double trouble in your case."

Matthew decided Squeaky gave good advice. He intended to remember his words in the future.

Squeaky continued, "Maybe you should just be friends with Alice."

Matthew nodded his head. "You might be right, Squeaky, although a good friend is a better description." Matthew pondered Squeaky's words, but decided to give his relationship with Alice a few more weeks.

They continued to sit in the cool, comfortable darkness, watching the bats flying in the open sky over the planted fields.

"I wonder if they're from Gregory's Cave."

"Could be," responded Matthew. "Or maybe the large one in Dry Valley. The old timers say the Indians knew about it."

"Did I hear a rumor that Gregory's Cave was to be opened to visitors?"

"The Gregorys may do that. This area's attraction for vacationers is increasing. They might do well."

"Did you hear that?" Squeaky craned his head toward the direction of the sound.

A barred owl hooted at the head of Tipton's Sugar Cove, only to be answered by a rival somewhere down the creek. A flash of flying black wings and body against the dark, blue night sky told of the owl's presence and response to its challenger. A few minutes later it hooted from a different perch.

Matthew got up and lit the lantern hanging under the porch eaves.

"I've enjoyed working with you this summer. My cabinets look great," said Matthew as dusk settled around them and the mists appeared in the hollow below.

"We've done well."

"I'm going to miss you staying with me. Where do you go from here?"

"Actually, I may be on the Maryville College campus soon. The Chaplain, I believe his name is Evens, needs more bookcases in his office at the House-in-the- Woods."

The Chaplain's new home was built in 1917, the same year the college hired him as its first Chaplain, and the year Matthew started to school. The college pastor stayed on campus. In this way he was more accessible to the students.

"I know Pastor Evens. I'll put in a good word for you. I've got to go down to Maryville on Monday and look for a new place to stay. My former landlady moved in with her daughter, and they're selling her house."

"If you find a place, see if they have an extra room. I'll need one if I move to Maryville and build the pastor's bookcases."

"I'll do that. It's time to turn in. I'll see you in the morning."

Matthew paused at the door, "By the way, when are *you* planning on getting married? Charlotte won't wait forever."

"We've set Thanksgiving weekend for the big day. I think I'll ask your father to perform the ceremony; that is, unless you want to."

"I'd be honored to do it. I've already been ordained as a minister, so the ceremony would be lawful."

"Then it's all arranged. Good night, Matthew."

"See you in the morning. Will Charlotte be coming to meet you at church?"

"I think so."

"Night, Squeaky."

Chapter Thirty-One

THE SENIOR YEAR – September, 1920

Matthew's senior year at Maryville College started much like the train he rode between Maryville and Townsend. It struggled to get going, but after it did, picked up speed and threw off steam along the way.

Looking back, he decided Fall 1920 and Spring 1921 was the worst and best year of his life. When summer of 1921 arrived, the train pulled into its destination, and he disembarked to start the rest of his life.

Matthew walked down Court Street. His new room was opposite the College Woods and five blocks from Carnegie Hall. He was headed to the dorm where he hoped to find Tim Brackett. School started on Monday.

He walked through the columned porch and entered the main doorway. Tim was on the front desk.

"I see you're still director of information for another year," laughed Matthew, crossing the foyer. His words echoed in the room, which had high ceilings, marble floors and huge, floor-to-ceiling windows in the front.

"It's not another year, it's just one semester."

"Don't remind me, my friend."

Tim put down some papers he'd been sorting and came around the desk. He gave Matthew a manly hug and slap on the back.

"I lo-o-ve my job!" exulted Tim, who did like his interaction with Carnegie Hall's "inmates" as he called them. "Miss Henry couldn't find anyone else who could do it better."

Miss Clemmie J. Henry, who was Director of Student-Help, liked Tim. She was happy to have him back. Maryville College and Miss Henry were determined to provide help for those students with limited financial resources. The college's program was one of the best in the nation. Tim's father was especially thankful for it.

"It's good to be back and see you, my friend. How was your summer?" The two friends hadn't corresponded during the three months since completing their junior year. Neither one was a letter writer.

"Oh, you've got to see my new cabinets. Squeaky Benson—and you've got to meet Squeaky, did a wonderful job. He's coming Saturday, so we'll get together." Matthew was excited to see his old friend. "Squeaky may be working at the Chaplain's House-in-the-Woods and staying next to me on Court Street."

"I see. Are your mother and father doing well?"

"They sure are. We spent quite a bit of time together, eating mostly. It's hard to turn down Mom's cooking." Matthew patted his stomach.

"You don't seem to have gained an ounce. Her cooking is one of my fond memories of Cades Cove," said Tim. "How about Donald? How's he doing?"

"Great. I think he's getting serious about Polly Herron."

"Really, it's about time. Although, I hate to think about our good times ending at the sugar cove. By the way, have you seen Alice since May? Heard from her?"

"She wrote me." Matthew decided to play down the shoebox full of letters he'd received.

"So, are you still seeing each other?"

"I suppose so," said Matthew matter-of-factly.

"She didn't break it off, did she? And you didn't?" asked Tim.

"No."

"I can tell you're really excited about nabbing the most beautiful woman on campus. I can't figure you out."

Tim stopped talking to help a new student find his room. "You're on the third floor. Go to the end of the hall and climb the steps. The doors are marked," he instructed.

He turned back to Matthew. "Where were we? Oh, yes. What about Alice? Where do you two stand in your relationship?"

"I don't know. That's one thing I've got to figure out and soon."

"I see." Tim shook his head. "I don't understand you, my friend, but we can talk later. I'll be off the desk in about one hour. Why don't you sit down and wait? We'll go up to the café on Broadway and eat. I actually have some extra money and guess what."

"What?"

"I'm on the ground floor this year. I don't have to climb three flights of stairs anymore. You'll need to go by and see my new room."

"I came here to see if you had time to walk over with me to see Ollie."

"Great, we can do that on the way back from town. Will that work?"

"Yes."

At that moment, another student came up to the desk.

"I'm going over to see Pastor Evens. I'll be back in about an hour. Where's your room?"

"Down the hall. It's 105," said Tim, pointing.

"Oh, I can remember that. It sounds like your temperature last year when you were sick with the flu." Matthew was laughing, although it was no laughing matter when his friend lay in bed pale as a ghost. The Spanish flu epidemic of 1918 was deadly to many strong men and women in the East Tennessee area, and it didn't stop with that year, as Tim found out. "I'll see you there."

"O.K." Tim screwed up his face into a wry smile and motioned for his friend to skedaddle. He turned back to the young man standing before him. The new student looked bewildered, confused, and newly estranged from his family. Tim and Matthew called it the "new freshman look."

I wonder if I looked like that when I was a freshman? Probably not, since I lived in Maryville while at Preparatory School.

As Matthew left, Tim was giving detailed instructions to the young man.

I can't imagine starting school again, and I can't believe this is my last year. The future looms ahead.

∾

Pastor Evens' door was open.

"Come in, Matthew," he said when he saw Matthew in the hall. He came around his desk and shook hands with one of his favorite pupils.

"Are you excited about your senior year?"

"I'm excited and already a little sad."

"I'm sure that's a normal reaction. It's been so long since I graduated from school, I don't remember my feelings." He paused. "Sit down. I was just thinking about you."

Matthew settled into one of the upholstered chairs in front of Pastor Evens's wooden desk. Its shining surface reflected the two large, undraped windows behind it. He looked around the room, which was illuminated by light streaming through the windowpanes and a lamp sitting on the Reverend's desk. Bookshelves and framed pictures lined the two other sides. He wondered why the pastor needed more shelves in his house.

"You have a lot of books, Pastor." Matthew twisted in his chair, turning his head to see the room's contents.

"That collection spans several years and many subjects. One of my joys is reading, any subject or kind of book."

Attesting to this truth, numerous books were piled on one corner of his desk and cartons of books rested on the floor underneath. Evens walked over to a picture on the wall and pointed to it. "Speaking of senior year and leaving school, that's my college graduation picture several years ago. My mother and dad were there."

"Where did you graduate from?"

"Harvard, believe it or not." He paused. "I went there four years."

"Did you live close by?"

"Yes, in Boston, Massachusetts. I was there when Charles Eliot was president. Did you know that Harvard is the oldest institution of higher learning in America? It was started as New College in 1639. It's also the oldest corporation in our country."

"I had no idea," said Matthew, although he was familiar with the name and the school's place as a famous school.

Pastor Evens walked over in front of Matthew and sat down on the edge of his desk. "I'm glad you came by. That way, I don't have to try to find you. You're familiar with our chapel each morning?"

"Of course," said Matthew, wondering where the conversation was headed.

"What you probably don't know is that each year I designate a senior with superior academic standing to help in chapel. That student's main goal is to enter the ministry, and this year I have a short list of choices." He picked up a list containing four handwritten names from his desk and looked over it. "You're on it. Do you think you would be interested in helping?"

Matthew was dumbfounded. This offer was totally unexpected.

But he didn't think long. "Yes Sir, I am. I would be honored if you chose me."

"Wonderful, you were at the top of the list." He showed Matthew the penciled list and pointed to his name. "I'm glad I won't have to look farther. The job is yours."

"Thank you, sir. I'll do my best."

"You've been in chapel long enough to know how it works, but I'll explain the more obscure details. Each morning you'll read the Bible lesson I've designated and say the first prayer. Mrs. Tate plays the piano, and Mr. Wilson leads the music. When I'm out of town or can't be present, it becomes necessary for you to take over the devotional part, unless I get another professor to do it. I'll be sure to let you know in advance if this happens."

"Do I come up with ideas for devotions from scratch, or do you make the suggestions?"

"You might want to prepare some ideas so we can discuss them, and I have several books in my library you can use, both here and at my home." Evens continued, "This job comes with immense responsibility. It will be good practice for your future in the ministry."

"I won't let you down, Pastor."

"I believe you will do well, or I wouldn't have chosen you."

"Tonight, after supper, I'll start developing some thoughts for you to critique." Matthew was nodding his head. "And I agree. This is good practice for me. I'm really excited. Thank you for the opportunity."

"Feel free to come by my college office or drop by the House-in-the-Woods at any time for assistance."

"Speaking of your home, that's actually the reason I'm here. My friend, Squeaky Benson, said he might do some work for you, building cabinets?"

"Actually, I need bookcases. How well do you know Squeaky?"

"He's my friend. He built cabinets into my kitchen in the sugar cove, and I was well pleased with his work. I wanted to let you know this.

"Your recommendation is enough for me. He's going to come by on Saturday to look over the project and talk about my ideas."

"I know. We planned on getting together while he's here."

Evens nodded his head. "Very good."

Matthew continued, "Guess I'd better go. Tim and I are walking into Maryville to eat at the café."

"I'd go with you, but it's the new school year, and I have a load of things to do. Enjoy yourself."

Matthew said his goodbyes and left.

After seeing Tim's room, which was exactly like the one on the third-floor, but without the view, and eating at the café, the two friends headed for Ollie's home.

"You're really talkative this year. What's eating you?" asked Tim. "You should be elated at being chosen for the chapel position. Your cup should be running over."

Matthew could have said "Alice." He didn't. He made up some lame excuse about this being his senior year.

"I don't know how I'm going to get along the second semester. You'll be returning to Asheville." Tim only needed one semester to graduate since he started college in the middle of the year.

"Is that what's bothering you?" Tim laughed. "You'll have plenty of friends left, including the love of your life, Alice. By the time I leave, you may be engaged."

"Let's don't rush things," said Matthew dryly.

Tim looked over at his friend with a question in his eyes. He couldn't understand Matthew's lack of enthusiasm. The rest of the short walk to Ollie's was in silence.

When the two came to the path leading to Ollie's house, he called to them from the front porch. He'd heard them coming.

"Matthew, Tim, I'm so glad you came. I've missed both of you."

The two men looked at each other. "How does he do that," whispered Tim.

"I heard that," said Ollie, who was laughing. "Come on up."

"How did you hear that?" asked Tim.

"My hearing, feeling, and smelling are my eyes. I can almost hear the fog coming in on cat's feet." Ollie was referring to Carl Sandburg's famous poem about the fog. "I do know when it's foggy by feeling the amount of moisture in the air."

Tim mouthed to Matthew, "That's uncanny."

"Are you mouthing something, Tim?" asked Ollie.

Tim and Matthew doubled over with laughter.

"Ollie, you won't do," said Matthew when he could talk.

"Come in the house and sit down." Ollie called to his mother, who was in the kitchen, "Mom, Matthew and Tim are here."

Mrs. Miller appeared in the doorway, bowl and spoon in hand. "Well, glory be! How are you both? Let me get rid of this." She went back into the kitchen and reappeared without her bread dough. "It's so good to see you." She hugged and kissed both of the young men. "Sit down. Sit down. How were your summers?"

"Mine was very busy," said Tim. "I helped my father in his office and applied for a substitute teacher's job that might become available after December."

"Do you graduate in January?" asked Mrs. Miller.

"Yes, I'll be out then."

"Matthew's going to really miss you. You two have been best buddies for several years," said Ollie.

"Then you'll have to step up, Ollie, and be his best friend." Tim was smiling at Ollie and Matthew.

"I'll certainly try." Ollie faced Matthew. "How was your summer, Matthew?"

"Very busy. We built cabinets in my kitchen at the sugar cove."

"Tipton's Sugar Cove sounds like a nice place. I wish I could see it."

"Ollie, I was thinkin' the same thing. Would you like to go?" asked Matthew.

"Oh, yes. When?" Ollie was so excited he was dusting the piano stool with the seat of his pants.

"Ollie, quit fidgeting," said Mrs. Miller.

"How about Thanksgiving? If Tim can go, we'll do it." Matthew looked at Tim. "What about it, buddy? That will be our next to last holiday together, and Squeaky will be getting married that weekend. Everyone can come to the ceremony, which I'm to perform."

"Who's Squeaky?"

"He's the one that installed my cabinets."

"Oh," said Ollie. "I'll plan on it."

"Thanksgiving at the cove sounds fantastic. We'll have a great time. Have you ever been on a horse, Ollie?" asked Tim.

Mrs. Miller was sitting in her chair, looking more anxious by the minute. When riding a horse was mentioned she said, "I'm not sure Ollie should ride a horse."

"Now, Mom, Matthew wouldn't let me get into trouble. Would you, Matthew."

"Oh no, I won't let you ride over a cliff or into water over your head." Matthew realized the minute he said these words it was a mistake.

"Oh!" exclaimed Ollie's mother.

Matthew was teasing, so he hurriedly continued, "Mrs. Miller there's plenty of places we can ride that are very safe, even for someone with Ollie's difficulties."

"Well, I'll think about it," she said.

"Now, Mom, I think I can make that decision myself." Ollie was indignant.

"I'll tell you what, Mrs. Miller. Why don't you come too?" Matthew looked at her to see what she thought.

She nodded her head. "That's a possibility."

"Ollie, are you going to church with me Sunday?" Matthew was ready to start taking his blind friend to church. He enjoyed his company.

"Sure. Come by and get me. Do we still leave at nine o'clock?"

"Yes. I'll be here exactly at nine." During his junior year at college, Matthew came to understand Ollie's needs very well.

Ollie liked regularity, reliability, stability, and permanence. He could tell the time within a minute and knew when something had been moved. Of course, he was an everything-in-its-place kind of guy since he couldn't see.

Everyone got up, including Ollie, who followed Tim and Matthew to the door. "Don't forget Thanksgiving," he whispered.

"I heard that," said Mrs. Miller from the kitchen door. Ollie wasn't the only one who had keen hearing.

❧ Chapter Thirty-Two ❧

September at Maryville College — Matthew

After leaving Tim to return to Carnegie Hall, Matthew continued down Court Street. His walk was through an interesting area of houses belonging to influential members of Maryville society, bankers, lawyers, business owners, and to professors at the college. The architecture did not detract from the high and many-columned facades of the college across the road. Instead, it was an extension of the academic look he lived in each day. The farther he walked the bigger the house and land area around the dwelling.

The homes had circle driveways, beautiful landscaping, and large porches. Quarried Knox County marble or local slate graced front porches and entrance halls. A few automobiles sat here and there in driveways and traveled by him on the gravel roads. Servants opened doors when visitors knocked and ushered them into regal parlors.

Matthew paused at a large red-brick, colonial-style house with several tall, white columns on the large marble porch. Thin slate, supported with a hidden angle-iron grid and attached with copper wire, covered the roof. The slate came from the Abram's Creek mine at Chilhowee on the Little Tennessee River. Shipped downstream by barge, it was sold at the builder's supply in town.

If I remember correctly, Tim said the Biltmore Estate at Asheville has the same type of slate roof construction.

The slate surrounded the chimneys on each end of the house. On the end facing Maryville, electrical and telephone lines were attached.

A circle driveway went up to the front entrance, where several steps led to the large front doorway. Five small windowpanes, arranged vertically, ran down each side of the expansive door.

Huge oak trees shaded the house and the surrounding area. Landscaping in the center of the circle driveway contained many small, well-trimmed bushes, a tall maple tree, and several rocks of different sizes. Pine needles and last fall's leaves mulched the shrubbery and fall flowers. Yellow chrysanthemums and orange marigolds grew in profusion along the side of the gravel driveway. Clumps of red Indian paintbrush and white daises grew within rock gardens on the clipped lawn.

Several wicker chairs sat on the marble porch where a young child, dressed in short pants, played with some kind of toy while a young woman watched over him.

Wonder if she's a servant?

Matthew saw her look in his direction. He waved at the dark-haired, young lady who raised her hand in salutation. The young child, his blond hair shining in the afternoon sun, stopped and looked his way. Matthew continued on down the street and turned right to his boarding house.

One street over from Court Street, the home owners rented rooms to college students and those who worked during the school's term. This was where Matthew now lived in a large, frame house. His room was on the second floor.

Because he was early for the school year, he had time to purchase the books necessary for his class load and set up his room so studying was comfortable. His intention was to get a head start on everyone else. Pulling out a chair at his new study desk, he sat down to think about the position as scripture reader in chapel. He looked out at the empty robin's nest in the elm tree outside his window, its leaves starting to turn autumn yellow.

I certainly didn't expect Pastor Evens to choose me for the chapel position. There were other students qualified for the job.

Matthew didn't get a good look at the list Evens waved through the air, but he did confirm there were only four names on it.

I'll write mom and dad with the news. They'll be surprised and delighted.

Matthew picked up a pen and paper and wrote a brief note to his parents. Then he started to mull over his new responsibility. For the first time, he started to doubt his ability. Matthew worried about standing before hundreds of fellow students and falling short. The Cades Cove church members were small compared to the college enrollment.

What if I freeze and can't say a word? Action is better than sitting around worrying about this new experience. I'm still in shock. I can't let Pastor Evens down. I'll start right now thinking about subjects to use. Hum-m, something associated with college problems and life.

Later, after pacing up and down the room, he had a list of ten possibilities.

The supper bell rang.

After supper, I'll write a line or two of summary for each idea.

Placing the newly written pages on his desk, he bounded down the stairs. The smell of freshly-cooked food met him as he entered the dining room. He felt better. Mr. Hembree sat in his place at the head of the table with the bell at his right hand. Mrs. Hembree served the meal and then pulled up a chair to eat.

"Matthew, we've been talkin', if your friend Mr. Benson needs a room, we have a small one off the kitchen that might suffice," she said.

"That's wonderful. Squeaky stayed with me this summer, and he's a great guest."

"We'll show it to you after we eat. The bathroom, where he can clean up, is beside the kitchen. Will he need it for long?"

"I don't think so, but you'll have to ask him. He'll be here Saturday, and I'll bring him by to meet you."

"That's good. Will that be in the morning or afternoon?"

"I'm sure it won't be in the morning," said Matthew. We're going to eat dinner at the college and go see Pastor Evens. That's who he will be working for this fall."

"What will he be doing for the reverend?" asked Mr. Hembree.

"He's going to put bookcases somewhere within the House-in-the-Woods."

"Oh, he's a carpenter?" asked Mrs. Hembree.

"Yes, and a very good one," answered Matthew.

"Harry, this might be a good chance to get more closets built into the house." Mrs. Hembree always complained to her husband about the lack of space.

"I'll talk to him about it," said her husband.

~

The next morning, Matthew decided to take a shortcut through the college woods and run his ideas by Pastor Evens. Matthew wasn't one to lag behind. He wanted to get a jump on his writing, especially in the event he might actually lead the devotions.

The college woods consisted of several acres of virgin forest. Mature, tall oak trees, maples, tulip popular, and white pines grew here with green ivy twined around their trunks and branches. Trails made by white-tailed deer and smaller animals ran helter-skelter through the woods. Matthew picked one of these to follow to the main road that passed by the House-in-the-Woods and the president's house.

When he knocked on the door of Pastor Evens home, the chaplain came to greet him in his housecoat.

"Matthew, good morning. Come on in." Matthew entered the parlor. The smell of fried bacon clung to the air. "You're up early. Are you an early riser?" asked Stevens.

Matthew laughed. "Yes sir. In the cove you start as soon as the sun comes up and end when it goes down."

"Good habits are hard to break."

"I think that's the other way around," said Matthew smiling.

"Ah-h, it works both ways," said Evens nodding his head and motioning to a chair that sat nearby.

"I'm only going to stay a minute. I'm headed for the library to study," replied Matthew, holding onto the books and notebook he carried.

"What brings you to the House-in-the-Woods so early in the morning?" The pastor had noticed the papers Matthew was holding in his free hand.

"I worked on some ideas for devotions and wanted to leave them with you so you could critique them." Matthew held them out to the pastor, who took the sheets and glanced at them. There were ten in all.

"You have ten suggestions. I'm amazed and pleased at your speedy response. I'll look over them this afternoon. Come by in the morning, and we'll talk about your ideas. By then, I should have the first week's Bible verses ready. Our first chapel on Monday will be special. It's our opening one."

"Come about eight?" asked Matthew, hesitating. He wished he felt comfortable enough to express his doubts to this man.

"Yes, that's perfect. I'll see you then." Pastor Evens ushered Matthew to the door and watched as he walked down the lane toward the college.

That young man will go places if he chooses. I need to find out about his ambitions for the future and find a position that suits his abilities.

Pastor Evens shut the front door and returned to his home study, stopping in front of another copy of his graduation picture. He was proud of his association with Harvard.

His family wasn't rich, and this necessitated a job during the school year, plus the summer break. There were times he took a semester off to pay his way. He was twenty-five years old when he graduated, old for a Harvard graduate.

After school, he lived with his parents, working for a year. Then he left for several months travel in Europe with money saved from his job. During this time of bumming around the continent, he'd mulled over several lucrative offers in the North. Eschewing all, he sacrificed a comfortable post to teach at Maryville College. Helping Appalachia's backward and disadvantaged young people was a prideful obsession. Matthew fit into this criterion. With his aid, those he'd picked to help with chapel had gone on to prestigious positions after graduation. He felt sure Matthew wouldn't be an exception.

Pride was a character trait he couldn't shake, and interference by anyone into his school affairs caused him to be distrustful and jealous. In many ways, he wasn't a happy man.

Evens walked over and picked up the suggestions from his desk, intending to put them into his desk drawer to look at later. The first one caught his eye.

He read the title and summary.

This is a very good idea.

Matthew's first suggestion was very basic. *Why Go to Chapel?*

He got up and searched his bookshelves, finding the exact volume he needed. Its title was *The Modern Chapel*.

This will help Matthew on his first thought and provide him with information to complete his idea.

The chaplain sat back down at his desk and looked over Matthews other proposed subjects, making notes as he read. At times, he punctuated the silence with "very good or good thought or he's on the right path here" as he looked at the handwritten sheets. One hour later, he placed the sheets on the edge of his desk with a paper weight on top.

He smiled and picked up the material he had been working on when Matthew knocked.

I look forward to our discussion on the morrow.

~

Matthew met Tim for lunch in the cafeteria at Baldwin Hall. He couldn't help but think that Alice would be there in two days.

I haven't thought about her in one whole day. I wonder if that's good or bad.

"Matthew," said a familiar voice behind him.

Matthew stood up. Dr. Elmore shook hands with him.

"Dr. Elmore, I didn't know you were going to be here for the opening festivities," said Matthew.

"I wasn't sure I would be, so I didn't send you a note. How are you, my young friend? You look like your summer agreed with you. Do I feel bigger muscles under your shirt sleeve?" While shaking Matthew's right hand, he had gripped his arm above the elbow with his left.

"Probably, I worked in my kitchen at the sugar cove building cabinets for storage over the new sink unit and counter top. The whole house seems different now that the new kitchen is in place. Then we replaced the roof of the barn. My hay will stay dry through the winter."

"Tim, how are you?" asked Dr. Elmore turning his attention toward Matthew's friend. "Did you assist with the kitchen installation?"

"No, I stayed in Asheville, helping my father at his medical office. I saw enough blood there without coming to the sugar cove and mashing fingers and digging out splinters all summer."

"Won't you sit down and talk with us? We were finishing up our meal. How is the Moore family? Is everyone well?" asked Matthew of his late uncle's in-laws as the elderly gentleman settled in a seat by the two young men. He always inquired of the Moore's when he saw Dr. Elmore, who was their pastor.

"They're good. The whole Moore family was at church Sunday. They said to give you their regards and extend an invitation to visit."

"I would love to go, but my senior year will be hectic enough without adding more activities to it."

"Yes, I heard. You're supposed to help lead chapel. That's a great honor, Matthew. Pastor Evens is very *careful* about whom he chooses." Dr. Elmore was nodding his head. "Have you signed up for your classes?"

"I have," piped up Tim. "My last semester will be a breeze, more-or-less. I saved some easy electives for it. Thank goodness, Shakespeare's out of the way."

"I haven't told anyone, including Tim, but one of my electives is piano. I want to acquire at least an understanding of music; learn how to read music, especially. I signed up for the class this morning."

"You did!" said Tim, incredulously. "I don't believe it. Men don't play the piano, do they Dr. Elmore?"

"Now, Tim, participating in some kind of music class is a good experience for entering the ministry. Matthew might have to lead music in a smaller church, such as the one in Cades Cove. You can't get too much education," said Dr. Elmore.

"I had my choice of electives and chose piano. I told my teacher, Mrs. Tate, that I knew next to nothing about reading music. She said if I practice, I would learn quickly. I think I'll enjoy piano."

"Good for you, Matthew. I must run along. Come by my office this afternoon so we can talk. I'll be free after three o'clock. See you later, Tim." Dr. Elmore got up and headed out of the dining room.

"I can't believe you're taking the piano." Tim looked at Matthew as if he'd lost his mind. "Tinkling the keys?"

"Well, why not take piano?" asked Matthew, getting ready for the condemnation he was sure would come.

"I've never seen a man play the piano."

"You've seen Ollie play the organ."

"But that's different," stated Tim.

Matthew decided he wouldn't even pursue that statement.

"Beethoven, Mendelssohn, Mozart, Chopin, or Johannes Brahms, you've heard these names, haven't you?" Matthew was perturbed at his friend's prejudice.

"Of course, I have, but—"

Matthew interrupted him. "They were all men and great composers who played the piano. How about Albert Einstein, the breakout physicist? He is an accomplished musician and plays each day."

"Okay, okay, I give. Play the piano, if you must," exclaimed Tim.

"I've been reading about many male piano players of yesterday and today. I was like you, but I think learning to play is an excellent objective after finding out about them."

Tim changed the subject. He still wasn't totally convinced that his friend needed the experience of playing the piano.

He and Matthew headed back to the library to study.

🦋 **Chapter Thirty-Three** 🦋

A Meeting with Dr. Elmore, Matty, and Abigail —
Matthew

D r. Elmore sat at his desk. As chairman of the Board of Directors, he was responsible for Maryville College's future. The school's growing enrollment necessitated increases in endowments for new buildings and courses. President Wilson and he spent many hours poring over campaign efforts to raise money to finance the school's rapid expansion. Most of the travel associated with their fund-raising efforts fell on the President's broad shoulders.

Dr. Elmore reached for his black, stick telephone and pulled it toward him. Taking the receiver off its cradle, he flipped the yoked-cradle up and down.

The operator answered. "Dr. Elmore, how may I connect you?"

"Susie, I need to talk to President Wilson." Dr. Elmore arose from his desk and, carrying the two-piece contraption, walked toward the window by his desk. Looking out the window, he could see the building where the president worked.

"Please hold," he heard the operator say.

He gripped the phone through a series of clicks. President Wilson came on the line. "Good afternoon, Edgar."

"Sam, I know you're busy, but I wanted to confirm your trip to Pennsylvania next week. I'm sure you've got your train tickets and made appointments with the list of people I gave you, but I need to verify these for our Board of Director's meeting."

"I gave all that information to Nancy, and I know she was working on it. Let me check."

Only a few moments passed before President Wilson spoke again.

"Yes, we're all set. Did you get in touch with Mr. Tallent? I hoped to meet him, since he expressed an interest in sending his son to our school. I believe he could be influential in getting us to the right people in Philadelphia."

"No, and I can tell you I've tried. He must be on a trip somewhere. I have his address. I'll see that you have it so you can visit him while you're in the area."

"Don't forget the reception tonight."

"It's penciled on my calendar, Sam. I'll see you then. Goodbye."

Dr. Elmore replaced the receiver, walked to his desk, and sat the stick telephone down.

Sam's trip north was important for the college. Most of the money for new buildings came from New England.

Under their administration, the combined Voorhees Chapel and Music building was built. The Lamar Memorial Hospital, where Tim spent several days with the flu was constructed. Dormitories for men and women and Fayerweather Hall for instruction, the indoor Swimming Pool, and the House-in-the-Woods took shape.

On his desk was a design for Thaw Hall, which would become the new library. It included some additional classrooms. Another drawing depicted the new Alumni Gymnasium.

He was busy studying the new proposals when Matthew knocked on his office door.

"Come in," he beckoned.

Matthew entered the room as Dr. Elmore approached from behind his desk and shook hands with his visitor.

"Sit down, Matthew. I'm happy to see you. How was your summer?"

"This summer was the best one yet." He continued with an in-depth description of the repairs he'd made. "I can't wait to stay at the sugar cove permanently." He paused and continued, "Of course, I'll miss school and Tim and seeing you."

"Life doesn't remain static. It always changes," said Dr. Elmore.

"Can you believe that Chaplain Evens picked me for his chapel assistant? I never expected an opportunity of this importance." Matthew trusted Dr. Elmore. He knew this wise man would give him good advice, and he was ready to lay several problems in his lap, expecting his sensible counsel.

"I *can* believe it. Matthew, you're qualified for it."

"Is that true? Last night, I sat for hours trying to develop several ideas just in case I had to lead chapel. I'm not sure any of them are good. I guess I'm worried about falling on my face and failing at my new job. Why did I jump at this chance? What if I get up there and freeze? Who am I to tell others about Christ and life?" Matthew dropped his head after he finished.

"You've started to doubt yourself?" asked Dr. Elmore.

"Yes, I have, and that's something I've never done before." Matthew was shaking his head from side to side. "Even when I was recuperating from the bear attack or facing the fact that Uncle Lazarus was gone, I always knew I'd make it through. This worries me."

Dr. Elmore smiled. "Standing up in front of several hundred people is different from a classroom recitation, especially if you've never done it before. That would scare me, too."

Matthew looked up at his mentor. "I'm really worried that I'll fail," he said with conviction.

"Look here, the first thing I want you to do is eliminate the word worry from your vocabulary. Replace it with wonder. Now say, I wonder what God has in store for me, or I wonder what He wants me to learn from this new opportunity. Go ahead, say it. Emphasize the word *wonder*."

Matthew cautiously repeated Dr. Elmore's words. "I *wonder* what God has in store for me . . . I *wonder* what He wants me to learn from this new opportunity."

"When you use wonder, you start expecting something *won-der-ful* at the end of your problem or predicament. I don't think leading out in chapel is a problem for you. You'll do fine. Now, give yourself a chance to do just that." Dr. Elmore was standing in front of Matthew and smiling. He placed his hand on the young man's shoulder. "I know how you feel. I was once there too. One step at a time, my friend. Take it one step at a time."

"But, Dr. Elmore, your grasp of the Bible is deeper than anyone else I know, including my father. I wonder," Matthew emphasized the word, "I *wonder* if I'll ever understand it like you do today."

"Matthew, we all start at the same place. It doesn't matter if we're young or old or if we have multiple college degrees. Once we feel the tug of the Holy Spirit, we must make a decision, to believe in Christ or not to have faith in Him. Once that decision is made, our journey in life takes a different course."

"I understand that, Dr. Elmore, and for me the decision to follow Christ was made at thirteen. Two years later, God called me to be a minister. Somehow, I haven't made the progress in understanding the Word that I thought I would make."

"Remember, we start as babes on milk and work our way up to solid food. No one understands without a lot of study, meditation, and waiting on Him to reveal His ideas to us. I didn't know anymore than you at your age, but many years of listening to Christ at the urging of the Holy Spirit increased my knowledge of Him."

"What do you suggest that I do?"

Dr. Elmore thought for a moment and then he said, "Matthew, there's head knowledge and then there's heart knowledge.

"Okay," said Matthew, waiting for the former professor to continue.

"You can get head knowledge here at Maryville College. Learning Greek and Latin, reading background information, geography and studying the customs of the day helps to set the scene of biblical stories. Commentaries give you information on each individual verse and scenarios or thoughts you might use in your exposition to your audience. You can also pick up examples from lives of people to use in reinforcing your thought. Read the struggles and views of the early church fathers and other pastor's sermons."

"I understand," said Matthew. "What is heart knowledge?"

"Heart knowledge comes from immersing yourself in His love. People who believe in God never attain a complete love for Him, all except Jesus, but that doesn't give us an excuse to quit trying or to quit growing. We become what we love."

"What do you mean a complete love?"

"There are many facets to this statement. Give Him your undivided attention. That's the best way to show love to anyone, including our Lord and Savior. In other words, put yourself in His presence. Enter your closet for prayer and slam the door, shutting everything else out. Seek a closeness that comes from Bible reading and prayer. Study the words of Jesus. Say them out loud. There isn't a word in the Bible that God didn't intend to be there. Study them singularly. Ask yourself, why did He put it there?"

Dr. Elmore paused to collect his thoughts. "The Word says we are to become like Him. Isn't it reasonable to think as we become more like Him that we will understand more of God's Word? That's Word with a capital W. The Word is Jesus."

Matthew was getting excited. Dr. Elmore was speaking about ideas he'd never considered. He nodded his head. "Please keep going."

"Go to the foot of the cross and meditate on the sufferings of Christ while He hangs there. Picture His suffering. My mentor as a young lad, Dr. John Marshall, once said to me, 'Go to the cross, linger there awhile, look deep into His eyes.' I might add, feel His love. Let it surround you."

"I wish I were perfect. I feel so unworthy. Maybe that's what I was feeling," said Matthew, examining his feelings. "My imperfection, my pitiful attempt to be like Him."

"Don't we all. Read King David's life interposed with the Psalms. One minute he was on the top of the world. The next he was in the pits. He was a terrible sinner, but he was also a man who had God's heart. David always gives me loads of confidence."

Dr. Elmore continued, "Christ is always there waiting for your presence. Remember that. We can't overlook the Holy Spirit who is our comforter and teacher here on earth. He reveals Christ's love to us and illumines the scriptures. Pray for His intervention in your thoughts."

"Finally, all of this requires discipline. Seek a time or times in your daily life to interact with Him, one on one." He added for emphasis, "And did I say shut everything out, empty your mind, and wait on Him to fill it with thoughts."

"Matthew, heart knowledge comes from the throne of God. It flows like the life-giving water from God's dwelling place. There's one other thing, God will reveal only what you can understand and apply to your life. What He reveals to you will bless the lives of those around you."

After the old teacher finished, Matthew felt like he was standing on holy ground. "I don't know what to say, but that my Christianity is very shallow."

"I've followed Christ for many years, but I still feel the same way as you do right now. Would you like for me to pray for you, my dear, young friend?"

"Yes sir, I would."

The elderly pastor, who shepherded one of the major colleges in the south, placed his hands on Matthew's head. After the prayer, Dr. Elmore covered his silver hair with his hat and said, "Come, Matthew, let's go to the chapel."

∽

Matthew followed his lead.

They walked down one of the aisles toward the stage. "Take a book and mount the platform," said the former teacher.

Matthew did as he was told.

"Now read to me out of the book." Dr. Elmore sat down in an aisle seat to listen.

After Matthew finished reading, Dr. Elmore said, "You see, the sky didn't fall on you. My suggestion is that you come here each day and practice. That will do you the most good and help you overcome your fear of the audience."

Matthew came down from the podium and embraced his counselor. "Thank you, Sir. Today's words will inspire me the rest of my life."

"They're good words, Matthew. Words that I learned from people more gifted than I. They'll never fail you."

"There is one more thing I need to talk to you about. Do you have time?"

"Sure." Dr. Elmore realized that Matthew had several nagging questions he'd stored up for some time. They sat down in two chairs at the back of the auditorium. "What's on your mind?"

Matthew swiveled in his seat, leaned forward, and looked earnestly at the pastor, "You met Alice last year when we went to the concert together."

"Yes, she seems like a nice young lady."

"I'm sure our relationship could escalate to an engagement. I know this would make her happy. But for some reason I'm not comfortable with the possibility of marriage, at least to her. I don't know why."

"Matthew, if there's any hesitation about a future with her, you'd better be careful. Wait until you're sure she's the one for you. Don't make a mistake and think attraction is love. Or because she is beautiful and all the males are after her, that she's the right one. Be very careful. Wait until you are sure and without doubt."

"How do you know you're in love?" Matthew was embarrassed to ask the question.

Dr. Elmore wanted to laugh, but he didn't. Matthew was serious. Instead he said, "If you have to ask, I'd say you're not. But-t-t, give her a little more time. Something will happen to tell you whether or not. That's one question you must decide for yourself."

"Okay, I'll be careful."

"Will I see you at church on Sunday?"

"Yes. I'm bringing Ollie and Tim."

Dr. Elmore stood up and looked at his pocket watch. It was late afternoon. "My how time flies when you're engaged in important discussions."

"Thank you, Sir. I'll see you Sunday."

~

Matthew walked from the chapel to Court Street. His burden was lighter after talking with Dr. Elmore, but he was exhausted after the day's events.

Whew. I can't wait to get home and rest.

Tomorrow was Saturday and Alice would be moving into her dormitory. In her last letter, she had asked for his help.

I should go and help her.

Matthew was lost in his thoughts when a small voice startled him. The young child he'd seen the day before played in the landscaping by the road.

"Hi Mister, my name's Matty," he said, approaching and holding out his hand. He carried a hand-carved toy. It was a beautiful rendition of a red fire engine.

Matthew stopped in his tracks and smiled at the little boy. The lady from yesterday was bent over, weeding a flower bed by the side of the house.

"My name's Matthew," he said bending over to shake Matty's hand. "What have you got there?" Matthew pointed to the toy.

"Don't you know? It's a fire engine," answered Matty, offering it to Matthew.

Matthew noticed the young lady had stopped weeding the flower bed. She stood up and was watching her charge's activities.

"I really like it. Who made it for you?"

"My papaw Chuck."

"He did a wonderful job."

"Ma-tew, are you goin' to school?" Matty had trouble pronouncing the "th" and the "sw" sounds and sometimes "r". Otherwise he could speak very well.

"No, I'm coming from school," Matthew squatted down so he could be on the same level as his new acquaintance.

"But my mama said you were goin' to school," insisted Matty.

Matthew laughed and glanced toward the woman. "Okay, in the morning, I'm going to school. In the afternoon, I'm coming from school. This is the afternoon. Do you understand?"

"Maybe," said Matty as Matthew handed his toy back.

"How old are you, Matty?"

"I'm not quite free."

"Oh, do you mean three?"

"No, I'm free."

"Okay, so you're free. Do you live here with your mama and daddy?"

"I live here wit' my mama and Aunt Mary and Uncle John."

"What's your mama's name?"

"It's mama. Don't you know any-ting?"

Meanwhile, "Mama" was catching bits and pieces of the conversation. She decided it was time to rescue Matthew. She walked over and took Matty by the hand. The faint smell of her perfume floated in the air.

"I'm sorry if my little boy is bothering you," she said, putting a finger to her lips as a signal for Matty to hush.

Matty didn't. "Mama," he said, pulling on his mother's hand to get her attention. "I'm not a little boy. I'm a big boy. Uncle John says so."

"Matty, go to the house," ordered his mother, jabbing her finger in that direction.

"Bye, Mister Ma-tew." Matty headed for the house, the siren on his fire truck blaring to its full capacity. The siren stopped. "Mama, I want some squeet milk."

"Okay, I'll get it for you in a minute. Wait on the porch," responded his mother.

"He never meets a stranger," said his mother.

"I'm Matthew Tipton, and he wasn't bothering me. In fact, I was enjoying the conversation," said Matthew, sticking out his hand as he introduced himself. *She looks vaguely familiar*, he thought. *Something about her . . . I don't know.*

Abigail knew Matthew immediately. A pained look passed over her face as she remembered another time and place.

"I'm Abigail. Matty and I live here with my aunt and uncle."

"It's nice to meet you, Abigail." Her eyes held him.

Matthew stood in front of her at a loss for words. Her eyes were so familiar, beautiful and brown with long, sweeping lashes. Her makeup was applied with expertise. Her thick, wavy hair was neatly coiffed and her oh-so-slim body was dressed in the latest fashion.

Where have I met her?

He cleared his throat.

He felt awkward.

Little boyish.

"I'll be going," he said and headed for the road.

Why does she make me feel so ill at ease?

Matthew looked toward the porch as he walked away.

Matty waved goodbye.

❧ Chapter Thirty-Four ❧

Maryville College, Alice Arrives — Matthew

Saturday morning seemed like it would never come.

Raining softly.

The rain of early fall.

The kind of rain common to the Smokies after several hours of gentle wind.

Matthew heard it softly sighing through his open bedroom window. Then the rustle was accompanied with the drip, drip of the rain on aged, soon to be cast-off leaves. He snuggled deeper into his warm, single bed, pulling the covers up to his ears.

At eight, Matthew headed to Pastor Evens home. It had stopped raining, but the leaden skies threatened to drop more. The two went over his chapel ideas, which passed muster with flying colors.

Confidence.

Confidence in his ability to produce the thoughts his chaplain needed was sown in his heart. He received the Bible scriptures for the following week and the schedule for the special service on Monday. He saw that his name was on the schedule for the scripture reading and final prayer.

President Wilson would officiate. Dr. Elmore would give the address and Chaplain Evens, the closing remarks. He was among friends.

Chaplin Evens suggested that he compose his prayer before hand. He would not be as nervous if he knew what he was going to say. Matthew intended to heed his advice.

He headed for the library where he planned to meet Tim and study until Alice arrived before noon. As he walked through the campus, the bright sun shone through a break in the clouds.

"What did Pastor Evens say about your suggestions?" Tim whispered as soon as he saw him.

"He liked every one of them and gave me some plans for proceeding. I have a book to study for the first one." Matthew held it up. "He wants me to give the devotion on Friday, even though he won't be gone."

"What's the title of that one?" asked Tim, wondering why Dr. Evens had given up his role so easily. "It must be very pertinent to school."

"Good guess," Matthew responded, "How about 'Why Go to Chapel'?"

"That's certainly original . . . and simple."

"What do you *mean* simple?" Matthew felt annoyed that his friend had touched on a subject that initially bothered him. He'd wondered at the importance of his down-to-earth suggestion.

"Uncomplicated, basic . . ."

"You're *digging* your hole a little deeper."

"Maybe I mean . . . I don't believe the subject's been raised the three years we've been here. The curriculum says, 'You are required to attend chapel in the morning but not at night.' I don't remember sentences about why."

"It's in there," said Matthew. "I looked it up, but *some* people have a tendency to gloss over what they feel are unimportant facets of college life. I thought I'd give our students a better, more in-depth reason to come," said Matthew. "The subject's complicated."

"I can't wait," Tim said, ducking his head back into the book he was studying. "Of course, it's a little late for me." Two eyes stared at Matthew over the edge of the book.

~

The two continued to study in a quiet truce until time to help Alice.

"We'd better go before eleven just in case she's early," Matthew said in a whisper. He started to collect his books.

"Why don't we leave them here? We can come back and study later," suggested Tim. "I don't want to lug them around."

"Good plan," agreed Matthew. "We'll pick them up after we meet Squeaky."

~

Tim and Matthew arrived at Baldwin Hall at ten-thirty.

Sitting in wicker chairs at the entrance turned out to be a bad decision. Every student and parent thought they were bellhops and asked for their help. Soon the two men were toting luggage, potted plants, and a menagerie of other supplies. One young lady brought her own desk, which Matthew and Tim hauled up two flights of stairs.

"Let's take the backstairs down to the ground floor, so we won't have to be pack rats for anyone else," said Tim. He was rolling his eyes, breathing hard, and leaning against the stair rail.

When Matthew could catch his breath he said, "We could do that, but we might miss Alice."

"What's so important about that?" teased Tim.

Matthew gave him a friendly poke in the ribs.

The two tote men were heading for the stairs with another co-ed's luggage when they heard a familiar voice.

"What do you mean carrying another woman's luggage?" asked Alice, a vision in a hot pink outfit. She was smiling and standing with her hands on her hips. She ran to Matthew and threw herself at him with such force that he staggered backward and dropped the two bags he was holding. She wrapped her arms around his neck and tried to kiss him on the mouth. Matthew turned his head in time for her lips to land on his cheek and held her at arm's length.

"Here, let me look at you," he said to cover his embarrassment.

If Alice was disappointed at her reception, she didn't show it. Instead, she turned her attention to Matthew's friend.

"Tim, it's good to see you."

"Same here," said Tim. "Who brought you?"

"My father. He's unloading the car."

"Alice, we need to take these bags to the second floor. We'll be right back." Before Alice could answer, Matthew turned toward the stairs with Tim on his heels.

"Man, what's wrong with you? That wasn't much of a reception for your intended," he exclaimed. "Why didn't you kiss her?"

"She's not my intended, at least not yet." He rubbed at the lipstick Alice smeared on his face. Intimacy was something he hadn't pursued in their relationship.

Matthew didn't say another word about the matter, although Tim continued to press the issue. They headed back to the lobby.

Alice's bags were piled outside the entrance door. Mr. Davis stood beside his automobile talking to his daughter.

"If you need anything at all, don't hesitate to call me at the bank," he said.

"Father, I know that, and I will call," said Alice. "Here's Matthew. He and Tim will help me carry my things to my room. You don't need to help."

"Matthew, good to meet you," said Mr. Davis. "Alice jabbered all summer about you. She must have written a box full of letters."

My daughter has good tastes in men, tall, dark, handsome, and blue-eyed.

"Yes sir, I'm pleased to finally meet you." The two men shook hands.

"And this is . . ."asked Mr. Davis.

Tim extended his hand. "Tim Brackett, Sir. Matthew's best man."

Matthew shot a dagger at Tim as Mr. Davis said, "Hello, Tim."

I'm going to throttle him one day. I hope Alice didn't hear that.

Alice was busy sorting through her luggage. "What room are you in, Alice?" After helping the others, Matthew and Tim knew the routine.

"I'll find out. There's Clara! Dad, you need to move so Clara's dad can pull in to unload." An excited Alice headed for her friend. "And Marsha's right behind her," she exclaimed.

Mr. Davis pulled over into a visitor parking space.

Clara jumped out of the car. She was joined by Marsha and a crazy scene of hugging and hellos took place.

"Looks like we'll be here for awhile," Mr. Davis said after walking back to the entrance of Baldwin Hall.

Matthew, Tim, and Mr. Davis sat down in the wicker chairs until Alice's friends started to unload their cars. The luggage was piled onto the sidewalk.

In the confusion that followed, bags were taken to the wrong rooms, but the conscripted bellhops decided the girls could straighten it out later. The classmates were all on the second floor.

"Thank goodness, we didn't have to carry another desk up to the top floor," said Tim after the last bag was safely on the second one. He flopped down onto a wicker chair where unloading continued.

"Tim, I don't think that's a good place to sit unless you plan on moving more luggage." Matthew was finished with moving heavy suitcases.

Alice and Mr. Davis came out of the entrance. "Remember . . ."

"Yes, Dad, I'll call if I need anything." Alice gave her father a kiss, and Tim and Matthew said their goodbyes to him.

Mr. Davis walked across the parking lot, started his car, and drove off, waving as he passed them at the front door.

Matthew suddenly remembered he was to meet Squeaky for dinner at Baldwin Hall. He and Tim needed to hurry. No need in telling Alice about his new friend. She'd have a whole bunch of questions about him.

"Alice, I'll see you tomorrow afternoon, after church," said Matthew. "I'm sure you need to unpack and visit with your friends, and I have studying to do."

"Can't I go to church with you?" she asked, raising soulful, begging eyes to his. She'd seen her mother use this tactic with her father, when her mother wanted results.

"We'll go next Sunday."

Alice didn't argue.

~

Tim and Matthew walked at a rapid pace toward Baldwin Hall.

"A shoebox full of letters, huh," said Tim.

"Don't start, my friend."

~

When Matthew jumped back at her attempted kiss, Alice's heart had turned stone cold. But, when she heard Tim's comment about being best man, her heart skipped several beats.

Matthew must be talking to Tim about our future relationship.

She pretended to rummage through her luggage so her countenance wouldn't show her excitement. She would bide her time. Not force the issue unless it became necessary. Things were looking up.

Wonder what studying he's doing? School hasn't started yet.

~

Abigail sat on the front porch watching Matty play. Seeing Matthew had dredged up long repressed emotions of that day long ago; bitterness she didn't wish to revisit. She ran her tongue over the scar on the inside of her mouth. It was rough and lumpy. For the millionth time, she tasted the blood and felt the pain of the attack.

"Mama, look I've found a worm in the grass." Matty ran toward her on his short, chubby legs. Abigail wondered how such an evil act could produce someone so wonderful.

"I see, sweetheart."

Matty laid the wriggling, red worm gently in his mother's hand. "Go find another one."

"Okay, I will." Matty headed back toward the area where he'd found the first worm. Several minutes lapsed as he searched in the wet grass and landscaping.

"Look under a rock," called his mother, watching from the porch.

It was hard enough dealing with her emotions after her rape without finding out she would have a child by her attacker. It was almost like being attacked twice. At first, she was angry.

So angry.

Angry at her father.

Herself, Kitty.

The whole world.

Angry at the man who raped her.

Her trips into the forest were filled with shouting against the criminal act perpetrated against her. And then, she was angry because she was pregnant. There were people in the mountains who dealt with unwanted pregnancies. She could get rid of the unwanted child if she decided to.

Those thoughts changed the minute she felt the baby move. Something happened. She fell in love with her unborn child. At that moment, she pledged to give it her full devotion and love.

She was sure marriage and an extended family was out for her. No man in his right mind would want a soiled woman for a wife, especially one with a baby. She set her heart to remain single her entire life.

Matty started picking up rocks and soon he found a small, wiggling red worm.

"Mama, I found a baby one." He was so engrossed in keeping the tiny specimen from falling out of his hand that he tripped on a maple tree root sticking up out of the ground. Down he went. Arms outstretched. He immediately started bawling.

Abigail rushed off the porch to her child's side. She picked him up from the ground and brushed him off.

Matty continued bawling. "I lost my worm," he cried.

"You've also got a boo-boo on your knee."

Matty looked down at the blood on his knee and bawled even louder, if that was possible.

"I thought you told me you're a big boy. I don't think big boys bawl like you. What do you think?"

Matty's cries decreased to a whimper. "But Mama, it hurts.

"Let's go in and put a bandage on it. Maybe Uncle John will give you a quarter for your boo-boo."

Abigail and Matty went into the house.

～

A few minutes later, Matthew walked past. He looked in the direction of the porch. He was disappointed that Matty and Abigail were nowhere in sight.

He was also disappointed with himself.

Why did I mention taking Alice to church the following Sunday?

She didn't know about Ollie, and Matthew wondered how she would react to his blind friend.

Will Alice be repulsed by him? But I shouldn't be concerned. As a pastor's wife, Alice must have compassion on those with physical handicaps.

"I still wonder how she will respond," he said to himself.

Matthew shook his head. *Oh, well. The damage has been done. No use in making a problem out of a situation that may not happen.*

I won't tell Ollie until next week. Tomorrow, we'll enjoy our Sunday together.

❧ Chapter Thirty-Five ❧

The Chapel and Matty — Matthew

On Monday morning, Matthew sat on the stage waiting to read the selected scripture. Chapel was the only college function scheduled today. It was primarily used to familiarize the new students to current and new curriculum. New professors would be introduced to the students. All teachers would be in office that afternoon for conferences with any student needing advice.

The opening chapel meeting was normally longer and from looking at the schedule, Matthew realized today wouldn't be different than the other three years he'd attended.

He watched as President Wilson walked to the podium and gave the opening prayer. The President welcomed several hundred students. After going through a list of announcements and making the faculty introductions and new curriculum offerings, he introduced Matthew and shook his hand as he moved to the microphone to read the scripture lesson of the day. It was Matthew 6:25-34.

> *"Therefore I say unto you, Take no thought for your life, what ye shall eat, or what ye shall drink; nor yet for your body, what ye shall put*

on. Is not the life more than meat, and the body than raiment? Behold the fowls of the air: for they sow not, neither do they reap, nor gather into barns; yet your heavenly Father feedeth them. Are ye not much better than they? Which of you by taking thought can add one cubit unto his stature? And why take ye thought for raiment? Consider the lilies of the field, how they grow; they toil not, neither do they spin: And yet I say unto you, That even Solomon in all his glory was not arrayed like one of these. Wherefore, if God so clothe the grass of the field, which today is, and tomorrow is cast into the oven, shall he not much more clothe you, O ye of little faith? Therefore take no thought, saying, What shall we eat? or, What shall we drink? or, Wherewithal shall we be clothed? (For after all these things do the Gentiles seek:) for your heavenly Father knoweth that ye have need of all these things. But seek ye first the kingdom of God, and his righteousness; and all these things shall be added unto you. Take therefore no thought for the morrow: for the morrow shall take thought for the things of itself. Sufficient unto the day is the evil thereof."

After reading the scripture, Matthew's next action was to introduce Dr. Elmore, whose list of credentials was impressive. "And now, I give you the Chairman of the Board of Directors and my friend, Dr. Edgar Elmore. Sir, on behalf of the students, we are honored to have you address us today." Matthew turned around as Dr. Elmore approached.

"Matthew, the roof didn't fall on you," he whispered and extended his hand. The genuine affection between the two men was obvious and noted by Chaplain Evens.

"No sir, it sure didn't." Matthew smiled at him and shook his hand.

The gist of Dr. Elmore's message was to take one day at a time. "Today you will make hundreds of choices and think thousands of thoughts. There isn't time for tomorrow's challenges."

He finished with, "Don't give up. Today may be everything you expected. The next one may not. Start each day with prayer and Bible reading, attend chapel, and don't worry. Instead, wonder what God has in store for you right now. Our hope is in the future, but we prepare for it each new day of our lives. Live this day to the fullest. *'Oh ye of little faith,'* today trust that He knows best. After all, He does."

Dr. Elmore returned to his chair, and Chaplain Evens got up to conclude the rest of the meeting. The chaplain feigned a cough when passing the Chairman of the Board. There was no friendly handshake.

Matthew's prayer was the last item on the schedule. Because of Dr. Elmore's address on living one day at a time, he changed his focus a little.

When he said, "Amen," Matthew's first chapel was over.

Those on the platform made it a point to shake Matthew's hand, including Dr. Elmore and Chaplain Evens.

"Tomorrow we will settle into a regular chapel schedule," said Pastor Evens. "See if you can have Friday's devotion by Wednesday so I can look over it."

"I didn't realize you were going to be gone on Friday, Evens," said Dr. Elmore.

"Oh, I won't, but Matthew's topic is relevant to this week, and although I didn't know it, ties right in to your address. I decided Saturday that he should give it soon.

"Well, Matthew what's the title?" asked Dr. Elmore, putting his arm around his young friend.

"It's '*Why Go to Chapel*,'" Dr. Evens answered before Matthew could respond. He had singled out Matthew, and he intended to steer him through his final year.

That was impolite. He should have let Matthew reply, thought Dr. Elmore. "I'd planned to go back home on Thursday, but I'll stay until Friday and leave for Chattanooga on the afternoon train. I want to hear you speak." Dr. Elmore looked at Matthew and mouthed the words. "I'll help."

Dr. Even's jealous nature, although he tried to hide it from those around him, was obvious to Dr. Elmore. The director didn't know if the problem concerned him personally or was directed at others also. This wasn't the first time.

~

Matthew stepped off the platform. Tim and Alice were waiting.

"You were great," was Alice's response. *I might want to set my sights on a larger church.*

"I can truthfully say that I'm glad it's over," said Matthew, breathing a sigh of relief. "Tomorrow we'll start our normal services. And Friday, Dr. Evens and I'll reverse rolls, and I'll give the devotion."

Alice grabbed his arm. "We should celebrate, don't you think, Tim? We have the rest of the day. Let's go into town and get a soda. Here comes Marsha. She can go with us. Hey, Marsha," Alice called.

The foursome set off for Maryville Café. It was the watering hole for college students and filled to capacity after the chapel service. Alice clung to Matthew, marking her territory. She intended to make sure no other female got any ideas. Her objective was so obvious that several girls snickered at her on the far side of the room, but no one approached.

Matthew felt uncomfortable; smothered might have been a better word, as he sat on a stool at the soda counter. They sipped on ice-cream sodas and made small talk for several minutes until Matthew suggested returning to the library to study so he could work on his presentation for Friday.

"We'll all go," said Alice, looking at Marsha.

Why did I open my big mouth? Now I won't get any work done.

The library was Matthew's last refuge. Now it would be inhabited by two females. He looked at Tim, who seemed to be getting along famously with Marsha.

"Marsha and I are ready to go, aren't we?" said Tim with a smirk on his face.

"Sure. I need to check out a book." Marsha was making eyes at Tim, and he was obviously enjoying it.

Matthew stood up, putting action to his words.

Maybe the girls could do something else. Let's see…

"Are you unpacked, Alice?" he said

"I'm completely done."

"How about you, Marsha?" said Matthew.

"Me too."

Matthew didn't see the slight kick Alice gave her friend under the counter.

Guess that wasn't such a swell idea. They're the only two females at the college who have everything in place.

"Okay, I'm heading for the library to study." Matthew walked out the door with Alice hanging onto his arm.

~

Matthew was tired that afternoon after a full day at school. The last three days had left him drained of emotion. He would've passed Matty up except the little boy saw him coming and ran to greet him.

"Ma-tew, I've got a boo-hoo."

Matthew threw his head back and laughed, relieving the tension he felt. Even though he was tired, seeing his young friend perked him up.

"I think that's a boo-boo," said Matthew, picking up the little lad and holding him over his head.

Matty giggled.

Matthew put him down on the ground. "How did you get a boo-boo?"

"A worm did it."

"What! A worm did it. I've never seen a worm make a boo-boo. Are you sure you didn't fall? Tell me the whole story." Matthew sat down on the grass at the edge of the driveway, positive this would take a while and felt the sun, warm on his shoulders.

Matty started to sit down but ended up flat on his back.

"Matty, that's not a bad position. I think I'll join you." Matthew stretched out on the green grass to listen to the little boy's story. He threw his arms over his head and crossed his legs, looking at the white, puffy clouds floating across the sky. The bright sun made hovering shadows of the wisps.

Bare skin, eyes closed.

Grass soft and cool.

If I'm not careful, I'll be asleep.

"Ma-tew, are you asleep?" asked Matty after he finished his narrative.

"No. I'm just restin' my eyes. I heard your story," responded Matthew. "What happened to the worm?"

"It fell. Let's to go see if we can find it" Matty started to sit up, but Matthew put out his arm, easing him back to the ground.

"I'm not much of a worm hunter," said Matthew, *or anything else at this moment,* he thought to himself. Matty stretched back out beside him.

"Do you see those clouds, Matty?" asked Matthew, pointing to the sky and changing the subject. "We might have rain tomorrow."

"Where does rain come from?" asked the little boy.

Whew, how can I explain that? I'm not used to relating scientific processes to little children.

"Uh...the clouds suck water from the air." Matthew pointed to the clouds, waved his hand around above his head, and made a sucking sound with his mouth.

Matty was watching, completely absorbed and forming his mouth to make Matthew's sucking sound.

"Then they suck water from the ground and air." He pointed to the ground and made the same sucking sound. "Once the water gets into the clouds, they get really heavy and the rain falls to the ground." That was the same explanation his mother had told him, well almost.

Matty looked intently at the clouds. "Ma-tew, where's its mou-t."

What on earth am I going to say? Think fast, Matthew!

"Matty, look at my head. What's this?" Matthew pointed to his eyes.

"Eyes," responded Matty.

"What's this?"

"Nose."

"What's this?" Matthew pointed to his mouth.

"Mou-t."

"Now look here." Matthew turned his head. "Do you see a mouth here?" He felt the back of his head.

"No."

"We can't see a mouth because we're looking at the back of the cloud. Do you understand?" asked Matthew, well-pleased with himself.

"Maybe," said Matty.

Matthew was wondering if that was a standard answer with Matty, when he heard a muffled laugh from the porch. Turning over on his side, he saw Abigail sitting in a chair partially hidden by shrubbery growing on the lawn. His face flushed, and he felt warm all over.

"Sorry," she said. "I couldn't stand it anymore." Abigail stood up and walked to the edge of the porch. Matthew's heart skipped a beat. She was a vision in a red dress that brought out her tanned skin, dark hair, and especially, her eyes. When she smiled, as she was doing, white, even teeth appeared between her lightly-colored lips. She was holding an embroidery hoop.

Abigail's beautiful.

"That was a rather unusual explanation about rain."

"It's based on what my mother told me years ago," said Matthew on the defense. He felt ill-at-ease, again.

319

"Matty's at the how, why, and where stage in life." Abigail apologized for her son's questioning attitude as she floated down the steps. "This can be a little maddening."

"I love it," said Matthew. "He's a bright little boy. You should be proud of him."

"Oh, I am, and I agree with you, he is very intelligent." Abigail continued down the driveway toward the two prone figures.

Matthew noticed she'd tucked the hoop under her arm.

"Do you plan on lying on your back long?" She was laughing at him, again.

I do look ridiculous.

Matthew pulled his long frame into a sitting position and then stood up. He reached down to help Matty up.

"Are you leaving, Ma-tew? We didn't play." Matty was hurt, and he looked like he would start bawling. Matty never cried, he bawled.

"Some other time, my little friend. Your mother's insulted me." Matthew said this in his most insulted voice.

"Mama!" said Matty in his most indignant voice. "You made Ma-tew mad."

"Mr. Tipton, I certainly didn't intend to offend you. Please accept my apology." Abigail said this formally and bowed. She knew Matthew was teasing — or was he flirting? She couldn't be sure. "Please come back and play with Matty."

"Since you've apologized, I will."

Matty stood silently watching his mother and Matthew talk back and forth. The conversation progressed rapidly, and he didn't quite understand what was going on. But he realized that Matthew was coming back later to play.

"Oh boy, Ma-tew's coming to play." Matty was jumping up and down.

"I must say playing is high on my agenda." Matthew smiled, showing his dimples.

Abigail laughed. "Playing with Matty won't get you a degree, but it might get you a hug from a swell little guy. I think I'd take the hug."

"I believe you're right," said Matthew.

When Matty heard hugging mentioned, he held up his arms to Matthew.

"Matty gives good hugs and kisses," he said. "Aunt Mary says so."

Matthew picked him up and two fat little arms were wrapped around his neck. A wet, slobbery kiss was placed on his cheek. This was followed by a loud smack.

"I think you've stolen my Matty's heart," said Abigail. "He's never taken to anyone quite this fast."

Matthew gave Matty a kiss on his forehead and handed the little boy to his mother. He felt the same tenderness toward Matty that he'd felt toward his Uncle Lazarus and a strange stirring in his heart for Matty's mother.

Ah, perfume.

The smell of her perfume lingered in the air.

"I'll try to come by soon, Matty. See you later, Abigail." Why did he have thoughts about Abigail? He was seeing another girl. It wouldn't do for him to be attracted to her.

Matthew walked down the street. Matty and Abigail were waving when he turned at the corner to say goodbye. At that moment, Squeaky appeared from the college woods.

"Wait up, Matthew." The two covered the distance to their home together.

～

Abigail watched Matthew go. She wondered what he would think if he knew that Matty was named after him and his Papaw. The little boy's full name was Matthew Charles White.

～

The next morning, it was pouring rain as Matthew went to school. He had to run to keep from being late to chapel.

The rest of the week flew by as Maryville College classes started in earnest. On Friday afternoon, Matthew went by to see Ollie and make sure his friend would be going to church on Sunday.

"Ollie, we will have a visitor this Sunday."

"We will, who?"

"Her name is Alice Davis from Knoxville. She's a classmate at college and a good friend. I hope that's okay with you," responded Matthew, dreading the next question.

"Is she your girlfriend?" asked Mrs. Miller who came through the kitchen door at that moment. She baked, boiled, or fried foodstuff most of the day. Some of her products were sold to regular customers who stopped by the house to pick up items. She was expecting one of her customers momentarily. "Well, Matthew," she prodded.

"Let me put it this way, she's a girl and she's a friend. I suppose you could combine the two into girlfriend."

"Well, glory be," said Mrs. Miller. "Do you have any plans to ask for her hand in marriage?"

Matthew chuckled. "None at present. I'm not sure she's the girl for me."

～

On Sunday, Matthew walked from his boarding house to Baldwin Hall. He buzzed Alice's room on the intercom and heard her voice.

"I'm not quite ready. I only need five minutes," she said.

"Hurry or we'll be late. Did you forget the time I said I'd arrive?" asked Matthew.

"No, I'm running late." Alice had stayed up the night before playing cards with Marsha, Clara, and another roommate. Hauling her body out of bed proved more difficult than she planned. She was still tired and grouchy.

When she finally appeared, she was twenty minutes late. This meant they wouldn't arrive at punctual Ollie's on time. Matthew was angry.

"We'll have to hurry to get to church," he said, the tone of his voice indicated his disappointment. This was the first time in the months Matthew and Ollie had gone to church that he'd be late.

"Why?" asked Alice. "It's only a short walk up Court Street and Broadway. We'll still be early."

"We have to make a detour and pick up my friend, Ollie Miller. He's going with us. He always goes with me on Sunday morning." Matthew was walking rapidly toward the street Ollie lived on.

Alice started to huff and puff, physically and emotionally. "Why didn't you tell me this?" she retorted, against her better judgment. She always handled Matthew with caution. Kid gloves, actually. She tried not to show him the impatient side of her personality.

"I would've if I'd known you were going to be late. I thought I would surprise you." They were at the path leading to Ollie's house.

"Well, you certainly did that. Who is this Ollie character any way?"

Matthew didn't have time to answer. Ollie stood at the door.

"I'm sorry I'm late," said Matthew.

"I've been worried that something happened to you, my friend." Ollie had heard Alice's comments as the couple came up the drive.

"I'm okay, Ollie. Let me introduce Alice Davis. She's the one I told you about." Matthew took Alice by the arm and steered her up the steps.

Alice extended her hand. At the same time, she saw Ollie's eyes. She recoiled and was in the process of withdrawing her hand when Matthew said, "Alice wants to shake hands with you." Matthew grasped her arm and pushed her hand into Ollie's. After making him late, she wasn't about to insult his friend.

"I'm pleased to meet you, Alice. Matthew's friends are my friends." Ollie was exploring her hand with his fingers, as he did when shaking Matthew's and Tim's hands.

"Likewise, I'm sure," said Alice pulling her hand out of Ollie's grasp, a shudder running down her body.

I won't touch the blind man again, and he's certainly not going to touch me. The sooner I get Matthew out of these situations the better.

When Matthew saw her shudder at Ollie's eyes, he wondered how she would react at the sight of the scars on his body. Scars she could not see, because they were hidden by his clothes.

"Let's go to church, Ollie." Matthew led his friend down the steps and out to the curb. Alice had to fend for herself. The threesome set off down the road with Alice lagging behind.

"Will we be very late, Matthew?" asked Ollie.

"Not if we walk fast, my friend."

"Okay."

Alice pouted the rest of the day.

On Monday after chapel, Alice apologized profusely and grabbed Matthew's arm. They walked together to the library and stayed there until Matthew's first class.

❧ **Chapter Thirty-Six** ❧

The Routine at College — Matthew

Matthew's life settled into a routine; breakfast at the Hembree's, chapel, classes, dinner, more classes, and somewhere in between and after, studying in the library. On the way home, he often played with Matty. Sometimes he talked to Abigail and sometimes not. Squeaky Benson finished Pastor Even's bookcases and went back to Cades Cove to work on another job. The weeks flew by.

In late October, he ran into Abigail on a Friday in the Music Department at Voorhees Chapel.

"Abigail," he called down the hall.

She turned around and waved. He walked down the hall to meet her. She had a music book in her hand.

"Are you taking piano lessons?" He held out the same book for comparison.

"I am. Are you?" Abigail was smiling at him.

"I wanted to know how to read music. This seemed the simplest way. I plan on becoming a minister in Cades Cove, and thought I might need it."

"Really? You hadn't mentioned that before. Is this going to take place in the white-framed church you see off Rich Mountain Road?" Abigail spoke before she thought.

"Why yes, are you familiar with the area?"

I've got to be careful here, or Matthew might suspect who I am.

"I've been in the cove on a horse and hiked some of the area," she said matter-of- factly. That was the truth, although she could have added much more. "How many churches are there in the cove?"

"We have three at present." Not thinking there might be more to the subject, Matthew changed it. "How's Matty?" asked Matthew.

"He's great. He asks about you every day and looks for you in the afternoon. It won't be long until the weather will force him to play inside."

"I've been so busy this week, staying late and working on several ideas for class projects. Then there's my term paper due at the end of next year before I graduate and practicing for piano. Have you had piano lessons before?"

"No," Abigail continued, "I've always wanted to take lessons, and now that Matty's older I have time. Aunt Mary's girls can sit with him. I'm enjoying my study. How about you?"

"Mrs. Tate is a great teacher. She's very patient with me."

"You have Mrs. Tate, also. She must teach all the beginners. When's your lesson."

"It's at four, after my other classes. When's yours."

"At three, or is that free?" laughed Abigail, using Matty's speech.

Matthew had never seen Abigail so unreserved, alive, and passionate. Taking music agreed with her.

She's not a raving beauty like Alice, but she has an inner beauty that shines in her face and creates deep pools of brown in her eyes. Matthew felt like he could drown in their bottomless depths.

"Matthew," Abigail looked at him with a puzzled expression on her face. "For a minute there, I lost you."

"I was only thinkin'." *Yes, about how pretty you are when your defenses are down.* "Did you ask something?"

"I asked if you were headin' home. I thought we might walk together," said Abigail.

"Give me five minutes."

"Where are you going?" asked Abigail.

"To the chapel. Pastor Evens left me some papers to pick up on the podium. I need them for chapel tomorrow."

"I've never been in the chapel." Abigail continued, "Did you know our recital takes place there at the end of the school year? All piano students are required to play a memorized piece in the program. It's a required part of our lesson assignments."

"I know. Don't remind me. Come on, you can go with me." Matthew grabbed Abigail's hand and headed down the hall. In the chapel, he walked up the steps to the platform and retrieved his material.

Abigail looked around at the cavernous building with seats arranged in rows. The center section had thirty wooden seats from aisle to aisle, and the two outside rows had fifteen. From front to back she counted twenty rows.

"Well, what do you think?" asked Matthew, bounding down the steps.

"This is a huge room," said Alice. "I didn't dream it was so big."

"We have several hundred students in here each morning." He walked over to an aisle chair. "I used to sit there," Matthew pointed to a chair about five seats over. "Professor Nita Echols sat here." He tapped the chair he was standing against. "She took role and marked us absent or present."

"You have to come to chapel?" questioned Abigail.

"Yes, in the morning it's required, and you get demerits if you don't come."

"Where do you sit now?" asked Abigail.

Matthew pointed to the stage. "I read the scripture and have the closing prayer."

"You've never mentioned that."

"We've never stood in chapel together either," said Matthew.

"That's true."

"Are you ready to go?" asked Matthew.

"Yes," said Abigail, taking one last look around.

The two friends walked out of Voorhees Chapel and headed for Court Street. Matthew was busy talking about the piano lessons they were taking and his participation in the chapel services. He didn't notice Marsha and Clara sitting on a bench next to a huge hemlock tree that partially concealed them. He didn't see them put their heads together, get up, and head for Baldwin hall at a fast pace.

◈

Within fifteen minutes, Abigail and Matthew were at the colonial-style home where she lived. Matty was sitting in the window, looking for his mother to come home. He ran to the large front door and tried to open it up. It wouldn't budge.

"Oh my," said Abigail. "He'll be bawling in two seconds."

"No, he won't" said Matthew, rushing up the steps and opening the door. "Hi Matty," he said. "I've brought your mother home."

"Ma-tew, can you play?" was the only thought in Matty's head, and he was ready. He'd been playing the quiet game for several minutes, waiting for his mother to show up.

"Oh, Matty, I need to go home and study. I have lots of homework to do." Matthew patted the stack of books he carried.

"What's homework?"

Abigail started laughing. "You're going to regret opening that door. I need to go inside for a few minutes. You boys have fun." She waved and disappeared into the house, leaving Matthew to Matty's mercy.

"Okay, let's play." Matthew put his books on the porch. "Where's your fire engine?"

"Papaw Chuck made me a truck." He walked over to a white column and "drove" it out from where he had parked it, making noises that a truck probably wouldn't make.

"Has your Papaw Chuck been here lately?"

"Yes. He came to see A.B."

"Who's A.B?" asked Matthew, driving the truck on the marble floor's cracks and making a noise comparable to Matty's.

"Mama, silly."

"But your mother's name is Abigail. Oh, I get it. Your Papaw has a nickname for your mama."

"What's a nickname?"

Matthew groaned.

"Are you hurtin', Matthew?" asked Matty.

"Yes," Matthew said, driving the truck toward the steps. "Ro-o-o-m, Ro-o-o-m," said Matthew.

"I'll get Mama." Matty took a step toward the door.

"Why," asked Matthew.

"She gives good apple a-pirn." Abigail put medicine in apple chunks for Matty to eat. The apple covered up most of the pill's strong taste.

"Matty, somehow I don't think that would help. Come here." Matty approached Matthew, who took him in his lap and gave him a big hug. "I love you," he said.

"I love you," said Matty, looking up at Matthew with eyes that looked a lot like his mother's, and holding on tight with his chubby arms wrapped around his friend's neck.

"Did you know there's an Abigail in the Holy Bible?" Matthew realized this would start a whole new conversation. It started.

"What's a Holy Bible?" asked Matty.

"It's a book that talks about God and Jesus and the Holy Spirit." Matthew hoped Matty would pick only one to talk about.

"Oh, what's God?"

"God is the reason you're here on the earth."

"But Mamma said the milkman brung me. His name is Jacob." Jacob was an elderly gentleman whose dairy route delivered milk, eggs, and butter to your doorstep.

He serviced this general area and came by the Hembree's with supplies from a local grocery store— sort of like a rolling store, which was a large truck stocked with groceries for people to buy in rural areas.

Matthew shook so hard with concealed laughter, he doubled over. "I guess we'll have to tell her the truth, won't we?" said Matthew when he could talk. Tears rolled out the corners of his eyes.

"Do we know a secret?" asked Matty.

"I guess so."

The door behind them swung open. Abigail shut it softly.

"So, what are you two doing?" she asked.

"We were having a deep conversation about God."

"Mama, you're wrong. The milkman didn't brung me. God did," piped up Matty.

"What?" asked Abigail, looking from one to the other.

"Matty," exclaimed Matthew in mock horror. "You told our secret."

"What are you two talking about?" exclaimed a mystified Abigail.

"It's a long story," said Matthew. He continued, "I was wondering, do you two go to church anywhere?"

"No."

"Could I take you and Matty to mine on Sunday?"

"I can't go, but Matty might like too." She hurried to ask Matty the question. "Would you like to go to church with Matthew," she paused and looked at Matthew, "next Sunday?" Matthew nodded.

"Maybe, what's church?"

Abigail shook her head in exasperation.

Matthew explained, "It's where little boys and girls go and learn about God. He's the one in the Holy Bible. Would you like to go and learn about Him?"

"Oh yes." Matty was clapping his hands. He'd go anywhere with Matthew. They often went walking in the neighborhood.

"Okay, I'll come and get you Sunday and we'll go."

Matthew had stayed longer than he intended. He said his goodbyes and headed home. For a fleeting second as he walked home, he wondered why Abigail couldn't go on Sunday. And how would Alice react to his little friend's company. Maybe, it was a good thing Abigail hadn't gone, because Alice didn't know about his relationship with the little boy, nor had Matthew ever mentioned Abigail.

❦ Chapter Thirty-Seven ❦

College Continues — Alice

A gloomy Alice sat at the open window of her dormitory room, wondering why her relationship with Matthew hadn't escalated. The bond she wanted hadn't increased one whit, and she was frustrated.

She wondered, *Could I have latched onto the wrong guy?*

She refused to believe she'd made such a bad mistake. He was handsome, intelligent, and malleable, exactly what she wanted. She didn't intend to give up — ever. Her mother had called to tell her of a possible opening at a church in Knoxville. It wasn't the biggest one, but Alice saw it as a springboard to something bigger.

I'm anxious to know what mother finds out on Sunday afternoon.

Alice got up and started pacing the room. Long discussions about Matthew with her school friends hadn't helped. Traveling home on weekends and engaging her mother in conversation hadn't solved her romantic problems. Those trips did help her avoid Ollie, but placed her in proximity to her loathsome parent's critical tongue and her single-minded suggestion of Three as the ideal mate — always Horace T. Blackwell, the Third.

Weekends.

Happy and filled with fun activities with her few friends.

Where have they gone? I came to college to get away from home, and now college has become as intolerable as my old prison.

Alice felt boxed into a corner. She writhed, twisted, and struggled to free herself from the maze she'd created. Caught in this web of deceit and circumstances she couldn't break free, but she had a goal. Her focus was on attaining that goal, and she'd try every wile, every scheme in her repertory to make it happen.

Once, she'd lied to Matthew, telling him she planned to go home but hiding out in her dorm room. She, Marsha, and Clara had spent the weekend playing cards, eating at Maryville Café, and shopping at the stores downtown.

Alice returned to her window seat. The Maryville College campus was a peaceful, serene place with oaks and maple trees turning the colors of autumn. People, including couples, walked the concrete sidewalks.

Speaking of people, isn't that Marsha and Clara coming across campus? Yes, it is.

She waved at Marsha and Clara as they walked rapidly toward Baldwin Hall.

Frustration.

Disappointment.

She hid both from family and friends.

No one knows the real Alice Davis. Ha, what a pretend life I lead. It's Matthew I want, and it's Matthew I will have.

His participation in chapel was a positive step in finding a large church, and everyone was praising his three chapel devotionals. They were well thought-out and interesting. She even thought they were, and getting her attention in chapel required major effort.

Alice's plan was to get Pastor Evens involved in pushing Matthew toward taking the position — if it was offered. She knew his feelings because of a conversation she'd overheard. Matthew, Pastor Evens, Tim, and another professor were standing in a hall of Voorhees Chapel.

"Matthew, you're wasting your talent by going back to Cades Cove," stated Pastor Evens. "Don't you think so, Professor Myers?"

"I think he could find a church in the surrounding area once he graduates. Cades Cove is *so* isolated."

"That's exactly what I've been telling him," Evens continued. "He's wasting his talent, if he goes back to the cove."

"It's not a good place to become known, especially if you want to grow into a larger pastorate."

"Exactly," said Chaplain Evens, punctuating Professor Myers's sentence.

Matthew responded, "Takin' or even entertainin' the possibility of a larger congregation isn't in my near future. The people of Cades Cove need a pastor as much as anyone." Matthew knew Pastor Evens's heart. This wasn't the first time he'd brought up the subject.

"I really think you're making a mistake." Even's was adamant, as unyielding as Matthew was resolute.

Alice's thoughts were brought to a sudden halt. She turned. At that moment Marsha and Clara rushed through the door into her room. They couldn't wait to tell Alice about Matthew's *new friend*.

"You two are out of breath," observed Alice. "What have you been up to?"

"It's not what we've been up to," said Marsha. "It's what the love of your life, Matthew's been up to."

"What do you mean?" Alice was all ears.

"We saw him coming out of Voorhees Chapel with another woman," Clara uttered as she nodded her head. "They headed toward Court Street."

Marsha spoke up, "They looked really chummy, too."

"Did you know this person?"

"No, we've never seen her on campus, but it was obvious that Matthew did."

The girls hung around, waiting for Alice to burst out in anger. But Alice quit talking and became strangely quiet. Marsha and Clara couldn't get out of the room fast enough. Alice had been weird, since coming back to college. Normally, their friend would have charged around the room, spouting words not becoming a young lady.

"Did she take that information well or not?" asked Clara, looking at Marsha. "I figured she would burst out in anger."

"We've seen her angry before, but I don't know. She was hard to read, too quiet and too reserved."

"I wouldn't want to be Matthew when she sees him tomorrow. We'll be able to hear her all over the campus," said Clara. "That'll be like my uncle's car radiator cap popping off. Steam explodes everywhere." Clara's attempt to describe Alice's reaction fell pitifully short.

"More like Yellowstone's Old Faithful blowing off steam," replied Marsha, whose family had vacationed there last year. The geyser was impressive, loud, and aggressive.

The two ladies went into their room and shut the door.

~

After hearing of Matthew's traipsing through campus with another woman, Alice turned white, compressed her lips, and otherwise did not show her quiet rage.

She seethed with anger for most of the night. Up and down she walked in her room. When she lay down upon her bed, she tossed about and, finally in anger, threw her coverings on the floor. She felt like picking up her desk chair and smashing it against the wall. But her plans for Matthew didn't change. Now, they became an obsession.

~

When she saw Matthew at lunch on Saturday, Alice didn't say a word about the other woman. She smiled sweetly and said, "Will you be here at the regular time to pick me up tomorrow?"

"I'll be about ten minutes earlier."

Inwardly, Alice groaned. She wasn't a morning person. Saturday and Sunday were days to laze around, eat breakfast in bed, carried by a servant, and luxuriate in a tub of water. No one in their right mind exited the house before twelve o'clock on either day.

~

On Sunday morning, a grumpy Alice waited downstairs for Matthew to pick her up. Since her first walk to Ollie's and to church with Matthew, she hadn't missed a Sunday. Well, except when she went home on weekends so the servants could wash and iron her dirty clothes. Alice did *not* do laundry. While at home, the usual perfunctory appearance at church wasn't on the agenda. Her parents went, but getting Alice up to go proved too difficult.

I'll show Matthew that I can be an obedient minister's wife.

Anyone knowing Alice would laugh at the word obedience applied to her manner. Since she was a young child and realized her powers of exploitation, Alice wasn't subject to or controlled by anyone but her own selfishness. Alice was a spoiled brat. An island unto herself, she often made an exception of her father and sometimes deferred to her young brother.

She and her mother argued about everything, except spending money. Here they were on the same page. Alice spent her share, buying the best of everything, including the latest fashions.

Where is Matthew? He's going to be late.

Alice stood tapping her foot on the wooden floor. Patience wasn't one of her virtues either. Walking to the mirror, she checked her outfit for the umpteenth time and then returned to the windows at the front entrance.

She looked across the campus where the morning mists hung low on the grass. Warm days and cooler nights with no wind caused this phenomenon. The leaves had changed to gold, orange, red, and brown. They hung damp and limp from the tree branches. Some fell gently to the ground and made rustling noises as you walked.

All of autumn's beauty was lost on Alice as she looked anxiously for her intended. Matthew was always on time. She kept watching the reception area clock and the campus path he used. No one appeared on it but a man with a small child on his shoulders. As the man got closer, she realized it was indeed Matthew.

Who on earth is that child? Is this another surprise?

They got closer, and Alice saw Matthew's face. It was animated, happy, and relaxed.

I didn't know he liked children. Of course, small children don't run wild on the college campus.

Alice was disgusted, but her face didn't show this emotion.

Why does Matthew always pick up strays, and whose child is this anyway?

"Duck, Matty," said Matthew, as the two walked through the door of Baldwin Hall.

"Good morning, Alice." Matthew slid Matty to the floor. "Let me introduce Matty White. He's my good friend."

Matty stuck out his hand, "Good morning, ma'am." He said this in his well-rehearsed best. He looked handsome in his long-sleeved, white shirt and dark pants. His hair was still wet after his mama's brisk combing.

Alice wanted to ignore Matty, but instead she did shake hands with Matthew's charge. "Where did you get *this* one?" she said, looking at Matthew.

Matthew chose to ignore her tone of voice. "He lives on Court Street with his mother, Aunt Mary and Uncle John. I pass his house on my way home. We play, don't we Matty?"

"Yes, we play with my fire engine and truck, and we look for worms and bugs," added Matty proudly, beaming from ear to ear. "And I have a boo-boo."

Matty turned his elbow over so Alice could see his badge of courage.

"Matty gets lots of boo-boos," explained Matthew.

"How wonderful," said Alice, showing a bit of the sarcasm she was feeling. She walked over to the full-length mirror to check makeup, nylon hose seams, and dress before walking out the door.

"Hadn't we better go, Matthew?"

"Yes," he said, raising Matty to his shoulders. "Let's go, little buddy. We're stopping by to get Tim and then pick up Ollie. Do you remember what I told you about him?" Earlier, Matthew and Matty had a long discussion about Ollie's sightless eyes. Matty looked sad and was quiet for several minutes after their conversation. But he didn't say anything.

Chapter Thirty-Eight

Going to Church — Matthew and His Gang

"Ollie," said Mrs. Miller, "Do you need me to check your outfit?"

"Yes, I'll be out in a minute."

"Better get a light jacket. There may be a chill in the air."

Mrs. Miller stood in the parlor, looking out the door at the beautiful autumn morning. Hearing a movement behind her, she turned around to see Ollie coming into the room. She started laughing.

Ollie did have a sense of humor. He was barefoot. His pants and shirt were inside out, and the felt hat he'd placed on his head was backward.

"What's wrong?" he asked as innocent as a babe.

"You know what's wrong. Get back in your room and fix your clothes," chuckled Mrs. Miller. "You have thirty minutes until Matthew gets here."

Fifteen minutes later he appeared and went to his round piano stool. It was round because he said it fit his bottom better. Putting his fingers to the keys, he played a few bars of a favorite song while thinking about Alice.

I should play a dirge in her honor.

Ollie was a good judge of character. He realized after their first meeting that touching Alice's face was impossible, so he refrained from asking her. There was something about her he didn't like, and in her presence he was uncomfortable.

"That looks much better," said his mother, coming into the room to check him out. Ollie knew his clothes by texture of cloth. He had on a brown plaid shirt, brown slacks, socks and shoes. "You look spiffy, but don't you need a jacket?"

"No, I'll be okay. By noon, it will be warm outside in the October sun. Mom, do you like Alice?" he asked, because she was on his mind.

"Alice is different," said Mrs. Miller.

"That's not what I asked. Do you like her?"

"I'll admit I have my reservations about her. I guess I don't trust her." Mrs. Miller returned to the kitchen.

Ollie got up and went to the front door to wait on his friends.

Trust...that is the word.

He didn't trust her, and his mother felt the same way. He didn't want to butt into Matthew's life, but he hoped somehow her real personality would become obvious to his friend. Ollie felt Alice would be a serious mistake, but he would not intrude.

She's Matthew's girlfriend, and I'll be friendly to her.

Ollie heard them coming. He stepped outside the door.

"Hi, Matthew," said Ollie. "You have Tim and Alice with you, and I heard another wee voice."

"You sure did. You need to meet Matty. He's my best friend. Tell Ollie how old you are, Matty."

"I'm not quite free," said Matty wriggling down from Matthew's shoulders and running up the steps. He knew he was supposed to shake hands with Ollie.

"He means three, Ollie, and if you'll bend down, Matty wants to shake your hand." Everyone was smiling but Alice. She had a pained expression on her face that said, "Let's get this over with."

Ollie got down on one knee and shook Matty's hand. He felt Matty's face and shoulders. "Matty, I'm so happy to make your acquaintance."

Matty was looking closely at Ollie's eyes. Matthew had a breathless moment when Matty put up his hand to Ollie's temple. But it was a gentle stroke on the older man's face. For once, Matty was silent and in awe.

"Shall we go to church everyone?" asked Matthew. Tim rode Matty on his shoulders and Ollie placed his hand on Matthew's arm.

"Alice, why don't you lead the way," asked Matthew.

They made a strange looking procession as they walked to church. The group passed several houses and arrived on Broadway Street, turned right and headed east toward Washington Avenue. Four blocks later, they walked up the steps of Broadway Church, and were greeted by a deacon at the door. Here, the group separated, each going to their respective teaching classes.

Matty and Matthew walked downstairs where the younger children played in a large basement room. Several ladies watched over them and one came over to introduce herself.

"Hello, I'm Mrs. Johnson, and who's this?" she said, ruffling Matty's hair.

"I'm Matty. I'm not quite free." Matty stuck out his hand, showing three fingers, and then turned his attention to several children playing on a rug near a window.

"Matty, you can go play," offered Matthew. Matty ran in the direction of the chattering children.

"I'll take good care of him. Is this his first time in church?"

"As far as I know."

"He's not your son?" Mrs. Johnson looked at Matthew curiously.

"No, he's the son of a good friend."

"I see." Mrs. Johnson looked back toward the children. "He makes friends easily, doesn't he?"

Matthew laughed, "Yes, he does. What will the children do during the morning class?" Matthew had no idea. He'd never had a child at church before. The whole area within Broadway Church was foreign to him.

At Cades Cove, services were all together, and there were no teaching classes. Children cried and the minister spoke over the usual disruptions. A woman or man scolding a child was frequently heard and sometimes a loud whack settled the youngster down. Crying babies were taken outside, nursed, or rocked to sleep in a mother's lap.

Mrs. Johnson responded, "We'll play some games, read a Bible story, learn to pray and have a snack. You'll pick him up for church."

Matthew nodded his head. "If there's a problem, I'm in Joshua Sterling's class."

"We'll come and get you. Leave quietly and he'll never know you're gone. I'll keep watch on him."

Matthew made no noise as he ascended the stairs.

When he went back later to pick up Matty for the church service, he was sitting at a low table eating crackers and drinking juice.

Matty saw Matthew and ran to him. "Ma-tew, Jonah swallowed a whale!" he exclaimed. He was so excited and interested in telling Matthew what he'd learned that he mixed up the famous Bible story. Pictures of a large whale and a bearded man were posted on a board in the middle of the room; a rug to sit on was in front.

"Matty, the whale swallowed Jonah," said Mrs. Johnson, chuckling. "But then what happened?" she continued.

"He got out. God helped him."

"That's right," said Matthew. "He did. Was Matty a gentleman, Mrs. Johnson?"

"Yes, he was." Mrs. Johnson bent over and gave Matty a hug. "Come back next Sunday, Matty."

Matty was tugging at Matthew's hand as they headed for the stairs. "What's a gemp-l-man?" he asked.

Matthew explained that he was someone who did what he was told. "And that's gen-tle-man."

"Oh," said Matty, "gemp-l-man."

Later upstairs, he sat quietly when the pastor spoke, as he was told to do. Finally, he crawled over Tim to Matthew, curled up, and went to sleep. Matthew hugged him close. He made a warm bundle in his lap. Alice moved to the side so the youngster's shoes didn't touch her immaculate dress.

At the end of the service, Matthew walked all of his charges to their respective homes. The final stop-off was Matty's. As he left him on the door step, he heard Matty telling his mother excitedly about church. This time he got Jonah and the whale straight.

"And I was a gemp-l-man."

Matthew reached the road and started walking toward home.

"Ma-tew," the child called and ran toward him, raising his arms to be picked up. He gave Matthew a hug and a wet kiss. "Matty wants to go again."

"Sure thing, little guy. Next Sunday and the Sunday after that." Matty ran back to his mother, who stood in the door. She waved, and Matthew waved back.

~

On Sunday afternoon, Alice's mother called.

"Alice," said Mrs. Davis as soon as she got to the phone, "The position is open at Grace Church. It's the one on Clinch Avenue. I talked to one of the deacons and he's interested in Matthew coming."

"Oh, Mother, that's wonderful. What's the deacon's name, and do you have his telephone number?"

Alice was so excited, she dropped the pencil she was holding. Retrieving the pencil from the floor, she managed to write down the information. After talking to her mother for several more minutes, she hung up the telephone, folded the paper, and put it in her pocket.

Now she would put her plan into action.

~

After Alice staked out Matthew as her territory, she was always hovering around him between classes, in the library, and at lunch. The only places Matthew managed to be alone were at his boarding house and Tim's dorm room. As her intrusion into his school life increased, he spent more time in Tim's room and the Hembree residence. He saw Matty and Abigail more and more.

❧ Chapter Thirty-Nine ❧

More Scheming—Alice

On Monday after chapel, Alice made an appointment to see Pastor Evens. He was the first on her list of recruits.

Alice knocked on Pastor Even's door. It was early afternoon.

"Come in."

"Alice, so good to see you. Come in, come in."

Alice was amazed. From ceiling to floor, the walls were lined with bookcases and pictures. She walked straight over to his desk. The piece of paper with the information she'd gotten from her mother fluttered in her hand.

"Please sit down," said the Pastor, looking across his shiny desk and indicating a chair. "How can I help you?" The sun shone in the window behind him, silhouetting him in the light.

Alice seated herself in the appointed chair. "You have an interesting office, lots of books and pictures." She waved her hand in their direction.

"Yes," said Pastor Evens and came around the desk. "I'm proud of my books, and this is my graduation picture." He indicated the tintype of his

Harvard graduation. Alice thought he must give this same speech often. It seemed practiced.

"But you didn't come here to talk about books and pictures, did you?" He sat in a chair opposite her and leaned forward, his elbows on his legs and hands together between his knees.

He certainly has long arms.

Alice suppressed an urge to laugh. "No, I didn't. I wanted to talk to you about Matthew."

"Matthew Tipton?"

"Yes, I . . ."

Before Alice could go on, Evens said, "Are you two engaged?"

"Uh no, not yet."

"I see. I just wanted to know. I see you together a lot. What about Matthew?"

"He wants to return to Cades Cove and take up his father's pastorate. From what I can gather, this is a *small* church with a *small* attendance." Alice said small as if it were a dirty word. "I can't imagine he would be paid much, and I think it's beneath his capabilities."

"Well, I have to agree with you there on both accounts. We've had some discussions about this. He's very adamant."

"If we found a place in Knoxville, do you think he might accept it?" Alice looked closely at Pastor Evens, hoping to witness a particular response. The change in his demeanor and eyes was almost imperceptible. They became slightly more calculating and shrewder.

"Have you found such a place?"

"I think I may have, but you know how Matthew feels. He'll have to be approached very carefully."

"Absolutely true," said Pastor Evens. "What church is this?"

"It's Grace Church. It's the one on—"

Evens interrupted her.

"Clinch Avenue in Knoxville." He stood up and snapped his fingers, looking at Alice excitedly. "I'm familiar with it. It's not the biggest one in Knoxville, but it would be a good start; a better start than most aspiring ministers could hope for. Hum-m-m." Pastor Evens started striding back and forth across the room.

"Yes," said Alice, swiveling in her chair to watch him. "I have the name of the deacon and his telephone number." She handed him the piece of paper.

"How do you want to proceed, Alice?" Evens could tell that Alice was clever and calculating. He was sure she already had a plan, and he wanted to see if he liked it.

"You would need to call the deacon. What's his name?"

Evens looked at the lined school paper. "Let's see, Jerome McGhee."

"Call Deacon McGhee and see exactly what the church is looking for, when they need that person to start, and how much it pays." Alice was more interested in the salary.

"Matthew would certainly be qualified for a pastorate almost anywhere. I'm much impressed with him. I'd like to see him get a church he could use as a springboard to something much better. How good this would look on his list of accomplishments. This would do it."

"That's exactly what I thought. I can't call but—"

"I could," said Evens, interrupting her as he sat down again. "Once I find out all the details, I could suggest Matthew for the position."

"Yes, but now we come to the hard part. How . . ."

"To approach Matthew." Evens finished her sentence. "We can't tell him they might consider him as a candidate for the position." He sat, thinking.

"No," said Alice. "We'll tell him they need someone to fill in on the Sunday he tries out. That's sorta the truth."

"Sure, that's a good idea. He's a fill-in while they're in transition between pastors. That will work!" Pastor Evens snapped his fingers, got up, and started pacing the floor. "I could even suggest that to the deacon." He was getting more excited each moment he and Alice talked.

Why didn't I think of that? Matthew's lucky to have someone like Alice on his team. With her behind him, he'll go far.

"I'll get in touch with Deacon McGhee and see if I can make arrangements for Matthew to give a trial sermon."

"Good," said Alice. She mentally patted herself on the back. She'd come to the right person. "Will you let me know how you're progressing?"

"I'll be glad to, and thanks for the information. If he gets the call, I don't see how he can turn it down. I'd be very disappointed if he did."

"So would I. Thank you. I'll let myself out."

"Matthew couldn't find a better girlfriend than you," he called after Alice.

～

Pastor Evens stood up and started to pace the room again. He couldn't call today, but he would tomorrow. He was excited at Matthew's prospects. Every candidate he'd picked for chapel had gone on to nice pastorates. He would do everything he could to see that Matthew did the same. He smiled.

And his girlfriend is on my side.

~

It took until the middle of November to set up the meeting, which turned out to be the Sunday before Thanksgiving. Pastor Evens called Matthew into his office.

"Matthew, a church in Knoxville called to see if I knew someone who could fill-in on the Sunday before Thanksgiving. They're looking for a pastor and in urgent need. Everyone they've contacted has a commitment or is tied up with family activities for the holiday. Since they're without a pastor and until one is found, they decided to give a young aspiring minister a chance to fill their pulpit. This is a great opportunity for you to practice. I've recommended you. Are you interested?"

"How much different would this be than chapel?"

"You'll need to have a longer message. At least thirty minutes. I can't imagine a problem with that. You can expand one of your devotionals. Getting there means riding the early train to Knoxville, and I'm sure I can get someone to pick you up at the station. They would drive you to the church, feed you, and take you back to the station." Pastor Evens said this, although he knew other arrangements might be made. "We'll work those details out."

"What's the church's name?"

"It's Grace Church on Clinch Avenue."

"How many people go there?"

"I believe Deacon McGhee said two hundred and fifty members. I've never been there, but some of the people are well-known in Knoxville—doctors and lawyers."

"I see," said Matthew. He didn't jump at the chance as he had chapel. He said a silent prayer while weighing the pros and cons.

"What do you think?" Pastor Evens held his breath, waiting for Matthew to answer. He hoped for a positive response.

"This opportunity would be another step toward becoming a minister."

"Yes, you would be involved in an actual church service." Pastor Evens tried not to show his impatience as he waited.

"I hadn't thought about doing something like this, but it doesn't scare me." Matthew sat still. The size of the congregation didn't bother him. He stood before several hundred at chapel each morning.

"I'll be glad to help them out. I'll do it."

"Good. I'll call Deacon McGhee and tell him you've accepted. He and I will work out the final details. I'll let you know them. Work on your message, and I'll critique it. I may have some answers for you by the end of the week or sooner."

"Okay," said Matthew as he walked out the door.

~

Alice had been sitting on pins and needles for weeks, waiting to see if her plan came to fruition.

When Matthew mentioned his talk with Pastor Evens while they ate lunch in the cafeteria, she squealed, "Oh, Matthew!" She jumped up and ran around the table to hug him. Matthew turned beet red, embarrassed when several other people looked their way.

Alice almost let the cat out of the bag. "Matthew, we'll have —" Alice bit back the words she was about to say. She and her mother had already made tentative plans for Matthew to stay at their home for the weekend. Her father was to pick them up at Baldwin Hall and transport them in his automobile to their home on Kingston Pike. Mrs. Davis and Alice intended to show Matthew what living with the affluent of Knoxville could be like. Neither one realized their extravagant life might cause him to run from it.

"That's wonderful. Tell me everything."

Matthew related the details of his conversation with Evens.

"Maybe my family can make some of the arrangements for you. I'll ask Mother."

"Pastor Evens said he would make the arrangements with Deacon McGhee. I'll know soon." In considering the chance to speak at a Knoxville church, Matthew hadn't thought about the Davis's. It was rather exciting, going to a big city and standing before a real congregation.

Maybe meeting the rest of Alice's family is a good thing.

But Chaplain Evens needed to make the preparations. He could imagine what Alice and her family might come up with, and he wasn't thrilled at the prospect.

Alice let the subject drop, biding her time. After they finished eating, the couple headed for the library to study.

~

The next day, Alice dropped by Pastor Even's office and told him of her family's arrangements for Matthew's speaking weekend.

"Sounds great. I almost wish I were going to speak," he said.

"How do you think we need to tell him?" For once, Alice was at a loss.

"I'm going to call Deacon McGhee this afternoon, that way he'll know Matthew is coming to speak. If your father could call McGhee and tell him of your plans that would solve one problem. Does your father know the man?"

"I don't know, but I'll find out. He'll be glad to call one way or the other."

"Let me know as soon as your father contacts him. Then we'll get with Matthew after chapel the next morning. I don't want to do this until I know for sure your plans are complete."

"Okay, I'll let you know."

"Convince your dad that time is of the essence. We don't need to delay but finalize our plans."

"Okay," agreed Alice. Things were looking up.

~

Mr. Davis's telephone call to Deacon McGhee took place on Tuesday before the Sunday Matthew was to speak. Alice, upon hearing, ran straight to Pastor Even's office with the good news.

"That is excellent news," he said.

"How do we break it to Matthew?"

"In the morning after chapel, I'll walk with Matthew down the steps to the auditorium floor. You be sure to meet me there. That's when I'll tell Matthew of the Deacon's plans. You'll need to speak up quickly. Uh . . . say something like, 'My father plans to pick us up on Saturday morning and drive us to Knoxville.' Then follow my lead."

"Okay."

"I'll continue with something that will help you."

"I see," said Alice. "I'll follow your lead."

~

Alice tossed and turned all night. The last time she hadn't slept was the night she learned that Matthew had left campus with another woman.

I wonder who she was. Well, no matter.

Alice felt sure that after he visited her home Matthew would see what her family could add to his life. Sunday wouldn't come too soon for her. But first, she had to convince Matthew that coming to her home was important.

And Pastor Evens was going to help. *Enlisting his help was a stroke of genius.* She had one more person to approach . . . Tim.

"I'm not sure of him," Alice said out loud in the darkness. She liked Matthew's friend, but sometimes he looked at her funny. She wasn't sure whether he liked her.

~

Wednesday morning dawned cold and clear. Frost edged the limbs of trees and blades of grass as Alice walked to chapel. Each cloudy breath reminded her that winter was on the way. Alice shivered. Winter was not her favorite season.

This was it. She would soon know if Matthew could flat-out refuse her help. If she and the pastor worked the conversation just right, Matthew wouldn't have time to refuse. She hoped that would be the case.

Her section of chapel seats was monitored by Prof. Myers who noted her presence on his list of names. Alice sat down. That morning, chapel seemed to drone on for hours, but finally Matthew said the last amen, shook hands with a special guest and headed for the stairs. Pastor Evens was tied up with greeting the guest and, after finally breaking away, hurried for the platform steps. Matthew was walking away, although Alice was doing her best to delay him.

"Matthew," called Evens, "wait up."

Alice breathed a sigh of relief as Matthew stopped to greet the pastor.

It's about time. I was about to have a conniption fit.

"I've got some information about Sunday. I called Deacon McGhee and everything's set for you to speak. He'll pick you up at the train station and make the other arrangements."

"That's great. I'm looking forward to meeting him and speaking at his church."

Alice turned toward Evens, speaking to him directly as though Matthew wasn't even present. "Pastor, when my family heard about his speaking engagement in Knoxville, they decided to help with his stay. My mother has made arrangements for him to come to our house for an overnight stay."

"Alice, that isn't—" Matthew was going to say necessary.

"I know you don't want to impose, Matthew, but my mother insists."

"This is a great opportunity, my boy. I wish I were going to speak." His idea was to make Matthew feel bad if he didn't accept the invitation.

Alice quickly added, "Last night, my father contacted Deacon McGhee, and he accepted an invitation to supper on Saturday night."

"But . . ." Matthew put up his hand in a futile effort to stop what was happening.

"No buts, Matthew. This is wonderful," said Evens.

"My father will come and pick up both of us for the ride to Knoxville in our family automobile."

"That's wonderful, Alice." Evens turned to Matthew. "Matthew, you can't refuse such a gracious invitation. I think that settles it. I'll leave you in Alice's capable hands." The pastor begged another appointment and abruptly left. His parting ended the conversation.

Studying that night in the library, Matthew complained to Tim about the previous conversation. "If I didn't know better, I'd think those two were in cahoots. Every time I opened my mouth to protest, one or the other cut me off. I was looking forward to the weekend. Alice's interference has put a damper on my trip."

Tim was strangely silent on the matter.

❧ ❧ Chapter Forty

Getting Dressed for Knoxville — Matthew and Abigail

On Wednesday afternoon, Matthew went to his teachers and begged off of his last two afternoon classes on Thursday. His explanation for being absent was accepted. His next step was to talk to Abigail.

He raised the doorknocker on the Anderson's front door and tapped. A servant answered the door.

"Yes sir. May I help you?"

"I'm here to see Abigail White." Matthew didn't often knock to see Matty. But after the weather became cold, he and Matty went for walks around the block with the little boy bundled up like an Eskimo. Matthew always waited in the foyer.

"Yes sir. Please come in." The servant led Matthew into the huge parlor. It had a grand piano sitting in one corner. "Please wait here, and I'll get Miss White."

Matty's childish voice could be heard coming from somewhere in the cavernous house. Sitting in Cades Cove, this house would look totally out of place. Many houses in the cove were two-story, white-framed homes, but marble and columns were out of place.

Matthew looked around the room where he sat. Ample upholstered seating was provided for guests. The tall windows were dressed in blue hangings, draped stylishly over the top and falling to the hardwood floor. An area rug containing blue flowers graced the floor, and a bowl of freshly cut flowers sat on a center table placed exactly in the middle of the carpet. Flowers in a vase were always on a cabinet in the foyer hallway.

I wonder where they got those this time of year.

Matthew wasn't used to seeing fresh flowers in the late fall. Early frosts killed any tender green plant growing outside. Abigail had pulled up the marigolds and other annuals, collecting seed for next year. He and Matty had helped her with some of the plants, putting their collections in envelopes and labeling each variety. He had used the opportunity to talk to Matty about how plants grow, giving Matty a perfect chance to ask a hundred why questions.

Matthew heard Abigail's footsteps as she came down the long hall leading from the foyer to the back of the house.

"Matthew, I had no idea my visitor was you," she said upon entering the room, her heart quickening at the sight of him.

"I'm sorry to barge in, but I need your help."

"I'll do what I can," she said.

Leaving the Davis family out, Matthew briefly explained his visit to Knoxville. "I need a suit to wear to the service and to any functions I may attend. And also, Squeaky's getting married the following weekend. I could wear the suit to the wedding. Would you go to town with me tomorrow and help me select one?" Matthew would have been embarrassed to admit to Alice that he didn't own a suit. He'd never had a use for one.

"Of course, I'd be glad too."

"I'll come by around two o'clock. Is that all right?"

"Perfect," she said. "I'll be ready. Would you like to see Matty?"

"I'd love to see him, but today I need to put the finishing touches on my message for Sunday. Pastor Evens wants to look over it. I'll have more time tomorrow." Matthew got up to leave.

"I understand. You'd better hurry and go before he finds out you're here."

They walked to the front door with Abigail leading the way. She opened it up.

"I miss seeing you." Matthew said softly. He smiled and walked out the door.

∽

Picking out a suit turned out to be a fun trip as Matthew and Abigail strolled from one department store to another. Finally, they returned to Badgett's on Broadway to try on the one they thought was best for the occasion. This store advertised the largest collection of men's suits. After much discussion, Matthew chose a navy suit over a brown one. It was three pieces with vest, coat, and pants. The pants needed to be cuffed. A salesman with cloth tape measure pinned them up to the right length.

"You look more distinguished in the blue one," Abigail stated as Matthew walked in front of the full-length mirror which stood next to the fitting rooms.

"I do like it," said Matthew, turning around to look at her. "The wool will be warm in the winter."

"And hot in the summer. Do you need a summer suit also?"

"I hope not. At least, not in the cove."

"You'll need to get the cuffs hemmed. I think my Aunt Mary would be glad to do that. I don't see any problem in them being done by Friday afternoon. I'll take them home with me and ask her."

"I need a hat also." Matthew walked toward men's hats at the rear of the store. Abigail stopped to look at a new cloche hat similar to the one she wore over her new shorter hair cut. It was chocolate brown felt with a band of multicolored ribbon around its small brim.

"That's beautiful," said Matthew, who stopped walking toward men's accessories and returned to see the effect of the jaunty hat when Abigail placed it on her head. Coming up behind her, he was looking at her in the mirror as she modeled it.

"Yes, it is." Abigail replaced it on the hat stand and continued toward men's hats.

"Would you let me buy it for you?" asked Matthew.

"Oh, I wouldn't think of it, but thank you for asking." They were at the men's accessories section with men's hats displayed prominently in the middle.

"We'll have to buy a fedora. They're the latest in fashion. My Uncle John wears one. Do you ever wear hats?" Abigail couldn't remember seeing him in one.

"Only in the cove when working in the fields," responded Matthew. "A wide-brimmed straw hat keeps the hot sun off your head. Men in my father's church are welcome to wear bib overalls. A felt hat would look ridiculous."

"Fedora's are easy to pack if you don't want to wear them. You roll it up and put it in your suitcase." Abigail demonstrated. "But I should think you'll need to put it on your head in Knoxville. I can't imagine any respectable man going outside without one."

"How about this navy one?" asked Matthew.

"The color works with your suit. There's an interesting story behind this style of hat." Abigail pulled the hat off his head and flicked a small piece of lint off of the dark felt. Looking up, her brown eyes met Matthew's sky-blue gaze.

"Okay, I'll bite. What is so interesting about it?" Her perfume made him weak.

Abigail looked back down at the hat and turned it around in her hands. "It was first worn by a woman, Sarah Bernhardt, in a play."

"Is that the truth? This is a woman's hat."

Abigail looked up, again. "Not now, silly. Men started wearing them a few years ago, according to my Aunt Mary. They're very stylish in New York. The last time she was there, she saw fedoras on the street and at church. She bought one for my uncle, rolled it up to carry in her valise, and gave it to him at Christmas."

"What a comfort to know that," said Matthew. He was teasing her and looking at his prospective chapeau with interest.

"That one will be fine," said Abigail, handing it back. "How about shoes?"

"I think my black ones will be okay. They'll have to be. I don't plan on spending any more money." Matthew headed for the sales counter.

Abigail picked up a pair of navy socks along the way.

"You might need these."

Matthew and Abigail left the store. Outside on the sidewalk, Matthew asked her if they could make a detour.

"Sure, what did you have in mind? I have to get back in time for supper, which, by the way you're invited to. My Aunt Mary wants to meet you."

"That's very nice of her, but I don't want to intrude."

"You won't be, and anyway Matty will want to see you."

"I need to stop by a friend's house and talk to him. It's not much out of the way."

They set off in the direction of Ollie's house. The sun had disappeared behind clouds from the west. There was a warning of weather moving in. Matthew wondered if it might snow. Underneath his overcoat, he shivered at the thought.

Because of the cold weather, the Miller's windows were closed, and Ollie didn't hear them until they walked up the steps and onto the porch.

"Come in, Matthew," he called before Matthew could knock on the door. "The door's open."

Matthew opened the door and held it so Abigail could enter.

"You've brought someone with you."

"Yes, Ollie. I brought Matty's mother. Her name is Abigail White."

"Matty's mother, really? How nice to meet you." Ollie stood up, took three steps, and extended his hand toward her.

Abigail looked at Matthew and pointed to her eyes while shaking hands with Ollie. Matthew nodded as Ollie explored her hand.

"You must garden quite a bit," said Ollie.

"How did you know?" said Abigail taken aback.

"Since I can't see your hands, I can tell by feel. And there's a scratch in-between two of your fingers. That's an odd place to find one. Was it a rose bush?"

Abigail laughed. "It sure was. How long have you been blind?" Abigail instinctively knew her inquiry wouldn't bother him.

"Many years," was Ollie's response. "Mom says it was a complication from measles as a young lad."

Matthew was watching this exchange. Abigail was looking at Ollie with . . . pity? No, it was tenderness, a deep tenderness.

How easily Abigail interacts with Ollie, and her compassion for him is obvious.

"Matthew, is this the weekend you speak in Knoxville?" Ollie returned to his piano stool and sat down.

"Yes, Ollie, it is," replied Matthew. "And Abigail and I have been in town, picking out a new suit for the occasion. I also have a new hat and socks."

"So that's what's in the bag you're carrying. Did you buy a fedora? You know there's an interestin' story behind that hat."

Matthew laughed. "Yes, so I heard. Did it have anything to do with Sarah Bernhardt?" asked Matthew, smiling at Abigail.

"Ah, did Abigail tell you?" Ollie knew Matthew's voice was turned in that direction.

"Yes," said Matthew. Then he continued, "About my trip to Knoxville, I wanted to make sure you understood this was the weekend, and we wouldn't be going to church."

"I hadn't forgotten. Matty will be sad."

At that moment, Mrs. Miller appeared from the kitchen. "I thought I heard your voice, Matthew. And who's this?" Mrs. Miller came over to be introduced to their visitor.

"I'm Matty's mother, Abigail White."

"So pleased to meet you. We think Matty's special, and Ollie enjoys going to church with him."

"What are those delicious smells coming out of your kitchen? I just realized I'm getting hungry." Abigail patted her stomach gently.

"I have freshly made bread and pecan pies. Last summer's pecans are coming in now, and also black walnuts."

"I love black walnuts. My father . . ." Abigail stopped talking. She didn't complete the sentence. She cleared her throat and coughed to cover up her abrupt end.

"Mrs. Miller bakes for many people. They come here to her home to purchase her products. I take bakery goods home for Mrs. Hembree at times."

"Then I may buy a pecan pie for my aunt before leaving, if you have an extra one," said Abigail.

"I do, and I'll send some cookies for Matty."

"Abigail, why don't you come and take me to church Sunday? Then Matty can go. What's Tim doing? Could he go, Matthew?"

"Well, I don't know. I'll ask him. What about it, Abigail?" Matthew knew that she had turned down his invitation. He wondered if she would turn down Ollie's.

"I don't think so, Ollie. I . . ."

Ollie interrupted, "Are you taking a trip, climbing Mt. Everest, or meetin' the president?" he asked.

"No," laughed Abigail. "None of them."

"Then you have no excuse. It's settled. I'll be ready at nine. That's the *appointed* time," he teased.

Matthew realized he'd heard something like that just recently.

When the couple left, Abigail carried a large pecan pie and a loaf of warm bread, fresh from the oven. She promised to bring the empty pie plate back on Sunday morning.

∼

Dinner at the Anderson's was a pleasant affair. Matty insisted on sitting next to Matthew with his mother on the other side. That way both of them could help him with his food. Mr. and Mrs. Anderson were gracious hosts, putting Matthew at ease. The conversation flowed around the table with chatter from the Anderson's youngest girls joining in the adult discussion.

Mrs. Anderson looked over at Matthew and Abigail. They made a handsome couple, and Matty adored Matthew. She was sure her niece was in love with this young man, but she wasn't sure Abigail knew it. She wondered if Abigail would deny herself Matthew's love, if he avowed it.

Chapter Forty-One

The Sermon in Knoxville—Matthew

Mr. Davis pulled up to Baldwin Hall in his late-model Buick. He was behind schedule. The spoke rims with whitewall tires flashed in the early afternoon sun as he stopped and applied the hand brake. He arrived bundled up in his overcoat, muffler, and driving gloves to ward off the cold wind.

A light skiff of snow had fallen overnight, but by dinner the white stuff had melted, and the roads were dry. Lateness was not one of his character traits, but keeping his car in top-notch condition certainly was one.

The car was immaculate, inside and out. It was a seven-passenger model he used to drive to work and ferry his customers to lunch. Like clockwork, his butler cleaned it each Saturday. It was a symbol of Mr. Davis's hard work at the bank and his wealth. As he approached Baldwin Hall, Alice and Matthew stepped to the curb, where a small pile of luggage rested.

He hopped out of the car, placed his fedora on the driver's seat, and looked at the mound of luggage. "I thought this trip was only for the weekend."

"Now Father, don't start," said Alice. "I'm taking home my summer clothes."

"I was only teasing daughter, dear," said Mr. Davis, smiling at her, giving her a bear hug and a kiss. "How are you, Matthew?" They shook hands.

"Good to see you, Sir."

Since Mr. Davis was a take charge kind-a-guy, he started giving instructions.

"Matthew, you'll ride up in the passenger seat beside me. Alice, come over and get in behind Matthew. I'll put the luggage in the back seat." He opened the door for his daughter to enter the car and closed it back. Then he rushed to the other side, and with Matthew's help, started placing assorted bags in the back, moving around in the vehicle's cramped interior. Matthew lifted the last two and wondered what was in Alice's bags.

If I didn't know better, I'd think she was transporting lead they're so heavy.

After the luggage was stored, Matthew strode to the passenger side, opened the door, and got in using the running board. The process was a little awkward for him, because he'd never ridden in an automobile before. When he traveled, he rode on trains or horses or walked. He had to admit, he was a little bit nervous and excited.

To cover his anxiety, Matthew turned to Alice's father and said, "Mr. Davis, I certainly didn't expect you to house and feed me while in Knoxville."

Mr. Davis put the car in gear, let out the clutch, and moved smoothly ahead. "Our family is glad to have you, young man. Alice's younger brother, Ike, looks forward to meeting you. He loves playing games, and he's hoping you will too."

"Father, Matthew won't have time to play kid's games." Alice made a face at the very idea. "Mother and I have a full afternoon and night of activities planned. We want to introduce him to Knoxville."

"Hear that, Matthew? Sounds like you won't have time to catch your breath."

Matthew insisted, "I do need time to work on my message and some down time to rest." Always before delivering his devotions, he took time out to meditate and pray for his delivery. This action calmed him and helped him concentrate on the important reason he stood behind a podium, to deliver the Word of God.

The car zipped off the college campus onto Washington Avenue. It passed the train depot and turned right onto East Broadway. Matthew held onto the inside door handle and looked out of its square windows at the passing businesses. They soon became houses and finally farms. Broadway Street turned into Maryville Pike. He was whizzing toward Knoxville at thirty miles-per-hour. The Davis's talked together in animated conversation. He was content to get comfy in the seat and enjoy the new experience of riding in an automobile.

Several minutes later, they were at the outskirts of the largest city in East Tennessee. Mr. Davis started pointing out different buildings and businesses.

They drove across Gay Street Bridge, positioned high above the river, its girders silhouetted in the sky above. Looking down, Matthew saw a barge in the river below. Its wake sent small waves crashing against the Holston River banks. On one side, cables dangled from a failed attempt to place a tram car across the river. The first trip ended in disaster, when a cable broke and a passenger lost his life. The suspended wires were a constant reminder of this accident.

At the end of the bridge, the car entered city traffic, and they stopped at the first traffic light at the corner of Gay Street and Kingston Pike. Mr. Davis called Matthew's attention to the bank building where he worked. Straight ahead, the downtown area with neon lights, signs, and center traffic islands was jammed with cars and street cars. Although it was Saturday, Gay Street was a beehive of activity.

"We aren't going down into that madness, Matthew, until Sunday. We turn here," said Mr. Davis, who did just that.

Turning left onto Kingston Pike, the road where the Davis family lived, buildings of the University of Tennessee appeared before him.

"This campus is the other "Hill" of East Tennessee," explained Alice and laughed.

"Really?"

"Yes. I was amazed that Maryville College campus has the same nickname." She was happy. Her plan to snag Matthew was set in motion. This weekend was important to its conclusion.

Matthew turned around and smiled at her.

She's as relaxed as I've ever seen her.

Matthew leaned over toward Mr. Davis, dipping his head to catch a glimpse of the vast university grounds. He saw several three-and four-story brick buildings sitting to the left of the road. The car drove through the congested university district and past a series of small businesses. The residential area started just beyond.

As they traveled down Kingston Pike, huge houses appeared to the left and right of the road. The farther they traveled, the bigger the house and estate. Turning left, the entourage entered the driveway of the Davis residence.

Matthew looked around. Magnolia trees and leafless shrubs lined the graveled path. They were mulched with rounded heaps of pine needles and recently fallen leaves, some still showing colors of yellow and orange. He caught glimpses of the columned mansion as they drove down the drive. Finally, the Buick sedan pulled up to the door. Matthew craned his neck and looked upward.

The Anderson house, where Abigail and Matty live, would easily fit into this mansion with lots of space left over. Living here must cost a fortune.

Matthew tried not to show his amazement, but Alice was watching him closely. She saw his incredulity at the size of the house.

So far, so good. How will he feel to be waited on hand and foot? Can't wait for him to see Grace Church. It should really impress him.

The butler, who was watching for the group to arrive, came out of the door and took charge of the luggage. He was dressed in a dark suit and wore white gloves on his hands. He smiled as he picked up Matthew's luggage from the marble walk and disappeared into the house. A young boy hurried down the marble steps toward them.

"Matthew, I'd like for you to meet Ike. Alice's brother."

"I'm pleased to meet you, Ike." Matthew shook hands with the young lad.

"Matthew, do you play games?" questioned Ike, who looked to be seven or eight.

"Not too many, but I'm willing to learn."

"Good. Let's go . . ."

"Wait just a minute, young man. I believe Matthew has more important things to do right now. First, he needs to unpack. Why don't you show him his room and then bring him downstairs when he's finished?"

"All right Father." Ike had found a willing victim. No one else in the household played games, except card games. He would wait patiently for an opportunity to get Matthew alone. He was used to leftovers.

The group walked into the foyer, passing the butler as he headed out the door for more luggage.

~

Matthew's room was almost as big as his cabin at Tipton's Sugar Cove. Shiny wood floors, upholstered chairs with gold trim, and a huge, four-poster bed were part of the opulence of the room. He walked over to the window. It looked out over the river down below. He could barely see another house hidden in the white pine trees, nestling between the Davis's and the waterway. Across the river, leafless trees lined its banks, and planted fields appeared as far as the horizon. A house with two chimneys was silhouetted against the sky. Smoke from the fireplaces inside lazily climbed to the sky.

His luggage sat on a low stool at the end of the bed. Matthew opened his suitcase, pulled out his new suit, and hung it in the closet. He put his new hat on a chair beside the door and placed his other clothes and toiletries on the dresser top or in the drawers.

What possessed me to accept this invitation? What on earth am I doing here? Why such a hullabaloo over one unknown person's speaking engagement?

Matthew was perplexed. He didn't understand that this was his coming-out party, much like the debutants of Knoxville's polite society. He was being displayed to the upper crust as a possible future son-in-law and a potential minister of a church in Knoxville.

Matthew started as a voice behind him said, "Sir, may I help you unpack?" The butler stood in the open door.

Matthew laughed. "No, I'm finished. There wasn't much," said Matthew. It was almost an apology. The butler was a tall, dark-skinned man. His demeanor toward Matthew was open and kindly. Matthew immediately trusted him.

"Sir, the bathroom's at the end of the hall. Pull the bell cord if you need anything. Someone will come to help." The butler pointed to a piece of decorative cloth hanging from the ceiling with a tassel on the end. "Are you sure I can't help you?"

"No, thank you," said Matthew, giving the butler a gracious smile. He sat down in a chair to catch his breath and look over his sermon. It lay on the bed where he'd taken it out of his suitcase. Before he'd read through the first paragraph, the door opened and Ike came in.

"Are you unpacked?"

"I am."

"I'm supposed to bring you down to the parlor. I think Alice is taking you driving in Mother's Roadster. Better watch her. She's not much better than Mother when it comes to driving." Ike rolled his eyes.

"Do you know where we're going?"

"I think she's going to show you the sites of Knoxville."

"In that case, a bathroom trip is in order."

Ike steered him down the cavernous hall and pointed out the closed door to this room. The click of their heels on the marbled floor echoed around them.

Matthew returned to his room, picked up his new fedora, and carried it downstairs.

The butler was waiting at the front door. "Miss Alice is outside at the car."

"Should I wear my hat while driving in the car?" he said, remembering Abigail's words.

"The car is open, Sir. You can or cannot, as you wish."

Matthew looked at the hat and at the butler. "Will you place it back in my room?"

"I will. Just ask me if you're in doubt . . . about anything. Remember to ring the bell, and I will come."

"By the way," said Matthew. "What's your name?"

"Nathan, Sir."

"Why, that's my father's name."

"He must be a good man." Butler Nathan was smiling.

"He is. I'm pleased to meet you, Nathan." Matthew shook hands with his new friend.

At that moment Alice barged in the door.

"Oh, there you are. I was wondering what was keeping you. It's cold outside." She gave Nathan a hard stare as she grabbed Matthew's hand.

"Yes, Miss. Mr. Tipton was headin' out the door."

Nathan closed it shut behind them.

After an hour of tooling around Knoxville, Alice headed for Clinch Avenue and the church where Matthew would speak tomorrow. In the open car, Matthew could swear he was frostbitten.

"Alice, it's cold. Don't you think we'd better head back for your home?" he suggested.

"We have one more stop," she said.

Matthew pulled his muffler up over his red nose, hoping for a pause in driving. The sun was warm when the car wasn't moving. "Aren't you cold?"

He wondered how she could drive in the cold air. He was beginning to wish he'd brought his hat, but it would probably be back on Kingston Pike in the gutter along the road.

"This is our stop," she said. "Then we'll head home."

Looking over his muffler, Matthew read, "Grace Church."

"This is where I'm supposed to speak." For a second, Matthew forgot he was cold. He leaned forward to get a better view. "Where's the marquee?" he asked Alice. The title of his message was rather unusual and should be posted there.

"It faces the other side." Alice turned around in the street as he examined the building.

The church sat on a street corner, facing two main streets as many churches often did. Those attending parked at the curb. As they pulled to the front entrance, Matthew looked at the church's exterior. It was of rough-hewn gray rock, and the stained-glass windows were arched with the same jagged stone in a light gray or beige. He wasn't familiar with it but guessed the main part was granite. The massive bell tower sat at the corner where the two streets met, surpassing the church's steep gables in height. Eight or ten steps led from the sidewalk to the entrance door, which was secluded under a roof in case of inclement weather.

"Did you think it would be this large?" Alice turned to look at him briefly and then stopped in front of the marquee.

Matthew was thinking. *It's big enough. I wish we could go inside so I could see the sanctuary. It reminds me of New Providence Presbyterian Church at home.* Matthew didn't go there, but many at the college did.

When Alice stopped in front of the church, she couldn't believe what she read on the marquee. It said:

> "All About Prunes"
> Guest Speaker
> Matthew Tipton of
> Maryville College

"That's a strange title," said Alice, frowning. "What's your subject about? Surely not dried plums."

Good heavens, how did he come up with such a silly title? What will the deacons think? What will anyone passing by think? When we're married, I'll have to —

"No, it's not about *them*." Matthew's emphasis was on the word them. "Guess you'll have to come and pay attention."

The word attention was a sore spot with Alice. Hers was of short span. Matthew often teased her by asking questions after chapel or church to see if she understood or even listened. She was interested in who was at these two gatherings, not what was said. Hats, dresses, and shoes were her main interest in going. When he asked her questions, she became annoyed and quiet. It wasn't likely she'd know any more at the end of his sermon tomorrow than she did right now.

Arriving back at the house, Alice announced that dinner would be at six o'clock. Matthew thought that would give him just enough time to thaw out and dress. If this evening soiree lasted past eight-thirty, he intended to make his excuses and go upstairs to his room. Devotions were always the last activity of his night with a quiet time before he started.

Nathan came at the ring of the bell.

"Am I appropriately dressed for tonight?" Matthew questioned. He stood in the middle of the room dressed in his new navy suit.

"You look spiffy, sir. Hum-m-m, I'll be right back." Nathan disappeared down the hall. When he returned, he carried a beautiful silk tie with diagonal stripes of charcoal, burgundy, and navy.

"Try this one and see how you like it." Matthew switched out the ties.

"Wow, it looks great."

"Yes, it does. Mr. Davis said for you to keep it. It's not one of his favorites."

"Great," said Matthew. "It's already one of mine."

"You'll need to come downstairs in about fifteen minutes, Sir. The Davis's always receive their guests in the foyer."

"Thank you, Nathan."

"Have a good evening, Mr. Tipton."

Several minutes later, Ike came flying into the room. "Come on," he said, motioning for Matthew to follow him. "We'll be late."

Matthew hadn't met his hostess. When he went downstairs to the parlor, he saw where Alice got her good looks. Mrs. Davis came forward and extended her hand.

"Matthew, I'm pleased to meet you. Alice has talked so much about you."

Matthew looked into two of the bluest eyes he'd ever seen. Since he couldn't come up with an original statement, he said lamely, "The pleasure is mine, Mrs. Davis."

"You've met our family?" Blanche Davis waved her hand at everyone except her husband. He wasn't there.

"Yes, I have and seen most of Knoxville." Matthew smiled at her.

My daughter has an amazing choice of men. If he's as intelligent as he is handsome, Matthew will be a good catch.

"How did you like the Roadster?"

"Nice automobile. A little cold with the top down."

"Alice," Mrs. Davis turned to look at her daughter. "Didn't you put the top up? It's freezing cold outside." Blanche exaggerated. It was cold, but not that cold in the afternoon sun.

"Mother, you know I hate to adjust that top." Alice bristled at her mother's reprimand.

Mrs. Davis let the subject drop. No use getting into an argument in front of Matthew. He'd find out sooner or later about her temper.

"We'll form a receiving line at the door. I believe I see our guests starting to arrive." Mrs. Davis headed for the door as Nathan appeared from nowhere.

Matthew got the distinct impression he was watching just out of sight.

"Ike, where's your father?"

"I'll get him." Ike disappeared up the stairs and reappeared with Mr. Davis in tow.

When he saw Matthew, he shook hands and said, "Nice tie."

"Thank you, Sir. It's a favorite of mine."

Mr. Davis roared with laughter. He liked this young man.

He took his place at the head of the line. As the guest, Matthew was next. Mrs. Davis, Alice, and Ike finished out the group.

Nathan opened the door as the first attendees arrived. The faces became a blur to Matthew as more and more people appeared.

Finally, Deacon McGhee grasped Matthew's hand. "I'm pleased to meet you, young man," he said, shaking his hand firmly.

"And I you. I hope we can talk during supper," said Matthew as other guests came through the door. Deacon McGhee moved on down the line and joined the roomful of guests milling about in the parlor.

When everyone had arrived, the greeters mingled with those attending. Alice latched onto Matthew's arm and steered him toward a couple she knew on the far side of the room. She noticed that Three and The Blackwell's weren't invited. Her mother was protecting her ace-in-the-hole.

⧸⧹

Matthew pulled a chair in front of the open upstairs window and looked out at the chilly, star-lit night. The moon's reflection danced on the river below. A slight wind blew from the west, moving the bare limbs on the trees and sighing in the pines. Lights twinkled in the dark below. Somewhere out there was Tipton's Sugar Cove. How he wished he was there. Being in this atmosphere of overindulgence was foreign to him. He preferred the peace and quiet of Cades Cove. Matthew was grateful for the experience of visiting Knoxville, but this life was not for him.

He had liked Mr. McGhee instantly, and they had talked much of the evening, much to Alice's disappointment. Matthew made plans to arrive early the next morning at the church. Mr. McGhee would pick him up and give him a grand tour of the facility before the other members arrived. Alice and the rest of the Davis's were coming later.

Shutting the window and pulling the curtains, he turned toward the bed and picked up his much-used Bible from the bedside table. Turning to John 15:1-6, he read his scripture for tomorrow where Jesus said:

> *I am the true vine, and my Father is the husbandman. Every branch in me that beareth not fruit he taketh away: and every branch that beareth fruit, he purgeth it, that it may bring forth more fruit. Now ye are clean through the word which I have spoken unto you. Abide in me, and I in you. As the branch cannot bear fruit of itself, except it abide in the vine; no more can ye, except ye abide in me. I am the vine, ye are the branches: He that abideth in me, and I in him, the same bringeth forth much fruit: for without me ye can do nothing. If a man abide not in me, he is cast forth as a branch, and is withered; and men*

*gather them, and cast them into the fire, and they
are burned.*

In the margin of his Bible was penciled the word
"Prunes."

After studying his sermon, Matthew got up and
practiced some of the passages, striding up and down
the room. It wasn't his intention to memorize his
speech, but to remember enough and be familiar with
his ideas so that he could deliver them naturally with
proper inflection and gestures. He checked his outline
again and prayed out loud, "Father, tomorrow's
message is in Your hands. Please take it and use it to
Your glory. Amen."

On Matthew's bed lay a pair of pajamas, placed
there by Nathan while he was at dinner. He knew they
were pajamas because he'd seen them advertised in
Harper's Bazaar. This was one of the magazines
available at the library and placed in his hands by
Alice, probably with an ulterior motive for him to
become familiar with today's fashions.

Matthew stood looking at them. For him, this
would be a first. All the men he knew went to bed in
their underwear or long johns. They considered
pajamas a frivolous or unnecessary piece of clothing.
Matthew removed his clothes, putting them on wooden
hangers in the wardrobe. He pulled on his pajamas,
tied the drawstring, and got ready for bed. Tired, he sat
on its edge. There was a light tap on his door. He got
up and padded across the room in his bare feet.
Opening the door, he saw Ike outside with his finger to
his lips.

"Do you want to learn a new game?" he whispered.

"Sure," said Matthew, realizing the young lad was alone and needed the companionship of someone who was a buddy to him. The two conspirators tiptoed barefoot down the hall to his room.

Ike's room was as big as Matthew's. Inside, Matthew saw a game board laid out before a window on an expensive, wooden card table. On it were several marbles on a six-sided fixture with multiple holes.

"What's the name of this game?"

"Oh, I can't say it, but Father taught me how to play. I think he said it's German."

"Does he not have time to play with you?"

"No. He works until late at the bank, and he's exhausted when he comes home, but he told me he's planning on retiring in a few years. Then we'll have more time together."

"Is this game hard to understand?"

"No, you'll catch on in no time."

One hour later, after getting a good trouncing and begging that he needed his beauty sleep, Matthew padded back down to his room. This time he got under his expensive sheets and coverlet and fell asleep.

He awoke the next morning when Nathan shook him by the shoulder. "This is the big day, Mr. Tipton." Nathan went to the window and pulled the curtains apart. It was still dark outside.

"I was so tired after yesterday. College isn't this bad."

Nathan laughed. "Yes, Sir. I could tell you were tired last night. If you hurry, you'll beat Alice, Mrs. Davis, and the rest of the crowd to the bathroom. You don't want them to get ahead of you."

"It's that bad, huh?"

"Yes, Sir. I'll lay out your clothes while you're gone. There's a towel and washcloth on the washstand. You enjoy your hot bath."

When Matthew returned to his room, a breakfast tray sat on a portable table by his bed. He feasted on oatmeal, eggs, bacon, and hot coffee. His mother would say it was a stick-to-your-ribs breakfast. Suddenly, he felt a longing for home. He wished his mother and father could be present for his presentation. He knew they were pleased by this opportunity.

❧ Chapter Forty-Two ❧

Knoxville, The Sermon — Matthew

Deacon McGhee arrived at the exact time they had discussed. Nathan opened the door. "Are you ready, Mr. Tipton?" he said.

"Yes, I am."

"I'll pack your things while you're gone, and they'll be ready when you return. I understand you're going to S. & W. Cafeteria after the service. You'll enjoy that."

"Nathan, I hope I can call you my friend."

"Yes sir, you can, and I'll be praying for you this morning."

"That's the best thing a friend can do."

Grace Church was only ten years old. Its sanctuary was coated with plaster and painted a cream color. A center aisle split two rows of pews. The pulpit was in the center of the platform with the choir loft behind. A large, circular stained-glass window rose to the top of the roof gable over the choir. This beautiful window couldn't be seen unless you were standing in the auditorium.

"It's a shame the public can't see the window," observed Matthew.

"I've said the same thing since I became a member here seven years ago." McGhee went on to explain the reasoning behind putting the window where it was located. "It catches the sun most of the day. Street-side, the sun wouldn't have revealed its beautiful design."

"Of course, it's on the southeastern side."

"Have you spoken with a microphone, Matthew?"

"Oh yes, we use one in our chapel services. No one could hear us if we didn't."

"Good, we'll get set up while our early Bible study is in progress, and you can practice on our equipment. Let's tour the rest of the church."

Matthew sat on the front pew as Deacon McGhee introduced him. He didn't see the Davis's until he mounted the platform. Thank goodness, the family sat near the back of the church. Their presence would not be a distraction. The text of his sermon lay before him on the podium with a glass of water to the side.

Matthew planted his feet firmly behind the wooden stand, looked out over his audience, and smiled. "I'm very pleased to be here and help out in the interim while you look for a pastor." He grasped the edge of the pedestal, because he had a tendency to move away from his stationary microphone. "This is an opportunity many aspiring young ministers never get, so I thank you for invitation."

Matthew picked up the glass and sipped some water. Then he started.

"Once I received a firm request to address you, I considered several topics. Some of them I have used during devotionals at Maryville College. But as I was turning the pages of my Bible, one word jumped out at me. You might've guessed what it is if you saw the marquee. If you expect me to talk on prunes, the dried fruit of the plum, I'm going to disappoint you. And, if you came to find out what on earth a college senior intends to say about prunes, then the sign out front did the trick. You're here to listen. I'm not going to ask for a show of hands for either idea."

There was subdued laugher in the audience.

"My father is a minister at a small church in Cades Cove. At an early age, he required his children to learn the books of the Bible and to carry a Bible to church each Sunday. I'm sure many of you have had the same experience. When we could read well enough, he expected us to follow along in the scriptures as he preached. I usually penciled notes, especially after being called to preach, on the margins of my Bible.

"You can imagine my shock at seeing the word *prunes* scribbled beside the fifteenth chapter of John. Did my father use the word when preaching from these verses, or did a child use the word to enhance his understanding of God's word? I prefer the latter explanation. Please open your Bibles to John 15:1-6." Matthew paused. The rustling of pages was heard throughout the congregation.

"I've asked Deacon McGhee to come and lead us in the reading of our selected scripture. Would you please stand and honor the reading of God's Word?"

After the reading of the scriptures, the worshippers resumed their seats. Matthew returned to the podium to continue his message. He was glad Chaplain Evens had grilled him on the protocol expected in today's service.

"May God bless the reading of His word."

"Amen," said several in the congregation.

"In our scripture lesson, Jesus teaches from a position the Jews knew well, using simple language that contained a deeper meaning. Historically, the Israelites were cattle herders and dressers of fruit trees and vine products, such as dates and grapes. In fact, when the twelve spies who were sent by Moses to check out the land came back to report, two-man teams carried huge clusters of grapes on poles across their shoulders. These edible products were and are important in Israel's diet. But to bear fruit, the absolute best fruit," Matthew emphasized his point by raising his hand to punctuate each word, "the grower prunes his trees, taking off extra or diseased limbs."

"I've often watched my father in his fruit orchard in early spring. He would take his big knife out of his pocket," Matthew pulled out his pocket knife, opened it, and waved it in the air, "and I can tell you it was much bigger than this one. He would take his knife out and cut off the smaller limbs of a newly planted tree. I thought the tree would die, because he pruned it so severely. Miracle of miracles, it didn't. Since he eliminated unneeded parts, the rest of the vine or tree became stronger and bore larger fruit." Matthew laid his knife back on the pulpit.

"This analogy of pruning a vine or tree was a good starting place for Jesus to talk about His relationship to his followers and explain one of the reasons problems, trials, and difficulties arise. Some, but not all, are prunes of bad habits, thoughts or other actions. In other words, Jesus is excising diseased or unneeded parts from His follower. His intention is to make us, His branches stronger and more like Him. To make us a stout, resilient, more perfect part of the vine.

"Look at the first verse and specifically at the first two words. First, Jesus must establish what kind of vine He's talking about and the importance of the vine. Jesus says that He is the vine. He is the trunk or main stalk. He's what holds the tree together, the glue, if you will.

"The branches attach to him. This vine, branches and all, cannot produce to its fullest or best unless it has a vineyard keeper or husbandman. Our Father or God carries out this work. Taking out His pruning knife, remember *the word is a two-edged sword*, He lops off or trims those appendages or branches which keep the vine from producing to full capacity.

"I've never heard a tree or vine say ouch, but I'm sure it would protest if it could. As humans, we often loudly voice our opinions to God when He teaches us a lesson.

"Who are the branches in this analogy? The ones left attached to the trunk are those who believe in Christ. They are Christ-followers. The others or unbelievers or lopped-off branches are cast away. Verse six says they are *cast into the fire and burned*." Matthew went on to explain in further detail his thoughts pertaining to the branches cut off from the tree.

"There's another idea expressed in these verses. It's directed to you, the person or believer. Let me preface my following remarks by saying this. God does everything in love. When He does surgery on us, it's because He loves us. Now, let me continue."

"Each individual branch, you and I, have character traits that the Father, or in this case, the Husbandman, needs to cut out of our lives. Once these are gone, we become better more perfect advocates for Christ. After all, Jesus admonishes us to become more like Him, so

He is constantly reminding us to look for areas in our lives that are offensive to Him, to other believers and to unbelievers. If we do this, let the Holy Spirit identify these areas or faults, we will achieve our reason for following Christ. And that is to become a light to other men." Matthew raised his hand to emphasize the final sentence.

"On December 16, 1811, a violent earthquake awoke the 400 terrified residents of New Madrid, Missouri. The earth rolled, cracks opened, and large areas of land either rose or sank. Church bells rang in Boston, Massachusetts, a thousand miles away. This upheaval was caused by a huge, underground fault. Sometimes *our* faults are hidden from us, embedded deep within our soul. Excising them causes pain, but the results are plain and recognizable in our lives. Faults can cause rippling effects in our families, friends, and businesses, and these people are the first to witness the results of God's pruning."

After pursing his subject for ten or fifteen more minutes, Matthew said in closing, "First, Our Father, in love, prunes us so we can bear more fruit, so we aren't a detriment to His kingdom. Sometimes, that process hurts. But as He rids us of sin, it is replaced with the fruits of the Spirit. Who doesn't want more peace, happiness, and joy in Him? Second, the sin in our lives divides us from the blessings God wants to give us. Third, we become a light to other men. And finally, fourth, we become more like Him."

"So, if you want to pencil "Prunes" in the margin of your Bible, it should remind you of your position in God's kingdom, and that as His child, we expect to be pruned more than once, and it will hurt." Matthew paused and looked over the congregation. Taking a deep breath, he continued.

"There is one other penciled note in my Bible. It says, 'Matthew, you are a branch.' Pencil that in your Bible using your name as a reminder of who you are in Christ. Thank you, for your attention."

Matthew looked at Deacon McGhee and nodded. He walked off the platform and sat in the front pew. The deacon concluded the service.

After the service ended, several people came forward to greet Matthew.

"I thoroughly enjoyed your message," said Deacon McGhee, shaking Matthew's hand firmly and thanking him for coming. The others said the same thing.

～

Alice stood to the side of those greeting Matthew until she made the decision it was time to go.

Matthew's made a great impression, but we can't stay longer. The line to eat will be around the block, and it's too cold to stand outside for very long.

She walked over and took Matthew by the arm, smiled sweetly at those around him and said, "Matthew, we must hurry." Gently but firmly, she steered him through the milling congregation toward the door.

"We've got to get to the cafeteria before the crowd gets there, or we'll have to wait in line an hour." She whispered. He continued to greet church goers, as she pushed him out the door.

The Davis's were already in the car, which sat on the curb in a no parking zone.

～

That afternoon Matthew prepared to head back home. He checked the guest bedroom, and went down the steps to the first floor. Nathan had his packed bags, which were sitting in the foyer.

"It's been a pleasure meeting you, Mr. Tipton," he said, extending his hand.

"I've enjoyed meeting you too," Matthew responded.

Ike came bouncing down the stairs, calling, "Matthew, I get to ride with you to Maryville." He hurried out the door to the waiting car, got into the back seat, and slammed the door.

Alice wasn't going because school was out until Thanksgiving holidays were over. She and Mr. Davis appeared together. She walked to Matthew's side and, as usual, put her arm through his.

"Are you ready to go, Matthew?" Mr. Davis asked.

"Yes sir, I am."

"Nathan, please put the bags in the car. I'll wait outside for you, Matthew." Mr. Davis went out the door and got in the driver's side of the car.

"Alice, I really appreciate your family's hospitality during this weekend. Everyone was very accommodating. Guess I'll see you at school after Thanksgiving." Matthew leaned forward to give her a friendly hug.

Alice whispered in his ear, "I'll miss you."

Matthew let go and hurried out the door.

～

Nathan watched him leave from the front steps of the mansion. "Dear God," he prayed, "don't let Matthew get caught up in her web. Let somethin' happen to open his eyes to her cunnin' ways." He turned and went inside as the car drove down the circular driveway.

When Matthew unpacked from his trip to Knoxville, he found the cleanly, pressed pajamas, two more ties, socks, three new shirts, and another fedora. It was dark brown. His extra pair of shoes was polished until Matthew saw his shadow in them. He smiled. Nathan was a very good friend, indeed.

Chapter Forty-Three

Thanksgiving! — Matthew

Whew! Thanksgiving holidays for Matthew were relaxing ones after the days leading up to his talk at Grace Church. On Monday morning, Tim went to get Ollie and bring him back to Carnegie Hall. They waited there until Matthew arrived with a surprise guest.

It was Matty.

Matthew had dropped by on late Sunday afternoon to tell Abigail about his morning meeting at Grace Church and to hear how she had enjoyed her church visit with Ollie. Matty had come running into the room when he heard Matthew's voice in the parlor. He explained that he was going home for Thanksgiving and wouldn't be back until the following Sunday. Matty stood in the parlor, holding his hand.

"Mama, I want to go home wit Ma-tew." He was determined to go. Nothing could persuade him otherwise.

"But, Matty, you'll get homesick," said Abigail. "Don't you think you would miss me?"

"No."

"Just a little bit?" Abigail held up her thumb and index finger and made a circle, leaving a small space between.

"No," said Matty, holding tightly to Matthew's hand.

"Matthew, I . . ." started Abigail.

"Do you think he would be okay? I don't mind taking him and my mother will think she has another grandchild. Ollie will be there and so will Tim. So, there will be people he knows." Matthew looked at Abigail for an answer.

"He goes to his grandfathers for a few days now and then."

"What do you think?"

Matty was standing in the floor looking back and forth at the couple as they discussed his future.

"Are you sure you want to go, Son. You can't come home until Matthew comes back." That wasn't quite true, because Matthew would bring him home if he became unhappy or homesick.

"Yes, Matty wants to go." Abigail threw up her hands, and that was the end of it.

~

Ollie and Matty loved the train ride to Townsend, where Matthew's father picked them up at the train depot for the ride across Rich Mountain in his new buggy. He drove them to Tipton's Sugar Cove and stayed to help Matthew and Tim start a fire. When he unloaded a basketful of food that Martha had cooked for them, he grinned at the strange group.

Just like Matthew. He always had a menagerie of friends and small pets.

"I'll see you men Thursday, if not before," he said and waved goodbye.

Ollie sat in front of the crackling fire, enjoying its heat while the inside of the cabin warmed. Matty stretched out on the bear rug, his short chubby legs crossed over each other. For the rest of the stay, the two were inseparable.

⤳

"Ollie, would you and Matty like to go feed the horses?" Matthew stood next to the cabin door after breakfast the following morning. "I'll get your coats. It's cold outside."

Matty jumped up. "Come, Ollie, let's see horses." Matthew helped the two down the porch steps and watched as the little boy took Ollie's hand to lead him to the barn, knowing that Ollie couldn't go by himself.

The path was downhill and fairly smooth, except for some boulders along the edge. *It's amazing that Ollie trusts a 'not quite free-year-old' to lead him around.*

"Wock, wock, Ollie!" warned Matty, making sure his friend didn't trip on one. He pulled Ollie to one side or other, steering him around the big boulders.

Matty's enjoying his new responsibility. Walking several feet in front of his two companions, he turned around to observe their actions.

"Matty, I want to feel a wock," said Ollie. Mattie guided his friend over to the side of the trail, took his hand, and directed it toward a stone.

Ollie ran his fingers over the hard stone, which was covered with mint-green and gray lichens.

"Do you feel a wock?"

"Yes, I do. It feels hard and rough. What color is it?"

Matty looked over at Matthew who mouthed, "gray."

"It's ray."

"Come here, Matty, and let me whisper it in your ear," said Matthew.

Matty let go of Ollie's hand and hurried over to Matthew.

This time he said the word right, "It's gray."

The group came to the barn and entered the stall area. The smell of fresh hay was strong in the air. In preparation for their coming, Donald Razor had cleaned the stalls and placed fresh matting within.

Matthew started feeding the horses with sweet feed out of a tow sack sitting in a barrel on a nearby bench. When it was cold outside, Matthew kept his horses in the barn, turning them out to pasture in the afternoon.

Ollie leaned against the stall wall, and Matty climbed the boards so he could see the horse inside. One horse came to check out Matty, nudging him with its silken nose.

"Ma-tew, he feels just like Mama's dress."

"I'm sure it does, my little man." Abigail often wore a green, velvet dress. She looked good in it, as she did in everything she wore.

When he had finished feeding the animals, he walked down to the pasture to look at the cows in the field. Ollie and Matty stayed behind to pet the horses and watch them eat. A fine haze of white appeared before his face each time he let out his breath. Matthew breathed deeply and pushed the air out of his mouth. A huge gust of white cloud appeared.

He stood holding a wooden post, part of the barbed wire fence. *This place is full of so many memories.* Walking in the woods and listening to the gurgle of the creek beside his home, brought back thoughts of others who had lived here.

I'm glad to be home, away from the pressures of school and Alice. He realized that his relationship with her needed to change, and facing her wasn't something he wanted to do. An inner sense warned him that Alice was volatile. *We have a different set of values, and I can't picture her living here at the sugar cove. I've let our relationship 'wock" on long enough. I'll tell her soon. As soon as the right opportunity presents itself.*

Standing there looking across the fields, reminded him of the wonderful home it could become for him in the future.

Later, smelling the bacon frying in the skillet, listening to Matty's childish give and take with Ollie and Tim made him wish for that future and the prospect of a wife and family.

He closed his eyes. As it happened many times lately, Abigail's face came before him. The scent of her perfume floated to his nostrils. His thoughts toward her were different than those for Alice. Analyzing his feelings, he realized he didn't long for Alice; instead he wanted to push her away. He loved seeing Abigail, noting her tenderness toward Matty and Ollie. If she held his arm or put her arms around him, he wouldn't push her away but draw her closer to him. Was he falling in love with her? Was he?

Analyzing his feelings, and realizing he yearned for Abigail shocked him, excited him, and thrilled him all at one time. His heart beat faster; throbbed was a better word. She would make a wonderful minister's wife.

But she refused to go to church, except for the one Sunday with Ollie. *I wonder why. I need to find out. Help her if possible. She can't be my wife and not be a Christ follower.*

Wife.

My wife. Is that what I'm thinking about?

⁓

Although it was cold outside, on Tuesday, the group went horseback riding. Tim held Ollie's reins, and Matty rode in front of Matthew. They rode slowly toward Razor's gristmill, past the tulip poplar, over the hills out of Tipton's Sugar Cove, and down the curvy road. At the mill, the newcomers met Donald and John.

On Wednesday, they rode in the buggy to see Squeaky's intended and finalize plans for his wedding on Saturday. Ollie promised to play the churches pump organ much to Matthew's surprise.

⁓

Thanksgiving Day dawned cold and clear. The Tipton's always got up early. By ten o'clock delicious smells permeated Nat and Martha's cabin. Two of Matthew's brothers and one sister arrived from Knoxville. They rode the train to Townsend and rented a buggy at the livery stable. Seven children of various ages ran squealing through the house. Matty soon found a friend and became engrossed in throwing wocks from the back porch. Ollie sat in the parlor, chatting with Nat while Matthew listened.

"Ollie," said Matty, coming close and looking up at his friend. "Do you want to frow wocks with us?"

Nat picked him up and placed him on his knee. "Whose wocks are you throwin', young man, and where are you throwin' them?" he asked in a rather stern voice, although he was teasing.

Matty just looked at him, his eyes big as saucers. He didn't know what to say. "I don't know."

Matthew started laughing. "Your hands are filthy. Let's go wash them. It's time to quit throwing wocks and eat." He got up and led Matty out of the room toward the kitchen where Martha and the other women were bustling around putting the finishing touches to the holiday meal.

"Matty, do you like sweet potatoes?"

"Yes ma'am, I like squeet 'tatoes and squeet milk," said Matty.

"That's sweet, s-s-wa-eat, s-s-wa-eat." Martha turned around and tried to sound the word so Matty would understand.

"Squ-ee-t 'tatoes," said Matty, trying really hard.

"God loves it. That's a hard word to say, isn't it," she said laughing and looking at Matthew. She bent down and gave Matty a quick hug, dropping mashed potatoes off the spoon she was holding onto her clean floor.

Picking up her dish cloth, she wiped the linoleum floor and pretended to head for Matty's face. He squealed and ran behind Matthew, laughing and peeking out at her.

"Have you found someone to play with?" Martha asked.

"Yes, we frowed wocks."

Martha laughed again. "He'll catch on soon enough, and then he'll chatter like a squirrel protecting its hickory nuts," she said to Matthew.

"I think he's already past that stage," said Matthew, ruffling Matty's hair. He had inched around Matthew's leg with caution and stood facing Martha again.

"It would be nice to have a grandchild like Matty." Martha looked at her son and smiled. "Do you have your eye on anyone?" Martha knew that was a loaded question, but it was one she and Nat were concerned about. After all, he was almost twenty-one years old.

"No, no one special, yet."

Martha searched Matthew's face. Was it a little redder? Had he blushed? She turned her attention back to Matty. *Hum-m, it wouldn't hurt to have a little more information about his family.*

"Matty, what's your Mama's name?" Martha continued mashing the potatoes, putting in fresh butter she had made from cow's milk.

"Mama."

Matthew answered, "Matty, your mama's name is Abigail, Abigail White."

"Okay."

During this conversation, Martha continued to finish the Thanksgiving meal. She checked the oven. Her rolls were brown and ready to remove. This was the last thing she had to do.

She grabbed a potholder from the nearby counter. "Matthew, we're ready to eat. Will you and Matty go get the others?" As they hurried out to call everyone to eat, she removed the rolls and wondered what Abigail was like.

"Dad, dinner's ready," Matthew called through the door.

"Ollie, I'm hungry," said Nat slapping his knee. "Are you ready to go?" The two men headed in the direction of the delicious smells, Ollie with his hand on Nat's shoulder.

～

Squeaky's wedding turned out to be the social event of the fall in Cades Cove.

The church was filled to capacity with some standing out in the afternoon cold. Somehow the busybody line had gotten details of the ceremony, including the blind organist, and passed it on to everyone they could reach.

There was an air of expectancy as Matthew, dressed in his navy-blue suit and a new tie, entered the church. Such finery, cove people weren't used to.

Ollie played wedding music on the out-of-tune pump organ. Its yellowed keys jumped up and down as his nimble fingers explored the keyboard. He cringed each time he hit a sour note.

The old organ, played in the church for many years and subject to heat, cold, and humidity, struggled through the music, screeching at times as Ollie played the wedding march for the bride. Although most of the families weren't familiar with the songs, they were familiar with the shrieking sound the organ emitted. The concert was dubbed wonderful by all.

Matthew used a wedding service provided by his father, as Squeaky stood, handsome in his newly bought suit. At the end of the service, the suit would become a recluse in the back of his cedar closet to be used in the future for important funerals or a special friend's wedding.

The bride wore a new dress carefully stitched by her mother. It was beige with smallish light green and yellow flowers and could be converted into a Sunday dress. Holly with red berries, twirled into a circlet, and placed on her dark hair, was the only ornament she wore. A blue handkerchief, carefully made by her deceased grandmother was carried in her left hand as she walked down the aisle.

At first, her father objected to walking his beloved daughter to the altar, but a few tears changed his mind. He did refuse to wear a suit, walking proudly in his new blue overalls and white shirt.

Fascinated by the ceremony, Matty sat quietly between Tim and Martha. He was still leery of Matthew's father after the wock episode.

At the end of the ceremony, everyone agreed it was the most beautiful wedding they'd ever been to, and Ollie was surrounded by admirers.

The busybody line worked overtime on Saturday night.

🍃 Chapter Forty-Four 🍃

Another Sermon at Grace Church — Matthew

Full and frantic were the days leading up to Christmas vacation.

Two weeks after Thanksgiving, Deacon McGhee called Matthew at the Costner's and asked him to speak again at Grace Church. This time Matthew made arrangements through McGhee to arrive early on Sunday morning. He didn't tell Alice or Pastor Evens until chapel was over the Friday before he was to speak.

"No, no, the arrangements are already made," he said, vetoing any suggestions the two wanted to make.

This was fine with Evens, who accepted Matthew's preferences. *I don't care how Matthew gets there or what he does when he gets there, he's going back to speak. That's the important thing. They're interested in my protégée. All I have to do is stand back, watch his progress, and encourage him. Hum-m-m, Alice is in a snit, but she'll get over it when Matthew takes the position.*

Alice controlled her anger but shot a fierce, withering look at Evens. *Matthew ignores me, and Evens is a traitor.* She couldn't believe he didn't support her attempts to control the situation. Securing her umbrella because it rained outside, she walked off in a huff before she exploded in anger, leaving Matthew to walk to his class in the rain.

∾

On Saturday morning, the mists of early morning, caused by yesterday's rain, enveloped the train as Matthew's parents traveled to Maryville from Cades Cove. The sun, burning through the low-hanging clouds as they pulled into the depot, was brilliant, emitting eye-squinting rays in the rain-washed atmosphere.

Nat had asked a retired preacher to speak on Sunday so he could go to Knoxville and hear his son preach.

"Matthew, I'd love to see Matty and Ollie," said Martha Tipton as soon as she arrived. Matthew picked up her bag and helped her across the street for the short walk to the Hembree's home where his parents were to stay the night. "I'd like to hear Ollie play on a good organ."

∾

After making his parents comfortable in their overnight room, Matthew made a trip over to Ollie's to ask them to Mrs. Hembree's for supper, but Mrs. Miller suggested they come to her home. In fact, she insisted. Then he went to the Anderson's and invited Abigail and Matty. Everyone planned to meet at Ollie's at five o'clock. This included Tim.

"Let's go early, Matthew. I'll help Mrs. Miller cook. She's going to have quite a crowd, and I know how much work that can be."

"Okay, mother, we'll go at four o'clock," said Matthew, who headed for the library to study for his sermon.

~

When the Tipton's arrived at the Miller's, it seemed everyone else had the same idea. Tim was there, setting up the dining room table and placing the dishes on their delicately crocheted mats. He greeted Matthew.

"Hi, buddy, I thought I'd help Mrs. Miller set her table." He was caught doing woman's work, and he knew it.

"All you need is an apron," said Matthew, teasing his best friend.

"I offered him one," said Mrs. Miller, pointing to the counter where the apron lay crumpled up in an untidy pile. "He mumbled somethin' about not looking like a sissy. I was hopin' he'd help with the cookin.'" Mrs. Miller was smiling from ear to ear. It didn't take long being around Tim until you found out there was men's work and women's work.

"Sounds like my good friend." Matthew slapped Tim on the shoulder and nodded his head up and down slowly. "Put it on and I'll tie the apron strings in a bow for you."

Tim took a playful swing at Matthew and said, "Oh, get out of here." He was red around the ears but continued to set the table.

Martha, who'd been standing in the door listening to the exchange, came into the room. Matthew introduced her to Mrs. Miller. "Tim, where's your apron? I'll use it."

"Oh, heavens. You're all on me." Tim handed the apron to Mrs. Tipton. "Here," and headed for the door.

"Matthew, let's go join Ollie and your father. The women can manage this."

"Tim, I didn't mean to run you off." Martha was tying the apron on.

"Don't worry about it." He exited through the door.

They'd just sat down in the parlor when Ollie announced, "Abigail and Matty are at the door."

Matthew jumped up, opened the door, and Matty rushed by him into the room. He headed for Ollie, who was sitting on his organ stool as usual. Abigail was climbing the steps. "I don't see how his chubby legs can outdistance me."

"It's all that youthful exuberance, Abigail. Br-r-r, it's cold out here." Matthew ushered her into the parlor, shutting the door behind them.

"I thought I would come early and help Mrs. Miller."

"Sure, come into the kitchen, and I'll introduce you to my mom."

"Wait up, Matthew," said Nat. "I haven't been introduced to this young lady."

Matthew introduced Abigail, who stopped to exchange a few words with those gathered in the room.

"Okay, now come and meet my mom."

Abigail followed Matthew into the kitchen where the two women were busy working. Mrs. Miller came over and gave Abigail a hug.

"Abigail, it's good to see you. Do you know Matthew's mother?"

Mrs. Tipton was looking back and forth at Abigail and Matthew. Was she the reason Matthew had blushed at Thanksgiving?

"No, she doesn't yet," answered Matthew. "Mom, this is my friend, Abigail White, Matty's mother. This is my mother, Martha Tipton."

At that exact moment, Matty rushed into the room and tugged on Matthew's sleeve. "Ma-tew," he said, "come see my bear."

"Uh oh, duty calls. I'll leave you three women alone." Matthew smiled at Abigail as he left the room.

After dinner, Ollie played the organ for his audience, who clapped until their hands were red.

~

Mrs. Tipton kept watching the interaction between Matthew and Abigail. As the night progressed, her intuition told her these two were in love. But, what about Abigail? Who was she? Where was she from? What had happened to her husband? There were so many unanswered questions; questions that needed to be addressed.

As they got ready for bed later at the Hembree's, she approached her husband, "Nat, did you notice how Matthew and Abigail acted around each other?"

"Yes, they're good friends, and Matty is such a cute child. I believe he's gotten over his fear of me. I didn't mean to scare him at Thanksgiving. Did you see him sittin' on my knee? He told me the story of Jonah and the Whale, and I talked to him about David's tussle with Goliath." Nat paused to lay his britches on a nearby chair. "He loves our boy."

"I believe the feeling's mutual, *and* I think our son and Abigail are more than friends. My woman's sixth sense tells me they might be in love with each other." Martha went on to explain her fears for the couple. "We don't know anything about her."

"She's easy enough to like," said Nat, looking over at his wife. He was standing in his long johns on the other side of the bed.

Martha gave him a do-something-stare.

"If it makes you feel better, I'll ask Matthew before we go home," said Nat, climbing into bed and noticing the heating register below the window made a clunking sound. "I hope we don't have to listen to that the rest of the night." Nat turned over and soon snored.

"Men," said Martha. "How can he go to sleep that fast?" She lay awake for awhile before turning over on her side and dropping off into a fitful rest.

~

The next morning after a good breakfast at the Hembree's, the trio headed across the Maryville College campus for the train station. Alice sat on one of the inside benches with her ticket in hand. When she saw Matthew, she rushed forward and attempted to embrace him. He recoiled and held her at arm's length.

"I am so sorry, Matthew, for being so cross. I've got a ticket," she held it out. "I'm going with you today."

Rather than cause a scene in the depot, Matthew accepted the fact that she was going. By now, he was sure Alice could explode at any minute.

Mr. and Mrs. Tipton looked at each other in amazement. Who was THIS woman?

"Mom and Dad, I'd like to introduce Alice Davis." There was no elaboration, no further introduction.

Martha noticed that he didn't introduce her as friend or enemy. Evidently these two must have had a spat or she wouldn't be apologizing. *Where does she come from and how does she fit into Matthew's life? This is amazing. I've gone from wondering about one woman and now there's two and unanswered questions about both.*

Alice turned her phony charm on the Tipton's. "Pleased, I'm sure," she extended her delicately gloved hand which was engulfed by Nat's rough, work-hardened paw. Then she latched onto Matthew's arm. He was her possession, and she was going with him to church in Knoxville.

Matthew's message had another provocative title, "The Stackpole in Your Life." A stackpole was used to stack hay in the field. It was placed in the ground at the center of a pile of pitchforked hay. The pole steadied the pile and held it together.

His message was a continuation of the vine and the branches. He told his audience that just as Jesus is the vine, whereby they are engrafted as believers into God's family and at the same time pruned of bad habits and sins, a stackpole in a believer's life steadies him. One who follows Jesus can expect certain things to surround him, much as the hay surrounds the stackpole. This is promised in the Bible.

As we are pruned of bad habits and sins, they will be replaced with the blessings of the Holy Spirit. These are peace, joy, love, etc. Then he explained God surrounds us with promises which we can depend on. The first one being God's faithfulness. Matthew picked out another couple and explained them.

After the sermon, Deacon McGhee and Matthew lined up in front of the pulpit. Several of the church came forward to greet the men and compliment Matthew on his message. Then McGhee loaded the foursome into his car, and they went to Vegas Restaurant, a well-known but expensive restaurant at the north end of Gay Street.

"Prime rib and velvet cake are specialties," said Deacon McGhee. "Feel free to try both." After waiting for several minutes, they were ushered into the dining room. Tables with white cloths, heavy silverware, and crystal glasses greeted them. After they were seated, maître d's with cloths over their arms poured water into glasses and opened menus for each diner.

Nat sneaked a look at Martha and raised his eyebrows. There were no prices on the menu.

～

Later, during a private moment on the train back to Maryville, he asked his wife, "I wonder what that meal cost?"

Martha replied, "A lot. Nat, I'm worried that Matthew will be taken in by such luxury. I liked Deacon McGhee, but there's something superficial about our whole experience today. And, I worry about Alice. She treats Matthew like a possession, hangin' onto his arm and gazin' into his eyes. That's flattering to a man, and she's such a beautiful girl. But . . ."

Martha paused and didn't finish her sentence. Suddenly she continued, "And where does Abigail fit into this puzzle?" She turned to look out the window of the railcar. She didn't want to consider what might happen to Matthew if he became more involved with Alice. "What's our son gotten hizself into?"

When the group arrived in Maryville, they remained in the train depot where earlier they had left their luggage. Nat and Martha's connection would leave in forty-five minutes. There was no need to walk back to the Hembree's.

Alice stayed latched onto Matthew's arm.

Nat looked over at his son.

I'd like to talk to Matthew. Wonder if I can pry Alice loose long enough to talk to him in private? I need to find out what's goin' on here. I didn't know about the first woman in my son's life; now there are two and one of them is from Knoxville's society. I get the distinct impression she's after him, and she's not exactly cove material.

"Son, let's go over and look at the new Baldwin." Train engines in the area tended to be Shays because they were workhorses and could be used timbering the forests of East Tennessee.

Matthew got up. Alice was still attached.

They walked around the steam locomotive engine, over the tracks, and back upon the loading platform. Alice was still attached.

Refreshments were offered inside the depot in a cooler.

"Martha, why don't you take Alice and get her a Coca Cola? There's a cooler inside."

Martha got her pocketbook and stood up. "Come on, Alice, we'll get a cold drink."

"Let's go get a soft drink, Matthew." Alice pulled him along with her. Frustrated, Nat decided to forget it.

I give up. She's like a leech, but a match wouldn't burn HER loose.

The train chugged into the station, belching black smoke and steam. The passengers hopped off and entered the depot, passing the group of four standing in a close circle waiting for the "All aboard." Nat and Martha were reluctant to say goodbye to Matthew. So many unasked questions hung in the air between them.

Finally, the two unhappy parents boarded for the trip to Townsend, waving to the young couple standing on the wooden platform.

~

When Nat and Martha came down for Matthew's sermon, they were pleased and happy for their son. They returned home confused and wondering what the future held in store for him.

Nat looked over at Martha's concerned face. "Wealth and power are deceitful masters," he said to Martha and sighed. "He's received the right training as a youth. We'll have to pray and trust in the Lord."

"Didn't he deliver a wonderful message?" said Martha.

"Yes, he did." Nat realized he hadn't even said so to his son.

That night during their devotions, Nat and Martha started praying in earnest for Matthew to make the right decisions. When Martha got up from the floor, there were tears in her eyes.

~

Matthew's school went through Friday, but he stayed until the next Sunday so he could take Ollie and Matty to church. When he and Matty arrived at the Miller's, he carried two mysterious bags, which he gave to Mrs. Miller for safe keeping.

"You and Matty will stay for dinner, won't you? I'm having meatloaf and mashed potatoes," she said looking at Matty.

"Ma-tew, I love mash' 'tatoes," said Matty.

"Yes, I know." Matty was tugging on Matthew's hand and looking up at him with pleading eyes. "Okay, we'll come back and eat with Ollie."

Matty went running into the other room to tell Ollie, and Matthew gave Mrs. Miller a hug. "Thank you for asking us. I'd told Abigail I wanted to treat Matty for dinner, but he'll love being here with Ollie and you."

After the service was over and they had eaten, Matthew picked up one of the shopping bags he'd given Mrs. Miller for safe keeping. Inside, were gifts wrapped in bright paper. He picked out one and handed it to Matty.

"Please take it to Ollie's mother."

Matty did as told but stood looking up at Mrs. Miller with soulful eyes.

"Do you want to help me unwrap it, Matty? Here, tear this piece of paper off the package."

Matty pulled at the end and there was a loud rip. When the package was unwrapped, Mrs. Miller found a baking dish inside.

"Oh, Matthew, thank you so much. I needed one just this size."

Then Matty carried a thin gift to Ollie. "Yes, Matty, you can help me unwrap it," said Ollie before Matty could ask. Once the paper was off, a phonograph record of contemporary music for his Victrola record player was revealed. Ollie got up and put it on. Music floated through the air.

"We have some gifts for you," he said.

Mrs. Miller came out of Ollie's bedroom with two packages. Matthew's turned out to be the patchwork quilt she'd been stitching on her quilting loom. "Mrs. Miller, I can't take this. I'm sure you need it."

"But I've been making it for you. That's the reason I kept asking you if you liked the colors and design I was using.

"I do like it. Thank you both so much."

A smaller box went to Matty, who was so excited he couldn't open his own package without Matthew's help.

Matty started to shake the box to see if it would rattle. "No, no, Matty, don't shake it, something inside will break." Mrs. Miller hurried over to hold the package level. When it was opened Matthew understood why.

Inside were layers of Christmas sugar cookies with faces and designs on them. Matty squealed in delight. "See, there's a snowman and a Christmas tree," said Mrs. Miller.

"I think you'd better give Ollie and Mrs. Miller a hug for these," said Matthew pushing him in Mrs. Miller's direction. Matty was happy to oblige. He liked hugs.

"Merry Christmas to you," said Matthew and Matty as they headed toward the Anderson's.

～

Matthew didn't stay long at the Andersons. When the butler answered the door, Matty rushed in with his box of cookies looking for his mother. Abigail appeared in the hall.

"Look, Mama, cookies. Can I eat one?"

Abigail looked into the box and pulled out the Christmas tree, giving it to her son. "Go to the kitchen, and when you get finished you can come back."

"Hi, Matthew. I suppose those are from Mrs. Miller and Ollie." Abigail led the way to the parlor.

"Yes, they are, and look at the beautiful quilt she gave me for Tipton's Sugar Cove." Matthew pulled it partially out of the bag to Abigail's ooh's and aah's. "I was stunned when I saw it in the package. I know she and Ollie could use it themselves."

"They're always ready to share, even though they have little, whether it's music or food. I always come away from their house in awe at the love they've shown me while I was there."

"You're absolutely right."

Matty ran back into the room. Abigail brushed a few crumbs from his cheek.

"I have something for Matty." Matthew pulled out a box and handed it to the little boy. "Is it okay for him to open it now or should he wait until Christmas?"

"Open it now, Mama," exclaimed Matty, holding the package above his head and turning in circles.

"Go ahead and open it, Matty. Put your scraps of paper in the paper box."

"I have something for you too, Abigail." Matthew held the package out. It was a square box with a ribbon tied around it.

"I think I'll open it also. Is that all right?" Abigail looked up at Matthew, her eyes bright with tears.

"I didn't mean to make you sad."

Abigail was untying the ribbon.

"Tears aren't always a sign of sadness." The ribbon came off. Tissue crinkled in the box. "Oh, the hat, Matthew. How did you remember?"

"You looked so beautiful in it, I thought you should have it."

Abigail came over and gave him a quick hug. Her face touched his. The smell of her perfume lingered in the air and on his cheek.

"Mama, look. It's some britches."

"Why, Matty, it's a fireman's outfit. You can wear it when you play with your fire engine that Papaw made you."

Matty ran to look for his toy.

Matthew thought this would be a good time to slip out. When Matty found out he was going home for two weeks, he would want to go. He waved goodbye to Abigail from the road. "Merry Christmas," she called.

"Merry Christmas to you," said Matthew.

Alice's gift was a different matter. Matthew was careful to choose something pertaining to the college. When he presented her with a small box and a large one, she squealed, ran to him, and hugged his neck.

"Two, Matthew," she said, looking at him as if one contained a big secret.

She opened the large box first. It contained a tasteful, short jacket with the words, Maryville College, on it. She shook the smaller box to see if it would rattle. It didn't.

Slowly she opened the package, taking off the ribbon and removing the colorful wrapping, noticing it was the kind of box which should contain jewelry.

Matthew watched her growing excitement. He'd made the wrong decision and immediately regretted his purchase. *Alice thinks she's getting an engagement ring.* He started to stop her and explain his feelings toward her. He couldn't do it.

Matthew! What's wrong with you? Why can't you tell her?

Alice's excitement grew at each stage. She looked at Matthew with glowing eyes. Opening the smaller box, she found inside a pin to wear on her lapel, indicating that she was a pupil at the college. No words could describe the look on her face; small box, wrong conclusion. Then another thought entered her mind. "Matthew, we're pinned." Pinning was another way of saying a couple was going together.

Oh, how could I have been so stupid?

But Alice was delighted. *Matthew takes it slow, but this is progress. Wait until I show Mother. She'll be so excited. Of course, it isn't an engagement ring.*

Christmas vacation passed quickly. Matthew returned to Maryville College to finish the last semester; his final one at school.

✣ Chapter Forty-Five ✣

The Last Semester at Maryville College — Matthew

When the call came, it was dialed to Pastor Evens office. He was elated. He sent word for Alice. Her response was immediate.

"Matthew's been called to preach at Grace Church. Isn't that wonderful?" Pastor Evens paced up and down his office.

"Oh, I can't believe it. It's like a dream come true." Alice had schemed and pretended this would happen for so long, that the actual happening was anti-climatic. She felt weak, faint. She sat hard in the chair closest to her and put her head in her hands.

Evens thought she was crying. "Are you okay?"

"Yes. I could drink some water.

Pastor Evens went to get the water. When he returned, he explained his plan. "We need to approach Matthew carefully. No pushing. No pressure. I think I'll tell him before chapel in the morning. Then, before he can refuse, I'll ask him to think about his answer and let me know before the end of the semester. Deacon McGhee wants to know as soon as possible."

Alice nodded her head. But for once, her scheming mind was blank. She was content to let Pastor Evens make the plans, but waiting until semester's end meant not knowing Matthew's response for several days. She would spend those days on pins and needles.

"Alice, don't act like you know anything about this. Don't say anything at all. Better yet, don't go around Matthew. If he wants you to know, he'll tell you. Remember, he needs to make this decision without pressure from me or you."

This was the longest and hardest two weeks of Alice's life. She stayed away from Matthew, afraid she would say the wrong thing. They studied in the library and sat with a group at dinner in Baldwin Hall. She went home both weekends.

~

It was tempting, taking the position in Knoxville. In a moment of weakness, Matthew considered his options. He would be recognized in the ministerial association of Knoxville and be the pastor of a newly established church of ten years. A larger congregation meant more money, and he could hobnob with those who had power and prestige. Any idea or project would be fully funded and supported by his congregation. Then, there was the opportunity of accomplishing good within the greater community rather than the confined area of the cove.

Much like World War I, Matthew's war was over before it started. The struggle couldn't even be considered a skirmish. He would not accept the position. The battle and his decision were made years ago down on his knees beside his bed in Cades Cove.

Matthew smiled. *My decision will cause a conflict with Alice and Chaplin Evens. It's time to tell Alice how I feel about both her and the offer. Buck up, Matthew. You can do this.*

⁓

After receiving the unanticipated call to Grace Church, Matthew sent a long letter to Dr. Elmore. He explained his predicament and asked him to come to Maryville College, if possible, by the third week of January. Part of the letter said:

> *I know that Pastor Evens will be terribly disappointed when I say no. My position as the future pastor of my father's church hasn't changed. It's been the same from the first day I started at Maryville College, but some will not accept my decision. I would like to have your support should my choice become an issue with the chaplain.*
>
> *I hope you and Mrs. Elmore are in good health and I look forward to seeing you.*
>
> *Best Regards,*
>
> *Matthew Tipton*

⁓

While waiting for a reply from Dr. Elmore, Matthew went home to discuss the offer with his father. The opportunity came as they rode to check on his Aunt Annie.

The two walked their horses toward Rowan's creek as the morning sun shone on the fresh snowfall. It sparkled, and thousands of ice crystals flashed with each step the animals made. The low murmur of their voices mingled with the joyful splash of winter-water over the rocks of Abram's creek. Father and son rode in the camaraderie of their physical and spiritual relationship.

Thunderhead Mountain's snow-white face was clear and brilliant as it towered over the two men. Matthew squinted as he looked upward toward the dazzling white knoll, as the sun warmed his upturned face. A feeling of peace and calm flooded him. He'd been tempted, but he'd made the right decision. Matthew assured his father that his intentions hadn't changed. He still planned to assume the pastorate when his father retired. It was a divine moment between an earthly father and son.

~

Given the situation facing him, seeing Dr. Elmore was an emotional experience. He knew his friend and mentor would give him good advice.

His problem wasn't in making the decision not to accept Grace Church's offer, it was the repercussions that might follow.

It was late afternoon when the two men embraced at the door of Dr. Elmore's office.

"Come in and sit down." Dr. Elmore shut the door behind him and sat with Matthew before his desk.

"So, you've gotten an offer from Grace Church in Knoxville?"

"Yes Sir. I went as fill-in a couple of Sundays, and they've called me for their pastor.

"How did you hear about the position?" Dr. Elmore needed to know more about the situation before he knew how to address it.

"Pastor Evens received a telephone call asking him to recommend someone for Sunday worship. He recommended me, and I went before Thanksgiving.

Then they called me personally and wanted me to come before Christmas to speak. I did. The people are really very nice, and I enjoyed my trip to their church, but I've never intimated that I was interested in the position. I don't know why they even considered me for the job." Matthew would have gone on with his narration, but Elmore put up his hand to stop him.

"Let me get this straight. You were told this was fill-in and not as a try-out for pastor?

"Yes, that's true. At least, that was my understanding."

"Matthew, are you sure you've made the right decision? Grace Church is an excellent one. I know some of the people who go there."

"Yes sir, I'm sure. The people of Cades Cove need a pastor too. They're as much entitled to the best as any other church."

"I'll try to get to the bottom of this and let you know what I've found out."

"I need to let Pastor Evens know my decision. We'll be in chapel together and—" Matthew stopped and remained silent.

"Go ahead and inform him. Do it today. Tell him you intend to go to Knoxville and deliver the news in-person. That way he won't call and alert them in advance. Make sure he understands you don't want anyone else to know your decision. I'll go with you to Knoxville later in the week."

"That's exactly what I was going to do. I'm glad you're going with me."

"I'll be here for two weeks and attend the graduation ceremony. Isn't Tim graduating early?"

"Don't remind me. I'm dreading his leaving. I'll be a ship without an anchor."

As soon as Matthew left his office, Elmore called his friend at Grace Church and made an appointment to see him at his business the next morning. He asked his friend to see if Deacon McGhee could meet them for dinner.

∼

Telling Pastor Evens wasn't easy, but Matthew didn't back down. The pastor handed him the scriptures for the following week and said coldly, "You're giving up a lot, you know."

"Maybe so, but my decision was made years ago. It's not my decision, but what God wants me to do. I'm going to Knoxville and tell Deacon McGhee in person, and I would prefer no one else knew at present."

Pastor Evens threw up his hands in disgust and turned his back on Matthew.

"I'll see you in the morning at chapel, Pastor."

Evens made no reply, and Matthew let himself out the door.

He took that like I thought he would. But after the last few days of waiting and dread, Matthew felt like a load was lifted from his shoulders. He was walking on air. It wasn't long until he crashed down to earth.

∼

As soon as Matthew left his office, Pastor Evens rang Baldwin Hall and asked for Alice, ignoring Matthew's request for his silence. When she came on the line, he told her Matthew had turned down the Knoxville position. He didn't mince words.

Alice did not hang up the phone. She was so mad she slung the receiver against the wall. Where was he? She rushed out of the front door of Baldwin Hall, slammed it behind her, and stormed across campus. She wanted to destroy something, anything.

Who does Matthew think he is? I found him a great position at a respectable church, and he turned it down. I'll see that he never gets another offer at any church in Knoxville. What a dud he is.

~

After leaving Pastor Evens's office, Matthew stopped at the library to get a book. He was heading across the campus in the gathering twilight toward Carnegie Hall when he saw Alice storming toward him, her shoes crunching loudly on the graveled path.

"Stop! Wait up!" she screamed at him, her fists clenched.

Matthew stopped in his tracks, wondering if he needed to defend himself. He hadn't seen much of Alice since starting school in January, and he wasn't unhappy about that. He wondered why she was so upset.

"What do you mean not accepting the position at Grace Church? How could you do that to me?" Alice was in his face, and hers was livid. The veins in her neck stood out clearly under her skin.

"How does it concern you?" Matthew felt like he was being flogged by one of his father's roosters.

"What do you mean? I thought we were a couple and someday we might be married. We've been together for months.

"Alice, I was going to talk to you," Matthew sputtered. "But—"

Alice cut him short. "Did you think I would give up my life in Knoxville? I certainly didn't intend to live in *the cove*," she yelled at him. "You must reconsider!" Alice was still in her fantasy world.

"I've never said anything about marriage, and you were the one who kept following me around. How did you find out about me not accepting the position? I told Pastor Evens only minutes ago." Matthew's calm demeanor made Alice even madder.

"What does it matter how I found out? Turning down this offer is idiotic. You need to reconsider!" Alice stomped her feet and slammed a fist into her palm.

"How did you find out?" asked Matthew, realizing something wasn't right, and beginning to lose his calm.

"Pastor Evens called me. He's really upset too. You've disappointed both of us," she stormed.

Matthew sucked in his breath. He felt like someone had punched him in the stomach.

Betrayed.

Betrayed by a man I trusted.

When he recovered, he said, "The decision was mine to make, and really it was made years ago. I've told you all along what I'm going to do. You didn't have any reason to think otherwise. I've never misled you." Matthew raised his voice another octave, resolving never to trust Evens again.

"But-but Tim said he was going to be best man and you gave me a pin," sputtered Alice.

"Tim say's a lot of things in jest. Go bless him out." Matthew started to realize his procrastination and lack of clearly stating facts had led to this situation. "I gave

you the pin in friendship. Anything else you assumed."
But I didn't correct her when she assumed it, did I?

"Why didn't you tell me that?"

"I wanted to, but the time never seemed right."

Alice floundered around for a way to hurt him. "You wouldn't have fit in anyway. You're too country and backward. I'll bet that blue suit is the only one you own." The edge of her mad had worn off, and she realized she was cold. She turned around and abruptly headed for Baldwin Hall.

"What do you mean? At least I don't put on airs I don't have," retorted Matthew. He was beginning to get a feel for cross retorts. So, what if they weren't quite accurate?

"Thank goodness, I wasn't raised on a pig farm!" yelled Alice, "I'd guess the air there is worse than mine." She threw this insult at him as she walked away.

"How do you know how I was raised? You've never been to my home," Matthew yelled after her as she hurried down the lane. "And anyway, what's wrong with a pig farm as long as its honest labor? I'm sure your family eats pork." His father raised pigs to kill and eat, and many of the farmers in the cove did the same.

~

Alice didn't turn around but threw her hand in the air in a defiant gesture. She continued walking toward Baldwin Hall; her mind a jumble of thoughts.

Why would he deliberately turn the offer down? There must be another woman. That's it. Maybe the one Marsha and Clara saw him with. I need to check that out. He'll be sorry he's embarrassed and humiliated me. Yes, I'll check that out.

Alice arrived at Baldwin Hall and headed straight for Marsha and Clara's room.

The brain-storming session lasted over two hours.

Chapter Forty-Six

Searching His Soul — Matthew

Several minutes later, Matthew stood on the steps of Carnegie Hall, looking in the direction of Baldwin Hall and running his fingers through his hair.

What was that? Never have I spoken in that tone to Alice. And what about her? Is that the real Alice Davis? Did I cause this outburst? Am I to blame for Alice exploding?

Matthew's mind was a jumble of unanswered questions.

I thought she was going to hit me. Then it occurred to him. *She's capable of that. I saw it in her eyes.*

He turned, entered the men's residence hall, and headed for Tim's room.

Advice.

Good advice from Tim.

That's what I need, and soon.

Matthew hurried down the hall. He didn't stop to knock but barged right in. Tim wasn't there. But Matthew knew he would appear soon. They planned to study before he went home to eat supper.

Matthew collapsed on the unmade bed, putting his hands over his eyes. He'd often wondered about Alice, especially if she was suited for a minister's life.

Yes, he admitted, *I did consider the possibility . . . but not lately. When did my interest in her change?*

When she recoiled at the sight of Ollie's eyes and touch.

The realization was so vivid, he could feel himself snapping his fingers.

Then I wondered, how would she react to the unseen scars on my body?

Matthew shook his head and involuntarily rubbed his chest with his hand.

They're not as noticeable now, but the grizzly sight might turn off a person with Alice's prejudices and delicate airs. Alice isn't a tolerant person. This is obvious in her standoffish way around other people.

Why does my future always depend on these terrible scars? He rubbed harder, trying to dislodge them from his body, and wincing because they hurt when moved roughly.

Tim entered the room.

"What's wrong, buddy?" Matthew never stretched out on his unmade bed. "Are you sick?"

Matthew might have said yes, but instead he laid out the whole scenario that had just taken place, including the fact that he'd just turned down the position at Grace Church. The words tumbled over each other.

"She thought we might have a future relationship. I guess that may have been possible, except Alice . . . I don't know, the more I came to know her, I couldn't see us together. I guess I should have told her."

"I guess you should have, good buddy." Tim's comment was rather stern. "Might-of saved you the confrontation you just went through."

"There never seemed to be a right time."

"You knew she would become angry, is that it?"

"The tendency to become upset was always there, beneath the surface. She would pout if she didn't get her way and apologize profusely later."

"Kept you off balance, huh?"

"Yes, that's exactly it." Matthew shook his head back and forth. "I can't believe Alice thought I would accept the call to Grace Church, and we'd be married. Can you believe that, Tim?"

"Yes, I can—knowing Alice."

"What do you mean by that?" asked Matthew, looking at Tim. Instead of answering his friend's question, Tim asked one.

"Matthew, if you never saw Alice again, would you be devastated or relieved?"

"What kind of question is that?"

"Answer me."

"I'd be relieved. I am relieved."

"Matthew you may be book smart, but you're the most ignorant man when it comes to women. When you run around with one woman for months, it's almost a given that there's something going on besides friendship."

"I never said—"

Tim cut him off. "Think about it. Wasn't she just a trophy hangin' on your arm? Granted, she's the most beautiful woman on campus. It would be easy to do that."

"No, no. She wasn't a trophy. Is that what you think? I may not understand women very well, but I wouldn't treat a woman like that." *Or would he?* The thought jumped at him.

"Are you sure about that?"

Matthew didn't answer Tim's question but asked, "And why didn't you like her?" Matthew heard something in his friend's voice bordering on disdain. If he didn't like Alice, he'd never said so.

"I didn't have a problem with her until lately. I always knew she was shallow and definitely not a deep thinker. Mentally, she doesn't match your capabilities."

"But what happened to change your mind."

"Alice proved to me that she's manipulative and self-centered. And according to what you've told me, she doesn't tolerate the sick or physically disabled. Some minister's wife." Tim's sarcasm was evident. "What do you think she will do at the sight of your scars?"

"Yes, what would she think? How do you know she's manipulative and self-centered? I've never understood that about her. What happened?"

"Really, but she kept you off-balance. That's a form of manipulation. Pins and needles, walking on eggshells, isn't that the way we all felt around her?"

"Exactly." Another mental finger snap.

"We rarely saw the real Alice. She's hidden behind the mask on her face. You said yourself there were doubts in your mind. You knew she wasn't genuine."

"Yes, that's true."

"How do you think you received the call to Grace Church? How many college seniors have an opportunity like that? Do you have any idea how that opportunity fell into your lap?"

"I thought Pastor Evens received the request and recommended me. Was that not true? Did he deceive me—again?"

Matthew could believe this now. He would have defended the Chaplain before.

"Partially true, but Alice's family knew one of the congregation at Grace Church. He was on the search committee. The family recommended that they look into you as a prospect. After reviewing your records, they decided to give you the nod to come and try out. Are you following me?"

"No. I was to fill-in." Matthew insisted. "Where did you get this information?"

Tim ignored the question and continued, "Then after your second time to speak, her family pushed the man to extend the call to you to become their pastor."

Matthew held up his hand. "I'm sure they called me on the merits of my qualifications and not Alice's family's recommendations."

"I'm sure you *were chosen* for your qualifications also. Let's hope she and her family didn't make *that* much difference."

Matthew sat with his head in his hands as Tim continued.

"Now to answer your question. What convinced me of her duplicity happened one day as I was leaving Anderson Hall after Bible class. She wanted to talk to me. We walked out and sat on the steps of the building. It seems she needed to enlist my help. She looked at me with those big blue eyes and told me exactly what was happening, everything.

"Her exact words were, 'Tim, I'll never live in Cades Cove. I can't stand the thought of leaving Knoxville for those snake and chigger infested woods. Matthew's got the opportunity of a lifetime if he gets a call from this church. He might eventually become the pastor of the biggest church in Knoxville or Nashville. Who knows where he will end up? He's a gifted speaker.' She kept on laying out plans for your mutual future, and none of them included a pastorate in the cove." Tim waited for Matthew to say something. But Matthew sat as Tim's words came at him like hammer blows.

"I thought she was very presumptuous since you weren't even engaged. I guess she's never been denied anything she went after. Then she asked me to persuade you, if I got a chance." Tim paused. He needed to collect his thoughts before he proceeded. "You know I didn't do that."

Matthew shook his head. "No, you didn't."

"When you told me your suspicions about Pastor Evens and Alice being in cahoots, you were right. They conspired to get you to Knoxville, to immerse you in luxury, and to convince you to take the job if offered to you."

"So that's how it all came to pass. I didn't know." Matthew sat for some minutes in silence. He felt like he'd been dealt several hard blows to the head. He was addled and couldn't think clearly.

"I got the feeling she picked you out, because you were *the one* she could mold into the man she wanted. You had all the qualities she needed. Let's admit it. You're a good-looking guy and one of the smartest on campus. You just weren't rich enough, and Alice needs money. She needs lots of money to exist. She was trying to assure herself of the part you were missing. I'm sorry, Matthew."

"Me too. Do you mind if we don't study? I need some peace and quiet." Matthew got up from the bed and walked to the door. "Thanks, Tim, I can always depend on you for good advice."

"It wasn't advice this time, Matthew. It was hurtful information. I believe I'd write her off as a necessary experience."

∼

Matthew headed for the Hembree's and the safety of his room. He sat on the edge of his bed, trying to figure out what had transpired. Moving to a chair at his study desk, he sat looking out of his upstairs window. The sun turned orange, and the clouds were tinged with a bright orange glow. The day was drawing to a close and so was part of his life.

Exhausted, he returned to his bed, stretched out on his back and then his side. Soon he was sound asleep.

When Matthew woke up his head was much clearer. Alice was nonetheless on his mind. He faced some tough questions about the last few weeks. Was she only a prize on his arm? He'd told Tim no, but was this true? Tim's comment about what man wouldn't consider her a trophy caused Matthew to start thinking. Was he like every other man on campus?

Pride?

Pride. Matthew shook his head. Could he stand in the pulpit and preach to those in front of him on the subject if he harbored it in his own life?

All Christ-followers are works in progress. They're not perfect, Matthew, and neither are you. A pastor speaks from his own failure. And, he begs for forgiveness when necessary.

He sat several minutes digesting this profound truth.

Matthew admitted to a feeling of pride when he thought of beautiful Alice walking around campus with him.

I put up with her possessiveness. In doing so, I led Alice to believe she had rights to me when her attitude was an aggravation. But the smugness and pleasure he derived out of the other men's envy was real.

How could I mislead her? It was my fault. No wonder she was angry.

Matthew thought about Tim's idea concerning Alice picking him and pursing him. And then there was the scheming to place him in another church besides the one where he was called to preach.

It all fits! Whew! I even momentarily considered it. I need to decide how to approach this new information. Hopefully, it won't escalate to a bigger problem.

"Matthew, you'll apologize to Alice for leading her on as soon as possible." He wouldn't write her off as a necessary experience as Tim suggested.

Pastor Evens was another matter.

I can't believe he couldn't keep my confidence. I'll never trust him again. Should I continue with chapel or let someone else take my place?

The rumble in his stomach alerted him to supper.

I'm hungry. Funny how bodily processes keep functioning. The world falls apart around you, but your belly tells you it's time to eat.

Bounding down the stairs, he entered the dining room and greeted Mr. Hembree. He took his table napkin, shook it out, and placed it on his lap.

I need to see Dr. Elmore and tell him what I've found out. Tomorrow's Saturday. He may not be in his office, but I'll find him. I hope it will be a better day.

"Matthew, would you like some green beans?" asked Mrs. Hembree.

Devotions were longer than usual that night.

❧ Chapter Forty-Seven ❧

A Decision Made and Dealt With — Matthew

Matthew didn't find Dr. Elmore in his office or on campus Saturday, but he did see him at church on Sunday. They made an appointment for Monday at dinner.

"I've got some information for you," said Dr. Elmore

"I've got some for you too," responded Matthew.

"We'll eat in my office and that way we won't be interrupted."

~

Their meeting lasted over an hour. When it was over, Dr. Elmore called President Wilson and set up an appointment for Wednesday. He asked for Pastor Evens to attend.

"Matthew, you need to come. If you need an excuse to miss class, I'll write you one now."

"I'll need one for my Advanced Latin class. What are you planning to do?"

"I haven't completely decided." Dr. Elmore handed him the excuse.

"I'm sorry to cause so much trouble."

Dr. Elmore shrugged his shoulders. "I've not been comfortable with Evens for some time. I couldn't quite put my finger on the reason. I believe you've exposed the problem. The college may owe you some thanks after this is over."

~

President Wilson's office was crowded with four people sitting around his desk. When Pastor Evens saw Matthew and Dr. Elmore come into the room, he started to sweat.

Guess this is not a pat-me-on-the-back meeting. Elmore's always been a thorn in my career and Tipton, well, I'll take the tack that I recommended him for a position, and he embarrassed the college when he turned it down. Evens realized any excuse he made would be a lame one.

~

President Wilson and Dr. Elmore graduated the same year from Maryville College. Their friendship included years of full confidence in each other's abilities and dependability.

"Edgar, you called for this meeting. Do we have a problem here?" President Wilson started the meeting.

"Yes, we do have a problem. It started when a young woman schemed to get a man she intended to marry established at a church in Knoxville. Grace Church was looking for a pastor. She enlisted the help of Pastor Evens. Together and without Matthew's knowledge they formulated a plan to make this happen.

"At the same time, Pastor Evens misled the church to think Matthew was interested in a pastor's position. He wasn't. His plans were and are now to go back to Cades Cove and speak in his father's church. Evens told the church elder to work with him and pretend

Matthew was a fill-in. This was supposed to take the pressure off the young man whom he gave a high recommendation.

"Matthew was told the purpose of his speaking engagement was to fill-in. The church was looking for a pastor but they needed someone to speak on this particular Sunday. The scheduled minister couldn't make it or some other catastrophe had taken place."

"Is this true?" Dr. Wilson was watching Evens's reaction.

"Not quite. I suppose both parties came up with their own ideas about what I said to each. I could have spoken like that, but they've misconstrued my words to their own point-of-view. The position was an excellent opportunity for Matthew. For a young inexperienced man to find such a wonderful position matching his abilities doesn't happen often. He could go to Grace Church, grow in his ministry, and not be buried in an area where he couldn't expect to advance his career."

"He's," Dr. Elmore motioned toward Matthew, "never intimated he'd take a position other than the one in Cades Cove, has he? So, why did you pursue this course?" Dr. Elmore looked at Evens for a response.

"I still think it was an excellent opportunity for Matthew. His girlfriend was for it and wanted it to happen. He's embarrassed the college by turning down the offer." Evens rubbed his sweaty palms together in a nervous gesture and kept searching his mind for a defense.

Dr. Elmore continued with the information he and Matthew had gathered. He ended with, "Matthew received a call to the pastorate. Pastor Evens was correct in his assessment of Matthew's abilities. The search committee at Grace Church thought the same. If there's any embarrassment here, it's been created by the chaplain because of his underhanded methods."

The meeting was not going well for Pastor Evens. *Caught like a rat in a trap. All I can do is throw myself on the president's mercy.*

When the discussion was over, President Wilson got up from his chair, hands behind his back, and strode around the room. His lips compressed together in a thin line as they always did when making a decision. His emotionless face didn't show the deep contempt he had for a faculty member who couldn't be trusted. That was one thing he demanded of his college employees, his ability to trust them.

Knowing the gravity of the situation, Evens started to make another lame excuse. "President Wilson, I—", but Wilson cut him off by throwing up his hand and looking sternly at him.

"Please, Evens, I believe I've heard enough. You've been in this office before over questionable activities." Wilson sighed, resigned himself to the inevitable and went back to walking. Dismissing one of his professors wasn't one of the jobs he enjoyed.

Evens being called on the carpet in the President's office was news to Dr. Elmore, but he didn't need to know every minute happening at the college.

Dr. Wilson continued, "I've given you chances to redeem yourself when other problems arose." The president stopped behind his desk.

Everyone in the President's office waited for his decision.

"But this time, I can't do that. I would like you to tender your resignation for the end of the year. I want it on my desk this afternoon."

"What!" Evens, anticipating this response, jumped up from his chair. "You can't do that. I gave up important opportunities in the north to come here and teach these backward, ignorant people." He was fuming mad, clenching and unclenching his fists.

Matthew thought, *He's as angry as Alice when she confronted me as I walked to Carnegie Hall. I wonder if he's telling the truth about his myriad of prospects in the north.*

"I have done it." Wilson calmly stated. "I won't tolerate an employee I can't trust." Wilson was not being delicate about his opinion.

"If you feel that way, I'll quit, effective today. You people don't know what you're losing." Evens banged his fist onto the President's desk, walked out of the office and slammed the door behind him. He stormed past Dr. Wilson's secretary.

"Pastor Evens, are you all right," Nancy said, startled by his demeanor and determined stomp. His chin jutted out at an angle pointing to the outside door.

"I'm fine," he replied, mumbling under his breath.

I'll show them. I can get any number of positions where I live. Goodbye and good riddance.

∽

"I'm sorry, Matthew," said President Wilson after Evens stormed out of his office. "It's hard to believe that someone called to the ministry could be deceitful, but it does happen. I wouldn't want you to think many of us are that way."

"President Wilson," Matthew responded, "he's the only one I know."

"Edgar, can you and Matthew handle chapel in the morning until I make a decision on what we need to do? And we'll want to start looking for a new chaplain for next year, but we can discuss that later."

The phone on his desk rang. The conversation was brief.

"Nancy says my next appointment is waiting outside."

"Will you have some time this afternoon?" asked Dr. Elmore.

"Why don't we do a supper meeting? Come to Willard House. I'll call my wife and tell her you're coming to eat."

Dr. Elmore nodded and opened the door. He and Matthew walked down the hall and out into the cold, sunshiny day.

As they walked back toward his office, Dr. Elmore filled his young friend in on the rest of his visit to Knoxville. "Matthew, we don't have to go to Knoxville to see Mr. McGhee. I've talked to him. He did send you a message. McGhee wanted me to tell you, if anything happens and you leave your pastorate in the cove, you should let him know. He and the church are still interested in you. There might be a possibility for you at Grace in the future."

"Thank you, sir. I can't imagine any reason for me to leave the cove, but I will keep his invitation in mind. Will you see that he knows I appreciate his offer?"

"Graduation is Sunday night. We'll be wishing Tim goodbye. He doesn't know it, but I received an inquiry from the school district in Asheville. They have a position available for a substitute until the end of the year. It won't be teaching English, but it's one he can fill until the fall session."

"That's great. He's been wondering what he would do until next year."

"Don't tell him. I'm telling you in confidence. I'll let him know."

"You mean don't act like Evens."

Elmore shook his head. "That's a sad situation. I'm always sorry to see someone in difficulty because they've acted dishonestly, especially if it's in the ministry."

Matthew realized Dr. Elmore was talking about his situation with Alice. *But was I dishonest? Sure, you were dishonest.* Add that to pride.

~

Tim walked down the steps at Voorhees Chapel, newly graduated from Maryville College. A critically ill patient of Dr. Brackett prevented him from making the trip to see his son get his sheepskin. Nat and Martha, along with Donald Razor attended the commencement.

To celebrate, the young men headed to Tipton's Sugar Cove for the weekend. Squeaky dropped by to wish him luck and told them he was moving to Maryville.

"That's where the work seems to be. You'll have to come over and eat supper with us, Matthew. We'll be glad to have you."

On Sunday, Tim and Matthew went to church and ate dinner with his parents. Nat gifted Tim with a New Testament Bible.

"It's easier to carry," he said as a reason to give it to him.

Martha packed cheese and crackers along with apples they'd stored in the cellar in a small box.

"I would put fried chicken in the package, but I'm afraid it would spoil. I did put two biscuits with bits of canned sausage from our winter hog killing in your dinner box. I believe you'll enjoy it on your trip home."

～

On Monday morning, the two friends stood on the depot platform.

"You'll write won't you, Tim? I want to keep in touch and hear how you're gettin' along."

"Sure thing, buddy. I hope you'll come and visit me. You haven't been to Asheville. We'll tool around the countryside in Dad's automobile. We might even get to accompany him to the Biltmore Estate. Some of the employees call him when they get sick. Talk about a chateau in the mountains. Whew, it's the biggest house you'll ever see."

Wheee . . . the high-pitched train whistle blew long and loud. Matthew almost jumped out of his skin.

"Guess this is it, Tim."

The two friends shook hands and embraced, a manly embrace, of course. Tim boarded the train, his supper box in hand.

After the train disappeared from sight, Matthew walked slowly across the Maryville College campus. He had no reason to visit Carnegie Hall, but absent-mindedly and automatically he headed in that direction. Not until he started up the steps did he fully realize Tim wasn't a resident now. The hole in the pit of his stomach reminded him of his loss.

Even with Alice hanging around, he and Tim remained close buddies, going places, studying together, and bouncing ideas off each other; sharing guy things.

He had lots of memories. For three and one-half years, they ate meals at Baldwin Hall, talked of secrets, hopes and dreams. They'd walked miles going to church in Maryville, to the café, and to class around the campus. They'd ridden on horseback in Cades Cove, fished in Abram's Creek with Donald, and hiked in the Smoky Mountains during the summer.

Matthew knew there was a chasm in his life. He still didn't realize how big it was.

Where should I go? Back to Hembree's or to the library to study?

He decided to go to the library and prepare for chapel in the morning. He needed to finish his devotion. After Chaplain Evens resigned, President Wilson assigned five people to hold chapel each morning. Matthew was one of the five, plus he still read the scripture and gave the last prayer before the students were dismissed on a daily basis.

As he walked to the library, he thought about Alice. She was no longer a worry. She remained in school but had her chapel seat reassigned so that she sat on the back row. She was so far back, Matthew very rarely noticed her. They hadn't spoken since the big blowup after Matthew turned down Grace Church.

Alice wasn't very approachable, not that he wanted a friendly relationship. But, Alice never went anywhere alone, either Marsha or Clara was with her, acting as her first line of defense. If they passed in the hall between classes, Alice's glare was enough reason for Matthew to avert his gaze. He wanted to talk to her, to apologize, but given Alice's hallway demeanor, he knew the time wasn't right. He hoped her rabid feelings would diminish enough for a civil chat.

Alice and Tim were gone.

He thought of Abigail and Matty. They were the one constant in his life. More and more, he depended on them for companionship. Although Matthew continued to ask her, Abigail refused to attend church with Ollie and Matty on Sunday morning.

❦ Chapter Forty-Eight ❦

A Friendship Grows — Matthew

If Matthew didn't go to the library to study, he and Abigail walked home after their music lessons were over.

"Abigail, I'll pick you up at six thirty for the faculty recital." Matthew held up his hand when she started to object. He'd waited until the last minute, because he knew she would protest. "We're both planning to go and it makes sense for us to go together. I won't take no for an answer."

The warmer March wind was blowing in spurts through the empty gray branches of the trees, whipping them back and forth as the friends walked along Court Street. Cool nights and warm afternoons meant spring was on the way. Earlier in the week, Abigail had pointed out crocuses and grape hyacinths peeking forth from the ground.

"Do you like flowers?" Matthew had asked.

"I love flowers, all kinds. When I lived at . . ."

Abigail stopped in mid sentence pretending to swat at a mosquito. She had started to say at Red Oak Flats. But she didn't want Matthew to know she'd lived there.

"When you lived where?" Matthew questioned, hoping he would learn something about her former life. She didn't always live with the Andersons.

"When I lived with Pa, I had a lovely garden full of flowers." Abigail meant her forest full of flowers on Rich Mountain and in Pawpaw Hollow. She'd never visited again after the attack but often wondered how they were doing. It had been almost four years since the assault and over a year since she'd visited her father. He always came down to Maryville to see her.

"Abigail, how long were you married?"

"Oh, I can't talk about that. Don't ask me again. Promise me you won't ask."

"But Abigail . . ."

"Promise you won't speak of it again." She stood facing him, one hand on her hip, music books in the other. She didn't want to lie to him about her former life.

This was an awkward moment between them but Matthew understood her intent. If he didn't promise, he might not see her or Matty again.

"Okay, I won't mention it." They walked on until Abigail said goodbye at the Anderson's circular drive.

"I'll be back at six-thirty."

"We'll go as good friends." She called. She would go, no complications and no involvement. She wanted Matthew to understand she limited their relationship to friendship, although her heart was a traitor. Long ago, Abigail admitted to herself that her feelings for Matthew were more than camaraderie.

Matthew agreed, "Friends, okay." He responded. At least she was going.

Questions about her previous marriage and life haunted Matthew.

Why wouldn't she talk about this? Why wouldn't she go to church with Matty, Ollie, and me? What happened to her?

His intuition told him there was an undisclosed happening or trauma in her former life. Maybe her former husband beat her. Was he truly dead? What was the truth behind her refusal to speak about all those things? Divorce was still an ugly word in the foothills of Tennessee. Was that the problem? Matthew shook his head. Too many unanswered questions.

Maybe I should stay away and not see her and Matty again. But Matthew realized he was in too deep. He was drawn to Abigail like a moth to a flame. He intended to pursue her until he knew the truth, no matter what it was. Then he would make a decision about his future.

Was I the one who wondered what love is all about? Love is taking a chance on getting hurt. It's wanting someone who will complete and complement your life. Like Lazarus and Sarah. He hadn't thought of his uncle in several months.

Matthew chuckled to himself.

How things change.

Over one month ago, he'd turned down a lucrative offer from Grace Church. He and Alice had fought on the campus of the college over his decision and he hadn't talked to her again. Chaplain Evens was dismissed from the college staff. Tim graduated and went home to Asheville.

Now, he realized he'd probably loved Abigail for several months. Was that one of the reasons he'd pushed Alice out of his life? He loved Abigail, wanted her, but he couldn't tell her of his admiration or he'd never see her again. What a mess.

"Matthew, you may get hurt," he told himself. "But Abigail is worth the effort." He thought of Matty. Tears came to his eyes.

"That's it. Until Abigail opens up, I'm at a loss. Graduation is in two months. What then?"

~

Each year the music teachers at the college held a recital to showcase their expertise in piano, wind, and stringed instruments. One participant played the pipe organ which filled the loft behind the platform. An orchestra accompanied the musicians when it was needed.

The recital was held in the chapel on Friday night and the community was invited to attend. The musical event lasted over two hours with one short intermission. The school provided a reception with refreshments afterwards.

"Hello, Mrs. Tate." Abigail walked toward her piano teacher. "The concert was wonderful. I enjoyed your piece by Beethoven. I think Concerto #5 is my favorite."

Mrs. Tate stood sipping fruit punch. She watched as her pupils approached. "It's one of mine also. I wasn't aware that you two knew each other."

"We've been friends several months. Abigail's little boy, Matty, introduced us. We play together. That is Matty and I do," Matthew was quick to add. He smiled at Abigail and turned back to Mrs. Tate.

"I've been wondering, Mrs. Tate. I have a friend. His name is Ollie Miller. He's blind but plays the pump organ really well. He even writes his own music. I've been wondering if I could bring him over so you could hear him play. I'd have to do this in the afternoon after class. Is it possible we could have a special guest play in the student recital next month?"

"Oh, Matthew," said Abigail. "What a wonderful idea. Ollie would love it. He does play beautifully." Her guard was down. She glowed as she looked toward him.

Both students turned to look at their teacher.

Mrs. Tate was more reserved with her answer. "By all means bring him over. I'll listen to him play and make a decision after I hear him."

"That's wonderful isn't it, Matthew?" She stood under the light with her hands clasped together. What Matthew observed in her eyes wasn't friendship.

Matthew turned back to Mrs. Tate. "What day is best for you?"

"Let's do it Monday after your class, Abigail. I'll expect your friend at that time. The pump organ and pipe organ are different. We'll see how he does on both." Mrs. Tate turned away to speak to other acquaintances who came up to greet her.

"I think Ollie will be amazed when he hears about this. How long have you been planning to ask Mrs. Tate?"

"I started thinking about asking her last Sunday when he gave Matty and I an impromptu concert. I think Mrs. Tate is the one who will be amazed."

"You're absolutely right."

"Are you ready to head for home?"

"Sure."

They inched through the well-heeled crowd toward the door. Matthew recognized several people. President Wilson and Dr. Elmore stood with their wives on the far side of the room. Matthew caught glimpses of the mayor of Maryville speaking to the pastor of New Providence Presbyterian Church. He spied his cousin, D.H. Tipton, who stood talking to a tall, distinguished man dressed in a suit and tie.

"Abigail will you wait here? I want to say hello to my cousin. That is unless you'd like to meet him."

"Which one is he, Matthew?"

Matthew pointed out his cousin. "He's the one in the pin-striped charcoal gray suit talking to the tall man in black.

Abigail looked in the direction Matthew indicated and recognized both men. "No Matthew, I'll wait here for you. In fact," she said looking furtively around for a safe haven, "I'll wait on the promenade outside." She slipped out the door as Matthew walked across the room. Both men knew her and she was sure one of them could relate her history. D.H. Tipton worked for her Uncle John at his bank, and Mr. Townsend was the bank's best customer. She hadn't thought about the two Tiptons being related.

~

Matthew returned. "Aren't you cold?" The promenade was enclosed but not heated.

"No. I'm fine. My coat is warm, and I pulled my gloves on my hands."

"You should have met my cousin. I asked him about the war in Europe. He was in some of the battles."

"Most of the returning soldiers don't talk about their experiences."

"You're right. He didn't say much. The man with him is his new employer, W.B. Townsend. He's the tall man in the black suit. From what I understand Mr.

Townsend and some of his friends own the Little River Lumber Company at Townsend. This is the first time I've met him."

"He's a fine-looking man," said Abigail as they headed for home. She decided to change the subject.

"Matty said to tell you hello."

"It won't be long until we can play outside. I'm looking forward to it."

"He's been wearing the fireman's suit and putting out fires all over the house. Uncle John acts as if he's afraid Matty will put out his pipe. And Matty comes roaring over with siren's blaring. The two get into a wrestling match with one or the other getting the best of the situation. It's hilarious watching a grown man play."

"I believe you've even laughed at me a few times." Matthew was teasing Abigail. They were walking close together in the moonlit darkness. Occasionally, the headlights of an auto illuminated the path. Their swinging hands touched. Matthew reached for hers and caught nothing but air.

"The concert was wonderful," said Abigail after walking up the porch steps at the Anderson's. "I never get tired of listening to someone who's accomplished at playing the piano. I especially liked the rendition of the old spiritual, 'Swing Low Sweet Chariot,' didn't you?" She was looking down at Matthew, her eyes twinkling in the porch light.

Pools.

Dark pools of brown looked back at him. I've never seen her so relaxed. Music does that to people.

Abigail looked beautiful in the dim light. Matthew's heart pounded in his chest. He couldn't open his mouth to reply. He was afraid of what would come out.

"Matthew, are you all right?"

He might have said no, instead he answered, "I'm just enjoying this moment with you. I did like the concert. I hope we can go again soon."

"We'll see," she replied, thinking it was nice to have a friend like Matthew.

He walked her on to the front door, took her hand, and wished her a good night.

"I'll come and get Matty on Sunday." He said as he walked toward the road. Turning, he called, "Think about going with us."

∾

Matthew was tired. His day included his normal schedule of classes, preparing for chapel, and working on a thesis for his major in Bible. The Bible Training Department and other learning divisions at Maryville College required seniors to pick a subject and develop a paper. It was turned in to an assigned professor within each section. The professor checked the term paper and returned it to the student. Corrections and other suggestions were noted in the margins for the student to pursue. This process might take several revisions but finally it was accepted, went to the review committee, and graded. After many long nights at the library, Matthew was almost finished with his.

That morning, he'd gotten out of bed and walked over to look out of his open bedroom window. A warm breeze, typical of the last few days of March, blew into the room. In celebration of the coming spring, Matthew chose a short-sleeved, blue-striped shirt. He often wore the shirt in Cades Cove but not at Maryville College because it revealed a deep scar on his left forearm.

∼

Matthew walked along Court Street. His habit on Friday afternoon was to take the rest of the day off after finishing classes. Heading for the Hembree's, he saw Matty and Abigail outside in the landscaping. She was bending over to check on the daffodils poking green points through the pine needles. He stopped to say hello.

"I'm tired. This has been a long week," he told her, and she suggested the arbor at the side of the Anderson house.

"We can sit down and rest."

This area of the yard wasn't visible from the road because mature shrubbery hid it from sight, but nothing blocked the view from the parlor window.

"Matty, come on we're going to the arbor to swing."

The little boy came running, waving his black bear in the air.

Matthew held the swing steady so Abigail could sit down and then joined her on the curved seat. The couple sat swinging in comfortable silence.

Matty played nearby. Happy to be outside in the warm sunshine, his wooden bear growled and scratched at the grass, threatening the two occupants in the swing with early demise.

Aunt Mary, book in hand, looked out the parlor window and waved at the young couple.

She mouthed, "Hi, Matthew," and disappeared within.

The warm air caressed their bare skin and ruffled Abigail's wavy hair.

"Matthew, what caused the deep scar on your arm?"

The question startled Matthew. He'd forgotten the place on his arm was showing.

Now's the time to tell Abigail about the scars on my body.

"That's a long story." Matthew turned in his seat toward Matty cupped his hand to his mouth and added a little louder, "and I might also add a bear story."

When Matty heard "bear story" he came running. Bears were his present obsession and hearing a story about his furry friends was always on the agenda. His bear growled as it approached the swing.

"Do you know a real bear story?" he said, laying his bear on the swing and attempting to crawl onto Matthew's lap.

Matthew pulled the child upon one knee. "Yes, I do, but you'll have to sit still and be quiet while I tell it." The little boy leaned back against Matthew's chest, holding his animal friend in his lap and looking up at his hero.

Matthew started his story on the day the drought ended in April 1917. He talked about walking up to Thunderhead Mountain and arriving there at dusk. Of standing in the open field and looking around at the vista before him, first Thunderhead, then North Carolina.

"I turned west and saw clouds appearing on the horizon. To the north toward Rich Mountain, lights twinkled along the cove road."

∿

Abigail sat listening to his story. The drought ended the night after she was assaulted. On this same day, she remembered walking to a high hill above Red Oak Flats and looking out over Cades Cove toward Thunderhead. To the west she noticed a bank of clouds was building on the horizon. While she was looking over at Thunderhead, Matthew was looking back at her!

∾

Matthew finished telling the story. He gently put Matty on the ground. The little boy stood with his arm draped over Matthew's knee. The bear uttered no sound at all.

Matthew turned toward Abigail. Their knees touched. Now was the time to show her his scars.

He was nervous as he started to unbutton his shirt and said, "If it hadn't been for my mother, I wouldn't have healed as fast as I did. Her daily prayers kept me moving forward. She put salve on the wounds, changed my bandages, and encouraged me to believe my recovery would be complete. It took several weeks for the deepest wounds to heal. Six weeks for my broken arm to knit back together. If I'm tired, I sometimes walk with a slight limp from the terrific thrashing the bear gave me in the laurel thicket."

Matthew opened his shirt. "But these are permanent."

"Oh, dear God," gasped Abigail, putting her hand to her mouth and reaching out to Matthew. She touched the longest ragged scar on his chest. He clasped her hand in both of his and rested it on his chest, relieved at her response.

Matthew pointed to a deep area on the scar she'd touched. "That was the last place to heal."

Abigail had listened to the horrific account of the bear's attack, but the full realization of the terrible conflict didn't make an impression until she saw the scars. She looked up at him with tears in her eyes.

"Ma-tew," said Matty. "That's a bad boo-boo." He leaned forward and put his finger on one of Matthew's scars.

Abigail and Matthew burst out laughing.

"Yes, Matty it is a bad boo-boo. But remember bears are dangerous, and they can hurt you."

"I need to tell Papaw. He sees bears in the woods."

"And deer, and skunks, and squirrels, and rabbits, and so on," continued Abigail hoping Matthew wouldn't pick up on the bears in the woods comment.

～

Abigail and Matthew took turns bringing Ollie for his organ lessons.

After Mrs. Tate listened to Ollie play the pipe organ, she decided to give him lessons twice a week. Ollie was an astute pupil, but after three weeks she understood he couldn't learn the principles of the instrument in time to play in the recital.

"Ollie is not going to fail. I know exactly what to do."

She arrived at President Wilson's office without an appointment.

"Nancy, does the President have time to see me?"

"I'll see, Mrs. Tate." She picked up the phone to inquire.

"Go right in, Professor."

Mrs. Tate went into the president's office and greeted him.

"What can I help you with, Irene?"

"I need a favor." She quickly explained Ollie's predicament. "I'd love for him to play. He's very good, plus the disappointment will be terrible."

"What did you have in mind?"

"There's an old pump organ in the basement of Anderson Hall. Do you think we could move it to the chapel and place it on the platform?"

"Maybe. Let's go see what condition it's in."

President Wilson picked up his hat and headed for his office door, which he opened to let Mrs. Tate walk through.

"Nancy, we'll be in the basement of Anderson Hall."

"I see, sir. I'll send all of your visitors over to that dark, musty hole." She said this tongue-in-cheek.

President Wilson smiled at his secretary. "Oh, you won't have to do that. I won't be gone long."

~

After pumping the bellows and running her fingers over the keys, Mrs. Tate realized the organ wasn't in such bad condition. A few days out of the dampness of the basement would work wonders towards its restoration.

"A thorough tune up and it will play as good as new," she said.

"All right. I want to hear Ollie Miller play and if he's as good as you say I'll have the maintenance men move it to the chapel. When do you think we can arrange this?"

"How about tomorrow afternoon? We'll go to his home. It won't take long. That way you can hear him play on a good instrument. Okay?"

"I'm sure my schedule is clear. Have you been to his home?"

"Yes. I've been there. I'll let Mrs. Miller know we're coming."

꧁ **Chapter Forty-Nine** ꧂

The Recital — Matthew and All

The student recital was held on the last Friday in April. Matthew's mother and father came from Tater Branch to hear him play. Abigail's Aunt Mary and Uncle John Anderson walked to Voorhees Chapel to listen to Abigail. Mrs. Miller and Ollie came with Squeaky Benson and his wife, Charlotte. Tim was the only one not present.

Matthew peered through the backstage curtains at the audience. The chapel was filled to overflowing with attendees and participants. Forty-five students were scheduled to play. The pump organ and piano were center stage. Stage fright or something close akin to it caused Matthew's heart to beat faster.

Matthew, old boy, get over it. You can handle this.

He looked to see where Abigail was standing and heard her describing the scene to Ollie, who stood close by.

Walking over to them, he whispered, "Well, recitalists this is it. Are you both ready?"

"I think so," said Abigail.

"How about you, Ollie?"

"Oh, Matthew, I'm reminded of a verse in the Bible. It's found in Isaiah 42 and goes like this. *And I will bring the blind by a way that they knew not; I will lead them in paths that they have not known: I will make darkness light before them, and crooked things straight. These things will I do unto them, and not forsake them.* Isn't that a great verse?"

"It's a wonderful verse, Ollie."

"Matthew, I wouldn't be here if he hadn't brought you into my life. And I most certainly wouldn't be walking out on this stage if you both hadn't helped me. God hasn't forsaken me, and music is the light in my darkness. I am blessed."

Abigail hugged Ollie.

"Matthew, where are you?"

"Here I am, my friend." He stepped over to Ollie and gave him an awkward hug.

∼

As the audience came through the doors of the chapel, they were handed a program. Each student's name was listed along with the piece to be played, all except Ollie who would be introduced by President Wilson at the proper time. Ollie's teacher had assigned him three selections intended to showcase his talent.

Most of the student's pieces were short, including Matthew's and Abigail's. As first-year piano students, they weren't required to memorize long musical selections. Each student walked across the stage, sat on the padded square piano stool and played their composition at the concert piano. At the end, the audience applauded whether the performance was perfect or not. Some pieces were serious, some funny.

Matthew's was serious, but Abigail's started with "Mary Had a Little Lamb" and Mrs. Tate had asked her to give the history of the song. Abigail was a quick learner. The best one Mrs. Tate ever had.

Abigail walked across the stage and stood before the microphone. "The composition I plan to play is a favorite of mine. It's a version of "Mary Had a Little Lamb" adapted by my music teacher Mrs. Tate. This American folk song originated from a poem by Sarah Josepha Hale in 1830. It's based on a true incident in Massachusetts when Mary Sawyer, at the suggestion of her brother, took her pet lamb to school. This piece is lively and lots of fun. I hope you enjoy it."

Abigail walked over to the piano, stood beside the stool, and bowed to the audience. Then she sat on the stool, hands in her lap and took a deep breath as she was trained to do. If she was nervous it didn't show. Lifting her fingers to the keyboard, she started to play.

Matthew looked on from the wings of the stage. The spotlights in the rafters above shone down upon her. In the streaming light she looked like an angel in her white, iridescent dress as it fell to the floor around her. She moved with the music she played and ended the piece with a crescendo.

Everyone cheered and applauded. She was the hit of the recital.

Until Ollie played.

President Wilson came to the microphone to introduce Ollie. "Our next participant is a special guest. He plays the pump organ and has for many years. He also composes his own songs. Besides going to church on Sunday, music is his one great passion." Wilson paused for effect and then continued.

"Ollie Miller is blind. He will tell you that his fingers are his eyes. I needn't say anymore but let

Ollie's fingers speak for themselves and be the window into his world of music and into his very soul. Ladies and gentlemen, Ollie Miller."

President Wilson walked over to the side of the stage and returned, leading Ollie to the organ stool as the audience clapped.

Ollie stopped beside the stool. His knee touched its edge and, bowing, he sat down. Feeling the seat with his sensitive fingers, he realized Matthew had sneaked his home stool onto the stage.

Matthew watched with bated breath as Ollie smiled, placed his fingers on the keys, pumped the organ, and played.

Matthew shut his eyes and listened to the sound as Ollie heard it. The rhythmic pumping of the bellows did not detract but added to the overtones, gladness or pathos of his playing.

Bach's "Prelude and Fugue in D Minor" for the organ was the first piece. Next, he played a medley of current favorites. Matthew recognized some of the melodies from the record he'd given him at Christmas.

Ollie's own composition was the last one. He liked hymns and this one had a verse and a chorus. Each stanza was played in a different key, but the refrain remained the same. Ollie's fingers flashed over the keys, up and down, as he blended the different parts of his song.

When Ollie was finished, he stood up and received a standing ovation. President Wilson walked to his side and whispered in his ear, "Well done, Ollie. Everyone is standing and applauding you. Take another bow."

President Wilson stepped back.

Ollie's bow was graceful and deep.

The audience's clapping died down but they remained standing.

President Wilson walked to Ollie's side and said in a low voice, "Sit back down until I dismiss the audience." He walked to the podium.

"That concludes our program for tonight. I'd like to thank you for coming and thank our participants. They've all done well. Let's give them another hand." After the clapping stopped, President Wilson bade them all, "Good night."

Matthew and Abigail walked across the stage. Abigail bent down and hugged her friend. "Ollie, you were great. Where did you learn all the newest songs?"

"Matthew gave me a record at Christmas. I've been practicing. Matthew, did you like my interpretation of your favorites?" Ollie stood up.

"I did. And your hymn was superb. Especially the runs you played between the verse and stanza. I'll never understand how you do that."

"I'd like to be able to play like you, Ollie." Abigail stood with her arm around his waist. "Could you give me some lessons?"

"Sure, when do you want to start?"

The three good friends stood on the platform waving at people they knew in the crowd. People were elbow to elbow. After several minutes the throng near the stage thinned out. It moved toward the entrances in the back of the auditorium.

"Come, friend. I'll help you down the steps. The crowd has cleared out enough for us to stand at the bottom. We'll wait down there. We're in no hurry." Matthew was an expert at shepherding Ollie. They descended to the auditorium floor; three happy people.

"We've been invited to the Anderson's for refreshments to celebrate our excellent performances." Matthew told Ollie. "Well, at least your excellent performances." He indicated his two friends.

"Matthew, don't we meet the others in the outside promenade and walk down Court Street together?" Abigail looked at Matthew and smiled.

"Yes, we do. Let's head there now."

∿

Several minutes lapsed before the group assembled. The crowd had departed as they started down the sidewalk toward the road to Court Street. Everyone was in high spirits, talking at once and congratulating the recitalists.

"Ollie, you were wonderful," said Mary Anderson. "I never dreamed you played with such dexterity and passion."

"As President Wilson said, music is my passion."

"Matthew, isn't that Alice?" His father pointed in the direction of a blond-headed woman coming toward them.

Matthew looked up. He caught glimpses in the street lights of someone staggering across the campus lawn.

It is Alice.

Is she drunk? He'd never known Alice to drink.

She came up and stood before him, her hands on her hips. For months she'd stored up her anger against her former intended, biding her time. She looked around the group.

This is perfect. Everyone who's important in Matthew's life is here. He'll rue the day he insulted me and ignored my wishes.

She put her hand up to her forehead and closed her eyes for a second.

"Alice, are you okay?" Matthew didn't know whether to touch her or not. She was swaying as she stood facing him. Her beautiful face was ashen. Her hair matted and unkempt. "May I help you?"

"Haven't you already helped me enough?" Alice looked at him and sneered.

Matthew was embarrassed. "Alice, this isn't the time for a discussion. What's wrong with you?" He meant she looked sick.

"Miss Davis, you don't appear well. Let me help you." Matthew's father reached out and put his hand under her arm to steady her.

Alice jerked away and ignored him, concentrating on Matthew.

Staring at him.

"You know what's wrong with me. You two-timing rat. You country bumpkin." Matthew had no idea she hated him this much.

Alice didn't take her eyes off her victim.

She'd dogged him around campus following at a discreet distance.

Watching.

Watching and waiting for the perfect time to confront him.

Seeing his adoration of *that* woman. The one who'd stolen him from her.

Hurt.

Hurt him as much as she was hurt. That was her aim.

"Alice, I never two-timed you. I—"

"Who's she then?" Alice pointed a finger in Abigail's direction. "I guess she's a mirage." Alice's sentences were short, like her breathing. She was gasping for each mouthful of air.

Matthew looked at the others. He was helpless to stop her.

"Alice, please."

"Good luck to you, sister." Alice tossed her head and pointed her finger toward Matthew. "Maybe he'll disappoint you. Like he did me."

"I think we'd better go." John Anderson took his wife, Mary, by her arm. Abigail and Ollie walked behind them. Mrs. Miller led the way, followed by Squeaky and Charlotte.

"Abigail, I'm sorry," said Matthew before they'd walked very far.

Hearing Matthew say her name caused Abigail to stop and turn.

Her stricken face told volumes.

"This is not what it seems."

After a quick glance at him she turned toward Court Street and walked quickly to join the others.

"He's sorry all right, dearie. If you never see him again," Alice gasped, "count yourself lucky," she called after the disappearing figure. She swayed again and Matthew thought she was going to fall but his father stood close by and she grabbed his arm.

Matthew's father said, "Young lady, that's enough. You must be out of your head. Matthew would never do what you claim to anyone."

Matthew closed his eyes and shook his head. This wasn't happening. When he opened them again Alice was still there in front of him.

"Why, Alice? Why are you doing this?"

"You know what they say about a woman scorned." Alice laughed coarsely. It was a strange sound that trailed off. "My head feels foolish." She said it in a whisper.

Alice fainted and would have fallen on the ground, except Matthew caught her in his arms. In amazement, he realized she wasn't very heavy.

Alice was burning up with fever.

"Mother, she's hot. The flu's been going around. I wonder if she got it."

Mrs. Tipton came over to feel of Alice's head. "She needs a doctor right now."

"Matthew, you owe us an explanation," said his father. "But at this moment we need to get your friend to the infirmary. We'll both carry her there."

～

It was almost midnight. Pitch black outside as Matthew looked out the front window of the infirmary at Maryville College. His emotions were raw, exposed, tingling, but he refused to leave until the Davis's came to stay with Alice. He owed her that much.

Where are they?

Agitated, he paced up and down the infirmary waiting room. What had Alice done? Ruined his life?

His father and mother stayed with him until eleven o'clock. During this time, he'd bared his soul and related the entire story concerning Alice.

"Now I understand why she was angry." Nat sat with his feet upon a footstool in the waiting room. His feet hurt. "But her attack on you was excessive and uncalled for."

"I wanted to talk to her, tell her I was sorry, but when I looked at her, I realized she was still in a rage. I hoped that time would calm her feelings."

"It does seem there's blame to go around, Son. You've got to settle this with her as soon as possible."

"I will Dad."

"I've got to ask you one more question. Where does Abigail fit into your life? Your mother and I want to know."

"After tonight, who knows? My feelings for her are more than friendship, but I'm proceeding with caution. We haven't talked about anything permanent." *We haven't talked about anything at all*, he thought.

"You love her," asked Martha.

"Yes, very much. But with Abigail there are so many unanswered questions. They might threaten any relationship with her."

"But you will find out the answers, won't you?" Martha stood up. "Nat, I'm tired." She was ready to go to the Hembree's. Eleven o'clock was two hours past her bedtime.

"She may never speak to me again after tonight. But I can tell you one thing. I intend to pursue her and find out the truth about her life. I don't want to lose her."

"Matthew, I'm going to take your mother over to the Hembree's and put her to bed. Where will you be tomorrow?"

"Here. At the Anderson's or the Miller's. Take your choice. I've got to apologize and explain what went on tonight to each of them. I can't imagine the experience being very pleasant." He shuddered at the thought.

"Martha, wait for me on the porch." Nat turned to Matthew. "Son, you can see what putting off inevitable problems can cause."

Matthew nodded his head.

Nat came over and put his arm around his son. They walked to the door. "Don't do this with Abigail. Insist on the truth and do it as quickly as possible."

"I'll start tomorrow. It isn't as if I haven't been trying to find out. I've asked, but I haven't insisted on answers."

"Your mother and I like Abigail and Matty. We worry about the questions surrounding his birth. I'm sure there's a reasonable explanation. I hope so. Your intention to become a minister of the gospel and stand in my pulpit requires you to be cautious and stand for the principles you've been taught. This is a tremendous responsibility."

"Yes, Dad, I know. I've been concerned about the same thing. I guess being busy with finishing my senior year here at the college is no excuse."

"We make time for those things that are needful. This is needful. Your mother's probably getting cold. We'll see you tomorrow."

Matthew went back into the room where Alice lay. She was asleep. *Where are her parents? Don't they care about their daughter?*

The Davis's came rushing in at twelve-thirty.

"Matthew, how is Alice?" Blanche Davis hurried over to her daughter's bedside and felt of her forehead. Alice's eyes fluttered open and closed again.

Mr. Davis stood close to Matthew.

"She's got the flu, Mr. Davis. Several of the college's students have had it." Matthew was tired. He walked over to a chair in Alice's small room and sat down.

"We didn't find out about her illness until we came home from the benefit ball. The servants have strict orders not to drive our cars and there wasn't a telephone in the building to call us. We changed clothes and came over immediately."

He walked over to his daughter's bedside and took her hand. Matthew watched as the two hovered over her. They seemed upset with each other. A short exchange of angry words proved his suspicion.

"You could have driven faster, and we'd have been here earlier."

"Really? I suppose your long-winded exchange with Madame Whitfield couldn't have been avoided, or the thirty minutes you took exchanging clothes after we arrived home couldn't be helped."

"You always turn everything back on me. It's always my fault." Mrs. Davis was very close to tears. Tears, she'd learned years ago, melted her husband's heart. They started to trickle down her face.

Mr. Davis sighed and returned to Matthew. "Sorry you had to hear that. I'm sure you're tired."

Matthew didn't say anything but nodded.

"Being tired is part of our problem." He lowered his voice to a whisper, "Blanche gets grouchy and sharp-tongued when she's worn-out." He resumed talking in his regular voice, "Go on home and we'll stay with her tonight. Will you come tomorrow?"

Matthew looked at him. Hadn't Alice told her parents of the separation? Apparently not, but why not? "Yes, I'll be by to check on her." What else could he say? One confrontation a day was enough. He got up and started toward the door.

"Matthew, thanks for staying with her."

"You're welcome, sir."

~

Seeing Abigail the next day was impossible. Although Matthew went twice to the Anderson's, he was told she was out of the house and no one seemed to know when she'd return. Talking to Ollie and Mrs. Miller was much easier.

"Matthew, you don't have to explain anything to us. I talked to Mama about Alice months ago. We both decided it would make us happy if you never saw her again. We didn't tell you, but we didn't like her."

"All the blame isn't Alice's. I put off telling her I wasn't interested in her for weeks and that led her to believe I was. I wanted to apologize, but she was angry and I was afraid to approach her."

"Have you talked to Abigail?" Ollie asked.

"I've been by the Anderson's twice. She won't speak to me. The butler tells me she isn't there."

"Maybe she isn't, Matthew."

"Surely the Anderson's wouldn't lie to you." Martha added.

"After last night, I wouldn't blame them if they did."

Mrs. Miller's heart went out to Matthew. He sat downcast and quiet, not like himself at all.

"Do you love Abigail?" asked Mrs. Miller.

Matthew nodded his head and said, "Yes."

"I think she loves you too."

"I hope you're right." Matthew got up from his chair. "I have to go. I'm going to the infirmary to see

Alice. As soon as she's better, we're going to have a serious talk."

"Are you going to see Abigail this afternoon?" asked Ollie. He was worried about his friend's subdued attitude.

"No. I'll go by in the morning to see if Matty's going to church."

"We're still going in the morning?"

"We are."

∾

Matthew knocked on the Anderson's door. When the butler opened the door, he asked for Matty.

"Good morning, I'm here to pick up Matty for church." Matthew held his breath as he waited for an answer.

"Master Matty isn't here, but Mrs. Anderson wishes to speak to you. Please come into the parlor, and I'll tell her you're here, sir."

Matthew was led into the men's sitting room where the smell of cigar smoke assaulted his nostrils. Comfortable chairs invited him to sit down, but pacing was more to his liking.

I'm not going to pace.

His heart had turned stone cold when the butler said Matty wasn't there. *I'm not going to think the worst. This can all be worked out.*

Mrs. Anderson entered the room. She came over and extended her hand.

"Please sit down, Matthew." She indicated a chair with her hand.

Matthew sat down and waited for her words.

"Abigail and Matty have decided to visit her father for a few days."

Matthew looked down at his hands in his lap and said, "Is she upset over Alice's outburst Friday night?"

"Matthew, I can't say. But something prompted her to leave here."

He looked at Mrs. Anderson. "There's an easy explanation for Alice's actions. I haven't talked to her since January. When she realized that I couldn't be manipulated into going against my principles, she decided not to speak to me again."

Matthew went ahead and explained to Mrs. Anderson the same thing he'd told his parents. He didn't hold anything back, including the fact that he loved Abigail and Matty.

"Alice is in the infirmary with the flu."

"Matthew, I'm sure Abigail will be back soon. You're welcome to stop by and check on her."

Matthew heard the clock strike nine. "Oh, I've got to go. Ollie's waiting on me to take him to church. He's a stickler for being on time."

They both arose, and Mrs. Anderson followed Matthew to the door.

"Didn't Ollie play well Friday night? I'd love for him to give a concert here and play for my friends."

"Yes, he's a wonderful organ player."

"I'll see you later. I need to go." Matthew ran down the driveway. The last Mary Anderson saw of him, he was still running down Court Street.

Mary climbed the stairs to the master bedroom. Her husband John, stood in front of the dresser mirror tying his tie.

"How did it go?"

"I think I'm on his side. Abigail should tell him the details of her life, and Matty's birth, and let Matthew make up his mind."

"You didn't tell him?"

"No, Abigail asked me not to. But if she doesn't come back, and he continues to come by to see her I may."

"I'll let you make that decision. What's the story behind the crazy girl's comments the other night?"

"I'll tell you the story as we go to church. Are you ready?"

"Yes, let's go."

John held the door for his wife, who said, "I like Matthew. He's honest. He and Abigail would make a charming couple."

"Yes, dear."

Matchmaker.

John smiled, closed the door, and followed his wife down the hall.

∼

Abigail sat on the hilltop overlooking Red Oak Flats. The shock of her feelings after Alice's declarations caused her to face reality.

What am I thinking? Years ago, I decided I can never marry. What man would want a soiled bride? A soiled bride with a child.

But Matty loves him, and he loves Matty.

Abigail sat for several minutes staring with unseeing eyes at Thunderhead in the distance. The day was balmy for April with a breeze rustling the laurel leaves. The noisy wind was changeable, stronger and then diminishing until it was so soft, she couldn't see it in the trees, or feel it on her bare skin.

What an amazing feeling being with him, hearing him talk about his school, his dreams for the future and his ministry.

His ministry. Abigail you've lost your mind.

Dream.

Go ahead and dream on. Even if there was a chance for marriage a minister is the last partner I could expect to marry. What was I thinking? And I was thinking about you. Something I promised myself I'd never do.

Never do about any man.

Alice brought me back to my senses. Made me realize how often I think about you, how deeply and yes, how I've fallen in love with you.

This Alice doesn't bother me. I've been around you enough to know her utterances aren't true. There's a good explanation. I know you wouldn't lead someone on. You would be true to the principles you've been taught.

How I wanted to hold him when he revealed the horrible scars on his chest. Reach out to him. Touch him.

Tears ran down Abigail's face as she groaned.

I have scars to. Take me in your arms. Tell me I'm acceptable.

"Oh, Matthew! Why did I fall in love with you?"

Thunderhead gazed down at the agonizing woman.

Abigail sat for several minutes much like Matthew had seen her on the fateful day they met on Rich Mountain. After a while she arose and with a sigh and a softer moan headed back down the mountain to the Flats.

The inward struggle pushed down deep within. Over for today.

❧ Chapter Fifty ❧

Preparing for Graduation — Matthew

The rest of April and the first two weeks of May were crowded with senior activities. In the midst of all the hustle and bustle, Matthew managed to have a long talk with Alice and apologize.

She saw his heartfelt regret and avowed her undying love. "There's still hope for us, Matthew." Tears trickled down her cheeks.

Matthew remembered the scene upon the Davis's arrival at her bedside. He was firm but gentle when he told her she needed to find someone else.

"Do you love the other girl?" Alice had asked.

"Yes, I do."

"What's her name?"

"Abigail."

When she would ask another question, Matthew held up his hand to stop her.

"Alice, we don't have anything else to talk about."

They could never be friends. It was better not to try. He turned and walked out the door of her infirmary room.

∽

Graduation was on Wednesday of the third week of May. Tomorrow was the long-awaited day. Then he would be released from school and be ready to return to Tipton's Sugar Cove. His days were non-stop college activities from daylight to dark.

The lower grades were still in school, but the seniors were finished with classes. His thesis was in and accepted with high marks. That morning he collected his cap and gown. In the afternoon, he'd met with the graduation committee to help with the final preparations for the ceremony. Later in the day, several hours were spent in the chapel supervising the stage setup.

〜

Matthew walked down Court Street, headed for the Hembree's. On an ordinary day, he and Tim would have studied in the library or his room. This wasn't one of those. Tim was gone and, with classes finished, he felt like a ship without an anchor. What to do with the rest of the day?

And I thought I was tired before.

As he passed the Anderson's he thought of Abigail.

No, I won't go there today.

The two times he'd stopped, the answer was the same. He didn't have time to pursue her now. Since his rent was paid until the end of May, he decided he would press the issue during the week after his graduation. This was his packing week as he finalized plans to return to Tipton's Sugar Cove on Wednesday.

I haven't thought about home in ages.

Paradise.

Peace and quiet in my Eden on earth.

How wonderful it will be to return and start life in earnest.

Sadness.

Sadness mixed with the thought of paradise? Why? He could answer that question in one word. Only he could solve the problem.

He bounded up the steps to the Hembree's and opened the door.

"Matthew," said Mrs. Hembree. "Look who's here." She was sitting in the parlor, entertaining someone he couldn't see. When he came in the door, she got up and headed for the kitchen.

"Tim!"

The two friends embraced, a manly embrace of course, while slapping each other on the back.

"How did you get here? I didn't know you were coming, you scalawag. Why didn't you write me?"

"I wanted to surprise you and, anyway, I wasn't for sure I could come. It was a last-minute thing."

"I think I like last minute things. Come on upstairs to my room so we can catch up. So much has happened since you left."

Matthew reached the first step when Tim changed the plan.

"I want to take you to the Maryville Café for supper. I haven't had potato and bacon soup since I went home. I told Mrs. Hembree we wouldn't be here to eat."

"Let's go." The two friends walked out the door and over to Court Street. They headed for town.

"Do you think Ollie would like to go with us?" asked Tim.

"I'm sure he'd go, but if you don't mind, I'd like to talk to you alone. Life's been hectic, and you've not been around to give me good advice."

"Nothing's changed, huh?" Tim shook his head. His friend Matthew could get into more messes than anyone he knew.

"Now don't start, buddy. I'm so glad you could come."

The young friends continued down Court Street and up the steep hill to Broadway Street. Turning right they walked a few feet to the café.

Ordering food didn't take long.

"Are you ready to graduate and become part of the real world, my friend?"

"I'm excited. Getting back to the cove has been a constant dream for two years.

"When do you start pastoring your father's church?"

"We'll split the responsibility for the ministry this summer, and in September I'll take over the pulpit. Dad says he'd still like to preach on occasion. Since you left, I've been going home to preach one Sunday each month. My reception has been enthusiastic. I'm grateful for the opportunity to preach God's word."

"I believe your cove life will be busy, but definitely not as glamorous as the Knoxville one would have been."

"It's going to be interesting, juggling my farm chores, studying the Bible, and preaching each Sunday. I've always wondered how my father worked all these activities into his life. I'll soon find out." Then Matthew added, "I don't think I'll miss the Knoxville scene."

"Your dad always went to the field early in the morning, before the hot sun rose overhead. I can see him now in bib overalls, denim shirt wet with sweat, and old straw hat pulled low over his eyes. I remember him saying he finished garden and field work before the heat of the day. Afterward, he'd come into the barn and sit in the old cane chair; the well-used one with its bottom almost gone, to pull off his muddy brogans."

"Yes, Mom always made him pull off his plowing boots in the barn and change into his regular shoes." Matthew chuckled. "I don't think he ever tracked mud into her kitchen."

"Your mom's even-tempered, but I believe she could communicate her displeasure to the reverend."

"And did many times. Dad was trainable, especially when it came to her."

Tim laughed, and Matthew continued.

"My habit here at school has been to study the Bible in the morning and have a short devotion at night. Earlier in the day my mind is fresher, more agile. Maybe I'll get up before daybreak. What about you? What are your plans?"

"There's no farm to tend, but I want to buy a small house. Teaching doesn't give you much opportunity to harvest fields, but a small garden would be nice." Tim had a secret, but he wasn't ready to spring it on Matthew. "What about Alice? What's happened to her?"

"Alice has been a thorn-in-my-flesh for several months." Matthew went on to explain the problems Alice's possessiveness had caused. "When she blew up the last time and was flat on her back in the infirmary, it gave me the chance to talk to her, apologize, and tell her there wasn't any future for us. I haven't spoken to her since."

"And Abigail."

The smile left Matthew's face. "I don't know. I don't know. Alice's words may have upset her. Probably did. She left and went home to her father. I don't know where he lives, but Mrs. Anderson does. Next week I intend to throw myself on her mercy. Beg her if necessary."

"You're a slow learner, buddy."

"I believe you've said that before."

"In an earlier life." Tim smiled. "School seems eons in the past."

"I realize my love intuition is slow, but I'm sure Abigail is my help-meet. I only wish I knew the story behind her marriage and life. She's been very close-mouthed about Matty's father. When I first met her, knowing was not a problem. Now it is. I hope the truth won't separate us forever."

Now, Tim laughed. "I recognize this is serious, but I can't help it. First, you have one girlfriend that you don't want and can't get rid of. Now you have one you want but can't have. She runs off and leaves you. Seems like you're unlucky at love."

"I don't believe in luck, Tim." Matthew smiled wryly, nodding his head up and down. "There's a purpose behind all this. I don't know what it is yet. But I believe, my intuition if you will, tells me this will resolve in the near future. Wait and see. As the Bible says when Moses parted the Red Sea," Matthew threw up his hand, *"stand back and see the glory of the Lord. I'm waiting on it."*

"I can't imagine a miracle like the Red Sea parting."

"A miracle is a miracle Tim. I've been believing in 'em more and more of late. Trust me, God has a reason in this."

~

"Matthew, I have a girlfriend." Tim said it so matter-of-factly the import didn't register with his friend for a second. They were finished eating and headed back to the Hembree's.

"What? You have a girlfriend, buddy, that's great. When did this happen? What's her name?"

"I've known her some time. We went to school together before I started to Maryville College. Her name is Alice."

"Alice! You're not telling me the truth. Alice!" Matthew haw-hawed. "I don't believe it."

"Rather ironic, isn't it?" Tim struggled to maintain his composure.

"It's hilarious."

"I've learned to wash dishes. No apron." Tim shook his hands and head back and forth. "No apron."

Matthew stopped in his tracks. He was bent over with laughter.

"Oh," he gasped, "And you question miracles. We've got to go by and tell Mrs. Miller the news."

"I didn't say I didn't believe in miracles. And we don't have to tell Mrs. Miller. I don't think so."

"She deserves to know. Come on, Ollie and his mother will want to see you."

They made a detour to the Miller's, but Matthew didn't bring up the subject of the apron.

~

"When do you plan to marry?" asked Mrs. Miller.

"Maybe this summer. We haven't set a date. All of my East Tennessee friends are invited."

"Ollie and I would like to come, but we don't travel far from home. We will pray for you and your future wife."

"Thank you. I can't think of anything Alice and I would want more."

~

Mrs. Hembree moved a cot into Matthew's room and the two young men spent their last night together for many months or years to come. Neither one knew when their next meeting would be.

Chapter Fifty-One

Graduation Day, 1921 — Matthew

If Maryville College had ordered a special day for graduating the Class of 1921 it couldn't have been more beautiful.

The sun came up over Chilhowee Mountain, shedding rays of light over the tree-studded campus and casting long shadows on the grass. The newly green leaves of spring danced in the morning breeze and the chirp of a robin on the lawn came clearly through the open upstairs window. A new day was dawning.

"I believe that's our wakeup call, Tim," said Matthew listening to the early bird and stretching his arms above his head. "After the graduation ceremony, we'll meet Mom and Dad for a special dinner at Baldwin Hall. Dr. Elmore and his wife will be there."

~

When the sun was almost overhead and the shadows directly under the trees, Matthew walked quickly across the stage, received his diploma, and shook the hand of President Wilson.

"Matthew, I hope you'll come and see me when you're in Maryville," he said.

"Yes sir, I'd like to keep up our acquaintance."

"Congratulations, young man." The handshake ended, and Matthew exited to the auditorium floor. He settled into his seat next to the aisle in the section reserved for graduating students.

Looking across the walkway, he saw his mother pull a handkerchief out of her purse and wipe tears from her eyes. Even his father's eyes appeared to be moist. He raised his hand and, with a slight motion, waved his sheepskin to catch their attention. The smiles on their faces were happy and proud. Thanks to his Uncle Lazarus, Matthew was the first person in the extended Tipton family to graduate from college with the intention of becoming a minister.

After the ceremony, Voorhees Chapel was alive with back slapping, hand shaking, and congratulations. Recent graduates milled around outside on the lawn, exchanging addresses, and saying goodbye for the last time. Packed trunks were either sitting at the depot or loaded into automobiles waiting on the rocked lane leading to Washington Avenue. Many of the students went straight home.

The rest of the crowd headed *en masse* for Baldwin Hall and a dinner hosted by the college for graduates, family, and friends.

As the happy Tipton family and friends walked through the chapel door for the last time, Matthew thought he saw a familiar figure in the crowd. Was it Abigail?

"I'll meet you at Baldwin," he said and hurried off in the direction of a disappearing familiar hat before anyone could protest. Bucking the moving crowd proved to be impossible and Matthew lost the well-known chapeau in the crush outside the chapel.

Advancing to the edge of the promenade, he strained to see her figure in the distance. If it was Abigail, the earth had swallowed her up. He stood for several minutes looking toward Court Street. She was nowhere in sight.

With a burst of energy, he ran toward Baldwin Hall and joined family and friends in the cafeteria line.

~

"Dr. Elmore, you've been my mentor and example to follow for four years." They stood outside Baldwin Hall. While everyone else visited, the two had a private moment. "Do you remember the first day we met? Uncle Lazarus brought me down from Cades Cove, and we had dinner together here in Baldwin Hall."

"I remember a young man with lots of dreams. I was very impressed with you."

"Four years have passed since then."

"Four busy years for you. You've changed, wouldn't you agree?"

"Yes. I have. I'm a much wiser man in two ways. I've absorbed all Maryville College could teach me. My ministry will be enriched because of the Bible and Bible related classes I've taken. Since we had our talk about studying and understanding God's Word, I've endeavored to spend more time reading and meditating on each individual word." Matthew smiled. "A couple of months ago I preached a whole message on one word."

"What word was that?"

"Fellowship."

"Ah, assembling believers together to study the Bible and to enjoy each other's company.

"Yes, and showing fellowship by visiting the sick, tending to widow's needs, and the most important fellowship, your one-on-one with Christ."

"I see. What is the second way you've changed?"

"I'm much wiser in relationships. I believe I understand people better. I didn't grow up around young people. Relating to others, the camaraderie of friends I've found has changed my life."

"You'll miss Tim?"

"Of course."

"What about the young lady we talked about? What has happened to her?"

"She's out of my life. She wasn't the person who'd complete my future. My interaction with her helped me understand women better, and most importantly, not to procrastinate."

"Is there anyone else?"

"I think so. But I haven't approached her. I hope she'll be a part of my life."

"Will you come to visit me in Chattanooga? My wife and I would love to have you. We'll take you around to the most interesting sites and feed you lots of good food."

"I'd love to come. Maybe before the summer is over?"

"Let's plan on it."

～

Nat looked over at his son, who was in earnest conversation with Dr. Elmore.

"Martha, I'm proud of Matthew. He's grown into a fine young man."

Martha glanced at her son. "We did a good job, didn't we?"

"I still wonder about Abigail. How will she fit into his life?"

"Remember, Nat, she's in God's hands."

Nat nodded his head and put his arm around Martha. It was time to say goodbye and head back to Tater Branch.

❧ Chapter Fifty-Two ❧

Solving a Conundrum — Matthew

Matthew sat on the edge of a comfortable blue couch in the parlor of the Anderson house. It might as well have been a blue rock. He was troubled.

He visualized himself sitting on the brink of a precipice. Below was a thousand-foot drop. If this conversation didn't go favorably, his hopes would crash off the brink with a distant thud.

There's a reasonable explanation for Abigail's reticence in telling her history, and Mary Anderson knows it. Oh please, God, let it be something we can surmount together. Matthew had been praying this prayer for weeks.

She sat down opposite him.

"How does it feel to be a college graduate?" Mrs. Anderson was smiling at him.

How can she be so calm?

"I don't feel any different. I won't understand its importance until I'm in Tipton's Sugar Cove."

"The cove must be a beautiful place. You talk about it often."

Matthew looked out the curtained window of the parlor. In the distance, Chilhowee Mountain appeared hazy blue in the afternoon sun, which cast mirrored patches of light on the rug. Although it couldn't be seen from the window, hidden beyond the rise in the foreground was Rich Mountain and past that Tater Ridge where his father and mother lived.

"To use a phrase out of the Bible, It's the Garden of Eden. Mrs. Anderson, I can stand on my front porch and look down into the shallow valley. There are huge fields of corn and wheat on one side and my cattle in another area. Right in front of my home and close to the barn, the horses graze in the pastureland. My first garden will be planted in a vegetable patch my Uncle Lazarus planted for years. It'll be a late start this year for peas and potatoes, but corn, tomatoes, beans, and okra will grow well and yield a good harvest." Matthew's enthusiasm covered his anxiety for a moment.

"I hope I can visit someday."

"Oh yes. You're welcome any time, you and Mr. Anderson."

"When do you leave for home?"

"I hope to head there on Wednesday."

Matthew took a deep breath and plunged on.

"Mrs. Anderson, please, you've got to help me. I need to talk to Abigail. Where is she? Where does her father live? Is it close by?"

"Matthew, Abigail asked me not to tell you, but I've talked to John, and he left the decision to me. I think you should know. My niece was raised on Rich Mountain in Red Oak Flats," Mrs. Anderson held up her hand. "I know the place doesn't have a good reputation, but my brother, Chuck White, protected his daughter from the general population. It was many years before she fully understood the happenings surrounding her."

Matthew was shocked.

He rode a horse or drove a buggy past the trail to Red Oak Flats every time he went home from Maryville. Abigail lived on up Tater Ridge beyond his secret perch on Rich Mountain. A two-or-three-hour walk would take him there, or he could ride his horse straight to the place.

"Why won't she talk about her past? I've poked questions at her, but she avoids answering them. And who was Matty's father?" Matthew wasn't sure he wanted to hear these answers, but he needed to know.

"Abigail's never been married." Mrs. Anderson waited for these words to sink in.

"She's never been married? But I thought . . . I guessed . . . maybe I assumed she had." Matthew sputtered. "Now that I think about it, she didn't answer the question when I asked her. So that's the reason. Matty — ?" He stopped. If someone had hit him with an oak board, he couldn't have felt more breathless.

"Before you think the worst, I need to tell you what happened." Mrs. Anderson went on to relate the assault in Pawpaw Hollow and Abigail's realization that she would bear a child.

"There are shysters in the mountains and other places that help you get rid of unborn children. The practice is dangerous and illegal. But Abigail wanted Matty."

Matthew sat speechless. One moment anger at the perpetrator filled his heart. The next, a genuine and heartfelt concern for a young girl in Abigail's position crossed his face.

Finally, rushing through his mind was the thought, *Abigail what you must have endured!*

Mrs. Anderson sat looking at him. "I know this is a shock. I can tell by your face. But Abigail did nothing to cause the attack. Her father ordered her to avoid the other inhabitants of the Flats like the plague, and she did. If Chuck White erred, it was in letting rogues who use women live in the Flats, creating the potential for abuse. In that respect he was wrong."

She continued, "Kitty McTeer was the only woman Abigail was allowed to socialize with. Abigail's mother died several years ago, and she's the only mother my niece has known since. I suspect she's my brother's girlfriend."

Mary Anderson sat looking at Matthew, trying to read his face.

"Moonshining made him enough money without building cabins for the dregs of society and charging them to stay there. I've talked to him, but he doesn't listen."

Mrs. Anderson paused. But Matthew said nothing. His mind was going in circles.

"I'm sorry. I understand what I've told you is a lot to absorb.

"Yes. It would have been much easier in bits and pieces. But I needed to know, and I wanted to know now."

Matthew asked the next painful question. "What happened to the man?"

Mrs. Anderson spread her hands in a helpless gesture. "I don't know. Maybe my brother can shed some light on the subject. When I asked, he said not to worry about it. The man would never cause trouble for anyone again."

Matthew was incredulous. How could Abigail's father make such a statement? Had Mr. White murdered the attacker in retribution for harming his daughter? He had to admit some feelings in that direction himself.

"Why did she leave here?"

"Abigail will have to answer that question, but I suspect she realized how much you mean to her. Abigail often told me she would never ever marry. This was a vow she made to herself years ago. She feels that no man in his right mind would want someone like her."

"Is that the reason she doesn't go to church. She doesn't feel worthy?"

"I think so."

Matthew rubbed both palms over his temples and hair. "I don't know what to say. I'm taken aback."

"I understand." Mrs. Anderson looked on. Her face filled with sympathy. "I can tell you that Abigail is a good mother to Matty. She's been a faithful companion to me. John and I wouldn't hesitate to call her a daughter."

Matthew rose and smiled at Mrs. Anderson. "Thank you for telling me her story. I'm going home and sort through everything you've said."

~

Mrs. Anderson watched as Matthew walked down the circular driveway toward Court Street. He looked like the weight of the world was on his shoulders.

I know he feels as if his world has collapsed around him. But Matthew is a survivor, and he will make the right decision. I'm sure of it.

◇

After his talk with Abigail's Aunt Mary, Matthew started home. In his mind, he saw a girl and heard her sobbing. She was dirty and her dress was torn. Her head was crowned with wavy chestnut hair and she looked at him with terrified brown eyes. Oh, those eyes.

Pools.

Dark brown pools.

How could I have been so blind? It was Abigail at my resting place on Rich Mountain. That was the reason she looked so familiar to me. No wonder she bounded past me and disappeared into the forest. She probably thought I was the man who'd attacked her, coming after her again. In any case, she was in no condition to talk to me.

Matthew shook his head. He hadn't thought of that day in some years.

◇

When Matthew arrived at his boarding house, Mrs. Hembree had his supper waiting, but he wasn't hungry. He pretended to eat, pushing the food around his plate. He thought about asking her advice but decided against it. Finally, he made some excuse and escaped upstairs to his bedroom.

He walked the floor in a quandary. What was he going to do?

I love her and in my heart I know she loves me. But hurdles I'd never thought of present themselves. Moonshining! Rape! Murder! Adultery!

The words shrieked at him.

What about my position in the church? What about my parishioners? People who look up to me for guidance. To be their shepherd. What would they think?

He couldn't get her to darken the door of a church. Of course, now he might know the reason why. She was a woman with a child who'd never been married. The people of his church would have to know. But she was the one abused. It wasn't her fault.

They should embrace her.

Love her. Comfort her.

I've been steadfast to God's calling to the ministry. Must I give it up to marry the woman I love? I know the answer to the question. I must be like the apostle Paul and stay the course.

Then there was his mother and, especially his father. How would they feel?

Pshaw! I'll go to bed and forget the woman and her son. My life won't end if they're not included.

For the first time in over a year Matthew didn't have devotions. He sat down in his upholstered chair and picked up his Bible, trying to read. Beautiful brown eyes stared back at him. He put the Book down on his chair table and headed for bed.

An hour later, Matthew rose and paced the floor again. Abigail and Matty had stolen his heart.

"They don't have a piece, they have the whole thing," he grumbled in the dark room. "Why, God, why?"

He walked over to the window and looked up at the starlit sky. Somewhere in the distance, he heard the low hum of an automobile. "There's a way, good buddy. You'll just have to find it. Please God, help me to find it," he pleaded.

He was relieved. From now on his path was clear.

There was a way for them to be together, he must find it. Matthew slid under the covers and went to sleep.

❧ Chapter Fifty-Three ❧

Home. Home. Home — Matthew

Matthew loved being home. The taste of bacon and eggs was twice as delicious sitting on his front porch, his legs dangling off the side.

After returning home, he'd hitched up the plow horse and cut up his garden patch. Disking came next, and then his dad brought his harrow to smooth out the plot. Matthew jumped on its flat surface and rode around the bumpy fields.

"Son, it's almost as smooth as peach fuzz on a young man's face," said Nat, who came over with seed and helped Matthew plant corn and beans. Nat had stooped down, picked up a handful of dirt, and was letting it run through his fingers.

"Uncle Lazarus's plot should grow remarkable vegetables," Matthew observed.

"Especially since the ground's been fallow for four years. Your plants will do very well. When do you plan on settin' out your tomato slips? I'll come over and help you."

"Next week, I think. Burchfield's Store has plans to get some on Wednesday."

～

Matthew bought two dozen. On Friday, he and his father planted them in hills with dried manure for fertilizer. They went into the woods and hauled out leaves for mulch, placing it around but not close to the tender plants.

"You're going to need a woman to can all this stuff when it's ready for harvest," teased his father.

"I'm going to throw myself on Mom's mercy." Matthew grinned. He planned to help her. After all, he'd helped her all his life. He wasn't totally unknowing about the process of putting up vegetables.

After two hard weeks of work, several blisters, and sore muscles, he was ready for a day of rest. Now with a head start on his planting chores, he decided to take tomorrow off. Since his father was preaching on Sunday, he didn't need to finish preparing a message to be delivered from the pulpit.

In the late afternoon on Friday, he sat on the front porch and watched as the shadows created by the June sun's setting crept across his fields and tipped the mountain beyond. He couldn't see Rich Mountain, but he looked in the general direction.

Moving back to Tipton's Sugar Cove proved to be lonely after the hustle and bustle of school.

It's time to go find Abigail, and tomorrow is as good a day as any.

~

Matthew decided to ride over to his mother and father's for breakfast on Saturday. He would leave his horse there and use the rest of the day for the hike to Red Oak Flats. If he had time after visiting the Flats, his favorite rocky outcrop was nearby. Six weeks had passed since the student recital, which was the last time, he saw Abigail. It seemed like an eternity.

Matthew stood on the front porch of his mother and father's house on Tater Branch looking toward Tater Ridge. At six-thirty, the sun hadn't topped old Thunderhead, but its brightness was evident in the cove.

"Dad, I think I'll go for a walk on Rich Mountain after breakfast. I'll be gone until late afternoon."

An hour later, he fixed a pack with his mother's food, took the tin cup hanging by the springhouse, and started up the trail. He planned to drink out of the clear-flowing streams along the way.

Nat watched as Matthew took the path along Tater Branch. He had sensed a marked change in his son's attitude since his return to the Cove. There was a sadness or melancholy which he caught glimpses of at times. Something was bothering his son. Something he didn't want to share. Of course, they weren't around each other as much, because Matthew lived in Tipton's Sugar Cove.

What was it?

Nat had remarked to Martha about his son's change, and she agreed with him. A mother always knew her children better than anyone.

"Don't worry, Nat. He'll tell us sooner or later. He always has," Martha said.

Nat sat down in his chair on the front porch, watched his son disappear into the forest and said a silent prayer.

Chapter Fifty-Four

Red Oak Flats — Matthew

Matthew headed for Red Oak Flats. He was determined to see Abigail. He remembered enough from her aunt's comments that he thought he could walk right to it. Since he was only a part-time resident and participant in the Cove's society for the last four years, he hadn't heard much about the happenings of the Flats.

What kind of reception will I get at that notorious place?

Aunt Mary told him Abigail was there and that she planned on staying the summer with her father. Matthew bypassed his favorite overlook and headed straight for Chuck White's cabins.

What will I say to Abigail? For sure, I'll tell her that I love her and Matty. How will she respond? I think I know why she left, but she needs to tell me, so I can help her understand this doesn't matter to me. After all, she didn't recoil at the sight of my scarred body but touched me with tenderness. How can I do anything but the same?

After walking steadily for over two hours, Matthew saw the tops of the seven cabins at the Flats. He stopped to get his breath and survey the area. Five of the cabins were close together and farther up the hillside.

All but one of them looked unused. Doors hung off the hinges, and roofs were caving in. Not at all the way Matthew pictured the place.

Two cabins sat away from the others. These weren't as roughly made as the ones on the hill. Matthew headed in their direction. He heard the faint sounds of a guitar, its strings being gently strummed.

Approaching the closest cabin, Matthew walked up the steps and knocked on the door. He knocked louder and no one answered. Descending the steps, he looked toward the other house and headed in the direction where the music was coming from. He didn't know it, but this was the same path that Abigail had walked each day for lunch with Kitty. Then he heard a familiar voice.

"Ma-tew, Ma-tew," Matty called. The little boy was running up the path to meet him as fast as his short legs could carry him.

"Matty," said Matthew, laughing and holding out his arms. He managed to pick Matty up and give him a kiss before being smothered in a big hug.

"That's the best hug in the world." Matthew closed his eyes and realized a tear was running down his cheek. The range of emotions he felt startled him.

He untangled little arms from around his neck and looked down into the childish face. Two brown eyes looked back at him.

"Let me look at you, little man. I haven't seen you for several days."

"Matty miss you." Looking at Matthew adoringly, Matty snuggled up close and placed his forehead against the curve of his neck. This was a familiar place for them both. Matthew hugged him close again.

"I've missed you, too." Matthew continued walking toward the second cabin. He saw a couple standing on the porch as he approached. He guessed one was Mr. White. Was the woman Kitty McTeer?

"Did you come to play wit me?" Matty was wiggling in his arms. He wanted down so he could show him a new toy.

"Matty, all you think about is playing." Matthew was laughing and poking his friend in the stomach. Matty giggled as he was gently deposited on the ground.

They stood at the porch steps.

"I'm sorry to disturb you." Matthew suddenly realized these cabins didn't get many drop-in visitors.

"I see that Matty knows you." Chuck White looked at his new caller to Red Oak Flats. He saw a tall, thin young man with brown hair and chiseled features. His nose was rather straight and slim and his mouth tighter than normal, because he was nervous.

"Yes. He and I have played together before. We lived close to each other in Maryville. Matty went to church with me on Sunday morning."

"Matty likes church. Plays with other boys and girls," said Matty, looking up at his Papaw.

"Who might you be, young man?" Chuck was amazed that Abigail never mentioned Matty's church going. But then, he didn't know his daughter very well these days. She was a grown woman, *a very beautiful woman*, he thought.

"Oh. I'm sorry. I forgot to introduce myself." In his anxious anticipation of this meeting and seeing Matty, he'd forgotten to state his name. "I'm Matthew Tipton of Tipton's Sugar Cove. My parents live at Tater Branch and my father is the pastor at the church you see on the other side of Rich Mountain."

Chuck White looked at him curiously with a question on his face.

"I wanted to talk to Abigail." Matthew blurted out.

I guess he wonders why I'm here to see his daughter, but I'm not going to tell him. I need to talk to Abigail before he knows how I feel about her and Matty.

"Come in, Mr. Tipton and sit a spell." Chuck offered a chair on the front porch. "Abigail isn't here right now. She's on one of her jaunts to the woods. She'll be back directly, I guess. I'm Chuck White and this here's Kitty McTeer. Abigail's my daughter." Matthew nodded his head at Kitty as Chuck paused for a second. "I don't often go to Cades Cove. Where is the sugar cove in that area?"

"It's off Parsons Branch Road. Are you familiar with the abandoned turnpike plans to connect a road from Cades Cove over the Little Tennessee River to North Carolina?"

"Seems like I heard about that. Part of it's in the lower end of the Cove, isn't it?" Chuck scratched his head and ran his fingers through his thinning hair at the same time.

"Yes. You continue past Razor's Grist Mill for a mile or so. Forge creek runs along my property."

"Do you like living there?" Chuck was curious about this young man who'd come to see his daughter, but it wasn't nice to ask personal questions to a stranger.

"Yes, I've lived there three years now. It's secluded, much like your home here. My Uncle Lazarus Tipton left it to me. He and his wife had no children. I spent my college summers fixing it up and my father helped some too. It looks good now, but I could use some comfortable furniture. For me, it's just fine." Matthew looked down and smiled at Matty, who was standing at his knee.

"Matty, do you want to sit in my lap?"

"Yes. See my train. Papaw made it."

Matthew pulled Matty into his lap and looked at the wooden train, turning it over and over and feeling the smoothness of the wood.

"This is a beautiful train. Your Papaw White makes great toys, doesn't he?"

"Great. Yes," agreed Matty.

"May I take it home and play with it?"

"Sure," said Matty. Matty made train sounds as he waved his toy in the air.

Mr. White continued the conversation, "I fixed this cabin up when I moved here and built some more." Chuck waved his arm out at his compound. "They're rough quarters, but then they served a purpose."

"Is no one else living here?" Matthew wondered where all the residents he'd heard about were hiding. He'd expected the worst imaginable characters, gambling, cussing and women. Where were they?

"No one else, just old Jake. He's my right-hand man." White grinned. "Everyone else is gone, and I'm not encouraging replacements. The last one left over three years ago, after—" he stopped. This young man didn't need to know the details. "It's been peaceful, hasn't it, Kitty?"

Matthew turned his gaze upon the lady who sat on the porch. She was pleasantly plump. Her attractiveness was obvious, although enhanced with makeup and diminished with age. He knew her connection to Abigail and Chuck.

"Very peaceful," Kitty said cordially. "I almost danced a jig when the last one left. I hope Chuck doesn't let anyone else live up here in the future. Hit wouldn't bother me if he set fire to those ramshackle cabins and leveled them to ashes." Kitty was looking over Matthew as she sat listening to the conversation. She knew a little of this young minister, because Abigail had confided her feelings for him. She loved his voice. It was deep and forceful. His words were precise and well stated. *Probably his ministerial training*, she thought.

"I must go," said Matthew, getting up and realizing he'd lost sight of his objective in coming to the area. "It's still a long walk home from here. It will be late when I arrive at my father's. Tell Abigail that I'm sorry I missed her, and I'll be back soon."

"We've enjoyed talking to you." Chuck stood up to shake Matthew's hand.

Matthew placed Matty on the porch floor after giving him a final hug. His young friend showed signs of crying.

"I'll walk out with you," said Chuck, picking up his grandson and bringing him along. Chuck's heart was tender when it came to his grandson and he didn't want Matty to start crying.

At the top of Rich Mountain, Matthew bid Chuck and Matty goodbye. He hadn't walked far until he heard his name called again.

"Ma-tew, you forgot your toy."

Matthew turned around and knelt on the ground. Matty was running toward him with his toy train in his hand.

"You'd better keep your toy so you can play with it."

"No. Matty wants you to take it." The little boy held it out to his friend. He was most willing to share his precious possession.

"Okay. I will, and I'll take care of it. I'll bring it back soon so we can play together. Will that be all right with you?" Matthew realized this was a good excuse to return.

"Yes."

"I'll see you really soon, Matty. Remember, I love you." Matthew gave him another hug, and watched him return to his grandfather, who hefted him to his shoulders.

Matty twisted around and waved as his papaw walked them both out of sight. Matthew waved back.

❧ Chapter Fifty-Five ❧

The Meeting—Matthew

When Matthew came to the next grassy spot, he sat down to eat his lunch, and then he continued along the crest of Rich Mountain. He had just enough time to visit his favorite overlook on his way home from Red Oak Flats. He detoured down a familiar ridge to come out at the spot.

The Flats wasn't anything like I imagined it would be. I wonder if Mr. White's still making moonshine. Nothing else seems to be going on there.

Matthew walked quietly as he cut off from the ridge to his sitting place.

I haven't forgotten my hunting skills, but I'm never going to hunt for bear in this lifetime; only small game like rabbits, squirrels, and 'coons, and maybe deer.

Some of the scars continued to smart even after four years. The doctor said it was a miracle he could walk after the damage done to his leg muscles. Determination and grit, like the Plott-mixed dogs possessed, brought him through. He remembered the softness of Daisy —

He stopped.

Someone was crying.

Soft sobs from resignation rather than hurt.

He walked forward and peered through the branches at a figure sitting in his retreat. The whole scenario was familiar. He stood there looking at the wavy chestnut hair and the curves of Abigail's frame. Like the first time, her head was on her knees and she rocked back and forth to comfort herself.

Matthew's heart skipped several beats as his eyes caressed her.

He placed the toy train and his food sack on a nearby limb. He wasn't ready to confess he'd walked to Red Oak Flats to see her.

"Darling Abigail," he said stepping forward into the open space. "What's wrong? Are you all right?"

Abigail jumped up and wiped the tears from her cheeks with the back of her hands, but said nothing. Matthew smiled, remembering another day.

"It was you that day years ago when I found a young girl here, sobbing her heart out." He wanted to reach out and hold her in his arms—comfort her. He stepped closer but didn't touch her.

"What happened that day to cause you so much grief? Can you tell me now?"

Abigail turned around toward the peaceful scene below. He saw her shoulders move as she sighed. It was time to tell all.

"Yes, I may as well tell you." Then she related the story of going to Pawpaw Hollow to visit her flowers and finding Dirk there. She told of the rape, of running and ending up here at the overlook.

"I wasn't in any condition for small talk. I couldn't concentrate on a word you said while we were here together. I suppose I was in shock." Abigail stopped talking for a minute.

"I didn't know your hurt, but I knew you were hurting. I'm sure I wouldn't have known what to say or how to comfort you then," said Matthew. The two were still standing and facing the peaceful, pastoral Cades Cove valley with Thunderhead Mountain in the background.

"Three months later, I realized I was going to have Matty. My father let me go to Aunt Mary's to have the baby. In Maryville, I was closer to medical help. No one but she knew the circumstances of my problem. We kept the secret very well, don't you think? As you know, we told everyone my husband was dead. But the truth is I've had no husband."

"What happened to Dirk?" Matthew was interested in knowing if he would turn up at a later date.

"I don't know, but I never saw him again. Pa said I didn't need to worry about him returning. When Pa makes statements like that, I shudder to think what might have occurred."

"So, you don't know?"

"I never found out."

"Abigail, you know this doesn't make a difference to me. I love you, and I love Matty." He wanted to hold her, to reassure her. He might have an idea how she felt, but until Abigail worked through the problem herself and was comfortable with the results, he was going to withhold his touch.

"Matthew, you're a minister. You can't marry a woman with a child who's never been married. Your parishioners wouldn't approve. You might lose your church, and coming back to the cove to preach has been your whole life." Abigail turned around to look at him. She wanted to observe his face—his eyes. They were full of concern and love directed at her. Dropping her gaze to the ground, she felt her resistance start to melt.

I can't give in — be strong, Abigail. I love him too much to let him throw away his life's calling. It's hopeless.

"Why can't I?" Matthew declared. "Jesus would not disapprove, so others shouldn't say a word." He wasn't so sure they wouldn't, especially the purists in his church. This was a future problem they might face. "Abigail, it's more important to have Jesus in your heart, than to have a church under your feet."

"How do you know Jesus wouldn't disapprove? He condemned many things, didn't He, like knowing someone out of wedlock? I feel dirty and used."

"That's true, but he also extended the grace of forgiveness and salvation to those who erred. You didn't err, Abigail. Dirk was the one who sinned."

Matthew continued to talk to Abigail about the woman prostitute at the well, the woman caught in adultery, and King David who committed murder. "Even though these people committed terrible acts, He didn't give up on them. He wanted them as His children. He doesn't condemn the person, unless we refuse to admit our sin. He abhors the act itself. If we ask for forgiveness, He is ready and willing to forgive, and receive us as his children. The secret is asking and receiving.

"Jesus gave both of those women and King David an opportunity to repent and know him after the sin. The Bible says his blood makes all things clean. Even though your problem wasn't your fault, if it bothers you, ask for His forgiveness." Matthew sensed a softening in her attitude and waited for her to ask the question.

"Matthew, I don't know much about God and things. Does He really want me? Will He take away this dirty feeling, this load I've been carrying, and save me after what happened over there in Pawpaw Hollow?" Abigail looked and pointed in the direction of her attack.

"Yes, Abigail. He wants you, especially you. He loves every individual and wants them for His very own. The Bible says He came to seek and save those who are lost. At one time in our lives, we are all lost. Why do you think He sent me into your life? Do you think meeting here at this place was an accident four years ago? And what about today? I could have gone on home." Matthew's voice was filled with pleading. He saw tears running down her face. He paused for a response and then continued.

"Abigail, I don't think it was an accident. I think God sent me to love you and Matty. I'll say it again, the problem of the attack was not yours. It was Dirk's. But if you feel that you are unclean, ask for restoration and His divine love."

"Oh Matthew, I wish that were true."

"It is true. Jesus is truth. He doesn't lie, and He is faithful. He'll accept you into His kingdom. Abigail you can trust me. I wouldn't lead you astray."

"Many times, I feel lost and without hope."

"Without Him you are lost and without hope, but with Him you are heir to His riches in heaven. You're loved to the uttermost." Matthew's voice was passionate as he talked to the woman he loved.

The fierce struggle going on in her heart was plain in her face. Finally, the fight was over. "Matthew, what do I need to do? Will you help me? I don't know this Jesus you're talkin' about."

"Would you like to know Him?"

Matthew waited breathlessly for Abigail's answer to his question. He saw another tear roll down her face. The response she made would determine their future together.

Abigail nodded yes.

"Come, let's sit here." They sat with their legs over the edge of the rock face. Matthew spent several minutes talking to her about the way to Christ. Abigail listened to him and nodded her head several times.

Matthew stood up and extended his hand to her. "Abigail, let's pray together."

Pulling her a little closer to him, Matthew put his hands on her shoulders and, forehead to forehead the couple stood while Matthew offered a prayer. Then Matthew stepped back.

"Abigail, you need to pray for yourself. Present your case to Him. I'll be back after you're finished."

Matthew walked out of the clearing into the woods. He felt strongly that Abigail needed to finish her petition by herself. He wanted her to be alone with the Savior. He lingered for some minutes and returned to the overlook.

～

Abigail stood looking down into the peaceful valley with the white-framed church in the middle. Turning around, she saw him approach, and she smiled. For the first time in several years, she felt clean. She was at peace with herself and Dirk, whom she had forgiven. She realized the old feelings were gone and something wonderful filled her heart to overflowing.

"Matthew, the weight of the world's been lifted from my shoulders. I understand now. I stood here four years ago and looked down into the tranquil valley of Cades Cove. I remember wonderin' how can there be peace anywhere when I'm hurtin' so badly. I didn't understand it then, but I do now. There is a stillness, a quietness. It comes with knowin' God, and that church," Abigail turned slightly to look at the church, "is a symbol of those who know Him. He wanted me to recognize this fact at that moment, when I was so confused and hurt, that there would be peace. God was here. He was right here that day four years ago, and He's here now. He sent you to show me that faith in Him brings hope *and love*."

The last obstacle was gone.

"Abigail, my sweetheart."

The imploring tone in his voice touched her heart as nothing else could do. Were the reservations she had against marriage and a union with him stripped away?

"You've come through more trials than most people suffer in a lifetime. Abigail, I love you, and I want to take care of you, minister to your needs and be your husband. I don't know what the future holds, but my one hope is that you will be by my side. Abigail, do you love me?" Matthew held out his arms and waited. He was only two feet from her, almost touching.

Abigail glided into his arms, pressing her face against his shoulder, her head nestled where Matty's had been earlier that day. Matthew's arms closed around her — tightly. He didn't intend to let go.

"Yes, Matthew. I think I've loved you from the first day I saw you playing with Matty. But I needed to know you accepted me as I am. I know that now." She drew back and looked into his eyes. Her face was bright and her eyes shining with tears. "I don't know" —

Matthew put his finger on her lips.

"My darling, may I kiss you."

The pain of the last bruising kiss was forever wiped out by Matthew's sweet kiss.

"You know when I start, I don't intend to stop kissing you," he said, teasing her as he smiled.

"Hum," she said. "I feel the same way."

Chapter Fifty-Six

Catching Up and Making Plans — Matthew and Abigail

Matthew strode in darkness toward his home. The stars twinkled overhead and moonlight lit his path. Cades Cove had turned in for the night. It lay sleeping like a baby in its cradle, innocent, peaceful and trusting. He wondered if the next few days, weeks or months would be the same for Abigail and him.

Thunderhead Mountain was a dark shadow against the sky, watching over all.

~

They'd lingered awhile sitting with arms entwined around each other and talking in the quiet, intimate setting about important things lovers talk about. They were as close as they would get before marriage. Abigail leaned her head on his shoulder. It was then she told him Matty was named after him.

Matthew Charles White.

Because he was kind that fateful day and she knew no other man she trusted. He was nicknamed Matty because one of the Anderson girls couldn't pronounce Matthew.

"When did you know you'd seen me before?" he had asked.

Abigail knew immediately who he was from the first day Matty had stopped him on Court Street. He was kind to her little boy. It was at that time she started to love him.

"You told me you planned on being a minister. I never intended to marry after the assault. If there was a chance, marriage to a preacher was the most impossible likelihood. My heart turned traitor and said you were the one." Abigail laughed a short, silvery tinkle that disappeared into the still depths of the forest. She'd never been this happy when she sat on the front porch at Red Oak Flats or walked to Pawpaw Hollow to talk to her flowers.

"I wanted more than anything to come to your graduation, so I rode the train down from Townsend on Wednesday morning. I saw you march in and walk across the stage. I almost lingered too long afterward, needing to be close to you. When I sensed you recognized me, I hurried from the chapel and hid behind the side door leading to the practice rooms. You didn't follow me."

"It was you. I thought my sight was playing tricks on me, you little sneak." He gave her a little squeeze.

They sat for several minutes in silence, looking at the pastureland and the church in the distance.

"How did you come to remember me?" she'd asked.

Matthew confessed that he didn't recognize her or place her at once. "You wore makeup and different clothes."

"They do change a person's appearance."

Smiling at her he said, "I did remember your beautiful, brown eyes. Deep pools of brown that have haunted me each time I revisit here where we sit." Another pause, then Matthew continued, "It was hectic during graduation, but I managed to stop and talk to your Aunt Mary."

"My Aunt Mary told you the truth?" she questioned.

"Yes, but it was at my insistence. I think she realized I wasn't leaving until I knew where you were."

"I'm glad she did. I forgive her. What's the answer to my question?"

"Your eyes, I couldn't remember where I'd seen them until I was walking home from talking with your aunt, and the puzzle pieces started coming together." He stopped to kiss her again. "What a shock that was to me. I couldn't eat that night and later, I paced the floor in my room. My mind was a jumble of thoughts. The problems surrounding a union with you seemed insurmountable. I decided to forget you," Matthew tightened his arm around her, "but that was impossible."

"You can't forget me?" she teased.

"You're right I couldn't. I got into bed, tossed and turned for an hour. I don't think the Lord intended for me to sleep until I made the right decision. You see He did want you, Abigail. I realized then that you and Matty had my whole heart. It was my intention to make you mine from that point on. But graduating from school was my first priority and then returning to the sugar cove. I needed to start gardening chores and ready the cabin to live in. But every day, every minute my thoughts were of you. How would Abigail like this or what would she say about that? I love you completely."

It was growing late. The sun was setting behind the trees, and mountain coolness was in the air. It was time to go. Traversing the mountain was dangerous in the dark.

Their parting was slow. Each lingered not wanting the time spent together in their newfound love to end. There were kisses and separating steps and returning to hold each other again. In the end a last, long kiss parted them for the night.

Matthew walked down the path for several feet before he remembered Matty's toy train and his pack. He turned around and retrieved them both.

After kissing Abigail goodbye, he walked back to his parent's house, arriving at dark. He stayed long enough to eat the food his mother had set aside for him, saddled his horse and left.

Today wasn't the day to tell his parents of his betrothal. He wanted to savor the day — not discuss any problems. He and Abigail had decided to do that next Saturday. She would ride with Matty to Tipton's Sugar Cove to see his home and eat dinner. Afterwards they would go to his parent's home and ask for their blessing on their future union, telling them about her former life.

The following day she and Matty would attend his church. Abigail would come down to the altar to acknowledge her faith in Christ, ask to join the church, and be baptized later in the summer in Abrams Creek.

On Monday afternoon, Matthew would ride his horse to Red Oak Flats to ask for Abigail's hand in marriage and eat supper with Chuck White.

~

Telling Matthew's parents turned out to be easy.

"We've been praying for you both," said his father.

"It's a relief to know about your life, Abigail. We both realized you two were a wonderful couple but not knowing the circumstances of Matty's birth caused us anxious moments." Martha's smile toward Abigail was genuine and open.

"What you went through happens to more people than you think. People just don't talk about it. At least your aunt and uncle were there to nurture and sustain you through this trial." Nat was leaning forward, his hands clasped together between his knees, watching Matty who was approaching him a step at a time. Nat wasn't surprised after their last meeting.

He opened his hands up, and Matty walked into the open space.

Matty looked up at Nat. "Ma-tew's going to be my daddy. Are you goin' to be my grandpa?" Serious brown eyes melted the elderly pastor's heart.

If Grandpa had any reservations left, they disappeared into the depths of those small brown eyes; eyes like his mother's.

"Yes, I think I will, but there's one problem." Nat's held up one finger and his face wore his most serious expression. "To be my grandson you must like to go fishin' and huntin'," he said.

"Matty's never been fishin' or huntin'."

"Guess we'll have to take care of that, Little Man."

"My new daddy calls me, Little Man."

"Don't go bear hunting with him, Matty," Matthew advised. He smiled as he sat watching the tenderness his father had toward the child.

Nat shot him a sarcastic glance. "Your experience was an accident son."

"I know. I know."

Martha was sitting on the edge of her seat. She couldn't wait another minute. Standing up, she walked over to Matty and picked him up, hugging the little boy.

"God loves it," she said. "I have some cookies in the kitchen. Would Matty like one and some milk?" They disappeared, only to return. Matty carried two cookies to everyone in the room and Martha followed with glasses of milk. Little Man wasn't satisfied until everyone shared his snack.

❧ Chapter Fifty-Seven ❧

The Busybody's Attack — the Pastor's Respond

The trouble started with the busybody line.

Church on Sunday went off without a problem, or at least it appeared to. Abigail and Matty sat with Nat and Martha. Halfway through the service, Matty curled up in Nat's lap and went to sleep.

Matthew finished his sermon and gave the invitation. The pump organ wheezed as Abigail came forward to proclaim her newfound faith in Christ and ask to join the church. She was accepted on condition of her baptism at a later date.

The enthusiastic worshippers crowded around, shaking her hand. They were curious but asked polite questions of Abigail and the Tiptons concerning her background. Deeper familiarity would come as they got to know her.

What was the connection between Abigail and Matthew? The congregation could add one-plus-one and noticed an obvious attraction between the couple. A few left unsatisfied with a need to know more about the young lady who might become the wife of their future minister. And the young lad, where did he fit into the picture?

Coming out of the church, Matthew offered Abigail his arm and helped her down the steps and into his father's buggy. The young people went home with the older Tiptons for the first of many family dinners.

From the church steps, two sets of curious eyes watched Matthew, Abigail, and Matty leave. Two minds started to churn and two mouths started to talk. Conjecture followed conjecture until the molehill of slander and false accusations became higher than Thunderhead Mountain. It only took a couple of days.

The busybody line was in full attack mode.

In many ways, Nat was responsible for Edna Akkin's and Precious Tipton's increase in gossiping. His procrastination in confronting them with the realization that gossiping wasn't acceptable for one who followed Christ was at least part of the problem. Not only had the two church biddies sinned, he had too.

By the middle of the week he understood the gravity of their hurtful words. The talk was about him and his family, a first for the Tiptons. No hint of gossip had ever touched his family.

Prostitute. Unwed mother. Red light district. Notorious. Unacceptable.

Preacher's son. His child. Fornicator. Pastor. Sinner. Unacceptable.

These sinister and untrue words hung in the air and buzzed on the telephone exchange for all to hear. The secluded cove and his congregation were in an uproar.

John Razor came with the disturbing news.

"Nat, there's talk of a confrontation after church Sunday. Some are saying Matthew should step down from taking over your pulpit. I don't believe the talk going around the cove, but many who don't know you well, they'll believe it." John sat in a chair in the parlor of Nat's cabin, concern showing on his face. "Something's got to be done about Edna and Precious. This isn't the first time they've spread slander, but it's the worst example of their dedication to spreading untruthful words. You decide what to do, and I and most of the congregation will back you up."

~

Martha heard the discussion from the kitchen. Stunned, she sat down at the kitchen table. "My word," she exclaimed in a low tone so the men in earnest conversation in the parlor couldn't hear.

She heard Nat tell John, "I don't know what to do, but I'll think about it. You'll be the first to know."

She heard the goodbyes and then silence.

The sound of footsteps in the direction of the Bible which lay next to her husband's chair, the turning of its leaves, and silence again told Martha volumes. Nat was seeking his answer in God's word.

Never one to be impulsive, he followed a routine he'd learned long ago – God first and then action.

Martha sat still. Love for him filled her heart to overflowing.

"Thank you, God, for such a wonderful husband. Give him and Matthew the knowledge and stamina they need to solve this problem. Continue to bless our church and its members with tranquility and love for each other. Don't let our fellowship be broken. Please God," she pleaded in a whisper. As always when confronted with important matters, tears rolled down her cheeks.

Chapter Fifty-Eight

The Busybody Plan — Nat

John wasn't the first to know. Martha was and she approved Nat's plan.

"Thank goodness the crops are in the ground, and I'll be able to concentrate on my message for Sunday."

"Nat, Matthew will have to be told."

"Yes. I'll ride over to the sugar cove first. This is as much his problem as mine. He can go with me to John's. We'll tell him together."

"Dad, I've always thought of Edna Akkin's and Precious Tipton's clattering tongues as laughable. Most of the cove residents do the same. But nothing they've ever said approaches the level of what you've just told me. Why now and why Abigail and me? The ladies are to be pitied."

"Matthew I'm not sure pitied is the word."

They sat on the front porch at Tipton's Sugar Cove. Down below the mooing of a cow for her calf was clearly heard.

"Get your Bible, Matthew, and read James 3:5-6.

Matthew retrieved his Bible from inside the house and leafed through it until he came to the book of James.

Even so the tongue is a little member, and boasteth great things. Behold, how great a matter a little fire kindleth! And the tongue is a fire, a world of iniquity: so is the tongue among our members, that it defileth the whole body, and setteth on fire the course of nature; and it is set on fire of hell.

"The Bible has harsh words concerning the tongue. I believe we're seeing the worst that can happen when it's loosed from its chains in Hell. It can be used for good or evil. But when used for evil this small piece of our body can spread slander and untruth like a raging forest wildfire which cannot be contained by any means but the saving grace of God's love, and a change of heart, a heart washed clean by Jesus' blood."

Matthew looked at his father. "Dad, I don't think I've ever heard you speak so passionately about a subject."

"I should have been speaking on this important verse years ago. I realized the two ladies had a problem, but the talk was never about me and seemed harmless. Now I understand it's cruel and vicious."

"Are you sure Edna and Precious started the insinuations?"

"I've talked to three of our church members and each said they heard the innuendoes first from Edna and then Precious followed up with more *information*. I don't understand Precious's need to hang around Edna.

"What do you intend to do?"

"First, go to the two ladies and tell them the truth about Abigail. Tell them how they've hurt our family and forgive them for this. What happens next depends on their reaction."

"Then I'm going with you." When Nat started to protest, Matthew held up his hand and said, "There's no discussion. I'm going with you."

"Okay. Go then."

"What do you expect them to do?"

"You have your Bible. Turn to Matthew 18:15 where Jesus lays out the procedure to follow. If we do as He commands, we will not err." Nat waited until Matthew turned to and read the Savior's words.

"If they don't talk to us, who do you plan to take with us for the next step?"

"Probably John and Ike Shields. Our congregation respect's their opinion."

John Razor and Ike Shields, Matthew thought. The same ones who'd gone on the bear hunt to Thunderhead Mountain. But now, the group would be together looking for forgiveness and restoration of two ladies who were valuable in God's sight. The bear needing to be killed in this case was an attacking tongue running loose with unspeakable untruths.

"Matthew, there's something you don't know about Sarah Tipton. Haven't you ever wondered why she and your uncle never had children?"

"I have wondered, but figured if they wanted me to know they'd tell me."

"Years ago, Sarah was attacked like Abigail, but Sarah's attacker was a well-known and influential man in Chattanooga. When Sarah went to her mother with her horrible story, her mother wanted to keep it a secret."

Nat continued to tell Matthew Sarah's story. "So, you see, I think Abigail did the right thing. The guilt or consequences of having a child aborted are terrible. I'm proud of your future wife for having her baby."

"Sarah must have gone through a period of terrible turmoil after she recovered."

"She did. But I've heard her say many times it was the 'grace of God through saving faith' that pulled her through. Sarah became a strong Christ-follower with Dr. Elmore's help and guidance."

"Funny, Dr. Elmore never mentioned Sarah's problems."

"No, he wouldn't. They were confidential admissions, Matthew. Just remember that."

They sat for some moments in silence.

Finally, Nat broke into Matthew's thoughts. "Son, we've got some serious problems to address today. Let's pray about them. We want God's will to be done."

Both father and son knelt on the rough planked porch of the cabin in Tipton's Sugar Cove. God heard their prayers.

∼

After talking to John Razor, Matthew and his father approached the home of Edna Akkins. She sat on the front porch, fanning, and saw them coming up the dirt path.

"Well, Pastor, what brings you here?" she said when they were close enough to hear. She began to squirm in her chair, uncomfortable at what might be said next. She laid her fan in her lap and crossed her arms over her chest.

"Matthew and I need to talk to you." The two men approached and stood near the bottom of the worn cabin steps. "Is Mr. Akkins here?"

"Naw, he's over at Burchfield's store. Went after groceries. What d'ya need? Maybe I can help you."

"You're the one we needed to talk to. May we come up and sit with you on the porch?"

Edna looked back and forth at the two visitors. Her suspicions were growing as to their visit. "Depends on what yer here fer."

Nat decided to plunge right in. "We need to talk to you about some untrue rumors or gossip being talked about in the cove. It's hurt my family, and I don't want it to hurt the church."

"I don't know what yer talkin' about or why yer on my property. Are ye accusin' me of somethin'?" Guilt was written on Edna's reddened face. She was leaning forward, her chin jutted out in defiance as she responded.

"We only wanted to get at the facts and tell you the truth."

"Facts! Truth! I'll tell you the facts and truth," she screeched. "Git off my property. The very idea accusin' me of gossipin'. Git, I tell you." Edna arose from her chair and made threatening gestures with a broom she'd grabbed that was standing by the door. "Git."

"But Edna, we only want to . . ."

"No buts! Git, I tell you!" Edna raised the broom over her head.

"We'll go."

Edna lowered the broom and watched from the front porch. Sure enough, they turned into the lane leading to Precious Tipton's place. She hurried through the front door and rang up her only friend.

When Matthew and Nat arrived there, Mr. Tipton stood on the front porch.

"Pastor, we don't want no trouble. It's best you jest leave us alone."

"Can we not talk to you and your wife? We're not here to condemn but to straighten out the facts and get at the truth."

"Some other day, Pastor, but not today."

❧

Nat called John and Ike Shields and explained the situation. Both men agreed to come over on Friday to accompany Matthew and his father to see the two women.

❧

The second visit turned out like the first. Edna refused to talk to the four men. This time she was backed up by her husband. Precious Tipton's husband sat on the front porch and at least listened to what Nat had to say. For the first time, he heard the real truth, but Precious never joined the men

Matthew thought he saw a window curtain flutter, but there was no way of knowing if a hand did it or the wind blowing through the open door of the house. He hoped the woman was listening in the dark interior of the home.

❧

"What are you going to do?" Ike Shields sat, looking at his pastors. They sat on the porch at Tater Branch.

"I've been giving this state of affairs a lot of thought, and Matthew and I have talked about it.

"Sunday, I intend to preach on a verse in James about the tongue. This won't be an easy lesson, but it's a needful one. I believe I'll offer my resignation pending what the church does."

John started to say something, but Nat held up his hand and stopped him.

"John, no minister can let schism go unchecked in his church. It must be nipped in the bud; stopped before it takes hold and creeps throughout the whole. If the pastor is the problem, he needs to step down, until the situation rights itself. I hope this will happen, but–"

"Of course, you're right."

"Go ahead and have a meeting after church on Sunday. Tell the people what has transpired this week. The next step is up to you and the congregation."

For several minutes after John and Ike left, the father and son sat in silent thought.

"Dad, I'm so sorry. I understood the details of Abigail's life would have to come out but hoped we could tell everyone later. I expected the people to learn to love her as I have. We planned to tell the congregation when we announced our engagement and approaching marriage."

"Your love for Abigail is not at fault. I am. I procrastinated. Isn't it ironic? I jumped onto you for not dealing with Alice in a timely manner and for not finding out about Abigail's past. Here I am guilty of the same thing. I hope you will forgive me, Son." Nat sat looking at Matthew, remorse on his face.

"Dad, please. There's nothing to forgive. This may be the most valuable lesson I've learned. Asking for forgiveness isn't easy."

"Are you ready to ride over to Annie's? I need to check on her."

"Sure, I'll get my hat."

Matthew went into the cabin to get his hat and say goodbye to his mother.

"Don't worry, Son. God is in control," she said.

The two men, father and son, walked off the porch. Nat put his arm around his son's shoulders.

"Son, you realize you may not be preaching in the cove after this Sunday?"

"Yes, Dad. But I can't believe God has brought me this far to take away my church. Don't you think He's still in charge?"

"Always," Nat said emphatically."

Chapter Fifty-Nine

The Hard Sermon — Nat

Nat finished his sermon. "Today I've spoken hard words, hard words because they needed to be said. Most of us can think of times we opened our mouths, when we should have kept them shut. I'm guilty of this also. When I realize I've done so, I must acknowledge my sin, and, folks, it is sin."

Nat paused and descended from the pulpit. He put his fingers together in front of his chest and chose his words carefully. Looking at the floor, he said, "I have been your pastor for several years. During that time, I endeavored to preach the truth, and I've taught my children to be truthful." He paused and continued, looking at Matthew and Abigail. "If there was anything in Matthew's relationship with Abigail which was unseemly, I would tell you about it. But there isn't."

He looked around at the congregation, his eyes passing over his friends. They stopped at John Razor. "I have tendered my resignation to John Razor pending the meeting you intend to have after church today. He knows the details of Matthew and Abigail's relationship — knows the details of Abigail's life, which he will relate to you. I hope this will clear up any misunderstanding you have."

Nat nodded and smiled at John. "There is one more matter to be dealt with. This is the gossip perpetrated by a few of our members. You are the church here and as such should deal with these hurtful words. Since they were against me and my family, I don't think I can lead you through this trial. Again, I've asked John for his help or whomever you select. What more can I say?"

Nat looked at Martha and smiled at her. Tears glistened on her face.

Matty leaned his head against her arm and looked up at her, sadness in his eyes.

Matthew stood up and walked down the aisle to stand next to his father, who put his arm around his shoulder.

"This may be the last time my son and I stand before you. I don't hold a grudge or anger against any of you. You've been my friends and family. And as God is my witness, my love and concern for you is great."

Nat gave the benediction. He and Matthew walked down the aisle. Tears ran down other faces and hands reached out to touch the two men as they passed by. Father and son walked out the church door, followed by Martha, Abigail, and Matty. Nat turned and closed the church door behind them.

The sun was shining brightly as the family climbed into their buggy and drove toward home.

With the church door closed, John Razor stood to tell the story of Matthew and Abigail's relationship.

A meeting of the leaders of the church was called for the evening since there would be no service. They would address the subject of gossip within the church.

~

Of the results of the meeting of the elders and what transpired afterwards Nat and Matthew heard bits and pieces. On Tuesday, five of the church leaders came to inform them of the outcome. They met in the evening at Tipton's Sugar Cove. John Razor was the spokesman for the group.

"Nat, we want to continue with you as pastor and Matthew as our future pastor."

"Did everyone agree?"

"Yes, the vote was unanimous."

"Praise the Lord," burst forth from Matthew's mouth.

John grinned. "I agree with that also."

The others in the group added, "Amen."

"We called a meeting on Sunday night to address the problem of gossip within our church. Several of us spent Sunday afternoon making sure all church members were invited to attend. We went to the Tipton house and the Akkins home."

John continued. "The meeting lasted over an hour, but we accomplished several things. Matthew, I explained *again* your relationship with Abigail and that she was your betrothed. After some discussion, we called for another vote to retain Nat as our pastor and you as our future one. Then we addressed the gossiping issue. Precious Tipton was there with her husband. The Akkins family didn't come.

"I told them your exact words about schism in the church and how you felt about it. I also reiterated that you didn't hold a grudge against anyone in the church but felt if the problem was your fault, you should step down. There was more discussion. Finally Precious Tipton got up.

"Brothers and sisters, I'm the one at fault here, not the pastor. I can't blame Edna for my problems. I knew better, but sayin' things gives you power over people. My husband's been talkin' to me, and he's right. Christian's don't act that way. The pastor brought that out in his message today. I was wrong, and I'm sorry I let my tongue run away with me. I beg for forgiveness."

"Nat, I thought people was goin' to shout, we was so happy. We accepted her apology, but told her she needs to apologize to you next Sunday when you stand in the pulpit."

This time Nat said, "Praise the Lord."

∿

The following Sunday, a glorious service was attended by all. Precious's apology was accepted with heartfelt praise.

That same day, Matthew and Abigail asked Nat to marry them on the first Saturday in July.

❧ Chapter Sixty ❧

O Happy Day — Matthew and Abigail

Matthew stood at the front of the church in the navy-blue suit. The same one his future wife helped him buy earlier in the year. His gaze met Mary Anderson's. She nodded at him and smiled. Chuck White and Kitty sat at the front of the church on the first pew, warming Matthew's old seat. It was the first time Chuck had ever been in a sanctuary. He was nervous and sweating.

Matthew's mother and Matty sat on the other side. Or rather, Matty stood in the pew. Grandma had told him his mother would come in the back door, and standing gave him a better view. He watched expectantly each time the door opened. Everyone was there but Tim who couldn't make the ceremony.

The sound of a horse and buggy could be heard outside. Squeaky and Charlotte pulled up to the door with Abigail. Squeaky helped both women from the buggy and this time when the church doors opened, Abigail appeared, framed in the doorway.

Matthew gasped. She was a vision in white with red roses in her hair. She carried a cluster of roses in her hands. As she came forward, Matthew said a silent prayer that the Lord would bless their future marriage. When she was close enough their eyes met.

Matthew saw deep pools of brown, swimming with love.

"Mama's beu-ti-ful," said Matty, who didn't whisper.

The audience chuckled.

Abigail gave her hand to his father, who placed it in Matthew's. They faced each other and said their vows. The couple was together and alone with their God. They exchanged two rings, something new among the church goers.

After the service, Matthew admitted he didn't remember saying his, "I do." All he could remember was drowning in Abigail's eyes. After the reception at his mother and father's house, the couple headed to Chattanooga to honeymoon in a guest house of the church where Dr. Elmore spoke. His father drove them to Townsend to catch the afternoon train.

At the end of the summer, Matthew took over his father's pulpit. Precious Tipton was the first one down the aisle to congratulate him. Although she was older, she and Abigail had become fast friends. Edna Akkins and her family sold out and left the cove. No one ever heard from them again.

At the start of September, the cool nights said fall was on the way. During the first week, Matthew was impressed to deliver a sermon from John. He'd studied each morning, rising early to leaf through the scriptures. One day, he'd ridden over to get his father's thoughts on the subject. Father and son were close, and Matthew valued his leadership.

Matthew got up from the altar where he'd knelt to pray after his sermon.

He looked back over his standing congregation as the song leader and organist started the hymn of invitation.

The message he'd just preached was one of salvation. The scripture was taken from John 4:13-14 where Jesus answered the woman at the well, *"Whosoever drinketh of this water shall thirst again: But whosoever drinketh of the water that I shall give him shall never thirst; but the water that I shall give him shall be in him a well of water springing up into everlasting life."*

Chuck and Kitty sat together on the very back bench. They'd been coming since the marriage of Matthew and Abigail, because the congregation was friendly and welcoming, something that Chuck never expected. Each Sunday after church, the two couples went to Nat's house or Tipton's Sugar Cove to eat dinner. The conversation always turned to theological questions; questions about spiritual issues that Chuck was determined to understand. Matthew realized he was probing for answers, and his prayers for his father-in-law increased in fervor.

Matthew felt the nudging of the Holy Spirit, "Go to Chuck. Go to Chuck." It wasn't his practice to walk down the aisle and talk to an unsaved person, but he did believe in following the Spirit's direction.

He headed down the aisle, while several sets of eyes followed him, and stopped behind the bench where Chuck stood.

He whispered quietly to his father-in-law, "There's an old sayin' that you can lead a horse to water, but you can't make him drink." Matthew looked down at

Chuck's white knuckles as the older man gripped the bench tightly. Matthew put his hand on Chuck's back, leaned forward and said, "Don't you want to let go of the bench and find the living water of Jesus Christ?"

That's all it took. Chuck let go of the bench and practically ran down the aisle. An old sinner was dislodged from his old way of life that day.

Later, he stood at the altar with tears coursing down his cheeks as he shook the hands of his brothers in Christ. At dinner with Nat and Martha, he said, "This Sunday is the happiest day of my life. A tremendous burden is gone. Henceforth, my life is different." Chuck meant his statement.

Another marriage took place the following Saturday. It was a simple ceremony uniting Chuck with Kitty. Only the family attended.

Chapter Sixty-One

Life Goes On — The Matthew Tipton's

Abigail strolled along the road leading to the cabin at Tipton's Sugar Cove. Down below her in the valley, Matty and Matthew threw hay at each other in the newly mowed field. The sounds of their laugher echoed throughout the area. Matty was now not quite four instead of free.

The September sun was warm on her skin.

She thought back to the day after her attack, when she felt her world had come to an end. She remembered the walk up to the hill above Red Oak Flats and looking across to Thunderhead Mountain. Was that almost five years ago? She remembered thinking the storm to come would be fierce, as the clouds piled up on the horizon. She was right. They were fierce. But the storms she and Matthew would face were unknown at that time. With God's help, they had weathered them, and in return God had given them a love *that passes understanding.*

She had no idea what the future held in store for them as a family. But she knew one thing, as long as her family placed their trust in God nothing else mattered.

She rubbed her stomach.

She knew a secret.

In the spring there would be a new visitor who would play under the watchful eye of Thunderhead Mountain and in the cool mists of Tipton's Sugar Cove.

∼

Later that same day, Matthew stood in front of the fire place, his head resting on his hand, which was placed on the mantle. All was quiet. Abigail and Matty were in bed, probably fast asleep. The light from the fire occasionally lit the dark recesses of the cabin and shone on his face. Turning to look out the window, he saw his Uncle Lazarus's rifle above the mantle where it rested in its cradle.

Lifting his hand, he rubbed the handmade stock, the one his uncle had made so lovingly from walnut growing in the sugar cove. The richness of the wood's grain shone through the layers of finish he'd applied.

"Uncle, I think you would be proud of your old home place and the people living here," he murmured.

At that moment the fire flickered brightly, and Matthew eyes were drawn to the tintype sitting on the opposite end of the mantle. He took a step toward it, held it in his hand. and turned the picture to the smoldering fire. The smiling faces, frozen in time, looked back at him.

"I shouldn't have wondered about finding another Sarah. She was out there, waiting until the time was right. God couldn't have blessed me with a better wife."

He continued to examine the picture.

"I wish both of you could meet Abigail and Matty."

He replaced the picture on the mantle, turned his back to the fire, and enjoyed the fire's warmth. Tipton's Sugar Cove was truly his beloved home. He closed his eyes and whispered a short prayer of blessing for the inhabitants and land.

"Matthew," Abigail called softly. "Are you coming to bed?" She stood in the bedroom door.

"Yes, my sweetheart." Matthew placed two large logs he'd deposited on the hearth on top of the fire and headed for the bedroom.

"A kiss is the price to enter, dear sir," said Abigail, teasing him when he reached the door.

"Ha, I can oblige you, fair maiden." Matthew picked her up in his arms, kissed her and carried her to the bed.

When they were comfortably settled in its warmth and Matthew's arms were around her, Abigail decided it was time to tell him her secret.

Laus Deo!

Matthew's motto is the Latin *Laus Deo* meaning ("Praise be to God). On Dec. 6, 1884 the largest piece of cast aluminum—the world's most precious metal at that time—capped out the Washington Monument. This same motto is found inscribed on that portion. The monument was dedicated on Feb. 21, 1885.

THE REAL TIPTON'S SUGAR COVE

By MISSY TIPTON GREEN

I met Carolyn Meiller (Reba Rhyne) years ago, and upon first meeting, we realized we had a couple of things in common. As soon as we started talking, we knew that we loved history and liked to put it in writing. We also have a common lineage in the Tipton's, of which we are very proud.

I have authored five books, two of them about the Tipton's or Cades Cove. Much research, many interviews, and digging for historical pictures was needed to get the information to do these historical books. Because he knew stories and information about Cadies Cove and the Tipton's who lived there, I relied on my great uncle, Lee Tipton's, memory.

The ones about Tipton's Sugar Cove kept my interest.

Tipton's Sugar Cove is accessible by Gregory Ridge Trail and sits right under Gregory Bald. I imagine the name came from the many Tipton's who lived there, and the abundance of Sugar Maple trees growing in the area. Sugar Maple trees were the best for obtaining syrup for sugar. You did this by drilling a small hole in the tree, putting in a "tap" for the sap to drain, and dangling a small bucket underneath the tap, to hold the dripping sap. Evidentially, there was a large quantity of Maple trees in this area, as well as the other Sugar Coves in Cades Cove. Sugar was not always available to many of the residents living in the Smoky Mountains, so they would substitute it with maple syrup.

This area also lived up to the definition of "cove", which is a small valley between two ridge lines that is closed at one or two ends.

My great-grandfather, Johnnie Tipton, son of George and Tuckaleechee Tipton, was born in Tipton Sugar Cove January 22, 1887, Mary Ann Burchfield Powell of Chestnut Flats was the midwife. At some point George and "Tuck" and their family moved out of the Sugar Cove and Johnnie and Louisa Myers Tipton moved their family into the house around 1919 to 1921. My great uncle, Lee Tipton, described the house as being a log house with one big room running east to west with a kitchen on the upper side with the chimney on the east end, the front door was on upper side of house.

A spring was nearby and water ran into a big trough, it was three to four feet in diameter and was made into a big tub. There was a picket fence on the upper side at the garden. The fence was made out of poplar wood and it was built to keep chickens and mules out of the garden. There was a pig pen to keep the pigs in. Everything was grown in the garden and stored as the Tipton family did not often travel out of Tipton Sugar Cove.

There were huge chestnuts trees close to the house and apple orchards where they gathered apples in the fall. The apples were taken by bushels to Maryville to sell. Johnnie and his sons, Roy and Vernie, stayed until sold out, returning to the cove.

The Tipton children, as well as other children that lived in the area, attended Laurel Springs School located on Parsons Branch Road. There was a trail that went from the Tipton House over to the school. William Abraham "Will Gull" Tipton and his wife, Susan Jane Burchfield Tipton, moved their family into the house in Tipton Sugar Cove where most of their children were born. "Will Gull" then moved his family to the Calderwood area. One of his sons, John "Gull" Tipton moved into the house in the Tipton Sugar Cove after he was married April 29, 1921. The house was home to many Tiptons.

John Franklin "Chicken Eater" Tipton and his family lived in a house in Tipton Sugar Cove. He farmed his land in the Sugar Cove and was a woodworker as well as being a master in the construction of wooden churns and buckets.

An ancestor of those mentioned above was William "Fighting Billy" Tipton, who acquired the first land grant for Cades Cove, Tennessee on March 23, 1821 for 1280 acres. Before this time the area was part of North Carolina. William soon began selling or giving some of his land to family and friends. He had a very successful role as the first large-scale landowner in Tennessee. William Tipton never lived in the cove. Two of his sons did.

Books by Missy Tipton Green:

Precious Memories
From Mineral Springs to Bed Springs
Arcadia Cades Cove
Arcadia Townsend
Arcadia Walland

Books of the Tipton Chronicles

Butterfield Station – 1858 to 1859
Chilhowee Legacy – 1911 to 1930's
My Cherokee Rose – 1930's and Present
Tipton's Sugar Cove — Matthew – 1917 to 1921

On the Way

The Six at Chestnut Hill – Present Day
The Tipton's at Tybbington, Before and Beyond – 550
    A.D. to 1690 A.D.

There will be sequels to some of my books. I can't write
but so fast. Be patient. R.R.

Ms. Rhyne may be reached at rebarhyne@gmail.com.

Made in the USA
Columbia, SC
28 January 2020